The Laughter of Love

A Pride and Prejudice Variation

Book II in the Her Unforgettable Laugh Series

Linda Thompson

The Laughter of Love - A Pride and Prejudice Variation
Series: Her Unforgettable Laugh Book III
First Edition

For information, please contact:
1700 Lynhurst Lane
Denton, TX   76205

Cover Design and Graphic Flourishes: Lori Whitlock, LoriWhitlock.com

ISBN-13: 978-1533088758
ISBN-10: 1533088756

DEDICATION

To my wonderful husband, Jim. Thank you for filling the nearly 28 years of our marriage with love and laughter. I look forward to an eternity of the same.

ACKNOWLEDGEMENTS

Thanks to my betas Julieanne Spoor and Betty Campbell Madden for their dedication, hard work, and endless support and encouragement.

Thanks to my wonderfully talented sister-in-law, Lori Whitlock for her beautiful cover design and graphic flourishes.

Special thanks to my friends in school, for all they teach me. I appreciate their confidence in me and their faith in my abilities. Their inspiration and assistance are invaluable.

My undying gratitude goes to my family for their understanding and love in spite of my occasional craziness. I would not be able to live my dream without their patience and help. I love each of you very much!

Her laughter will be mine forever as we start our life together! Its joy will fill our home and the lives of all those who come within her sphere of influence. Blessed are those who may enjoy her laughter and her loving care.

PROLOGUE

HER TIME IN London was coming to a close. Tomorrow, Elizabeth Bennet would be returning to her childhood home, Longbourn, in preparation for her wedding.

Elizabeth could never have imagined some of the things that occurred during her brief sojourn in town. Pleased with her reception by the Fitzwilliam family, Elizabeth grew to love them dearly during the short time of their acquaintance. She happily made several new acquaintances, including neighbors from Derbyshire, and believed many of the friendships developed would last throughout her lifetime.

Many trials faced her, as well, during this time. There were several people, among them Darcy's aunt, Lady Catherine de Bourgh, who did not find Elizabeth socially suitable to be the next Mrs. Darcy. However, neither she nor Darcy was bothered by this. Among those who did not find her worthy were a tremendous number of young ladies whose hopes of attaining Darcy for themselves, Elizabeth dashed. Two of the disappointed, Lady Marjorie, the daughter of an impoverished earl, and Miss Caroline Bingley, whose behavior bordered on vicious, caused near disastrous consequences for Darcy and Elizabeth. They attempted to arrange for their perceived rival to be compromised. The gentleman they solicited to assist them developed a great respect for Elizabeth, precisely because she was unlike most of the ladies of his acquaintance. Lord Wescott reported the information to Darcy and helped to expose the ladies and their misdeeds.

What would happen to Lady Marjorie when word of her father's financial reverses and her despicable actions were made known to the ton was yet to be seen. Elizabeth hoped to never again encounter Lady Marjorie, but she knew that someone as angry and resentful as she might still cause problems in the future.

As for Caroline Bingley, she had abused Elizabeth and her family from the very beginning of their acquaintance. While residing at Netherfield Park in Hertfordshire, she made several attempts to cause Elizabeth harm, hoping to keep her from Darcy, but her plans met with failure and eventual discovery. Consequently, her brother banished her from his leased estate. When she learned of Elizabeth's coming to town, Caroline tried to spread rumors of her unsuitability. This too had failed when a former friend, Evelyn Pottsfield, made Caroline's words look like nothing more than sour grapes for losing her chance to gain Mr. Darcy's attentions. Caroline had used Evelyn to attend the Netherfield ball after being banished by her brother. At the ball, Evelyn had met Elizabeth and Jane and thought highly of both. Banished to Yorkshire for her part in the attempt to ruin Elizabeth, Caroline now resided with a strict maiden aunt. Elizabeth hoped that her sister Jane, who was betrothed to Mr. Charles Bingley, Caroline's only brother, would be spared any further ill-will from Miss Bingley.

However, the greatest danger Darcy and Elizabeth faced came from George Wickham.

Wickham held a grudge against Darcy caused by his false sense of entitlement. As the son of old Mr. Darcy's steward, he had believed himself to be the favorite of Darcy's father and mistakenly expected Mr. Darcy's will to provide him with a life of ease for the remainder of his days. However, Wickham's delusion left him extremely disappointed when he learned his bequest was a mere one thousand pounds and the future possibility of a church living. Wickham refused the position in the church and requested money instead but frittered away the several thousand pounds in a matter of months. Hoping to gain what he felted was owed him, Wickham attempted to kidnap Darcy's younger sister, Georgiana, three times. Fortunately, each escapade ended in failure. Elizabeth's involvement in two of the failed endeavors caused his hatred to extend to her. Wickham managed to shoot Elizabeth as she intervened during the last undertaking.

While the Darcys and Elizabeth spent the winter in London, Wickham tried to run the Darcy, Elizabeth, and Georgiana down with a carriage and made an attempt to take Georgiana from Hyde Park before taking a shot at Darcy in disappointed frustration. Wickham successfully spirited away Darcy's carriage, with Elizabeth and her sister, Mary, inside, at the conclusion of the ball celebrating the engagement of Darcy and Elizabeth. The young ladies had been quickly rescued after suffering only minor injuries, and Wickham, fortunately, suffered a fatal gunshot during the rescue.

Despite all of this, Elizabeth dreaded most what she might face upon her return home. Fanny Bennet, Elizabeth's mother, never cared for her second daughter. In an atrocious letter to Elizabeth, Mrs. Bennet harshly denounced her least-favorite daughter with numerous unfounded and hurtful remarks. The unfeeling woman went so far as to refuse to prepare the simple, elegant wedding and wedding breakfast Elizabeth and her betrothed requested. Mr. Bennet offered his wife an ultimatum: to plan the events as requested or to be excluded from the wedding, which now included Jane Bennet and Charles Bingley in a double ceremony.

Mrs. Bennet pretended compliance, but it was discovered two weeks before the wedding that no arrangements had been made. Elizabeth's aunt, Mrs. Gardiner, and Darcy's aunt, Lady Matlock, left a few days ago to travel to Hertfordshire and take care of all the necessary arrangements. In spite of her confidence in the two ladies, Elizabeth was very worried over what she would find when they arrived at Longbourn, and she particularly dreaded facing her mother.

With all these memories and worries swirling around in her head, Elizabeth eventually drifted off into a restless slumber.

CHAPTER 1

As THE CARRIAGE containing Elizabeth, Mary, Georgiana, and Mrs. Annesley approached Longbourn, Darcy could see Elizabeth's tension increase with each passing mile. He and his cousin, Colonel Richard Fitzwilliam, were riding along the side of the carriage nearest to where his betrothed sat. Darcy leaned close to the window and said, "Elizabeth, my love, you must stop worrying, or you will give yourself a headache. You will not have to see your mother, and you must put that concern from your mind and think of other things. I know you are eager to see your father, and you have expressed your curiosity to see the changes in Kitty. You will also be able to see Miss Lucas again, not to mention being reunited with Jane and our aunts."

Elizabeth took a deep breath and rolled her shoulders, trying to release the stiffness she felt. She looked at William and said, "Thank you, kind sir. How is it you always know what to say to make me feel better? You are correct. With our aunts in charge, everything will be perfect. It will also be wonderful to see my father and the others again. Unfortunately, I cannot dispel the feeling of impending trouble." The concern in her expression worried Darcy. He silently cursed Mrs. Bennet for distressing his beloved Elizabeth at what should be one of the happiest times of her life.

"We have only six days until the wedding; I am sure we can manage to enjoy six pleasant, calm days without some catastrophe befalling us." Darcy gave her a beguiling smile. "After all, we thwarted Lady Marjorie and Miss Bingley, Wickham will never harm anyone again, and your mother is on the far side of the estate where you will not see her, unless by choice," he said confidently. "We have certainly earned a little peace, have we not?" asked Darcy with a smile.

The carriage turned into Longbourn's drive only to find another vehicle already there. As it came to a stop, Darcy and the Colonel dismounted, tossing the reins to a groom who appeared. Colonel Fitzwilliam stepped up to the carriage and handed down Miss Mary, offering her his arm to escort her inside. Darcy then assisted Miss Darcy and Mrs. Annesley before reaching in to lift Elizabeth from the carriage. Before the group reached the entrance, the door opened and out spilled a large crowd of people, all talking at once. Mr. Bennet stood in the entry, his usual amused grin on his face, before calling everyone to attention and inviting the newcomers into the house.

Once everyone was settled in the parlor, Mr. Bennet officially welcomed his daughters and visitors before demanding to know the state of Elizabeth's and Mary's health. "I look forward to conversing with you about your most recent adventure," he said, "and must admit to relief that those who were plaguing you in London have been effectively handled."

The conversation then turned to the plans for the wedding—what had been done and what still needed attention. "Has everything proceeded smoothly?" asked Elizabeth, nervousness in her voice.

"Do not worry, Lizzy; all will be well," said Jane.

"It certainly will, Elizabeth," confirmed Mrs. Gardiner. "We have been making excellent progress with your wishes for the wedding. Rebecca and I have searched the shops in Meryton, getting the majority of the things we need for the wedding celebration."

"Yes," continued Lady Matlock, "and we have a delivery coming from London on the day before the wedding that will bring all the things we were not able to acquire. So, there is absolutely nothing for you to worry about or even to do."

"There *is* one thing you need to do," said Mr. Bennet, "Reverend Winthrop wishes the four of you to stop by the church to talk with him at your earliest convenience."

Darcy looked at Bingley and the ladies, saying, "Shall we take my carriage into Meryton tomorrow to visit with Reverend Winthrop?"

"It is fine with me," said Elizabeth.

"I believe that would be acceptable," said Bingley after receiving a nod from Jane.

Mrs. Hill entered the door carrying the tea service, followed by a maid with more refreshments. The group settled in to enjoy the refreshments and visit. Eventually, it came time for the Netherfield party to depart to prepare for dinner, for they would be returning to dine at Longbourn that evening. Before doing so, Darcy carried Elizabeth to her room to rest until their return, "I will be back to bring you downstairs before dinner," he said as he deposited her on the bed and dropped a kiss on her forehead. "Will you please wait for me and allow me to return you to the party?"

"I will behave," she said, "but only because I long to be healed enough to take one last walk with you to Oakham Mount before leaving the area for my new home. I also wish to be well enough to explore all of the wonders I have been told can be found at Pemberley." The happy, expectant expression on her face as she thought of Pemberley warmed Darcy's heart.

"And I cannot wait to show you all the glories of your future home," said Darcy with a happy smile as he turned and left the room.

Before Elizabeth had time to fall asleep, Jane knocked but did not wait for an answer before slipping into the room.

"How are you feeling, Lizzy?" her sister asked.

"I feel perfectly well but am abiding by the doctor's orders to stay off my ankle for one more day. Then I will be back to my morning walks so that I can visit all my favorite places before the wedding. I wish to say a proper goodbye to my home before embarking on the next phase of my life."

Jane could not but laugh at her sister's answer. "Well, then, I will be sure that no one looks for your help with anything before ten in the morning so that you may take your walks. Of course, your aunts seem to have everything well in hand and will not allow me to do anything."

"Well, if they will not let you do any work, what have you been doing with your time for the past few days?" asked Elizabeth curiously.

"First, we met with Mrs. Hill and reviewed the menu and all of the dishes, tableware, and linens that we would need. Then, I took Aunt Madeline and Lady Rebecca into Meryton and introduced them to Mr. Wilkens in the general store and Mr. Johnson at the butcher shop, so that orders could be placed. Mr. Bingley has offered the use of his staff. There are several maids who are helping to clean the house in preparation for the wedding breakfast and several footmen who will assist during the event."

Finally, Elizabeth asked the question she was most interested in and most fearful of having answered. "Have you seen Mama?"

"Seeing Mama caused ambivalent feelings in me, but Lydia said that Mama had specifically asked that I visit after I returned from London."

"How was your visit?" asked Elizabeth tentatively.

"It started off well with Mama offering her congratulations and saying how she knew it would be this way when Mr. Bingley came to the neighborhood. She asked about the clothes I had purchased and the events I attended," said Jane placidly.

"What are you not telling me, Jane? You indicated she asked about your clothes and your activities. Did she not ask after me at all?" asked Elizabeth sadly.

"She did mention you, Lizzy, but that was when I decided it was time to leave, and I will not waste my time repeating the ridiculous things she said, so do not ask," said Jane firmly.

Elizabeth's eyes began to well with tears, but she dashed them away with the back of her hands. "If you would not mind, Jane, I would like to rest. Will you please let Margot know to wake me an hour before dinner, so that I may prepare."

"Certainly, Lizzy. I will have her bring up a cup of tea when she comes to assist you," said Jane as she exited the room, closing the door behind her.

As Elizabeth lay down to sleep, she did her best to think only of the pleasure she would experience with her family and friends for the next few days and of the joy she would have in sharing her future life with William. Unfortunately, she could not put aside the feeling that all of their troubles were not yet behind them.

When Margot brought Elizabeth her tea, Elizabeth was surprised to find that she had actually enjoyed a restful nap. Elizabeth donned the yellow gown she had received from the Gardiners at Christmas for this first night's dinner. She was excited to be home again, back in her comfortable room and looked forward to seeing some of her friends and neighbors in the days before the wedding.

Jane opened the door to Elizabeth's room and popped her head in to announce that she was going downstairs and would send Mr. Darcy up when he arrived. With the door open, Elizabeth could hear Lydia's whining voice complaining about wanting a maid of her own, like Jane and she had. She heard Mary calmly explaining that the servants were paid for by their fiancés and not Papa, so she should stop her fussing. "Besides," said Mary, "you always hogged the maid that we shared, so you have practically had your own maid for years." They heard Lydia's "humph" and the sound of her steps as she flounced down the hallway to the stairs. Jane rolled her eyes at Elizabeth and followed after Lydia as Mary appeared in the doorway.

"I see you were right about Lydia," said Elizabeth with a look of commiseration at Mary. "Try not to let it bother you. Just keep reminding yourself that she will be leaving for school shortly, and you shall come to visit us."

"Lydia is going to school?" asked Kitty in surprise as she appeared in Elizabeth's doorway. "I have not heard a word about such a plan, so perhaps you should not say anything. I do not think Papa has told her yet. I am sure he did not wish her complaints to begin before the wedding and probably does not plan to say anything until after everyone has departed," said Kitty wisely.

"You are most likely correct, Kitty."

"Does Papa plan to have Mama return to the house when everyone is gone?" Mary wondered.

"I do not know if he has decided that yet," came Kitty's reply. "They had the worst disagreement I had ever heard when he asked her about preparing for the wedding. Then when he told her it was to be a double wedding, Mama became even angrier. When she still refused to do the things that Lizzy had asked for, Papa banished her to the dower house. She tried to say she was much too ill to be moved, but Papa had the maid pack her trunks. Then Mr. Hill retrieved them and loaded them onto the small wagon to deliver them to the dower house. He asked Mama if she would like to dress before joining Mr. Hill in the wagon for her move. When Mama refused to leave, Papa threw her over his shoulder in her gown and dressing robe, carried her down the stairs, and dropped her onto the back of the wagon with her trunks. He told her that if she did not improve her behavior, he would not even allow her a maid to care for her."

"When she first moved there, I would try to visit every day, but since she only complains and speaks unkindly about everyone but Lydia, I finally stopped going."

"Does Lydia visit her regularly?"

"Yes, she goes daily, and she constantly complains about not having Mama here with her and how unfair it is that Papa sent her away," concluded Kitty.

"How has Lydia's behavior been when Lady Matlock is present?" asked Elizabeth, worry lines on her forehead.

"At first, Lydia tried to impress Lady Matlock, bragging about how popular she was with the members of the militia and what a brilliant match she would make if only she had the opportunity to go to London for the season. Lady Matlock looked her up and down only saying that she was much too young to be out in polite society and, based on her behavior, she doubted that Lydia would be ready for several years. Lydia has done nothing since then but whine and complain about the attention everyone else is getting, how unfair it all is, and that everyone is being mean to her," finished Kitty. "I have grown tired of listening to her and have been spending my time sketching, visiting with Maria Lucas, or learning from Mrs. Hill."

"I am very proud of you, Kitty, for being so responsible and mature. Mary has also told me how talented you are. Perhaps you would be kind enough to show me some of your drawings," said Elizabeth encouragingly.

"Would you really like to see them?" Kitty's question showed both trepidation and excitement.

"I would, and I am sure Miss Darcy would also enjoy viewing them since she loves to draw, as well."

The sisters' conversation was interrupted when Mrs. Gardiner appeared in the doorway. Smilingly, she said, "I believe we should head downstairs, Mary and Kitty, as the guests should be arriving very soon. Lizzy, would you like me to send your father up to assist you down the stairs?"

"No thank you, Aunt. William said he would retrieve me as soon as he returns. I am content to wait for him," said Elizabeth, a dreamy look in her eyes.

The ladies departed, and Elizabeth reached over for the book of sonnets on her bedside table. She did not have long to read before she heard William's familiar tread on the stairs. He soon appeared in her opened doorway. He was dressed in dark blue evening clothes with a gold vest that complimented Elizabeth's gown.

"Good evening, my Lizzy. Were you able to rest?"

"Surprisingly, yes, and I have also had the opportunity to talk with Kitty some this evening. She has promised to show me her drawings tomorrow, and I hope that Georgiana will be able to join us in the afternoon to see them as well, for the girls have that in common."

"I will be sure that Aunt Rebecca brings her along when she comes to help Mrs. Gardiner. That way she will also be able to spend some time with your sisters."

"Perhaps her presence will encourage Lydia to improve her behavior. Kitty said that she had not been the most pleasant company lately," finished Elizabeth.

Dinner that evening was a cheerful affair. The children had been invited to the table, so they could welcome back Elizabeth and the others. Edmund was delighted to be seated beside Miss Darcy, while Susan and Hugh were seated next to Darcy and Elizabeth, respectively. Kitty and Mary were seated on either side of Colonel Fitzwilliam, who spoke pleasantly to both girls throughout the meal as Lydia cast angry glances their way. Mrs. Gardiner had wisely seated Lydia between her and her husband to minimize her disruptive effect on the meal.

There was a short separation of the sexes after the meal, and Lydia peppered Mary and Kitty with questions about the colonel and his personality. They gave her brief responses, and she soon flounced away. Lydia moved to a chair near the entrance of the room where she would be the first to see the gentlemen when they returned.

In the library, Darcy was inquiring as to Mrs. Bennet's status. Mr. Bennet explained what he had said upon his return home and reported the necessity of removing her from the house, including the manner in which she had been removed.

"Do you believe we need to have the house guarded during the days leading up to the wedding?" Darcy asked with concern.

"It is quite a walk from the dower house into Meryton, and Mrs. Bennet does not like to expend herself in such activities. Unless you and Elizabeth make a trip to see her, I do not believe that you will encounter her during your visit," Mr. Bennet responded.

When the gentlemen rejoined the ladies a short time later, Lydia latched onto the colonel's arm the minute he walked into the parlor. He made every attempt to disengage her from his arm as he moved across the room in Mary's direction. Seeing where Colonel Fitzwilliam was heading, Lydia gave his arm a tug and said, "Sit with me, Colonel. I am much more fun than Mary and promise not to recite any scriptures to you while we talk." Lydia cast a smirk in Mary's direction as she spoke. Richard noted the embarrassed blush that spread over Mary's cheeks and once again attempted to remove his arm from Lydia's grasp.

Mrs. Gardiner spoke up, saying, "Lydia, I believe it is time for you and the children to retire. Please take them up to the nursery and help the nurse prepare them for bed. I will be up shortly to kiss them good night. Please be sure you read them a story or two while they are waiting for me."

"But, Aunt," Lydia began to whine. She was unable to say more before the firm voice of her father said, "It is time for you to depart now, Lydia."

Lydia flounced from the room without waiting for the children, and she was soon heard stomping up the stairs. Kitty quickly offered to take the children up to the nursery for her aunt and waited patiently as they offered their goodnights to everyone in the room and quietly exited to make their way to the nursery.

Before the Netherfield party departed for the evening, Darcy said he had sent a note to Reverend Winthrop upon arriving at Netherfield, asking if it would be convenient for him to receive the two couples at half past ten in the morning and that Reverend Winthrop had replied in the affirmative. He advised the ladies that Bingley and he would arrive by ten in the morning to pick them up for their appointment with the minister.

As Jane walked out to the waiting carriage with Bingley and the others, Darcy carried Elizabeth upstairs to her room.

"I am sad to see this day end."

"Why would that be, William? You are usually counting down the days until the wedding each night before we must separate."

"Yes, that is true, but after this evening, there is no longer an excuse for me to carry you in my arms," Darcy said somewhat forlornly.

"Yes, but it is only a few more days until you can carry me whenever you wish, and I find there is no place I would rather be than in your arms," said Elizabeth with a bashful smile.

Darcy leaned in and kissed Elizabeth's forehead quickly before removing himself from the temptation she presented. "Until, tomorrow," he said with a longing look from the doorway. "Good night, my Elizabeth. Sweet dreams."

Sitting alone at Rosings, Lady Catherine wondered how all her plans had gone awry. She looked back over her life, trying to determine what she could have done differently to achieve her desires. After many unsuccessful seasons, Lady Catherine Fitzwilliam had been forced to accept the hand of Sir Lewis de Bourgh. He was fifteen years Lady Catherine's senior, and she did not find him to be handsome. The gentleman had readily enjoyed the freedom of being wealthy and well-connected but had finally reached the point where he wished for more in his life. Lady Catherine was a handsome woman with a good pedigree. A connection to the Earl of Matlock could only improve his social standing. Sir Lewis had found Lady Catherine intriguing. He saw the disappointment and confusion she felt at having received no offers and hoped to eventually break down her defenses.

He felt he was making some progress until the announcement of the engagement between Catherine's younger sister, Anne, and James Darcy. It was a love match, and Catherine was green with envy. She had admired Mr. Darcy, but he never noticed her at all. In her jealousy and anger, Catherine had tried on more than one occasion to disrupt the relationship, but her brother had always interceded and asserted his authority as head of the Fitzwilliam family. When the marriage finally took place, Catherine hardened her heart further, and, in spite of Sir Lewis' many kindnesses, Lady Catherine could not bring herself to be accepting of the man she had felt forced to marry.

When nothing he tried could improve his relationship with Lady Catherine, Sir Lewis focused all of his love and attention upon his children. Their first child, a son, was born in the late summer and died a few months later after catching a winter cold. Next Lady Catherine experienced two miscarriages.

Two years after her sister, Lady Anne, gave birth to a healthy son, Fitzwilliam Darcy, Lady Catherine again gave birth, this time to a daughter, Anne. When Anne was two, Lady Catherine was again with child. This time, she gave birth to a healthy son. When the boy was three, he was playing in Rosings' formal gardens while his mother walked the paths. Lady Catherine was not giving the child the proper attention, and the young boy managed to climb up onto one of the fountains. He fell into the water, hit his head, and drowned.

Sir Lewis had been furious with Lady Catherine and forbade her from being alone with their remaining child. He assumed all the responsibility for hiring and instructing the staff to watch his only living child. He made sure that Anne had a loving nurse and a governess who would remain as her companion as she grew older. When Anne was eight, she was stricken with scarlet fever. She eventually recovered, but the high temperatures had affected her heart and left it weakened. When Anne recovered, Sir Lewis doted on her even more. Anne was well loved, and she adored her father in return. Her mother mostly ignored her unless it was to harshly correct her behavior. Anne was fourteen when Sir Lewis died, and she was heartbroken, becoming ill for some weeks following her father's death.

At the reading of the will, Lady Catherine received a severe shock to her senses. Sir Lewis had left everything to Anne. At the time of Anne's marriage or at age five and twenty, when she reached her majority, Lady Catherine would be relegated to the dower house with an income of one thousand pounds per annum. If Anne died before either of these events occurred, the estate would pass to Richard Fitzwilliam. There were no de Bourgh's remaining to inherit, and Sir Lewis had been fond of the happy and hard-working young nephew who was attending Cambridge and was preparing for a career in the army. His other nephews would both inherit estates, and Sir Lewis wanted to afford Richard the same opportunity to have a secure future.

It was shortly after Sir Lewis's death that James Darcy began making annual visits to Rosings at Easter, bringing his son with him. Catherine thought that since they were both now alone, Anne Darcy having died four years previously, she would be able to convince James to marry her. She was unaware of the fact that Mr. Darcy only came as a result of being one of the executor's of Sir Lewis's estate. The earl also made a trip to Rosings each year at the completion of the harvest for the same purpose.

Now Darcy was to marry, and it was not to her daughter. All the years that Darcy had visited Rosings, Lady Catherine had told him of the plans she and his mother had made when Anne was still in her cradle. She told him of their desire for their children to wed and join the two estates. Lady Anne had never agreed to this plan, no matter how many times her sister would bring up the subject. However, Lady Catherine was determined to catch Darcy for her daughter since she had not been able to capture his father for herself. Consequently, she drummed into Darcy her tale of the union being his mother's greatest wish.

Lady Catherine's most recent attempt to end the relationship had been a misguided attempt to disrupt the engagement ball of her nephew, Fitzwilliam Darcy, and the country upstart, Elizabeth Bennet, to whom he had engaged himself. She had been infuriated that her own daughter had thwarted her this time. After her latest mischief, Lady Catherine had been forcefully ordered to return to Rosings by her brother, the Earl of Matlock. He gave her strict orders to desist in her attempts to disrupt

Darcy's engagement. The Earl went so far as to threaten his recalcitrant sister with dire consequences should she ignore him.

Lady Catherine knew the only way she would retain her place as the mistress of Rosings was for her daughter, Anne, to marry Darcy. Then Anne would remove to Pemberley and leave Lady Catherine in charge of the estate in Kent. With that in mind, she summoned her parson, Mr. Collins. Collins was not too bright, but he was devoted to his patroness and only too happy to carry out her orders, no matter what they were. She whispered her plans to him and sent him on his way.

Mr. Collins stood looking around his accommodations. The Meryton Inn was small and noisy. He had registered under the name of Mr. Smith because his patroness, Lady Catherine, insisted that no one know of his presence in the neighborhood. She had given Mr. Collins explicit instructions and ordered him not to fail her. Because he had not ventured into the village on his previous visit to Meryton, none of the villagers had ever seen him. With his generally unappealing appearance and odoriferousness, very few of the villagers paid much attention to the newcomer.

Lady Catherine had timed his arrival in Meryton for the same day as Elizabeth was due to return to Longbourn. As he lay in bed that night, he thought back to his visit last autumn. He had been ordered by his patroness to marry and to select a bride from among his cousins. He initially chose Jane, who was the eldest and most beautiful. However, Mrs. Bennet had hinted that she expected Jane to be soon engaged and pushed Mr. Collins to choose Elizabeth.

He had noted her beauty and her more voluptuous figure and quickly agreed. Collins had lurked around Longbourn in hopes of catching his intended alone. He had every intention of making her his proposal and stealing a kiss, more if he could. Elizabeth had avoided him as much as possible, which had angered him. He had an over-developed sense of his own importance and found it inconceivable that she would not desire to be his wife. When forced to be in his company she had been barely civil and always remained very near to one of her sisters. He had heard of young women playing hard to get and determined that Elizabeth was doing just that. His thinking she desired him as well lead to even more lascivious thoughts of his intended. He had been furious at the treatment he received from Elizabeth, Mr. Darcy, and Mr. Bennet when he had been refused Elizabeth's hand. He had desired his revenge upon them since that time. Tomorrow he would make his way to the area surrounding Longbourn and watch for his chance to carry out his patroness's wishes. William Collins drifted off to sleep with a lecherous smirk on his face.

Mr. Collins gazed in the mirror at his appearance. Lady Catherine had procured some clothes for him to wear rather than have him appear as a parson. She had given him explicit orders to do whatever was necessary to compromise Elizabeth Bennet, thereby ending the engagement to her nephew, Fitzwilliam Darcy. Collins was delighted at the opportunity to gain his revenge and looked forward to having his way with Elizabeth. He tried to devise a plan that would allow him to come upon his cousin unaware. Smiling to himself, Collins relished the fact that he would be able to take what he wanted from Elizabeth. Then when she was ruined, he would offer to save her reputation and that of her sisters by marrying her. He looked forward to having Elizabeth in his control and promised himself he would show her his displeasure for her past behavior.

Never once did it occur to the obtuse parson that he had never actually proposed to Elizabeth, only assumed her acceptance as Mrs. Bennet had granted her approval of the arrangement. He determined his best opportunity would occur when she took one of her imprudent early morning rambles. Collins would have to rise very early and make his way to the area beyond the gardens of Longbourn. Surely he would be able to accomplish his goal as she walked out one morning.

CHAPTER 2

ELIZABETH WOKE EARLY the next morning with a smile on her face as she noted the sun seeping into the room. She swung her feet off the bed and gently stood, testing how her ankle felt as she put her whole weight on it. She was delighted to realize that there was no discomfort from the action. She dressed quickly in one of her old dresses and carefully made her way down the steps. She wished Mrs. Hill and Cook a good day, requesting bath water in one hour as she grabbed a freshly baked roll and let herself out into the garden by way of the kitchen door. This first morning she did not traipse far beyond the gardens as her ankle adjusted to her weight and the exercise. She ventured beyond the back garden wall only briefly to gather some wildflowers for a bouquet in her room.

As she gathered the flowers, she heard the rustle of leaves and the crack of a twig and looked about to see who else was abroad so early in the morning. Though she could not see anyone, Elizabeth had the eerie feeling of being watched. She knew that Wickham was gone, and no longer posed a threat, but still she felt uneasy. Deciding her bath water was most likely ready, Elizabeth turned and ran lightly across the lawn to the house. Collins was frustrated that she had moved away so quickly. Had Elizabeth returned to gathering flowers, he would have been able to get closer and carry out his patroness's desires. However, it was not the wishes of Lady Catherine he was contemplating, but the fact that with the compromise she would have to marry him. He would have her in his power for the rest of his life. Collins rubbed his hands together and looked forward to teaching her obedience to his wishes.

Collins carefully made his way to the trees across the road from Longbourn's drive. Perhaps, she would venture to town, and he would get another opportunity to extract his revenge.

Stopping in the kitchen only long enough to put the flowers into a vase of water, she carried them up to her room. She found Margot awaiting her, having just put some of Elizabeth's lavender bath oils in the tub. Margot quickly had Elizabeth undressed and in the tub. She helped Elizabeth wash her hair, then left her to soak for a few minutes. Elizabeth had finally managed to put her troubles behind her and slept well last evening. She was determined to put the nagging feeling of worry aside and enjoy these remaining days in her family home.

Elizabeth's eyes popped open as she heard the sound of the door opening and realized that Margot must have returned. It took very little time before she was dressed and ready to join her family to break her fast.

"Good morning, Papa," she said as she entered the dining room and placed a kiss on his cheek. She took her usual seat on his left and acknowledged the others there before her. "Good morning, Aunt Madeline, Jane, Mary, Kitty." Looking about she asked, "Where is Lydia this morning? Is she still asleep?"

"No, she was up surprisingly early and has gone to see Mama already this morning," replied Kitty.

"Has she been a good help with the children, Aunt Madeline?"

"Not so much as I would have hoped, but Kitty has been wonderful with them. She is even teaching Susan to sketch some. She will be a loving mother someday, just as you girls have shown you will be," said Mrs. Gardiner fondly.

They enjoyed a pleasant breakfast while Mrs. Gardiner reviewed for Elizabeth all the plans that had been made and what still needed to be done. She asked if there was anything she could do to help or anything she could pick up while they were in town for their meeting with Reverend Winthrop.

"No, Lizzy. You just go and enjoy yourself. Why don't you stop in to see Mr. Stevens? He was asking after you the other day," said Mr. Bennet.

Elizabeth and Jane had just returned to the sitting room when Mrs. Hill announced the gentlemen. "Good morning, everyone," said Bingley in his usual ebullient way. "What a glorious spring morning it is. Just perfect for a carriage ride."

"Good morning, Mr. Bingley, Mr. Darcy," said Mr. Bennet.

"Good morning, sir," said Darcy.

"I believe we had best leave if we are to make our appointment with Reverend Winthrop," remarked Darcy.

When the couples stepped outside, there was a surprise for Elizabeth and Jane. Because of the beautiful weather, the gentlemen had both brought curricles for the ride into Meryton.

"Oh, how exciting!" cried Elizabeth.

The gentlemen helped the ladies ascend into the carriages and climbed up beside them. They set off at a smart pace with Bingley leading the way. It did not take long before they arrived at the Meryton church. At the sounds of the vehicles, Reverend Winthrop exited the chapel and waited for the couples to join him.

"Good morning, Miss Jane, Miss Elizabeth, Mr. Bingley, Mr. Darcy. Welcome to you all! I am glad that you could come to see me today," said the white-haired reverend with the rosy cheeks and sparkling blue eyes. "Please come in and let us talk," he said as he stepped aside to allow the others to enter before him.

The two couples settled in the Bennet family pew, Reverend Winthrop standing before them. Telling Elizabeth that she and Mary were included in the prayers for the sick last Sunday, Reverend Winthrop asked Elizabeth how she and Mary were fairing. He asked Mr. Darcy about their trip from town on the previous day and spoke of his pleasure at being asked to officiate at the wedding of the two young ladies he had known since their birth.

"Now, Miss Jane, if you and Mr. Bingley will follow me to my office, I would like to speak to the two of you privately. When they return, Miss Elizabeth, you and Mr. Darcy should join me. Mr. Bingley and Jane followed Mr. Winthrop towards the altar, exiting the chapel through a door there. When they were settled in his small office in the rectory, he asked questions about how they met and their feelings for one another. Having baptized the ladies, he was delighted to see that they had both made matches with fine young men. After their individual interviews, they met together again, and Reverend Winthrop talked about the ceremony. He walked them through who would stand where and what they should say in response to his questions. After nearly hour, the meeting ended with Reverend Winthrop walking them out.

When they stepped out, Darcy turned and asked, "Reverend Winthrop, would you mind if we left the curricles here? We thought to walk about town a bit and plan to stop in at the tea shop."

"Certainly, Mr. Darcy, they will be fine in the shade of these old trees." With that, the couples waved and walked on. They strolled down one side of the street, looking in all the shop windows. Occasionally, they would enter a shop and look around, visiting with friends they encountered and making small purchases.

When the bell above the bookshop door rang, Mr. Stevens stepped out from the back of the shop and cried out his usual welcome. Seeing who stood there, Mr. Stevens face lit with pleasure as he rushed forward to welcome his old friends. "Miss Lizzy, Mr. Darcy, how wonderful to see you both again. I heard you would be back soon. News of a double wedding for two of the brightest jewels of the county created quite a stir. Please accept my congratulations to you both. I hope you will be very happy together."

"Thank you, Mr. Stevens."

"Indeed, Mr. Stevens," said Darcy. "Have you put aside anything special for us to look over now that we have returned?" asked Darcy with a smile.

"Well, now, it just so happens, I did set aside a book or two I thought you might like, sir. Would you like me to bring them out here for you or would you prefer to follow me into the back?"

"Oh, by all means, let us go to the back for old times' sake!" he answered, smiling widely. Mr. Stevens turned and led the way as Elizabeth's laugh rang out.

Almost half an hour had passed before Darcy and Elizabeth left the bookshop. Darcy carried a wrapped package under his arm as they departed. The couple strolled down the street to join Jane and

Bingley at the teashop. The group was happily settled and enjoying a cup of tea and a sweet when a harsh, angry voice was heard.

"So you have finally returned home you willful, selfish girl. Do you think yourself so high and mighty now that you are engaged to a man of ten thousand a year that you need no longer be kind to your mother? You were ever the same, never minding anything I told you. It is a wonder that you managed to catch a man at all!" sneered Mrs. Bennet

At the sound of her mother's voice, Elizabeth froze as the color drained from her face and tears welled up in her eyes. She could see her mother from the corner of her eye but did not turn to look at her.

Darcy reached under the table and took Elizabeth's hand in his. He leaned towards her and whispered in her ear. "She acts no differently than Lady Marjorie or Caroline Bingley; treat her as such." He leaned away and turned his head to look at his future mother-in-law. The look of anger and disgust he cast at her made Mrs. Bennet cringe before wrapping her indignation around her like a cloak.

Elizabeth slowly turned to look at her mother. "Good morning, Mama. How are you today?"

"How would you expect me to be when I have been banished from my home and none of my daughters care enough about me to visit, except my dear Lydia. And why do I find myself banished? Because of a selfish girl who made her father throw me from my home as though she were some sort of princess. You are no princess! You are nothing more than a tart, selling herself for ten thousand a year!" screeched Mrs. Bennet.

"That is enough, Madame! How dare you speak to Miss Elizabeth in such a disrespectful manner? She is the best lady I have ever known. Now, please control yourself, or I shall be forced to help you do so." Darcy's tone and his look both held menace.

"How dare you speak to me in such a fashion, Mr. High and Mighty Darcy! This has nothing to do with you," she returned with equal coldness.

"There you are mistaken, Madam. It was my understanding the opinions which matter most in regards to a wedding are those of the bride and groom, or, in this case, brides and grooms. It is their wishes that should be satisfied, not your own. You want a big fancy show to give you consequence. You care more for your own selfish wishes than those of the daughters who should be most precious to you. But your failure to prepare a wedding for them will not be a hardship for them. My aunt, Lady Matlock, and your sister-in-law, Mrs. Gardiner, are more than happy to arrange things to Elizabeth and Jane's liking."

"Maybe so, but I know how selfish Elizabeth is, and I am sure she did not take Jane's wishes into account when she made her plans."

"That is not true!" said Jane quietly. "Now, please, Mama, lower your voice. You are causing a scene and embarrassing the entire family by behaving in this fashion."

"Oh, hush, Jane," Mrs. Bennet snapped. "After all I did to help you gain Mr. Bingley's attention, so that you could marry well! You repay my kindness by siding with your sister to embarrass us with such a poor excuse for a wedding."

"I beg your pardon, Mrs. Bennet, but please do not speak to my future wife in such a manner. The only thing you did for Jane was to embarrass her with your poor manners," said Bingley stiffly.

Mrs. Bennet let out a screech as she turned to Jane, saying, "Are you just going to let your betrothed speak to me in such a manner?"

Sitting up straighter, Jane replied, "Why should I correct him for speaking the truth, especially in light of the way you are acting at present. His point is clearly proven by the poor behavior you are currently exhibiting, Mama!"

Finally Elizabeth found her voice. "Since it is going to be such an unacceptable event, you should be relieved Papa has forbidden you to attend. And, should you try to do so, you will be denied admittance."

"You cannot keep me from attending my dear Jane's wedding. I am the mother of the bride and have every right to be there."

"You are the mother of both brides, but that does not seem to matter to you," Elizabeth reminded her mother quietly.

Before Mrs. Bennet could reply, Jane said, "Lizzy is absolutely correct, Mama. We would not want to disgrace you with our poorly planned wedding. You would not enjoy it, so I am saving you the trouble of being embarrassed by attending. Please do not come."

Darcy and Bingley looked at their young ladies with pride, giving them each a warm smile, but Darcy had reached the limits of his patience. Placing several coins on the table, he stood up and offered his arm to Elizabeth. "Come, my dear, I am sure your aunt will be holding lunch for us. We have been gone longer than expected." Bingley rose and offered his arm to Jane as well. They brushed past Mrs. Bennet and exited the shop without speaking another word to her.

As soon as the couples had departed, the remaining patrons began to buzz with conversation. Mrs. Bennet stood stock still, almost shaking with rage. She was unaware of the words being spoken, but Mr. Thompson, who owned the shop, was not. He stepped from behind the counter and moved to where Mrs. Bennet stood. He straightened to his full height and said, "I do not appreciate your disturbing my customers in such a way. Now leave, Mrs. Bennet, and do not return." So saying he took the woman by her elbow and escorted her to the door. He quickly opened it and pushed her outside, closing it firmly behind her.

Arm in arm, the two couples walked slowly down the sidewalk toward the church. When they arrived, they climbed into the curricles and took off in the direction of Longbourn.

"Are you alright, my love?" Darcy asked quietly, once they were underway.

"I am well, William. You were right in what you said; my mother is no different from Lady Marjorie or Caroline Bingley. They each put their own selfish interests ahead of any other concerns. My mother or not, I finally realized that none of her ridiculousness mattered. If she had been willing to try, if she had been willing to grow and improve herself, Mama could have had a part in our life and the society she has always desired. Instead, she chose banishment. She chose not to see her daughters wed. It was Mama's choice to be lonely and isolated by alienating her daughters. She made her own bed and shall now have to lie in it. I do not plan to waste another moment worrying about my mother. I shall always be thankful to her for giving me life; however, I no longer wish to have her be a part of that life."

Darcy looked proudly at Elizabeth. "You are truly the most remarkable woman I have ever known, and I love you very much."

"I love you as well, William, and I would not have been able to survive all of the trials we have had lately without you by my side."

"Your father said that your mother did not like walking, which was one of the reasons he put her in the dower house so far from town. He also expected it would help to curtail her expenses. I did not expect that we would run into her there. She, however, did not seem at all surprised to see us. I wonder how she knew where we would be?"

"Oh, the answer to that is very easy. It seems that Lydia left much earlier than usual to visit Mama this morning. I am absolutely certain she is fully informed of everything that goes on in the house, including our plans. In the future, we may need to be sure that we do not discuss sensitive information if Lydia is present," said Elizabeth.

"I will be sure to inform your father about today's events when we have an opportunity. It appears we will need to employ the guards to keep her away from the wedding."

Mr. Collins had seen the curricles departing Longbourn in the direction of town, and he had followed as quickly as his rotund body and short legs could carry him. Sweating profusely and panting to catch his breath, Mr. Collins arrived in the village as the couples exited the church. He ducked out of sight behind a large tree near the church. Collins watched as they made their way around the village. When Darcy and Elizabeth entered the tea shop, Collins was about to move closer to see if he could overhear their plans when an angry looking Mrs. Bennet stormed into the shop. Collins took a position near an open window on the side of the store and heard her rant at Elizabeth. Collins barely managed to conceal himself as the two couples abruptly exited the shop and headed for the curricles parked near the church. They were quickly underway in the direction of Longbourn.

Mr. Collins was wondering if he could make use of Mrs. Bennet's dislike of her second daughter to complete Lady Catherine's request, but he decided she could not be counted upon to keep his presence in the area a secret. Though he was eager to have his revenge, he did not wish to face Mr. Darcy's wrath. He needed to complete his assignment and leave the area before his presence was discovered. Collins had moved again to stand near the window and was able to hear the owner removing the Bennet matriarch from the shop as well as the comments of many of the patrons about her deplorable behavior. No, he would definitely not confide in Mrs. Bennet.

When their curricle arrived at the front door of Longbourn, Darcy jumped to the ground and helped Elizabeth down. They entered the house in good spirits to find the others in the parlor. Both Darcy and Elizabeth noted the smug, deceitful look on Lydia's face as she looked up, asking, "How was your trip to town, Lizzy. Did anything exciting happen?"

"We had a lovely meeting with Reverend Winthrop, and Mr. Darcy was able to find some first editions he had been searching for when we stopped in to see Mr. Stevens. We also enjoyed a visit to the tea shop, but I would not call any of it exciting, Lydia."

"Oh," said Lydia with a look of disappointment.

"Were you expecting something to happen, Miss Lydia?" asked Darcy. "Something that might spoil our outing?"

Flustered by the penetrating look Darcy was giving her, Lydia stuttered, "No, no, not really. Nothing exciting ever happens in Meryton. Things will be even duller when the militia departs next week," she finished with a pout. "I have been invited to go to Brighton with Mrs. Forster when the troop leaves, but Papa refuses to allow me to go."

"As well he should," said Mrs. Gardiner. "You should not even be out in society at your age; letting you go off alone would be quite ridiculous as you do not seem to know how to behave properly."

"Oh, you are just being mean to me like everyone else, Aunt. Jane, Lizzy, and Mary have all been to town and gotten new gowns, and Lizzy and Jane even have personal maids. It is not fair. I never get anything!"

"That is enough, Lydia," said Mr. Bennet entering the room. "You have gotten far too much indulgence from your mother for far too many years. You will no longer be going out in society until you have turned eighteen and only then if you can prove to me that you have the sense God gave a goose."

Lydia began to whine and cry and was promptly sent to her room by her father. The others sat down to a light luncheon as Elizabeth and Jane talked about their meeting with Reverend Winthrop, and Darcy told Mr. Bennet of the books he had purchased.

After a brief look at Elizabeth, who gave a slight nod, Darcy turned to Mr. Bennet. "Sir, there was one bit of unpleasantness to our trip into Meryton."

"And what was that, sir?"

"We encountered Mrs. Bennet as we were enjoying refreshments at the tea room."

Gasps were heard from the other ladies present and Mr. Bennet inquired, "Well, Lizzy, you seem to be in good spirits in spite of the encounter. Are you truly well?"

"Yes, Papa, I am fine. After listening to Mama's harsh words and silliness, I told her she was fortunate that you refused to allow her to attend."

"Yes, and when she said no one could keep her from attending my wedding, I told her she was not welcome there," said Jane.

Mr. Bennet was extremely surprised to hear such words from his eldest daughter but quickly recovered. "I am very proud of you both. You handled yourselves very well."

"Yes, you did," agreed Mrs. Gardiner.

"Papa," said Elizabeth, "I suspected Lydia told her we would be in town today, and after her question when we returned home, I am even more convinced of it. If she is willing to encourage Mama in her poor behavior, I do not believe I wish to have her at the wedding either."

"I believe, Mr. Bennet, it may be necessary to employ the guards for the wedding day. Do you wish for me to send for some of the men from town?"

"That may be best, Mr. Darcy. We have only one footman here, and Mr. Bingley is loaning us several of his to assist at the wedding breakfast. I do not believe we will have enough left to guard the cottage as well. How many do you think we will need?"

"Tell me a little about the cottage first. Is it small or large? How many doors and windows does it have?"

"It is not particularly large. It has two doors, and there are windows on each side of it."

"Are there any nearby trees that would allow escape from the second floor?"

"No, there are not."

"I know, there are only two women, but I would rather err on the side of caution and have a guard for each side of the building. If I may use your library, sir, I will write a letter to Travers and arrange for the men to come as soon as possible and stay until the day after the wedding. Let us hope that she will not cause any difficulties for the one day in between," he said positively.

They talked about plans for the next few days. They were dining at Netherfield that night and again on the night before the wedding. Elizabeth suggested a picnic with the children for tomorrow if it was not too much bother for Mrs. Hill. Bingley offered to have his cook assist, so that it would not be a burden. Mary quickly stepped away to speak with Mrs. Hill, returning with her promise that she would have a cold picnic prepared for them at half past eleven.

The gentlemen remained a short time longer before departing. The Bennets would be dining at Netherfield tonight, so they would be in company again soon.

After all of the guests had departed, Mr. Bennet called for Lydia to attend him in his study. When she appeared, he wasted no time on pleasantries. "Lydia, did you tell your mother where Elizabeth would be today?"

"Yes, Papa."

"For what purpose?"

"Mama said that it was all Lizzy's fault that she was sent away from home. She wanted to talk to Elizabeth and convince her to let her come back. I do not like it here without, Mama," she pouted. "I want her to come home!"

"Elizabeth had nothing to do with my sending your mother away.   Your mother wrote a reprehensible letter to your sister, saying many unkind things to Lizzy. She even said that Elizabeth could not be married before Jane. Jane and Mr. Bingley were not engaged at the time. How would you like it if she said you could not marry until all of your older sisters had done so, as she said to Lizzy? I am certain you would not like it one bit, and you would make sure that everyone knew it," said Mr. Bennet, shaking his head. "Your mother also refused to arrange the wedding as Lizzy had requested. I gave her a choice to apologize and plan the wedding as requested or to be sent to the dower house until after the event was over. Your mother made her choice."

"How could you be so mean to Mama?" Lydia cried.

"How could your mother be so insensitive to two of her own daughters?" he flashed in return. "If you were her least favorite instead of her *dear* Lydia, how would you feel about having all of your wishes ignored?" her father asked. "Now you have a choice to make. Will you improve your manners so as to join the adults for a family dinner at Netherfield this evening, or would you prefer to dine in the nursery with your cousins?"

"Of course I do not want to dine with the children. I have been out for a year. I am no longer a child!" she cried indignantly.

"Being out in society is not just about attending parties, young lady. It is also about accepting more responsibility, being dependable, and making wise decisions. Your behavior of late has not been that of an adult. You are shirking your responsibilities to help with your cousins and are tattling to your mother about things that displease you or are none of your concern or hers. You will behave like a proper young lady at dinner this evening. You will keep the tone of your voice low, think before speaking, and above all, you will not whine or pout. If I observe the behaviors of a child, then you will be treated like one. So, if you wish to attend the dinner party tomorrow evening, you will behave appropriately this evening."

"But, Papa, I have to be there! I know that in addition to the colonel there will be a viscount in attendance. If I am not there how can one of them fall in love with me?"

"Neither of them will be falling in love with you. The viscount is already engaged, and the colonel's feelings are also attached, though he has not yet declared himself. If you earn the right to attend through proper behavior tonight, you, as the youngest female present, will not address either of these gentlemen without having been first addressed by them, or you will be sent from the room. Do I make myself clear?" asked Mr. Bennet sternly.

Lydia pouted but agreed.

"Remember, Lydia: this is your choice. If you cannot abide by these strictures, you will be sent to the nursery immediately. And your behavior at dinner tonight will determine whether or not you attend the ball Mr. Bingley is hosting before the wedding. And, if you attend the ball, you will not be permitted to dance."

"But, Papa, I always dance every dance when we go to a party or assembly. Why would I not be allowed to dance?" she cried indignantly.

"You are too young to be out in society. Both your aunt and Lady Matlock agree. I was too lax with your mother in allowing her to push you all out into society in hopes of marrying you off. I have learned from my mistakes and do not intend to continue in the old ways. You will have to adjust your behavior going forward, or you shall find your activities very limited. I have learned of an event in town where a young lady, whose behavior was as improper as yours, was thrown from a ball for her actions and also lost her admission to Almack's. With your current behavior, that is exactly what could happen to you. Now I want you to go to your room and think about all that I have said. We will see you at dinner." Mr. Bennet waved his hand in dismissal, picked up a book from his desk, and settled in for a little peace and quiet before the evening meal.

This evening, the children remained behind at Longbourn as the others journeyed to Netherfield Park for dinner. The meal was a pleasant experience for almost everyone. Lydia was unusually quiet, but her expression was not a happy one. After dinner, her sisters tried to get her to join in their conversation, but Lydia refused. She seated herself across the room and watched them with a sulky expression on her face.

Later that evening, after she was ready for bed, Jane knocked on the door to Elizabeth's room and slipped inside. She had barely settled herself on the bed when another knock was heard. When the door opened and Mary looked in, Elizabeth said, "Why do we not invite Kitty to join us as well?"

"I will get her and return momentarily."

By unspoken consent, no one suggested having Lydia join them. She refused their company earlier in the evening, and they expected she would do so again. Once the sisters were all settled on Elizabeth's bed, Mary said, "Was your meeting with Mama very unpleasant, Lizzy?"

"It was not so unpleasant as her letter. Much of what she said was quite silly. It was when she said it did not matter that Lady Matlock had approved the wedding plans, they were still poor, that I realized how truly ridiculous her opinions are. Lady Matlock is one of the leading hostesses of the ton; she would not have allowed me to plan anything that would be inappropriate. She tried to blame me for being put out of the house. Papa told me he would give her an ultimatum: She either arranged things as we requested or she could go to the dower house. Her current situation is of her own choosing. I will not allow her to place the blame on me, nor will I allow her to make me feel guilty for her situation."

"I am so proud of you, Lizzy," said Mary.

"I wish I had the courage to stand up to Mama and Lydia," said Kitty sadly.

"But you do," said Elizabeth. "Mary told me how you would not blindly follow Lydia any more, and you do not let her distract you from your art. You stood up to her in your own way. It does not always have to be with words."

Kitty's face brightened at Elizabeth's comments. "Thank you, Lizzy," she said, tears glistening in her eyes.

"Jane, how do you feel about the encounter with Mama? I believe speaking up for yourself to her was a first for you."

"I must admit I was feeling somewhat guilty for my behavior, but as you wisely pointed out, it is her behavior that is at fault, and I do not have to let it affect me."

Elizabeth told her sisters what she had said on the ride home with Darcy about honoring her as a parent, but not allowing her in her life until she apologizes and changes her behavior.

"I find that both wise and respectful," said Mary thoughtfully.

The girls moved on to other topics, talking about the picnic and what things they should take with them. Elizabeth asked Kitty to please bring her sketchbook, saying she would like to look at it and was sure there would be something for Kitty to sketch as well. Mary and Kitty talked about their hopes for the future, and Elizabeth invited Kitty to visit as well. It was nearly midnight when the sisters said good night to one another and finally retired for the night.

CHAPTER 3

THE MORNING DAWNED bright and sunny perfect for another walk. Elizabeth dressed quickly and left the house through the kitchen, taking a roll to tide her over until breakfast. This time, she headed farther afield, knowing that her ankle was up to the challenge. Elizabeth walked towards the fence that separated Longbourn from Netherfield. From there she planned to go on to the pond where she and William would often sit and talk.

Elizabeth's face lit with a huge smile when she saw William approaching on horseback as so often happened in the early days of their acquaintance. A matching smile appeared on his face as he sent his mount flying over the fence. Once on the Longbourn side, Darcy dismounted and swept Elizabeth up into his arms twirling her around in a circle.

"I had a feeling I might find you here," he said with a laugh as he set Elizabeth back on her feet.

"I could not imagine leaving Hertfordshire without visiting what has become one of my favorite spots," she said with a loving glance.

"Were you planning to continue on to where we would sit and talk?"

"How did you ever guess?" Elizabeth asked with a laugh.

"Please allow me to accompany you, my lady," replied Darcy with a bow before offering her his arm.

Darcy tied his horse off at the edge of the copse, and they walked on until they came to the flat rock where they settled themselves comfortably.

Elizabeth told him stories of her childhood adventures while he laughed at her exploits.

"I hope that we have a beautiful daughter one day who is just like her mother. Perhaps she would allow me to attend her on some of her adventures. I did not have that opportunity with you, but it would be almost as enjoyable, I am sure."

"You may wish to ask my father about my childhood before you wish for a daughter like me. He has often said that I am the cause of much of his gray hair," she laughed. They talked on about their hopes and dreams for the future, until Elizabeth finally said, "I must return home, or I will not be ready for the picnic when you arrive."

Darcy rose and reached a hand down to help Elizabeth to her feet. They returned to where his horse was tied. He reached out suddenly and lifted Elizabeth onto the saddle. He untied the horse and quickly mounted behind her. "The children would be very disappointed if you were late for the picnic. I cannot allow that to happen, now can I," he said with a laugh.

They rode quickly to the back wall of Longbourn's garden. Darcy quickly dismounted and reached up for Elizabeth. He slid her down his body and set her feet on the ground. He kissed Elizabeth's forehead and stepped away from her, saying, "Only four more days, my love." With another quick kiss to her forehead, he mounted and galloped away.

Collins had overslept this morning and was running to see if he could find Elizabeth. He had skirted the garden as he had done on the previous morning, carefully looking through the back gate to see if she was within the walled garden. Not finding her there, he turned about, looking in every direction.

A flash of color caught Collin's eye, and he moved off in that direction. Sheltered behind an ancient oak tree he was finally able to observe Elizabeth on Mr. Darcy's arm as they walked through the field. He took a seat at the base of the tree, watching the area where he had seen the couple, and waited for Elizabeth to return.

Mr. Collins' thoughts wandered as he waited, and the rustle of the grass startled him. Scurrying behind the tree upon which he had been resting, Collins was able to see Elizabeth mounted upon Mr. Darcy's horse as they returned to Longbourn. He heard them speaking of a family picnic that afternoon and knew he would have to wait for another day before he could carry out Lady Catherine's wishes.

Mr. Collins remained out of sight until Mr. Darcy's horse had again passed him on its return to Netherfield Park. When he was sure of not being observed, he returned to the inn, cursing his ill luck in oversleeping.

At the sound of carriages arriving, the occupants of Longbourn rushed to greet the newcomers. A surprise met their eyes when a farm wagon and a small open carriage pulled up in front of Longbourn. Darcy and Bingley sat on the bench of the wagon with the reins in Darcy's hands.

"Is everyone ready to go?" called Darcy.

"I am, I am, I am!" cried the children, who were nearly jumping up and down with excitement. Darcy and Bingley both hopped down from the wagon. Bingley moved to open the carriage door and offered his hand to assist Mrs. Gardiner. Darcy first lifted Elizabeth into the conveyance, then handed up the children. She helped to situate them on the blankets that had been placed into the bottom of the wagon where Georgiana sat. Once the children were in, Darcy helped each of Elizabeth's sisters into the carriage. Lydia, who had avoided all contact with her sisters the previous evening, now seemed anxious to be out of the house.

As Mrs. Hill rushed out of the house with a large picnic hamper, followed by the maid carrying a box with crocks and two bottles of wine, Elizabeth called out, "Papa, please come with us. It will be the last time we can do something like this for quite some time. Please come!"

As he looked at her pleading expression, he quickly reconsidered. "Just give me one moment, and I shall be happy to join you." Mr. Bennet hurried back inside the house only to return a short time later with his hat on his head, his walking stick in his hand, and a book tucked under his arm. He climbed into the open carriage with the older ladies and the group set off. They headed around the side of the house, past the barns and the stables to a track that led off across Longbourn. Elizabeth had selected a special place for their picnic. They traveled for nearly half an hour before arriving at the edge of the river that ran through Longbourn. Set back from the banks of the river was a beautiful stand of English Oak trees that offered plenty of shade from the warm spring sunshine.

Mr. Bennet helped the ladies down from the carriage as Bingley and Darcy lifted the others from the back of the wagon until only Elizabeth remained. She reached down and lifted out the hamper and box of beverages, fishing rods, kites, a ball, and all of the blankets that cushioned the bottom of the wagon, then handed things down to the others to carry. Darcy set down his burden and lifted Elizabeth down from the wagon. The group moved off towards the shade of the trees. The blankets were spread out with the food set in the middle until it was needed. Darcy carried the box with the beverages down to the water's edge. He pulled the bottles and crocks from the box and set them in the shallow water to keep them cool. Lydia found a place in the shade and leaned back against a tree, just watching the others but not joining in any of the activities. Darcy, Bingley, Elizabeth, and Georgiana ran with the children as they played tag and then catch. When Darcy and Bingley moved to flying kites with the children, Elizabeth and Georgiana joined the other ladies on the blankets.

Kitty had been sitting, her back against a tree, sketching as the others played. Elizabeth asked Kitty if she could see her drawings. Kitty moved to sit nearer to the others and placed the book in Elizabeth's lap. As Elizabeth opened the book, she gasped at the astonishing picture before her--Kitty had sketched Maria Lucas on the swing in Longbourn's garden. "Kitty, this is amazing. You have caught Maria's likeness perfectly!" Kitty beamed and blushed at her sister's praise, as Elizabeth turned the picture for the other ladies to see.

"It is lovely, Kitty!" said Jane.

"That is wonderful, Kitty!" cried her aunt.

"You have an impressive talent, Miss Katherine," said Lady Matlock.

Elizabeth turned the pages of the book to show the others many of Kitty's sketches. Soon the sound of Hugh's voice proclaiming his hunger was heard. Elizabeth set the sketchbook aside, and the ladies began unpacking the food, as the children and Darcy joined them on the blankets to enjoy the repast Mrs. Hill packed for them. A few steps behind them came Bingley carrying the drinks, which had been cooling in the river.

Mrs. Bennet looked around the corner of the back garden wall. She saw no one about so she moved to stand against the back wall of the house. She looked in the window to see that the kitchen was empty. She tried the door, but it was locked, so she took a key from her pocket and slipped it into the lock, quickly gaining entrance to Longbourn. She could hear the rattle of china and the murmur of voices. Just as she hoped, the staff was partaking of the midday meal. Sneaking through the kitchen, she gained the hallway that went past Mr. Bennet's library leading to the stairs. She paused briefly outside of the library but did not hear any sounds within. Advancing to the stairs, she mounted carefully, trying to avoid all the squeaky boards.

Gaining the second floor, she advanced down the hallway to the door of Elizabeth's room. She entered the room and began going through the drawers and wardrobe. Finally, she found what had to be Elizabeth's wedding bonnet. She pulled a pair of scissors from the pocket of her gown and began shredding the bonnet, cursing Elizabeth with each breath. She threw the last of the bonnet onto the floor and turned again to the wardrobe looking for her wedding gown. As she began yanking gowns from the closet, the door opened, and Margot came in, carrying some mending she had just finished. Upon seeing the stranger and the condition of the room, Margot let out a scream for help.

Mrs. Bennet shoved the young woman and rushed out into the hallway. She headed for the stairway and reached the bottom just as Mr. and Mrs. Hill appeared from the kitchen with Cook behind them. Mr. Hill grabbed Mrs. Bennet's arm to prevent her from escaping, as Mrs. Hill rushed up the stairs. She found Margot sitting on the floor in Elizabeth's room, blood coming from a small cut on her forehead. She helped the young maid to her feet and down the stairs to the kitchen. Mr. Hill had dragged Mrs. Bennet to the kitchen, as well, and locked her in a small storeroom. Her screams and curses could still be heard. Mrs. Hill sat Margot down and moved to get her bag of medicines, as Cook brought over a bowl of warm water and began to clean the cut. Mrs. Hill examined the wound carefully; it was not too long and very shallow, so did not require stitches. Then Mrs. Hill applied a small amount of salve and covered the wound with a bandage.

After the luncheon items had been packed away, the gentlemen, along with the three older children, moved to sit along the banks of the river, fishing rods in hand. Susan caught the first fish, but she would not touch it to remove it from the hook. She quickly lost interest in the activity and moved to sit on the blanket with the rest of the ladies. All of the gentlemen had success with the fishing; however, Darcy had to let his get away to rescue Hugh before his fish pulled him into the river.

They placed the fish in the box with the empty crocks of lemonade and tea and soon had everything and everyone loaded up, ready for the return to Longbourn. As the wagon pulled up in front of the door, Mrs. Hill came running out calling Elizabeth's name. "Oh, Miss Elizabeth, come quickly. I am so sorry! I do not know how she got in." Elizabeth jumped from the wagon rather than wait her turn to be handed down, and she followed Mrs. Hill into the house and up the stairs to her room. When she looked in, Elizabeth saw the wardrobe doors open, clothes were strewn about, and Margot on her hands and knees, gathering up pieces of fabric and lace.

"Margot, what on earth happened?" cried Elizabeth.

When Margot looked up, Elizabeth noticed the bandage on her forehead. "Oh, Miss Elizabeth, I am so sorry. Your wedding bonnet has been ruined beyond repair."

By this time, nearly everyone else had followed Elizabeth into the house and upstairs; only Kitty and the children were not present. Lydia hung to the back of the crowd with an odd look on her face.

"How did my bonnet become damaged?" asked Elizabeth with tears in her eyes.

"I am unsure, Miss Elizabeth. I came into the room to return some mending. I found a lady pulling things out of your wardrobe and this all over the floor. When I called for help, the woman shoved me and rushed out of the room."

"Is that why your head is bandaged?" asked Lizzy concerned.

"Yes, miss."

"Did you recognize the person?" asked Darcy.

"No, sir, I have never seen her before."

"Mrs. Hill, did you all see anyone leaving the house?"

"We did see someone, Miss Lizzy, but she did not manage to get away."

"Who was it that broke into my home, Mrs. Hill?" came the stern voice of Mr. Bennet.

"It was Mrs. Bennet, sir. We locked her in the storage room off the kitchen, sir," said Mr. Hill nervously.

"Gentlemen, will you join me in my library as we talk with Mrs. Bennet?" Darcy and Bingley nodded. "Mr. Hill, would you please bring Mrs. Bennet to my library."

"Yes, sir."

As the gentlemen departed to deal with the intruder, Elizabeth moved further into her bedroom and picked up pieces of her wedding bonnet. "What shall I do?" she asked the others in a voice thick with tears.

"This problem is quite easy to solve," said Lady Matlock with authority. I will send an express to Madame Colette for a replacement." She moved towards the writing desk in Elizabeth's room and quickly wrote her letter. She prepared a second one to her daughter, asking that they stop to pick the item up before coming into Hertfordshire. "I will stop in Meryton on our way home to arrange for these to be sent."

Elizabeth dismissed Margot to get some rest, and she and her sisters finished cleaning up the floor and returning the clothes to the wardrobe. Mrs. Gardiner went up to check on her children while Lady Matlock and Georgiana descended the stairs to return to the carriage. After leaving word for the gentlemen with Mrs. Hill, the ladies departed in the carriage, heading to the express office in Meryton.

Mr. Hill brought Mrs. Bennet to the library door, knocking sharply. At Mr. Bennet's call to enter, he opened the door and maneuvered Mrs. Bennet into the room, closing the door behind her. At Mr. Bennet's request, he stayed outside the door to prevent her from leaving.

Mrs. Bennet glared at the men present, a look of loathing on her face.

"Would you care to explain why you broke into my house?" asked her husband.

"It is my home as well. I should be permitted to come and go as I please."

"You gave up the right to live in this home with your disgraceful treatment of our second daughter," said Mr. Bennet coldly.

"Oh, yes, your precious Lizzy. Heaven forbid that your darling girl should not get her way in every little thing," sneered Mrs. Bennet.

"Lizzy gets no more special treatment from me than Lydia gets from you, and we were both wrong to show favoritism to any of the girls. We should have loved them all equally and encouraged what made each of them unique," said Mr. Bennet in a voice tinged with sadness.

"There is nothing to love about any of them but my beautiful Jane and by my dear, sweet, lively Lydia. What is your Lizzy but a willful, headstrong girl? Mary is hopeless, always quoting those stupid sermons, and the only thing Kitty is good for is attending to Lydia."

"There is much more to Jane than just her beauty. She is the sweetest, kindest, most gentle person I have ever known," said Bingley angrily, "but to you, she was a pawn in a game to capture a wealthy husband. Did you care that you embarrassed her at every turn? Would you have even cared if the man were a decent person or not so long as he was rich?

Would you have cared whether or not Jane was happy?"

"Mrs. Bennet, despite the fact that you are to be my mother-in-law, you are without question the most ignorant, unkind woman it has ever been my misfortune to meet. The only one of your daughters you deserve is Lydia, as she is exactly like you—selfish and spoiled. She is also an outrageous flirt whose behavior is completely unacceptable in polite society. All of your other daughters are excellent young women, and they became so in spite of the poor example they had in you." Darcy turned to Mr. Bennet saying, "I am sorry to have interrupted, sir, but I could not allow such slander to go unchallenged."

"Not at all, Mr. Darcy, and you, Mr. Bingley. It does my heart good to know that my daughters have such champions to protect and defend them. Now, Mrs. Bennet. You have yet to answer my question. I forbid you to enter this house until after the wedding at the earliest. Why did you enter?"

"There were belongings that I forgot in the rush when you forced me out. I knew the house would be empty, so I thought this would be a good time to get them," Mrs. Bennet replied haughtily.

"How could you possibly have known the house would be empty? And if you had forgotten things, why did you not just apply to me to come to retrieve them?"

"The way you threw me out, how could I expect you would agree to allow me my missing belongings?"

"Be that as it may, what possible belongings could you have had in Elizabeth's room, since that is where you were discovered?"

"You must be mistaken. I heard a noise coming from Elizabeth's room and opened the door to find a stranger there," remarked the Bennet matron defiantly. "You should have that person arrested for housebreaking."

"That young lady is Elizabeth's personal maid and is currently residing here. It was you who broke in; perhaps it is you who should be arrested."

"I believe you could easily make the case, sir, for breaking and entering as well as for destruction of property," said Darcy. "I am sure we could quietly arrange for her to be transported in punishment. I am not without connections, after all."

For the first time, Mrs. Bennet's bravado failed her, and her face blanched, but she countered, "No one would believe that I broke into my own home, and since I have a key, it was not breaking in."

Ignoring his wife, Mr. Bennet turned to Darcy. "Mr. Darcy, do you happen to know the penalty for destruction of property?"

"I do not know the exact sentence, but if we were to call the magistrate, I am sure he could tell us."

"You would not dare!" screamed Mrs. Bennet. "If you tried to do such a thing, I would see that all of you were ruined with me, except my Lydia."

"Oh, but your Lydia would be charged as an accomplice as she was the one who told you when the house would be empty so that you could break in," challenged Darcy. "Perhaps we should keep her locked in your storeroom until the guards arrive tomorrow?" he suggested with a twinkle in his eye as he spoke.

Mr. Bennet gave a chuckle. "I believe that just may do, Mr. Darcy. What an excellent suggestion!" A snicker, quickly smothered, was heard from Mr. Bingley.

"Perhaps the law is not the proper punishment for this, Mr. Bennet."

"What do you mean, Mr. Bingley?" Mr. Bennet looked at his future son with a raised brow.

"Perhaps any mother who could so discount four of her own daughters is unbalanced. Her erratic, uncontrolled behavior makes her more suited for bedlam than prison. There she would also be unable to harm anyone else."

"You are both monsters!" cried Mrs. Bennet, "How dare you treat me in such a fashion!"

"And how would you suggest we treat you? As my wife, you have no rights and may only do what I allow you to do. Who do you think will assist you in defying me? Do you think your brother Phillips, who is very fond of our daughters, would approve your current behavior and support you? Or, perhaps, you believe your brother Gardiner will offer his assistance? We know his wife's opinion of your behavior, and I can tell you, when he read your despicable letters to Elizabeth and his wife, he would have happily throttled you had you been present. It would not surprise me if you found your behavior has left you quite friendless."

"I am not friendless! My sister, Phillips, Lady Lucas, and Mrs. Long are all my dear friends!"

"Your sister Phillips would be horrified by your behavior to our daughters. You know how dear they are to her since she has no children of her own. I highly doubt she would approve your current behavior regarding the wedding of our two eldest daughters. As for Lady Lucas and Mrs. Long, with all the bragging you have done over the years, I am sure they would be delighted to see you get your comeuppance," finished Mr. Bennet in a satisfied voice.

Mrs. Bennet's confidence faltered as she recognized the truthfulness of her husband's words. Suddenly her shoulders slumped as she collapsed into the nearest chair.

"It is all that hateful girl's fault," she muttered.

"That is where you are wrong, madam. The fault lies squarely with you. Miss Bennet and Miss Elizabeth did what any loving daughters would do; they asked their mother to prepare things for *their* wedding in accordance with *their* wishes," said Darcy coldly.

"And, if that were not enough, you refused to accept the date our daughters chose for their wedding; you verbally attacked both of our eldest daughters in public; you additionally insulted our second daughter and sister in letters, you refused to allow Elizabeth to marry before Jane, and, finally, you have destroyed Elizabeth's wedding bonnet. You have insured that Jane and Elizabeth will want nothing more to do with you," said Mr. Bennet.

Mrs. Bennet was shocked to hear the situation described in such terms. Could her perspective truly be so wrong? No, no, it was just Lizzy being contrary. *I have done nothing wrong,* she thought! "I am sure neither Lady Lucas nor Mrs. Long would allow their daughters to dictate to them how a wedding should be arranged. They would certainly take my side," she huffed.

"I would not be too sure about that. I would not be surprised to find that you are the subject of the gossip you so loved to share after your little scene in town yesterday. Who do you think the gossips would choose to blame for yesterday's show—the two couples quietly enjoying refreshments together or the ridiculous woman who verbally assaulted and insulted them?"

Mrs. Bennet was shaken, but she attempted to maintain her brave demeanor. "My friends would not desert me!"

"However, whether or not you choose to accept responsibility for your actions is beside the point. The point is that we must determine what to do with you for the time being. We have some guards arriving tomorrow, but where to put you until then?" mused Mr. Bennet.

"Bingley, could you spare a footman or two to watch over the dower house until the other guards arrive tomorrow," asked Darcy.

Upon reflection, he replied, "I believe that would be possible."

"Mr. Bennet, if you were to lock the cottage doors from the outside, could they be opened from within without a key?"

"No, they could not, and Mrs. Bennet has the only key to the cottage. Speaking of keys," said her husband holding out his hand, "I believe you have a key that belongs to me." He continued to stare at her until she reached into the pocket of her gown, removed two keys, and dropped them into her husband's outstretched hand.

"Now, gentlemen, we have one other problem to deal with—Lydia. When I spoke to Lydia yesterday about telling her mother that Elizabeth had returned and that she would be in Mertyon, I placed restrictions on her behavior and warned her what the consequences would be for disobedience. Assuming she is again responsible for giving her mother information about the house, I believe I must speak with her again. I must ascertain if and how much she knew about her mother's plans before I determined what to do about her. Mr. Bingley, would you mind sending for your footman to come here before we return Mrs. Bennet to her home while I go upstairs and talk with Lydia?"

"Certainly, Mr. Bennet."

"If you gentlemen will excuse me, I will go to check on Elizabeth while you attend to these matters."

Mr. Bennet rose from his desk, and Bingley moved to take his place. As he opened the door, Mr.

Bennet directed Mr. Hill to come into the library and watch over Mrs. Bennet until he returned. Mr. Bennet moved towards the parlor to look for Lydia, as Darcy mounted the stairs to Elizabeth's room.

He stopped at the open door to take in the scene. Three of her sisters were still with her. Elizabeth sat on her bed with a lap full of scraps, her face showing signs of tears. As he tapped on the doorframe, she looked up and gave him a small smile.

"Elizabeth, my dear, are you well?"

"Yes, William, all will be well. It appears since mother cannot influence the plans for our wedding, she hoped to ruin it by destroying my wedding clothes. I am very fortunate that all she could find was my wedding bonnet. Aunt Rebecca feels certain Madame Colette will either have a suitable replacement or be able to recreate my bonnet. She and Georgie left to send the letters off by express. She sent one to Madame and one to Julia to stop to pick up the replacement from Madame before departing to join us in Hertfordshire. I think everything will be fine. It was a lovely bonnet, and I was just sad to see it destroyed."

"Bingley is sending to Netherfield for men to watch the house until the guards arrive tomorrow, and your father is speaking to Lydia to determine her part in what happened today. I believe her answers will help him decide whether she remains here or joins your mother in the dower house. Bingley and I will need to leave shortly if we are to get back to Netherfield before it gets completely dark. While we wait, would you care to take a turn in the gardens with me?

"That would be lovely, William. Would you excuse me, dear sisters?"

"Certainly, Lizzy, we shall await your return in the parlor," said Jane as the sisters stood to follow the couple downstairs.

As they passed Lydia's room, they heard raised voices but could not hear what was being said, so they continued on their way.

Inside Lydia's room, her father glared angrily at his daughter. "You admit to telling your mother that all of us would be out of the house today."

"Why should I not tell her? She is my mother, and this is her home," the young girl replied saucily.

"And did you know what she planned to do while she was here?"

"It is her house; I am sure she can do anything she pleases. What does it matter that she destroyed Lizzy's bonnet? Mr. Darcy is rich; he can just buy her a new one."

"It was not just any bonnet as you well know. It was Elizabeth's wedding bonnet."

"Knowing Lizzy's taste, it was probably just a plain old boring bonnet and probably not nearly special enough for a wedding."

"It is unfortunate for you that you choose to follow your mother's example in every way, as it seems you both need to learn the same lesson. As a woman, you have only the rights and possessions a husband, father, uncle, or other guardian chooses to give you. They can also punish you in any way they see fit. I believe that your callous behavior will earn you the same punishment as your mother. You will be banished to the dower house until after the wedding. Come with me, young lady."

With a pout on her face, she followed after her father. When they reached the first floor, Mr. Bennet turned towards the parlor. Finding three of his daughters there with their aunt, he said, "Girls, would you please go and pack Lydia's belongings? She will be joining her mother at the dower house until after the wedding."

"No!" shouted Lydia as everyone turned to look at her in surprise. "I do not want them touching my things!" she concluded angrily.

"At the moment ,what you want does not matter. Now come with me, young lady."

When Mr. Bennet and Lydia entered the library, Mr. Bingley was still within. "Sir, is there anything else you need from me? I believe Darcy and I should head back to Netherfield before it gets any later."

"By all means, Mr. Bingley. We will see all of you for dinner tomorrow evening." Bingley nodded to the ladies and exited the room.

"Mr. Hill, would you please wait outside of the door until further notice?" Bowing to his employer, Mr. Hill exited the room and took up his assigned post.

Taking his place behind his desk, Mr. Bennet looked at his wife and youngest daughter. Indicating the chairs in front of his desk, Mr. Bennet said, "Take a seat. I had hoped to put this off until after the wedding, but your actions have forced my hand." He waited until the women were seated, then leaned back in his chair, folding his hands into a steeple on his chest. As the ladies began to fidget in their seats, he finally spoke. "I am infinitely to blame for the condition of our family. I have tried for several months to correct some of my errors, and I have seen both Mary and Kitty try to improve themselves. They are turning into fine young ladies, very much like their older sisters."

"However, every suggestion I made to the two of you has been summarily ignored. You two utterly refuse to recognize that your behavior is not at all appropriate. Neither of you will attend the ball or the wedding. Beginning immediately, you are both confined to the dower house. You will no longer have any pocket money. I will determine your needs and make purchases for you as I deem fit. I will also notify all of the shops in Meryton that you two are not allowed to charge anything to the family accounts. You will have only one servant at the dower house, so you will have to assist in the work. You will not have a cook, so you will have to learn to do that as well."

Mrs. Bennet and Lydia sat, their mouths agape, just staring and hardly able to believe what they heard.

"Also, Lydia will be leaving for school in the middle of June. Since she has refused all her family's efforts to improve her behavior, she will be attending a school for unruly young women. Her future success in life, very likely her future happiness, will depend totally on her efforts. She will remain at school until the winter break in mid-December when she has two weeks off. Your time at the dower house will be good practice for your time at school as you will have daily chores there as part of the curriculum. The more enjoyable activities you would most want to participate in are earned with good behavior."

"No, you cannot take my Lydia from me," cried her mother.

"She must be sent away, as you only encourage her in her poor behavior. If you can both improve, you will certainly have the opportunity to spend time together in the future. But, Lydia *is* going to school very soon."

"Well, then, when will we be shopping for Lydia's new wardrobe for school?" asked Mrs. Bennet with excitement.

"There will be no need for shopping. They wear uniforms at the school. There is also a list of items indicating what can be taken to school and things that are forbidden. They do not have any shopping close by, and so pocket money is not needed."

"It sounds positively horrid. I will not go!" cried Lydia with a stamp of her foot.

"Lydia, we spoke just yesterday about your behavior, and I gave you strict instructions about what I would and would not accept. You could not follow those instructions for even one short day. You decided for yourself how you would be spending your time when you chose to ignore my instructions. There will be no ball for you, nor will you be attending the wedding."

"You and your mother will be mandatory guests of the dower house until after the wedding. At that time, I may allow you to return to the main house. However, you will not be permitted to go into Meryton, nor will we be receiving visitors. I plan to let the neighbors known Mrs. Bennet is ill, and her dear Lydia insisted on staying with her to care for her. I will say that I moved her to the dower house to protect the rest of the family and our guests from getting sick before the wedding. My words will most likely not be believed after Mrs. Bennet's display yesterday, nor will they be openly questioned. You two will remain here until Lydia's belongings are packed and the guards from Netherfield arrive. Then you will be escorted to the dower house."

Suddenly there was a loud knocking at the door, and the agitated voice of Kitty cried, "Papa, you must see this!"

Mr. Bennet opened the door to find a very upset Kitty on the other side.

"What is it, child? What must I see?" She grabbed his hands and pulled him towards the stairs. When they reached Lydia's room, he found all of her sister's staring into her small trunk with angry looks upon their faces. Mr. Bennet stepped over to the trunk and glanced down, his eyes widening in surprise. "What is this?" he asked confused.

"We had finished packing Lydia's clothes in her larger trunk and pulled this one out to pack some personal items in, but when we opened it, this is what we found," said Elizabeth.

"Where did it all come from?" he wondered.

"Some of it is mine," said Kitty angrily. "It was not unusual, Papa, for something to go missing if you refused to allow Lydia to borrow it, but as she never wore it, we had no proof that she had taken it.

The girls began to sort through the items to determine to whom they belonged. There were items belonging to all of Lydia's sisters, as well as to Mr. and Mrs. Bennet. There were also missing household items and items that could not be identified. There was a small box that, when opened, was discovered to be filled with money.

"What was she going to do with all this money? She always said she was broke and borrowing from us, but she never repaid any of it," said Elizabeth in frustration.

"Count what is there, and I will trust you to each take only what is owed you. You may also put your belongings away. Mary, would you please give the items belonging to me to my valet? I shall take the items that belong to your mother, and Jane, if you would give the household items to Mrs. Hill. I will have to turn over the unknown items to the magistrate, but I do not have any idea how I will explain having them," said Mr. Bennet woefully. "If it were known that Lydia had been stealing things, she could be put in jail or worse, depending on the value of the items."

"Please finish up Lydia's packing. I imagine the help Mr. Bingley is sending will arrive shortly." So saying, Mr. Bennet took the things for his wife and departed the room.

When he returned to his library, he set the items he carried on the edge of the desk and asked, "Do you recognize any of these items, Mrs. Bennet?"

"I certainly do as they are all mine! Some of them went missing quite some time ago. Wherever did you find them?"

"Perhaps you would care to ask your daughter Lydia that question."

"Why ever would Lydia know about them?" the woman asked, confused.

Mr. Bennet stared at his youngest daughter but spoke not a word. Finally, Mrs. Bennet turned to look at Lydia in confusion. Still Mr. Bennet did not speak, though by now the girl had begun to fidget in her seat.

"Lydia?" said her mother, "Do you know something about this?"

Lydia's face was bright red, and she looked at her hands in her lap when she finally answered, "I took them."

Mrs. Bennet was very confused. "You took them? Whatever for?"

"I wanted them," she said defiantly.

"Well, wanting something is certainly not an invitation to take things that belong to someone else," declared her mother indignantly.

"But you always said that I was beautiful and lively and that I could have anything I want," Lydia whined. "So when someone would not let me borrow something I wanted, I just took it."

"If that is the case, whatever did you want with my silver shaving cup?" asked her father.

"It was shiny, and I liked it," said Lydia quietly.

"How long have you been taking things from others, Lydia?" her father asked.

"I do not remember. It seems like it is something I have always done."

"There were several things that no one in the family recognized. Do you remember from where you took everything?"

Lydia shook her head but did not say anything.

"Well, young lady, your sisters have retrieved their belongings and the money you borrowed but failed to repay. However, you have left our family, and your future in particular, in a very precarious position. By law, Lydia, what you did was stealing. Do you realize that you could go to jail for this? Based on the value of some of the items you took, you risk being transported or hung. How I am to return some of these stolen items without explaining how they came to be in my possession, I do not know." Lydia was staring at her father, her face white and reflecting her fear.

"I hope, Mrs. Bennet, this points out to you how poor an example you provided for our daughters."

"That is not true!" she cried. "I never told her she could just take what she wanted, and if I had known, I would have told her it was wrong and done something about it," she finished with an irritated sniff.

"Yes, but I am sure when you reported it to me you would have put the blame on someone else," said Mr. Bennet with a raised brow. Mrs. Bennet blushed and looked down, proving her husband's statement.

"Lydia, do you realize that if anyone else were to have discovered the stolen items you could go to jail? You must stop this immediately! If one more thing goes missing after this warning, I will have only two choices. First, I could allow you to face the consequences of your actions. Or, second, I could have you committed. It would save you from the gallows or being sent to a penal colony, but I am not sure what kind of life it would be. Lydia, you have attended church since you were little. You know that stealing is not only a crime but a sin. It is far past the time you should have learned this lesson and so many others. Everything we say or do has a consequence—some good and some bad. I expect you to correct this behavior immediately. Is that understood?"

"Yes, Papa," she whispered without looking up.

"Lydia, despite what your mother has said, the world does not revolve around you and your desires. You are the daughter of an insignificant country gentleman, and it is time you recognize your place in the world. You are a ridiculous, silly child—spoiled, selfish, and far too flirtatious. It is extremely inappropriate in such a young girl. You will not get a husband in such a way. It will only lead to your downfall and the disgrace of our entire family. Your mother did you absolutely no favors by encouraging your wild behavior. I am equally at fault for allowing it to go on as long as it did. I am sending you to school in hopes that you will improve yourself. It is only by emulating the behavior of your oldest sisters that you will ever find a good life. It is only by being a good and kind person that you will every find real happiness."

"I do not believe that I will bring you and your mother back to the main house after the wedding. It is imperative that you be separated from her poor influence. I will allow you to return, but your activities will be severely limited, and you will be required to spend time with me, working to improve your mind."

"No, no!" cried, Mrs. Bennet. "You cannot take my dear girl from me even before she is sent to that horrible school. I must have my sweet Lydia with me."

"No, madam. It is better that you be separated as you seem to bring out the worst in each other. The behavior that both of you have exhibited for so many years will no longer be tolerated. Enjoy these few days you have for they are to be your last together until both of you have made significant improvement in yourselves. And, if again being in each other's company causes either of you to slide back into bad behaviors, the separation will become permanent."

At that point, a knock was heard at the door. Opening it, Mr. Hill informed Mr. Bennet that two men had come from Netherfield. Mr. Bennet asked Mr. Hill to show the men in, then see that the carriage was prepared and that the trunks in Lydia's room were loaded into it. A moment later another knock came and at Mr. Bennet's call of "Come" two men entered the room.

"Gentlemen," began Mr. Bennet, "did Mr. Bingley explain to you what you would be doing here?"

"He only said that you needed someone watched, sir."

"Did he also explain to you the need for discretion?"

"Yes, sir."

"You will be maintaining the security at the dower house on my estate. My wife has some objections to the upcoming wedding of my two eldest daughters. So rather than allow her to upset my daughters or disrupt their plans, my wife and youngest daughter are to reside there under lock and key for the next several days. Mr. Darcy has arranged for some guards to come from the city to take over for you, but they will not arrive until sometime tomorrow. I do not expect them to offer any trouble, but prefer to ensure that they do not disrupt the planned events. The only real rule is that you not let them out, short of the building being on fire, and I would again ask that you tell no one of the situation here. I would not wish for anything to tarnish this special time for my eldest daughters."

"We understand, sir. You may depend on us."

"Well, then, if you follow me, the carriage should be ready, and my daughter's trunks stowed. Gentlemen, if you will lead the way to the carriage. Mrs. Bennet, Lydia, please follow the gentlemen."

The ladies quietly followed the two guards from the room with no protest. The revelations of the evening appeared to have taken a toll on both of them.

CHAPTER 4

THE ATMOSPHERE AT Longbourn the next morning was somewhat subdued. Elizabeth had shown the things discovered in Lydia's trunk to Mr. and Mrs. Hill and Cook, who each recognized an item that belonged to them. Elizabeth apologized for the items having gone missing and thanked the staff for their dedication and loyalty to the family. She also showed the items to Aunt Madeline, who recognized some things that belonged to both her husband and her.

"What is your father going to do about the unidentified ones?" Mrs. Gardiner asked in concern.

"He has few options. He does not wish to get Lydia into trouble without first giving her a chance to change her behavior. Consequently, I believe he is going to turn it over to the magistrate and tell him it was found in a bag at the dower house. He plans to let the neighbors know Mama is sick and Lydia is tending to her. He will say we have moved them to the dower house to keep the rest of the family and guests from becoming ill. Then he can claim the bag was found in the house when they moved Mama and Lydia there."

Elizabeth continued. "William told me of what occurred when Mama was confronted, and Papa spoke to us of his remarks to Lydia before and to Mama after the discovery of the items Lydia had secreted away. It was pointed out to both of them that their activities could have serious criminal consequences. Papa said they were both quiet and subdued when they left for the dower house."

"Well, then, let us hope they will seriously consider their behavior while they have this quiet time to themselves. Perhaps there is hope for them yet," said Mrs. Gardiner encouragingly, as she wrapped Elizabeth in a hug.

Elizabeth spent much of the day overseeing the arrangements for the family dinner to be held at Longbourn that evening. Mr. Bingley's aunt and uncle from Scarborough were arriving today, as was Mr. Hurst. Mr. Gardiner and the remainder of the Fitzwilliam family were also expected. Lady Penelope would be traveling with them as well, and Elizabeth was excited to see her friend.

It was as she was arranging some flowers for the dinner table that a knock came at the door. She heard familiar voices in the hallway and moved to greet the newcomers. "William, Colonel Fitzwilliam, what a lovely surprise, and Uncle Edward, we are glad you have come."

Elizabeth's greetings were interrupted by running footsteps and calls of "Papa, Papa, we missed you!" Darcy, Elizabeth, and the colonel stepped quickly out of the way as three small bodies hurled themselves at Mr. Gardiner amid laughter and squeals.

Elizabeth and Darcy looked on the scene with identical expressions. Their eyes were soft, almost misty; their smiles were almost wistful. When they turned their gaze upon each other, both faces colored softly. Darcy reached out for Elizabeth's hand, entwining their fingers, as he gently rubbed the back of her hand. Mrs. Gardiner had followed the children, Rachel in her arms, at a more sedate pace. When she arrived at the bottom of the stairs, she was overwhelmed by the loving looks upon the faces of her niece and Mr. Darcy. Mrs. Gardiner smiled as she thought of the wonderful life they would begin in just a few short days.

Mrs. Gardiner moved forward to greet the newcomers, saving her husband for last as she placed a kiss upon his cheek. "Edward, dear, I'm glad you have arrived safely. Lizzy, would you ask Mrs. Hill to send some refreshments?"

"Certainly, Aunt Madeline," she answered, moving in the direction of the kitchens.

"Mrs. Gardiner, we need to speak with Mr. Bennet before we join you," said Darcy.

"I believe you know the way, Mr. Darcy. We shall see you in the parlor whenever you are free," she said, as she moved towards the stairway to show her husband to their suite.

The colonel followed Darcy down the hallway to Mr. Bennet's library. He knocked and entered at Mr. Bennet's call. "Good afternoon, sir," said the cousins as they entered.

"Good afternoon, Mr. Darcy. Good afternoon, Colonel. It is good to see you again."

"You as well, sir."

"The guards have arrived, sir. I hope you do not mind, but I sent them to your kitchen for refreshments before they take up their positions."

"Not at all, Mr. Darcy. I am glad you thought of it. When they are finished, we can take them out to the dower house. Is there anything that they will need to do their job?"

"Well, Mr. Bennet, the men and I were speaking on the trip over from Netherfield. They would prefer to do two men, twelve-hour shifts. We discussed the layout of the house from the description Darcy gave. They believe if they were stationed on opposite corners they could effectively watch two sides at a time. If we could furnish them with chairs or benches and a place for two of them to sleep when they are not on duty, that would be sufficient. Meals are the only other thing they will need." the colonel informed him.

"I would not wish to burden Mrs. Hill with additional mouths to feed at such a busy time," said Darcy. "I thought perhaps to purchase a ham, wheel of cheese, and bread from the shops in Meryton. That should allow them to eat as needed during the upcoming days."

"That is thoughtful of you, Mr. Darcy. As for sleeping, there is a small stable at the rear of the dower house. It has a room with two cots that they could use for sleeping."

"That should address the situation quite nicely," said the colonel.

"I have briefed the gentlemen on what they will need to do, sir, and as soon as they have refreshed themselves, we can take them out to the dower house. Would you like for my cousin and me to do this, or would you wish to handle the situation?"

"I believe that I should like to accompany you gentlemen when you go. I would like to see what frame of mind they are in today after all that transpired yesterday," said Mr. Bennet.

"And how are you handling the events of yesterday, sir?" Darcy asked, concerned.

"I shall be fine, Mr. Darcy. You need not worry."

A knock at the door revealed Mrs. Hill arriving to inform him that the guards had finished eating and were ready to leave. The gentlemen stood and moved towards the hallway. Mrs. Hill returned to the kitchen and told the gentlemen the carriage would appear around back to pick them up momentarily. Meanwhile, Darcy stopped into the parlor to explain to Elizabeth what was happening before he exited the house with Mr. Bennet and the colonel.

Elizabeth was nervous as she waited for the guests to arrive. Her aunt had put her in charge of this evening; she had planned the menu, table decorations, seating plan, and after dinner entertainment. She prayed that she had not forgotten something or made a dreadful mistake in her plans. *If I cannot handle a simple dinner party at Longbourn, how will I ever manage to be a suitable mistress of Pemberley?* she worried.

The family was gathered in the parlor when the sound of carriages was heard. A short time later, Mrs. Hill was showing the visitors into the room. First came Darcy, Georgiana, and Bingley, followed by Lord and Lady Matlock, Viscount Gilchrist, Lady Penelope, Colonel Fitzwilliam, Lady Julia, and, surprisingly, Miss Anne de Bourgh. Then came Mr. and Mrs. Hurst, and the last to enter were Mr. and Mrs. Albert Bingley.

This Mr. Bingley was the youngest brother of Charles Bingley's father and was the acting manager of the family business. Mrs. Bingley, Barbara, was the daughter of a clergyman who was the youngest son of a gentleman. She was happy with her husband. They had a lovely home, several delightful children, and a comfortable income. She had no aspirations for more. She was just happy to enjoy the blessings she had been given and to give back wherever an opportunity presented itself.

The Albert Bingleys were unlucky enough to have been visiting London when Caroline was abruptly returned to town. Barbara had no patience with Caroline's ridiculous behavior. Just as with Elizabeth, Barbara Bingley was of a higher social status than her niece but was treated by Caroline, with all of her ridiculous airs, as inferior. Barbara had been forced to listen to all of the hateful accusations made by Caroline regarding the poor manners and connections of Jane and Elizabeth Bennet. As a consequence, she was very much looking forward to meeting them and felt certain she would enjoy their company.

After all the introductions had been made, the group settled in for conversation. Half an hour later, Mrs. Hill announced that dinner was ready, and everyone departed for the dining room. Elizabeth had arranged for four courses, each containing a variety of dishes. The guests seemed pleasantly mixed, and everyone enjoyed the excellent meal and stimulating conversation. At the conclusion of dinner, Jane, who as eldest was acting as hostess, invited the ladies to join her in the parlor.

As the ladies departed, Aunt Rebecca said, "Elizabeth, could you and Madeline join Julia and me in your room for a brief moment?"

Elizabeth and her aunt quickly agreed, and the group moved up the stairs. Noting the small packet that Julia held as they entered Elizabeth's room, she asked nervously, "Was Madame Collette able to find something to replace my bonnet?"

"Yes," said Julia. "However, she did not send a new bonnet. She said this is what they use in several countries on the continent, and she believes it will become all the rage in England before too long."

Julia held out the package to Elizabeth, who gingerly accepted it. She placed it on the bed and began to unwrap it. Inside was the most delicate of items.

"She showed me how you wear it," said Julia. "May I show you?" At Elizabeth's nod, she picked it up and positioned it on Elizabeth head. Then picking up the extra fabric, she guided Elizabeth to the mirror, shook out the material, and adjusted it properly.

Elizabeth just stared at her reflection with tears in her eyes. In the mirror, she could see her aunts behind her, their expressions reflecting her own. Julia faced the three women with an expectant smile on her face. "Madame will be delighted that you were happy with her idea," said Julia.

"Oh, Lizzy, you look utterly beautiful," said Mrs. Gardiner.

"I believe," said Lady Matlock, "that Darcy will be left speechless at your beauty. Madame Colette's idea is inspired."

The ladies hung up the delicate article to allow the wrinkles to fall out and returned to the drawing room to join the others.

In the dining room, Mr. Hill brought both port and brandy to the table for the gentlemen to enjoy before they adjourned to join the ladies. They talked about many things, including the best ways to provide for their families. Each of the men cared greatly for those under their care and wanted the best for them. They talked of the good fortune they had to become acquainted through the upcoming marriages and what they hoped for each of the young couples.

As they were returning to the parlor to join the ladies, Mr. Bennet asked both Mr. Darcy and Bingley to join him for one moment in his library. When they were all in the library with the door closed, Mr. Bennet said, "I would appreciate it if you gentlemen would look over these items. Do you recognize any of them? If they belong to you, please feel free to take them with you when you depart."

Darcy did not see anything familiar, but Bingley picked up two small figurines. Looking at Mr. Bennet with confusion, he said, "I assumed Caroline had broken these in one of her tantrums. However did they come to be in your possession?"

With obvious embarrassment, Mr. Bennet explained what the girls had discovered when packing Lydia's belongings the previous evening. He told them of her comments and how her mother's remarks lead her to believe she could just take what she wanted. He further explained that he had made Lydia aware of what the consequence of her actions could have been and that he would allow her to suffer those consequences if anything should go missing again. As they left the study, Mr. Bennet asked Mrs. Hill to wrap the figurines and put them with Mr. Bingley's hat so that he could take them with him when he departed.

The evening ended some time later after more pleasant conversation and performances by most of the ladies.

The next morning Elizabeth arrived at their meeting spot, but there was no sign of Darcy. She climbed the fence and perched herself upon the top rail, facing toward Netherfield and waited for his arrival.

Mr. Collins had followed Elizabeth after she left Longbourn. He watched as she climbed the fence and turned her back to him. An evil smirk covered his face, for he knew his chance had come. Looking carefully about to ensure there were no others in the area, Collins crept closer. Silently, he reached up and grabbed the neck at the back of Elizabeth's dress, pulling her backward. With the sound of ripping fabric, she tumbled to the ground. Elizabeth's head bounced slightly when it hit the ground, dazing her, and she could feel the breeze on her legs as her skirt landed about her. Startled, she looked up to see the leering face of William Collins.

"Dear Cousin Elizabeth, I have come for what your mother promised me, and I will not be denied! I shall take you now, and you will have no choice but to marry me, and Mr. Darcy will again be free to marry Miss de Bourgh as his aunt wishes."

Elizabeth felt a prickle of fear, for she could not hope to overcome Mr. Collins' greater bulk and strength. However, she would never let him see her fear, so she used the anger his words provoked and spoke sharply. "Mr. Collins, every fool knows that only a father or male relative can grant permission for a marriage. My mother may have hoped for a match between us, but only my father could grant your request. Also, you never proposed to me and, had you done so, I would have refused. We are in no way suited to one another, so I suggest you return to your parsonage and leave me alone." Elizabeth attempted to rise from the ground, only to have Collins give her shoulder a shove and lean over her with a menacing expression.

"You will be going nowhere until I have completed what I came here to do." He had moved to stand over her and was unbuttoning the fall of his breeches. Thinking quickly, Elizabeth kicked up her foot as hard as she could, aiming for the despicable parson's groin. He doubled over in pain, his knees buckling as he fell towards her. Elizabeth raised her arms and shoved as hard as she could. Unfortunately, she could not move his bulk far, only managing to push his upper body to the side. Her legs were trapped beneath the lower half of him. She tried to pull them free, but could not. She managed to sit up but was unable to move the corpulent parson off herself. Mr. Collins was still moaning, but Elizabeth did not know how long he would be incapacitated. She knew that she needed to get away from him. At the sound of hooves, Elizabeth looked up. Seeing her beloved William, she waved her arms.

Darcy was looking forward to meeting Elizabeth for today's journey to Oakham Mount, but he was delayed leaving Netherfield when he encountered his cousin also preparing for an early morning ride. Richard decided to accompany his cousin to greet Miss Elizabeth but promised not to remain with them for long. They headed for the fence that separated Netherfield and Longbourn at an easy pace. As he crested the hill that gave him the first glimpse of their meeting place, Darcy saw a brief flash of color that quickly disappeared. He scanned the area, but did not see any sign of Elizabeth, so they continued their leisurely pace. As they approached the fence, he saw Elizabeth seated on the ground, her arms waving in the air. She appeared to be pinned down by something. His horse sailed over the fence to the Longbourn side, and he dismounted before the animal had come to a complete stop. Having seen the same thing as his cousin, the colonel followed closely behind him. Richard leaned down to release Elizabeth from the encumbrance. When he pushed the brown lump, a groan was heard. Richard rolled the mass over and cried, "Good Lord!"

Darcy turned at his cousin's cry, shock and anger appearing on his face as he too cried out in surprise. "Mr. Collins!"

Turning back to Elizabeth, Darcy placed his hands on her shoulders to check her for injuries and was surprised to feel bare skin. His eyes opening in shock, Darcy quickly removed his coat and gently placed it over Elizabeth's torn dress. His gentle touch caused her fears to be released, and she began to sob. Darcy wrapped her in his embrace, cupped her cheek, and stared into her eyes. "Are you well, my love? Did he hurt you?" Elizabeth shook her head, continuing to cry.

Darcy none too gently prodded Collins with his boot. "Explain yourself, Mr. Collins." Darcy's voice was cold, his anger apparent.

"I was here to wish my cousin well, and she practically threw herself at me."

"If you planned to wish her well, why did you follow her on her walk and not present yourself at Longbourn to do so properly? Try again, Mr. Collins. We both know that Miss Elizabeth cannot abide being in your presence. We are happy together, and I trust her, so I know that she did not do as you said."

Richard gave the man another kick. "Why are you really here, Collins? Did my aunt send you?" the colonel barked, his hand resting on his sabre.

"I told you what happened," said Mr. Collins, not meeting their eyes.

"So you did," said Darcy. "However, this time, I suggest you tell us the truth."

Beads of sweat broke out on Collins' forehead, but he said nothing.

"We should turn the miscreant over to the magistrate, Darcy. Based on what we observed, it appears like assault to me," remarked Colonel Fitzwilliam.

"It was assault," cried Collins, "but I am the one who was assaulted!"

"Miss Elizabeth is a proper lady, sir. Of what do you dare accuse her?"

"When I refused her advances, she delivered me a cruel kick. I am permanently injured, I am sure of it!"

"How dare you make such an accusation? Miss Elizabeth would only act in such a way to defend herself. What did you do that prompted her to assault you, sir?"

"Not a thing. Come, gentlemen. We are men of the world." Darcy and Richard glanced at each other and rolled their eyes. "My cousin, Miss Elizabeth, first used her arts and allurements to lure you from your betrothed, Miss de Bourgh, while she was promised to me. She must have realized the error of her ways and wished to, again, gain my attentions."

Collins' smirk was quickly erased as Darcy's fist made contact with the parson's face. Blood ran from his nose and mouth, and it appeared that a couple of teeth had been knocked out.

At hearing the parson's words, Elizabeth, whose tears had finally stopped, cried, "I would rather be a spinster than married to such a miserable excuse for a man." She pulled back her foot to deliver him another kick. However, this time, Collins saw it coming. He reached out and grabbed her ankle before she could make contact, giving it a hard wrench. Elizabeth cried out in pain and would have fallen if she had not been firmly held within Darcy's embrace.

"Are you recovered enough, Lizzy, to tell us what happened here?"

Elizabeth nodded and related to Darcy and Richard all that had occurred. When she spoke of the kick she had delivered to Collins, both gentlemen began to laugh.

"Well done, my dear!"

"That was very clever, Miss Elizabeth!"

"Elizabeth, did he say 'I would be free to marry Anne as my aunt wishes?'" Darcy looked at his cousin as he asked the question.

"Yes, those were his exact words."

"Do you think it was his idea or did Aunt Catherine put him up to it?" queried Darcy. Richard shrugged.

"How dare you accuse either Lady Catherine or me of such reprehensible behavior! No one will believe such slanderous things about a parson and a peer, especially coming from such a loose woman."

Darcy's fist, again, shot out. This time, there was a satisfying crack, and Collins cried out in pain. "How dare you speak of my betrothed in such a fashion! *If* you were a gentleman, I would call you out for such an insult."

"Darcy, do not put yourself to the trouble. We will just turn him over to the magistrate. I am sure he would keep him locked up until after the wedding. Father and I can deal with him at that time."

"We cannot bring this to the magistrate, for it could damage Elizabeth's reputation and that of her sisters," worried Darcy with a frown.

The men thought briefly of the best way to handle the scoundrel. "I know! We can lock him in the shed near the dower house. Then our guards will be able to keep an eye on him."

"Excellent, Richard!"

"You have no right to do that," cried the parson. "No one will believe her word over mine."

By this time, Richard had hauled Mr. Collins to his feet. Elizabeth bravely faced the ridiculous man, anger evident in her expression. Unable to bear looking at the stupid man any longer, she glanced downward. The sight that met her eyes made Elizabeth gasp and blush before looking quickly away. Hearing her and feeling the shudder that briefly ran through her body, Darcy looked towards the man with narrowed eyes. Taking in his appearance, Darcy realized what had caused Elizabeth's reaction. Mr. Collin's breeches were mostly undone.

Looking back at the man Richard held firmly by the arm, Darcy coldly remarked, "I believe your untidy appearance puts the lie to your words, sir. Seeing you thus, it will not be a matter of Miss Elizabeth's word against yours, for we are both witnesses to what you attempted to do."

Mr. Collins started to argue, but the men ignored him. "Richard, will you bind and gag him and deliver him to the cottage and the guards?"

"Of course, perhaps I will drag him behind my horse. At the very least he will get some much-needed exercise as he will have to run along to keep up."

At the colonel's words, Collins' eyes grew wide, and he began to splutter. Darcy's glare quieted the man.

"I will see Miss Elizabeth home to Longbourn and explain the situation to Mr. Bennet. Then, I will write to my godfather, the Bishop of Derby. He is in London on business at present and hoped to be able to attend the wedding. An express could reach him today. Perhaps he will be able to come immediately. He will know what to do to remove this miscreant from his living and his service to the church."

"You would not dare!" cried the suddenly nervous parson.

"I am sure that my godfather, who is greatly looking forward to meeting Elizabeth, will be quite interested to hear the actions of today. Besides, any parson who would attempt what you did—even if it is at his patroness's orders—does not deserve to hold such a position of trust and responsibility."

"You cannot treat me in such a manner! Lady Catherine will be very displeased with you. I must complete her request."

Richard gave Mr. Collins' arm a tug, saying, "Be quiet! After the treatment Miss Elizabeth was afforded at your hands, be glad you are still breathing. I am sure Darcy would much prefer beating you to a pulp to allowing you to continue your miserable existence." Richard grinned at the fearful look in the parson's eyes.

Darcy balled one hand into a fist, rubbing the other one across the knuckles, a scowl on his handsome face. "I would find that most satisfying, indeed," was Darcy's reply. Collins again looked pale and began mumbling.

"Quiet," said the colonel. "We can and will treat you any way we wish, as there is no one here to stop us. Nor do I believe Lady Catherine will concern herself with what becomes of you. She will have plenty of trouble of her own when my father finds out what she attempted. I will be speaking to my father immediately upon returning to Netherfield. I imagine he will be leaving for Kent shortly after your wedding." Darcy and the colonel both chuckled at the thought of what their uncle might do to the meddling Lady Catherine.

"I almost wish I could be present when he confronts her," said Darcy, "but, I expect to be far more pleasantly engaged at the time." Darcy looked at Elizabeth with such intensity that she blushed profusely, all the while feeling weak in the knees.

Breaking eye contact and begging her pardon, Darcy knelt down and tore several strips from the bottom of Elizabeth's petticoat. Handing the strips to Richard, Darcy again clasped Elizabeth in his embrace, and they watched the colonel attend to matters. Starting with his hands, Richard drew Collins' arms behind his back. He pulled the fabric so tightly that it cut into the skin of the parson's fleshy wrists.

"Must you make it so tight?" Mr. Collin's whined.

"Stop your sniveling," said the colonel, who took one of the strips of fabric, wadded it up, and shoved it into the prisoner's mouth before tying another one over it. Collins continued to complain, but the words were no more than an inarticulate mumble. When he had finished his task, the colonel commanded, "You will march before my horse to where you will be detained. Do not try to run away, for you will be unsuccessful. You are in no condition to get far, and I am armed with my sabre. Do not give me cause to use it." Sweat again began to bead on the parson's face, which paled at the colonel's words. Drawing his sabre, Richard mounted, "Now move, Collins." The man stood trembling, rooted to the spot in fear. Richard pulled his sword from the scabbard, nudging the man between the shoulder blades to get him moving.

Darcy and Elizabeth stood watching the two move away. Finally, Darcy broke the silence. "I know that you wished to say goodbye to Oakham Mount this morning, dearest Lizzy, but I believe that we should get you back to Longbourn as soon as possible. We will try another time before the wedding, perhaps even this afternoon. It may not be sunrise, but we will try again," Darcy promised.

"After I have changed and you have written your letters, could we visit the tenants? I would like to say farewell to them, but I do not have the time to walk to each of their homes before time to prepare for the ball."

"Could it be done on horseback?"

"Certainly, but you know that Papa does not keep horses that would be appropriate for us to ride," Elizabeth reminded him.

"I will return to Netherfield after the letters are written and return with another mount. Then we will visit the tenants."

"That would be wonderful, but you do realize that I am not the most skilled of riders."

"Perhaps not yet, but we will change that once we get to Pemberley. Many of its most beautiful spots can only be reached on horseback. I shall help you improve your riding skills so that we can explore the wonders of Pemberley, together," he concluded with a smile.

"Both prospects sound delightful."

"Let us return to Longbourn then. The sooner I prepare the letters, the sooner we will be off on our visits."

"With a horse and saddlebags, I will be able to bring the small gifts I have made for the children," said Elizabeth with a pleased smile.

Darcy lifted Elizabeth onto his horse and mounted behind her, settling himself in the saddle. The couple quickly arrived at the house. Elizabeth led the way inside and went immediately to her room, as Darcy strode towards Mr. Bennet's study. Elizabeth was pleased that she did not encounter anyone until she had changed. She hid the gown in the bottom of her wardrobe and changed into her riding habit.

She returned downstairs and knocked on the door of her father's study. Entering at his call, she found her father pacing the room. The stiffness of his body and determined step were a clear sign that he was furious. Seeing who entered, Mr. Bennet rushed forward and pulled his daughter into his arms, hugging her tightly. "Oh, my dear girl, are you well? Did that scoundrel actually lay his hands on you?"

"I am well, Papa. I was able to inflict damage to him before he could do the same to me. Then my white knight appeared to rescue me before Mr. Collins could recover." Elizabeth flashed a smile at Darcy as she spoke. "William, I was wondering if you think it would be possible to force Mr. Collins to renounce his inheritance of Longbourn because of his misdeeds?"

Darcy gave her a delighted smile. "I doubt that he will agree to do so. However, we will see if we cannot change his mind." Darcy's words were very determined.

Darcy stood. "Mr. Bennet, would you arrange for these letters to be sent express immediately? I promised Elizabeth we would travel to see the tenants today, as she wishes to say farewell. I must return to Netherfield for a mount for her, unless you would agree with her sharing my horse." Darcy grinned at his future father-in-law as he spoke.

"Though I would not mind your doing so, sir," the young couple's faces began to brighten at his words, "we would not wish to shock the neighbors or tenants with your behavior." He smiled as their faces fell.

Darcy bowed over Elizabeth's hand, kissing the back, "I will return as quickly as possible. Be ready, my dear."

The young couple spent a pleasant morning riding the paths and fields of Longbourn, as Elizabeth said farewell to the tenants she had helped to care for over the past several years. Darcy often looked on tenderly as he watched the children express their affection for *his* Elizabeth.

After luncheon, the sisters began their preparations for the ball that evening at Netherfield. They gathered on the carpet before the hearth in their mother's room, as it had the largest space to sit together. They laughed and talked as their hair dried, and the bond between them grew much stronger. They spoke of future times together and the hopes each had for their marriage. They knew that today was truly a gift, and they made the most of their togetherness. Each of the sisters would remember these moments for the rest of their lives. Jane and Elizabeth had each chosen to wear the gowns they wore when attending the opera in town.

They arrived early at Netherfield, where Mr. and Mrs. Hurst welcomed them. The engaged couples stood with them in the receiving line as the Bennet sisters welcomed their neighbors for what could be the last time they would all be together for a while.

Those close friends that had been invited to the wedding had arrived in time for the ball. Several were staying at Netherfield, but the inn in Meryton was also enjoying a brisk business.

Mrs. Hurst, with the help of Lady Matlock, had done a splendid job of putting the ball together in such a short time. Many in the community would not be invited to the wedding and wedding breakfast, so it was determined that a ball would be the best way for Elizabeth and Jane to say goodbye to their neighbors.

The ballroom was lovely, the food and drink delectable, and best of all, there were no surprises. All in all, it was a delightful evening. Elizabeth danced with many of the young men of the neighborhood, as well as Mr. Parkington, who had been denied his dance at the engagement ball in London. He had come without his sister, as he had noticed her disagreeable behavior towards Elizabeth.

When the last dance of the evening came, it was again a waltz. Darcy took Elizabeth to the floor and pulled her into his embrace for the dance. As he stared down at her intently, he watched the blush rise from the bodice of her dress until it covered her face. At her blush, he raised an eyebrow, as the corners of his mouth turned up slightly. The blush deepened, but Elizabeth did not break eye contact with her beloved. So lost were they in each other that they continued to turn to the music for a moment or two after it ended. The couple's failure to cease dancing brought a laugh from the crowd and many calls of best wishes. Darcy and Elizabeth were too happy to be embarrassed, so they took a bow to the crowd before Darcy raised her hand to his lips and escorted her off the floor.

On the morning after the ball, the brides, grooms, and all of their friends who were in attendance for the wedding met at the fence between Longbourn and Netherfield. They were to walk to Oakham Mount. Elizabeth wished to say goodbye to one of her favorite spots. It showed off the area surrounding her home beautifully, as well as made a delightful place for a picnic lunch.

It was a large party, and laughter and gaiety were frequently heard as they walked. Both the Netherfield and Longbourn cooks had contributed to the picnic. Darcy had also ordered a large selection of sweets from the teashop in Meryton. Darcy had sent his footmen ahead in the wagon with blankets as well as all the food and drinks. They would set everything out before returning to the bottom of the hill to await the need to take the items away. In addition to the engaged couples, Mary and Kitty were in attendance, as well as Georgiana Darcy and the Fitzwilliam cousins with Lady Anne and Lady Penelope. Tim and Helena Whitman, who had come for the wedding bringing Mr. Parkington with them, were along for the outing. Also present were the Westinghams and Hughes, plus a few of Bingley's closest friends.

Perhaps the most unexpected guest was Lord Wescott. He had performed an invaluable service to Darcy and Elizabeth on the day of their engagement ball in London. Elizabeth had come to like him during their encounters in town, and he had earned a good measure of Darcy's respect with his actions. In fact, as they had an opportunity to converse during the picnic, Darcy discovered an intelligent man who wished to improve himself and his estate. Darcy offered to be of assistance if he could, telling Westcott to feel free to write to him at Pemberley should he have issues he needed to discuss. Wescott found himself delighted to find Miss Evelyn Pottsfield also among the guests. They sat near to each other during the picnic and conversed frequently. Having already succumbed to the beauty of her eyes, Lord Wescott began to notice the softness and shine of her hair as it sparkled in the sunlight. She also had a charming laugh that tinkled with the clear tones of a bell. Evelyn was clearly intelligent and possessed a great deal of common sense, as well as a naturally happy disposition. Wescott suspected she was slightly older than Elizabeth and was surprised to find himself quite drawn to her. He had toyed with some of the most beautiful women of the ton, all of whom had been easily manipulated due to their shallow, grasping ways. Conversely, this quiet, unassuming woman made him feel peaceful and happy.

While the young people were enjoying the views from Oakham Mount, Lady Matlock traveled to Longbourn to help Mrs. Gardiner with the last minute details for the wedding and wedding breakfast. There were the shipment from London to be received, the flower arrangements to be created, and the bouquets for the brides to prepare.

While the ladies were busy with the final preparations, Lord Matlock, and Philip Cavendish, Bishop of Derby, were dealing with the matter of Mr. Collins. The Matlock footmen who had accompanied the earl's carriage were dispatched to bring Mr. Collins to Netherfield's main house while everyone was out. Now the three gentlemen were ensconced in Bingley's study.

Upon entering the study and observing the men present, Collins bowed so low he nearly toppled over. Righting himself, he assumed a humble expression. "Lord Matlock, it is a pleasure to meet the brother of my esteemed patroness, Lady Catherine de Bourgh. She is the greatest lady it has ever been my privilege to know. She was in excellent health when last I saw her," the cleric bowed again in the direction of the earl. As Collins paused to draw breath, the two men looked at each other in astonishment.

Turning to the bishop, he knelt and reached for the bishop's hand, placing a kiss on the ring that designated his office. "Your Eminence, it is a great honor to meet you. I am grateful for your arrival and your assistance to this humble servant of the church."

The bishop withdrew his hand and discreetly wiped it against his robes, attempting to remove the evidence of the man's obeisance. Collins continued, "There has been a misunderstanding, and I am sure that you will be able to clear up the situation."

Glancing at each other again, the earl and bishop seated themselves. The bishop took the chair behind the desk, with the earl seated somewhat to the side, and both men faced Collins. Mr. Collins was surprised that he had not been invited to sit and began looking around the room for another chair, but the only thing he saw was a screen in one corner. The study was quiet as Lord Matlock and Bishop

Cavendish stared at the man before then. Collins began to shift uncomfortably before the bishop finally broke the silence. "What do you have to say for yourself, Mr. Collins?"

"Your Eminence,"

"Bishop Cavendish will do," said the man with a frown.

"As I was saying, Reverend Bishop," the man behind the desk merely shook his head in frustration, "a young woman of my acquaintance has cast aspersions upon my reputation as a clergyman. She has no scruples when it comes to getting what she wants from gentlemen. She went so far as to inflict physical harm upon my person. I am sure that you shall be able to see through her innocent façade."

"Are you saying that the young lady is lying about what happened, Mr. Collins?"

Failing to hear the disapprobation in the bishop's voice, Collins nodded. "Indeed, Your Grace," again the bishop shook his head. "The young lady has previously used her arts and allurements to entice a gentleman away from his betrothed. Lady Catherine's daughter, Miss Anne de Bourgh, was engaged from her infancy to Lady Catherine and the earl's nephew, Mr. Fitzwilliam Darcy. However, when he met my cousin, Miss Elizabeth Bennet, he forgot his duty to his family and abandoned Miss de Bourgh. Miss Elizabeth threw herself at Mr. Darcy in spite of her engagement and the fact her hand had been promised to me. Lady Catherine has repeatedly expressed her displeasure with the new engagement, and since my cousin can in no way bring harm to her ladyship, she is attempting to strike through me, her ladyship's humble parson."

As Collins was speaking, the earl's face grew dark with rage. Finally, he could contain himself no longer. "You must not be in possession of your faculties to be spouting such nonsense! How dare you speak so disrespectfully about one of the finest young ladies I have ever met? Miss Elizabeth is incapable of behaving in the manner that you suggest!"

"I am sorry to say it, Lord Matlock, but I witnessed her hanging on your nephew's arm within a month of their meeting. Who knows how much more forward her behavior with him may have been when they were alone? I also heard from Lady Catherine about my cousin's scandalous behavior in London. Surely, Mr. Darcy would not forsake his duty to Miss de Bourgh and his family without sufficient *encouragement*?" The two men were disgusted by the leer upon Mr. Collin's face and the implication of his words.

"You told the gentlemen who discovered you and Miss Bennet that you were on your way to her home to offer your congratulations on her wedding when she 'threw herself at you,' is that correct?"

"Indeed it is, Your -- "

"Mr. Collins," shouted the bishop in annoyance.

"Your pardon, Bishop Cavendish," said Mr. Collins with another low bow.

"Why would you be offering your congratulations, if you have such a poor opinion of your cousin's match and in opposition to your patroness's wishes?" the bishop questioned sternly.

"I did not wish to cause a breach with my Bennet relations. It is my obligation to offer my counsel and forgiveness. I also hoped to do my duty to my patroness by trying one last time to convince my cousin that she was doing wrong to break Miss de Bourgh's heart by wedding the young lady's betrothed."

A muttered "Humph" was heard from the earl.

"Mr. Collins, your words are nonsensical and your efforts, at cross-purposes. You cannot try to offer your congratulations at the same time you try to convince her to break the engagement," said the bishop with a growl. "This gives me cause to doubt your words and actions."

"I assure you, Bishop, my reasons for coming here were most noble and undertaken with the best of intentions. If my actions could benefit Lady Catherine, Miss de Bourgh, Mr. Darcy, and the Fitzwilliam family, I would feel it a great blessing to be of service to them. These same actions, though, could benefit the entire Bennet family and my humble self through a closer family tie and the protection of the women in the family upon Mr. Bennet's demise."

"As their closest male relation and the heir to their family home, not to mention a member of the clergy, you should be willing to provide care for your nearest relations at such a difficult time." Again, the bishop's voice was stern.

Mr. Collins' face flushed, and he hurried to reassure. "I would, of course, your eminence, but . . . but would it not be more appropriate for me to be wed to one of my fair cousins rather than just to reside in a home with so many unwed young ladies?"

The bishop raised his arm to halt any further speech. "Mr. Collins, I wish to verify the facts. Are you telling me that you were properly betrothed to Miss Elizabeth Bennet with the approval of her father?"

With only the briefest of hesitations, Collins replied, "Yes, I was betrothed with the approval of her family."

"Sir, will you join us, please," called the bishop.

From behind a screen in the corner of the room stepped Mr. Bennet. His face bore an angry expression, and a bundle of brightly-colored fabric was clutched in his arms. The color drained from Mr. Collins' face at his cousin's appearance.

Mr. Bennet stepped to the side of the desk standing near Lord Matlock. The bishop looked at Mr. Bennet. "Sir, did you give permission for Mr. Collins to marry your daughter Elizabeth?"

"I did not. In fact at the time he accuses my Lizzy of hanging on Mr. Darcy, she was, in fact, being returned to our home after recuperating from a serious injury that occurred while visiting at Netherfield. When he made reference to being betrothed to my daughter, I specifically told him I would not permit any of my daughters to marry him."

"Thank you, sir," said the bishop. Turning to the parson, the bishop asked, "Is that the truth, Mr. Collins?"

The man's face grew red in embarrassment and anger as he tried to think of an answer that would not make him look bad in the bishop's eyes. "That is what Mr. Bennet said, your eminence, but I had already been promised Miss Elizabeth's hand by her mother. She was very anxious for the wedding to take place."

"As a member of the clergy, Mr. Collins, you are aware that the permission of the nearest living male relative is required before a marriage can take place. Why did you think yourself betrothed with only the mother's agreement?"

"Mrs. Bennet indicated that Mr. Bennet would agree with the arrangement provided I allowed her and her remaining daughters to live at Longbourn after the marriage took place. I believed I had the proper authority at the time."

"That may have been true, but your actions at the time you were found at Longbourn a few days ago indicate you still feel you have a right to marry Miss Elizabeth. In fact, your words express a great deal of anger at the young lady and her father for refusing you. Is that correct?"

"I am the heir to his estate and currently hold a prestigious living, thanks to the preferment of Lady Catherine de Bourgh. I am eminently suitable to marry any young lady—particularly those as low-born as my cousins. He had no reason to deny my request to marry Miss Elizabeth, especially after agreeing to provide a home for his family after his death."

"That is enough, Mr. Collins!" came the firm voice of the bishop. "Whether you agreed with his decision or not, you were well aware of Mr. Bennet's refusal of any relationship between you and Miss Elizabeth."

Mr. Collins looked as if he would like to disagree with the bishop but thankfully remained silent.

"Now, Mr. Collins, please explain to me your encounter with Miss Elizabeth two days ago," said Bishop Cavendish.

"Sir, as I told Mr. Darcy and Colonel Fitzwilliam, I was on my way to Longbourn to offer my congratulations to my cousin on her marriage. I came across her on her walk, and she threw herself at me. Perhaps she had been bothered by her conscience for taking Mr. Darcy from his true betrothed. I can only assume that she wished to regain my attentions rather than to be seen as abandoned." Mr. Collins offered smugly.

"Just what were Miss Elizabeth's actions when she 'threw herself at you,' sir?"

"She approached me and wrapped her arms around my neck. I was forced to push her away, and she fell to the ground. That is when she behaved most disgracefully, kicking me in a sensitive spot, Bishop."

"If she approached you from the front, could you please explain to me how her dress was torn?"

"She ripped it herself in an attempt to compromise me and force me to agree to marry her."

The bishop looked at Mr. Bennet and held out his hand. "May I have the dress, please?"

Mr. Bennet placed the bundled fabric into the bishop's hands. The bishop stood and shook out the material. "What you have said Mr. Collins cannot be true." He held the dress up for all in the room to view. "I know that because there is no way that Miss Elizabeth could have torn the back of her dress in this fashion—at least, not while wearing it."

"I . . . I . . . perhaps I was mistaken. Perchance it was torn when she fell to the ground," stammered Collins.

"The only way something like this could have occurred," continued the bishop relentlessly, "was if someone grabbed the back of her dress and pulled it hard."

"Would you like to try again, Mr. Collins, to explain what occurred? This time, I suggest you tell me the truth. Your future depends upon it."

"I . . . I . . . have told you . . . what happened," stammered the parson. The three other men in the room stared coldly at him. Mr. Collins was stammering, wringing his hands, and shifting from foot to foot. The silence lengthened, and Mr. Collins grew more distressed. Finally, he huffed softly. "I was following the orders of my patroness. She said that I should do whatever it took to end her nephew's engagement to my cousin."

The bishop, earl, and Elizabeth's father were all shocked at the parson's words. "Just how far were you prepared to go?" demanded the bishop?

"It is my great pleasure to serve such a benevolent patroness. I would do anything Lady Catherine asked of me. She is far above my cousin in rank, and it is her wishes, not Cousin Elizabeth's, that take precedence." Straightening in his chair, Collins glared at Mr. Bennet. "My cousin was at fault in denying me his daughter's hand and dashing the hopes of Miss de Bourgh and her family. My cousin does not deserve such a gentleman as Mr. Darcy! He is far too good for her! She should have been grateful for my condescension and willingness to marry such a penniless nobody," Collins cried angrily.

"Exactly what were your plans?" demanded the bishop. He stared at Collins.

"I was to compromise her, thereby, forcing her to end the relationship with Mr. Darcy. I would have magnanimously offered to marry her and looked forward to expressing my displeasure with her previously disgraceful behavior. How dare she deny me what I wish? She needed to be taught to behave like a proper parson's wife." His angry words were made more menacing by the cold look in his eyes.

"Mr. Collins, your actions are unworthy of a clergyman. For you to speak of a young lady in such a disgraceful manner is cause enough to discipline you. However, by your own admission, you planned to cause her physical harm as well as to ruin her socially." The bishop stared coldly at the man before him. "You are not worthy to be a clergyman."

"But . . . but . . . Lady Catherine has given me the living at Hunsford. The gift is for life. As I was doing what she desired of me, she will not wish to withdraw the living," said Collins smugly.

"She will not be able to retain you if I strip you of your office. Not only that, but the living can be taken from her and given to the church to grant."

Collins' eyes grew wide and his jaw slacked. "You cannot do such a thing to someone like Lady Catherine!"

"Indeed, I can. We have had complaints from the parishioners at Hunsford about your care of them, as well as concerning Lady Catherine's interference. Having a living to appoint does not give her the right to control the lives of others. You gave all your care and concern to her and not to the good people that you were there to serve. You are a disgrace. Now, you are faced with a difficult choice. I can see you stripped of your position and the living and turned over to the magistrate and sheriff to stand trial for assault, among other things. I expect with the power of the Fitzwilliam family behind the charges, you could be sentenced to death."

The earl nodded vigorously, muttering, "As you should be for what you tried to do."

Collins faced blanched at the bishop's words, and he began to plead for mercy. "But I was unsuccessful. I did not hurt her. She was in no danger from me, as the pain she inflicted on me proved. There is no reason for me to be sentenced so harshly. Please. Your Lordship, Your Eminence, please save me from this fate." Collins' blathering was nearly incoherent, and tears streamed down his cheeks.

"There is another option. You may retain your position as a clergyman, but you will serve the remainder of your days as a missionary in Australia. This option also requires that you renounce your inheritance and claim to Longbourn. You will not be permitted to return to England. If you do so, you will face the charges that I previously mentioned."

"You cannot force me to give up my inheritance!" Collins cried. "I may someday have a child, and he will then become the heir. Why would I deny him his due?"

"Well, you can choose the first option, but you will lose your inheritance that way, as well," the bishop reminded him.

Collins turned a hateful glower on Mr. Bennet. "I assume this was your idea."

"Indeed, no," he said with a grin, "though I was delighted when Elizabeth asked Mr. Darcy about the possibility." He and Lord Matlock both chuckled, and the bishop worked to contain his smile.

"Well, Mr. Collins, which option do you prefer?"

"I cannot make a decision without speaking to my patroness. If Lady Catherine were here, I know she would protect me from such an injustice."

"That is where you are wrong, Mr. Collins. As the head of the Fitzwilliam family, Lady Catherine is subject to obeying my commands. Soon she will be in no place to offer a living to anyone, as she will no longer be the mistress of Rosings Park."

Paling again, Collins realized that he had no other options. In his usual sycophantic tones, he said, "I shall be glad to accept a position as a missionary serving the church and our Lord. If you will allow me a few weeks to return to Hunsford to retrieve my belongings . . . ," Collins trailed off as he turned to leave the room.

"One moment, Mr. Collins. There is some business which must be attended to first. Mr. Phillips, will you join us?" the bishop called.

Another man stepped from behind the screen, carrying a case and bringing a chair with him. He placed the chair beside the desk and opened the case. Shuffling some papers about, he said, "Mr. Collins, these papers summarize the agreement that was reached here. I wrote down your confession as I sat listening, and it will be kept with these documents. I need you to sign here. This letter states that you are accepting a position with the church as a missionary in Australia and that you plan never to return. You are thereby renouncing your inheritance and naming Miss Elizabeth Bennet heir in your stead."

"No!" Collins shouted. "I may have to renounce my inheritance, but I refuse to name that tart as my heir."

"Would you prefer the first option, then?" asked the bishop.

Collins scowled and grabbed the pen, signing the document where indicated. "There, now I shall leave for Hunsford, and I hope never to see you again, cousin."

"The feeling is mutual, Mr. Collins," was Mr. Bennet's reply.

As Mr. Collins turned, he was again stopped by the bishop's voice. "You will not be going anywhere at present, Mr. Collins. You will return to where you were being held until after the wedding. Then you will be accompanied to Hunsford to pack and then escorted to London where you will embark for your new home on the next transport ship. Your work will begin immediately upon boarding. The captain will be given a letter explaining your circumstances, and he will turn the letter over to the church leadership in Australia upon arrival. I suggest that you work hard in serving the Lord, Mr. Collins, for though you will escape earthly judgment for your many misdeeds, you will still face the judgment of the Lord," the bishop's softly spoken words caused a chill to settle on the unrepentant clergyman.

Mr. Bennet opened the door to see the footmen who had brought Collins to Netherfield waiting to return him to the shed at the dower house. He beckoned the men, and they stepped up beside the parson, each taking an arm as they lead him out.

As they heard the front door close, Mr. Bennet sighed in relief. "That went better than I expected. Will these signed papers be sufficient to break the entail on Longbourn?"

"I believe so, Brother."

"I will have my solicitor assist you any way necessary to see that things are properly arranged," offered Lord Matlock. "Well, gentlemen, I believe I could use a drink. May I pour for you gentlemen, as well?"

Everyone nodded, and, after retrieving another chair from behind the screen, the gentlemen settled down to enjoy some peace before the other guests returned from their outing.

The evening brought those from Longbourn and the Netherfield Park guests together for a simple dinner. The conversation over drinks in the dining room following the separation of the sexes consisted of a great deal of teasing and advice for the grooms. In spite of Richard's occasionally pushing the boundary of good manners with his suggestive comments, the gentlemen generally had a pleasant evening.

In the largest drawing room, the ladies instead spoke of wedding trips and made plans to meet again. Mr. Bennet agreed to allow Mary and Kitty to return to London with the Gardiners. Then they would join them on their trip to Derbyshire later in the summer.

When the two groups came together, Mary, Kitty and Georgiana requested everyone's attention. "If we might have your indulgence for a few moments, we sisters would like to present a small gift to our siblings," said Mary. "When we were in London and my sisters and their betrothed decided to hold a double wedding, there was a moment when they leaned in together and kissed one of Papa's cheeks. I whispered to Miss Darcy that I wished I had my sister Kitty's talent in drawing so I could capture the moment."

Georgiana took up the story. "I, in turn, whispered a suggestion and offered my help. I made three sketches of the room and the chair where Mr. Bennet sat, just as it appeared that day, and brought them with me to Longbourn when I came.

"And I sketched the three members of my family as they would have appeared. Even though I was not able to see the event as it occurred, I had often seen my sisters kiss Papa goodnight and have used the days since Georgiana's arrival to finish the three portraits," added Kitty.

"When Kitty completed the first one," said Mary "I took it into Meryton to have it framed. We would like to present the finished portrait to Papa as a reminder of his beautiful daughters who will be leaving his home tomorrow," said Mary, as Georgiana and Kitty carried a wrapped package to him.

With tears in his eyes, Mr. Bennet unwrapped the picture to gaze upon that sweet moment that he knew he would always remember. He gasped at the quality and looked at the three girls. "Young ladies, you have given me a priceless gift," he said. "Miss Darcy, Kitty, your drawings are flawless, and, Mary, thank you for the thought and excellent framing. This lovely portrait will forever hang on the wall in my study."

As Mr. Bennet turned the picture for the others to see, there were many exclamations upon the quality of the work, the wonderful idea, and the sweetness of the moment.

"Lizzy, Jane, we have a copy for each of you as well, but we were unable to get them framed in time. We will send them or bring them to you when we come to visit in the summer," concluded Mary.

It was on that sweet note that the evening ended. Tomorrow would be a very busy day. Mr. Bennet escorted his two younger daughters out to the carriage with his picture clutched tightly to his chest. The gentlemen escorted their fiancés out, each taking a moment to say a private goodnight.

As Darcy and Elizabeth stood at the back of the carriage, he took both of her hands tightly in his. "This is the last time I will have to say good night to you and leave your company. Tomorrow is the beginning of our life together. The last few days have been perfect in the company of those we love best and our dearest friends. I will be waiting for you at the altar tomorrow, and after our vow and a few short words, you will be mine forever more. I love you, Elizabeth, and there are no words that could ever express how much. You are my first thought in the morning and my last thought at night. My heart beats for you; each breath I take is for you, and my greatest joy will be in having you for my wife and sharing with you all that the future has in store." He kissed the back of first one hand, then the other. He turned them over for a lingering kiss to each palm and then to the bare skin of her wrists.

Elizabeth's eyes misted at his words, and a lump in her throat made it almost impossible for her to speak. She swallowed several times before she was able to whisper, "I love you too, my William. You reside in my soul, and only when I am with you, am I truly complete and truly happy."

"Until tomorrow, my love," Darcy murmured as he handed her into the carriage.

CHAPTER 5

THE SOFT SOUND of Margot moving about the room caused Elizabeth to open her eyes. She glanced at the window to see bright sunshine attempting to find its way into the bedchamber. As her gaze focused on other things she was surprised to find a wrapped box on the bedside table. Picking up the card, she noted her name written in William's strong, neat hand. Breaking the seal, she read:

5 May, 18 ___

Dearest, loveliest Elizabeth,

 Today is the day you become my wife. There can be no greater honor in my life than having earned your hand in marriage. You are the most remarkable woman I have ever known, surpassing all of the qualities I one day hoped to find in a wife.
 I promise to spend every day we have together devoting myself to you and to the family I hope we will someday be blessed to

have. Everything I do will be to honor my love and commitment to you and to them.

I saw this even before we were engaged and knew it was meant for you. Its delicacy and brilliance seemed to match those same qualities in you perfectly.

I await the moment we are united as one.

Yours forever,

William

Elizabeth unwrapped the package and opened the black velvet box. She softly exclaimed "Oh, my!" as she gazed upon the diamond and pearl jewelry set the box contained.

Her exclamation drew Margot's attention. "Is everything all right, Miss Elizabeth?" she asked, turning to her mistress. Elizabeth nodded as she moved the box for Margot to see the contents. "Oh, my, indeed! They will be beautiful with your gown," the maid said as took the box from Elizabeth and placed it on her dressing table. "Your bath is ready, miss."

Elizabeth scrambled out of the bed, quickly removing her nightclothes and sinking into the warm bath. Margot washed and rinsed Elizabeth's hair and left her to soak while she retrieved a tray for her.

It was not long before Elizabeth was seated in front of the fire in her robe and enjoying her breakfast, as she waited for her hair to dry. After she had finished her meal, Margot filed and buffed her nails until they shone. Next, she was slipped into her undergarments and seated before the dressing table for Margot to dress her hair. She sectioned

Elizabeth's hair, twisting and looping it up on her head. She pinned them in place with the diamond and pearl pins Darcy had gifted to her. Then Margot wrapped the ends around her finger, leaving delicate curls all over Elizabeth's head.

Margot had just finished putting on the necklace and earrings when a knock came at her bedroom door. Mrs. Gardiner entered at Elizabeth's call. "I came to help with your dress, Elizabeth. Is that a gift from Mr. Darcy around your neck?" she asked. At Elizabeth's nod, she remarked, "Your young man has exquisite taste, my dear." Again, Elizabeth nodded.

First, Elizabeth stepped into a petticoat, which her maid pulled up and secured. Then Margot and Mrs. Gardiner lifted the wedding gown over Elizabeth's head. As Margot hooked the many small buttons, Mrs. Gardiner placed the bracelet on Elizabeth's wrist and secured her headdress.

Stepping back, Elizabeth moved to stand before the full-length mirror and stared at herself in astonishment. Madame Colette had designed many beautiful gowns for Elizabeth, but she had outdone herself with this one. It was the most exquisite thing she had ever seen, and the headdress Madame had chosen was indeed the perfect compliment.

Mrs. Gardiner and Margot wore pleased smiles as they gazed upon the picture Elizabeth made. At a knock on the door, they all turned. Mr. Bennet entered the room and stopped dead. Elizabeth could see him in the mirror, and the look on his face, she felt sure she would never forget.

"Where has my little Lizzy gone? It is not she I see staring back at me, but a beautiful young woman, who looks more like a princess than my little nature girl."

"It is really me, Papa, though I can hardly believe it myself," said Elizabeth with a self-deprecating laugh.

"Ladies, would you excuse us for a moment?" asked Elizabeth's father.

Both Mrs. Gardiner and Margot exited the room and closed the door behind them. When they were gone, Mr. Bennet turned to look at Elizabeth. "My dearest girl, there are so many things I should have said and done through the years before we arrived at this moment. But in spite of my failings, you have become a remarkable woman. Your kind heart and caring nature, combined with your intellect, make you a rarity among females. I am so glad that you have found such a good man, one who is truly worthy of you. I pray that you will know happiness every day for the rest of your life. Now come, we must head downstairs. Your sisters and uncle are waiting to see you, and it is almost time for us to leave for the church.

With tears misting her eyes, Elizabeth gave her father a large smile and said, "I love you so much, Papa. Thank you for everything you have done for me."

Mr. Bennet offered his arm, and the two of them descended the stairs. Margot had remained in the hallway and picked up the train of Elizabeth's gown as she negotiated her way down the stairs. Margot would ride with the coachman to the church to help both sisters with their gowns before they took their walk down the aisle. When Elizabeth arrived in the parlor, it was the first time anyone saw her in her wedding dress. Jane was already present as Mr. Bennet had collected his eldest daughter first and had a talk with her as well. As Elizabeth entered the room, all conversation ceased.

Before anyone could speak, Mrs. Gardiner turned to her husband and said, "I believe we should leave. Kitty, dear, you will be riding with us." As Mrs. Gardiner moved the boys towards the door, Mr. Gardiner and Kitty both took a moment to compliment Elizabeth on her gown and appearance. Kitty kissed both of her sisters on the cheek and told them how happy she was for them before rushing out the door.

Mary and Susan remained. Mary was to stand up with her sisters and Susan was to drop rose petals before the brides as they walked to the altar. Mary and Susan both wore pale lavender dresses trimmed in yellow ribbons with ribbons of both colors wound through their curls. Susan carried a small wicker basket filled with yellow and white rose petals and lavender blossoms.

Mary and Susan moved to the foyer to await the others. Mr. Bennet followed them, leaving Jane and Elizabeth alone in the room.

Elizabeth looked at her elder sister and said, "Oh, Jane, you look so beautiful. It is easy to understand why Mr. Bingley always calls you his angel, for you truly look like one."

Jane's gown was made of silk and of a color just off-white. It had a v-neck and small puffed sleeves. Narrow golden lace in a rose pattern edged the neckline and sleeves. Down the front of the gown was a trail of roses embroidered in a slightly darker silk. The roses continued around the hem of the gown, and there were pearls stitched into the design. A bonnet, covered in the same silk the gown was made from and trimmed with the gold lace, rested upon Jane's head. The bonnet was adorned with silk roses, and the ribbon that tied beneath her chin was embroidered to match her dress. She had delicate slippers on her feet decorated with the same roses as her bonnet. She wore a double strand of pearls that Charles had given her as a wedding gift and pearl drops in her ears.

"You have always been the most wonderful sister anyone could ever have. You have been my confidant, my best friend, and the person closest to my heart. I love you, Jane, and even though we will no longer see each other every day, you will always remain my dearest sister and friend."

With tears in her eyes, Jane hugged her sister and stepped back. "It is you, Elizabeth, who looks truly beautiful. The gown Madame designed for you is magnificent, and the veil on your dark curls gives a delightful contrast." Elizabeth's gown was truly a triumph of design. It was made of cream satin. The bodice had a deep, scooped neckline and was covered in Alencon lace that also formed the fitted sleeves that ended just below the elbow. The same lace adorned the hem and demi-train of her gown. Instead of a bonnet, a veil of tulle trimmed with the same lace as the gown covered Elizabeth's head. The full-length veil was shaped to match the train of the dress, but slightly larger. Madame Colette had stitched pearls and crystals into the pattern of the lace, and Elizabeth wore the pearl and diamond jewelry Darcy had gifted her that morning.

"Oh, Lizzy, I shall miss you every day, but we will come to visit soon. Charles and I agree we would like to look for a permanent home close to you and Mr. Darcy, and, until then, you must promise to write often. I think it is your laughter I will miss the most, for it makes anyone within its hearing happy."

After one last hug, the sisters linked arms and headed out to the foyer where Margo waited. She gathered up the train on Elizabeth's gown as the sisters exited the house. Mr. Bennet stood beside an open carriage. He had already assisted Mary and Susan into the carriage, and they sat in the rear-facing seat. Mr. Bennet handed in first Jane and then Elizabeth. He then gave Margot help up to the driver's seat before entering the carriage to seat himself next to Mary.

The carriage moved forward, and Elizabeth and Jane were surprised to find that Longbourn's tenants lined both sides of the driveway, waving and calling out good wishes to the two young ladies for whom they had both respect and affection. In a short time, the carriage pulled up before the church. Mr. Bennet stepped down, then turned to hand down Mary and Susan, who quickly entered the church. Margot had climbed down and was there to keep Elizabeth's dress from dragging in the dust when Mr. Bennet handed her down. As Margot and Elizabeth moved to the church door, Mr. Bennet helped his first born down, and they followed the others. They entered the church to find Charlotte standing in front of the closed doors that lead into the church's sanctuary. She had lined up Mary, followed by Susan, and was reminding Susan what she was to do. Elizabeth was standing towards the left side of the doorframe as Margot straightened her train and veil. Mr. Bennet stepped up on her right with Jane to his right. Margot brushed some wrinkles from the back of Jane's dress, straightened the ribbons on her bonnet, and tugged the hem of her gown down into place. Convinced that both the sisters looked just perfect, Margot slipped open the door, stepped into the sanctuary, and stood quietly against the back wall. She would have the pleasure of seeing the ceremony and would be available to assist the sisters with their gowns as they exited the church.

Charlotte complimented her dearest friends and wished them well. She gave Jane a bouquet of yellow roses, with one white rose at its center, tied with the same ribbons as her bonnet. Then Charlotte turned to Elizabeth and handed her a bouquet of white roses and lavender tied with a strip of the lace on her gown. When their bouquets were in their hands, Charlotte turned and opened both doors to the sanctuary. As the doors opened, the music could be heard, and Mary began her walk. She could see Mr. Darcy and Mr. Bingley at the front of the church with Colonel Fitzwilliam beside them. Mary noted how handsome he appeared with the sunlight on his light brown hair. His eyes had a mischievous glint, and he smiled broadly at her. She gave him a soft smile in return, just before she took her place opposite him at the altar.

Susan had started after her at Charlotte's direction, and she stopped at each step to sprinkle the flowers on the ground. Darcy could not help but smile at the little girl as she so carefully performed her task, but he soon turned his eyes to the back of the church, again awaiting his first look at his Elizabeth.

All the guests stood as the brides began to make their way down the aisle, blocking Darcy's view of Elizabeth as she came towards him. She had almost reached him before he could truly get a look at her, and when he did see her for the first time, it took his breath away. The look on his face as he saw her was not lost on anyone present. The utterly pure love displayed there touched the hearts of many, causing their thoughts to turn briefly to their own dear loves. Many hands were discreetly clasped as everyone heard the first words spoken by Reverend Winthrop,

"Dearly beloved, we are gathered together here in the sight of God, and in the face of this congregation, to join this Man and this Woman in holy Matrimony; . . . "(1)

Elizabeth and Darcy both held their breath when he said,

" . . . Therefore if any man can shew any just cause, why they may not lawfully be joined together, let him now speak, or else hereafter for ever hold his peace."(1)

When no objection was heard, Darcy and Elizabeth released the breath they had been holding, and at the slight sound; they turned to each other with relieved smiles gracing their faces. The couples stood before Reverend Winthrop, listening to the words of the service. Finally, he reached the first question, asking Bingley first and then Jane, who each responded positively. Then he turned to Darcy and said,

"Fitzwilliam James Darcy, wilt thou have this woman to thy wedded wife, to live together after God's ordinance in the holy estate of Matrimony? Wilt thou love her, comfort her, honour, and keep her in sickness and in health; and, forsaking all others, keep thee only unto her, so long as ye both shall live?"(1)

In a firm ringing voice, Darcy responded, "I will."

Turning to Elizabeth, Reverend Winthrop asked the same questions, and her reply of "I will," was clearly heard. Then the Reverend said,

"Who giveth these women to be married to these men?"(1)

In a voice husky with emotion, Mr. Bennet said, "I do," as he turned to take his seat beside Kitty in the first pew.

Darcy and Elizabeth listened as Jane and Bingley exchanged their vows. Then Elizabeth listened as Fitzwilliam vowed his love to her and plighted his troth. When it was Elizabeth's turn to repeat the words, she took Darcy's right hand in hers, and though her eyes had misted with tears, her voice could be clearly heard as she said,

"I, Elizabeth Diana Bennet, take thee Fitzwilliam James Darcy to my wedded husband, to have and to hold from this day forward, for better for worse, for richer for poorer, in sickness and in health, to love, cherish, and obey, till death us do part, according to God's holy ordinance; and thereto I give thee my troth."(1)

Darcy and Elizabeth watched as Bingley gave Jane her ring. Then Reverend Winthrop again called for the ring. Colonel Fitzwilliam handed him Elizabeth's ring, but those in attendance were surprised when Mary also gave him a ring. After taking Elizabeth's ring from Reverend Winthrop, Darcy placed it on the third finger of her left hand as he said,

"With this Ring I thee wed, with my body I tee worship, and with all my worldly goods I thee endow: In the Name of the Father, and of the Son, and of the Holy Ghost. Amen."(1)

Reverend Winthrop handed Elizabeth Fitzwilliam's ring, and the words were again repeated as Elizabeth placed a wide gold band on the third finger of Darcy's left hand, a satisfied smile on her face.

The couples knelt as Reverend Winthrop pronounced several prayers upon then. He then concluded the service with these words,

"Those whom God hath joined together let no man put asunder."

"Forasmuch as Charles and Jane and Fitzwilliam and Elizabeth have consented together in holy wedlock, and have witnessed the same before God and this company, and thereto have given and pledged their troth, either to other, and have declared the same, by giving and receiving of a Ring, and by joining of hands; I pronounce that they are

Man and Wife together, In the Name of the Father, and of the Son, and of the Holy Ghost. Amen."

"God the Father, God the Son, God the Holy Ghost, bless, preserve, and keep you; the Lord mercifully with his favour look upon you, and so fill you with all spiritual benediction and grace, that ye may so live together in this life, that in the world to come ye may have life everlasting. Amen."(1)

It is done, Darcy thought with relief; *now no one and nothing can separate us!* Darcy squeezed Elizabeth's hand and turned such a blindingly happy smile on her that the tears in Elizabeth's eyes spilled over even as her joyous laugh was heard. After signing the register, Darcy and Elizabeth followed Jane and Bingley down the aisle and out of the church. Bingley assisted Jane into the open carriage and climbed in after her, taking the rear facing seats. Then Darcy handed Elizabeth into the carriage and took the seat beside her. The streets appeared to be filled with neighbors and friends wishing to see the lovely Bennet sisters in their wedding finery and offer them their best wishes. The carriage slowly moved away from the crowd for the short trip to Longbourn.

Upon arriving at the estate, the couples quickly entered the house to grab a moment of privacy before the other guests arrived. Jane led Bingley to a small parlor at the back of the house, while Elizabeth and Darcy entered Mr. Bennet's library. The door had barely closed behind them before Darcy swept Elizabeth into his embrace and kissed her with all the passion he had been holding back. When he finally broke the kiss, they were both breathless, and Elizabeth sagged in his arms, as her knees went weak beneath her. Darcy gave her a roguish smile that showed how happy he was to have affected her so!

As he leaned to kiss her again, they heard the sound of voices in the entry as their family and guests began to arrive. Regretfully, Darcy gave her a quick kiss as he whispered, "Soon, my love, very soon."

They quickly exited the library and moved toward the foyer. A quick look at their faces told the newcomers what activity they had interrupted, and there were several soft chuckles heard as well as a few smiles of commiseration. The couples lined up in the entryway to accept the good wishes of their guests as each entered. Because the guests were few, the two couples were soon free to visit with all of their friends and family in a more relaxed manner. The doors between the parlor and music room were thrown open so that everyone could comfortably mingle with extra chairs placed about to provide seating for those who chose to enjoy the buffet. Darcy and Elizabeth wandered through the rooms, speaking to everyone. Once they had done so, they found a quiet area with a pair of chairs and were provided with plates by one of the footmen.

"We have a drive of several hours before we reach our destination for tonight; will you be ready to depart soon?"

"I will be ready whenever you tell me we need to leave, William. Just allow me a few moments for last minute goodbyes when the time comes," Elizabeth replied.

They continued to talk quietly as they ate. They saw both Georgiana and Kitty with their sketchpads trying to capture some memories of the event. They were laughing and talking to each other as they worked. Across the room, they saw the colonel seated beside Mary and talking with her as they enjoyed some of the refreshments. After they had finished dining, Elizabeth requested to be excused to refresh herself before their departure. She climbed the stairs to her room and looked around one more time. The furnishings remained, but all of the little things that represented her life had been packed to go to Pemberley with her. A knock was heard at the door, and Mrs. Gardiner asked to enter. Elizabeth opened the door to admit her aunt, then closed the door behind her. "I thought you might need assistance with your gown," offered her aunt as Elizabeth took care of her needs in preparation to depart. When she had finished, Mrs. Gardiner took both Elizabeth's hands in hers. "I want you to know how proud and happy your uncle and I are. You have always been a delightful girl, and you have grown into a remarkable woman. I know that you and Mr. Darcy will be blissfully happy, and it is what your uncle and I always wanted for you. Do you have any questions or concerns about tonight?"

"No, Aunt Madeline, I am a little nervous but more than that, I am excited. I love William so much and look forward to tonight."

"Well, then, give me a last hug and let us return to the party so that you can make your farewells."

Darcy and Elizabeth stopped to speak with their acquaintances from Derbyshire and made plans to meet in a few weeks' time.

They exchanged farewells with the Fitzwilliams, inviting them to Pemberley for Christmas. When saying goodbye to Bingley and the Hursts, they extended the same invitation. They also spoke with Bingley and Jane about when they would come to look for an estate. Darcy promised to have his steward begin a search for possible options. The Bingleys would be staying at Netherfield for tonight. Then they would travel on to Bath to honeymoon for a fortnight, before going to York to meet the rest of Charles' family. Jane moved with Elizabeth and Darcy as they said farewell to their sisters, including Georgiana. Georgiana was to go back to London with the Matlocks and would then travel with them into

Derbyshire when they came to their estate for the summer. Darcy stepped back, and the sisters embraced each other in a big group hug. There was laughter, followed by tears, expressions of love, and promises to write as they parted for what they knew would be a longer period of time than they had ever before been separated. Finally, Elizabeth moved on to say farewell to her father. Her emotions swirled as she tried to find the words she wished to say. They had spoken earlier, and Elizabeth had been able to say much to him then. "I love you very much, Papa," was all that she could get out now.

Mr. Bennet patted her cheek fondly as he said, "Be happy, my Lizzy; that is all that I could want for you." He kissed her forehead and turned to Darcy extending his hand. "Take care of her and be sure she is happy," he begged.

"I will, sir. You have my promise on that."

Elizabeth and Darcy moved to the foyer where Mr. and Mrs. Hill stood. Elizabeth hugged Mrs. Hill and thanked them both for the kindness they had shown her growing up. She begged Mrs. Hill to take good care of her father while he was alone and received her promise that she would. Mrs. Hill returned to the kitchen, and Mr. Hill opened the door. As Darcy and Elizabeth exited the house, most of the guests followed. Darcy handed his wife into the carriage and quickly mounted, taking the seat across from her. Elizabeth leaned to the open window, waving goodbye to everyone.

They heard Georgiana wave and cry out, "Goodbye, William. Goodbye, Lizzy. I shall see you soon!"

With that, the carriage moved down the driveway and turned towards Meryton. Elizabeth continued to watch out the window and waved to friends that stopped to admire the coach as it passed through the village. Soon they were on the road that carried them towards the first stop on the journey to Pemberley. Elizabeth's tears had ceased, and a smile showed on her face.

"What causes your smile, my love?"

"I was thinking how much I love you and that now I can stare at you without worrying what people will think," Elizabeth answered flirtatiously.

Darcy's gazed darkened with passion as he moved to sit beside his new wife. He took her hand in his and turned it placed a lingering kiss in her palm. Looking at her with his intense stare, he asked, "Are you ready, my love--ready for our honeymoon and the start of our happy life together?"

Her unforgettable laugh rang out as a blush appeared on her cheeks, a sparkle, in her eye, and a smile, on her face. Elizabeth nodded, saying, "Yes, my William!" Before she could say another word, Darcy wrapped her in his arms and kissed her passionately.

CHAPTER 6

JUST AS THE sun was setting, bathing the world in its golden light, the carriage turned into a long, tree-lined drive. "Wake up, my love. We have arrived," Darcy whispered softly to the woman sleeping in his arms. The days leading up to their wedding had been very busy, and some had been fraught with difficulties. They had survived, but there had been an emotional toll to pay, coupled with the fact that neither had slept well the previous night. They had both dozed as the carriage traveled towards their destination.

As she glanced out the window, the carriage turned off the road between two brick columns onto a tree-lined drive. "Where are we?" Elizabeth questioned her new husband, as she rubbed the sleep from her eyes. Darcy had kept his plans for the first nights of their honeymoon as a surprise.

"This is The Elms. The estate belongs to a friend of mine, Owen Stanhope, who recently departed for a trip to the Americas. Before he left, I spoke with him about using the estate tonight. I did not wish our first night together to be spent in a noisy, crowded inn. I wanted to insure your comfort and our privacy for this very special night." Elizabeth's cheeks flooded with color as she thought of what was to come.

As Darcy finished speaking, the drive veered to the right, allowing the house to be seen. It was a lovely building in the Palladian style. The numerous windows and graceful symmetry were pleasing to the eye. The setting sun bathed the tan brick in its rich, gold light. Lights appeared in several windows on the ground floor. The carriage continued around the circular drive, coming to a stop before the entry. Before the footman could climb down and place the steps, the front door of the manor opened, and a small, trim woman with silver hair and black button eyes stepped out to greet them. Darcy handed Elizabeth down and mounted the stairs.

"Mr. Darcy, it is a pleasure to see you again, sir. I am Mrs. Buxton, the housekeeper. Please accept my compliments on your marriage. Please come in," the housekeeper finished in a rush, a pleased smile on her face and a bright expression in her dark eyes. Darcy and Elizabeth exchanged a glance as they followed this tiny bundle of energy into the house.

As a maid appeared to take their outerwear, Darcy said, "It is a pleasure to be back at The Elms, Mrs. Buxton. Please allow me to introduce my bride, Mrs. Elizabeth Darcy."

"It is a pleasure to meet you, ma'am. We are delighted to have you with us."

"Thank you, Mrs. Buxton," said Elizabeth with her friendly smile. "The house is lovely and looks very inviting. It was a delightful surprise to realize we would be staying here rather than in an inn this evening."

"Yes, yes, just so. Now, we have a cold collation prepared for you per Mr. Darcy's request. Let me show you to your rooms, and you may freshen up before dining." Without waiting for their agreement, she turned and headed for the staircase. With a shared glance, where Elizabeth could barely keep her countenance, Darcy offered her his arm, and they followed the housekeeper up the stairs.

The woman stopped before a doorway and opened it for the couple. They stepped into a beautiful sitting room, causing Elizabeth to remark, "What a lovely, tranquil room."

"I believe your servants have already arrived, and hot water was sent to your dressing rooms. Dinner will be served in half an hour if that suits you?"

Darcy looked at Elizabeth and receiving her nod, replied, "That should allow us enough time, Mrs. Buxton."

"Just follow this hallway to the left and it will take you to the main staircase. The dining room is to the left at the bottom of the stairs." With that, the little woman bustled away.

When Darcy had closed the door, Elizabeth released the laughter she had been holding back. "Mrs. Buxton is delightful, but please tell me, William, that Mrs. Reynolds is not like that!"

"Mrs. Reynolds is certainly as efficient, but somewhat more sedate and reserved," came his laughing reply.

"Thank goodness," said Elizabeth.

Two knocks were heard, and at Darcy's call, Margot and Chalmers entered the sitting room from opposite sides.

"The water is getting cold, sir."

"I am coming, Chalmers." Darcy took Elizabeth's hand and raised it to his lips. "I shall wait for you here, my love." Elizabeth squeezed the hand he still held and moved to join Margot. When the door had closed behind her, Darcy sighed before going to join his valet.

After washing and changing, Darcy returned to the sitting room to await Elizabeth. He was staring out the window at the night sky as he recalled that the gardens at The Elms were some of the finest in the area. *Perhaps we shall walk them tomorrow and take a picnic lunch with us* he thought. A noise behind him caused him to turn in the direction of the door to Elizabeth's room. The sight that met his eyes was indescribably lovely.

Elizabeth had changed into an off-white gown, with a pale rose underskirt. The neckline, Empire waist, sleeves, and hem were all trimmed in a darker rose with lace edging the neckline and sleeves. The bottom of the gown was drawn up every few inches and held in place with a rosebud made of the dark rose. It created a scallop around the hem, allowing the underskirt to show. She had a wrap of the same pale rose draped across her elbows. She had also had her hair redressed, and now there were several curls resting tantalizingly on her left shoulder.

"You are beautiful, my love." The look in her husband's eyes as he spoke set the butterflies in her stomach to fluttering madly.

"Thank you, William. You are very well turned out, as well, my handsome husband."

Darcy gave Elizabeth his dimpled smile as he took her hand, bringing her fingers to his lips for a kiss before he tucked it into his arm and led the way to the dining room.

Mrs. Buxton bustled into the room after both of them had been seated. "I hope everything is to your liking?" Darcy and Elizabeth looked over the beautifully set table where could be observed a wide assortment of dishes.

"Everything looks delicious," said Elizabeth to the housekeeper.

Agreeing, Darcy said, "Thank you for your efforts, Mrs. Buxton. I am sure we shall enjoy our repast."

"I thought you might prefer to serve yourselves this evening, but please ring if there is anything you need. Well, then, I will leave you two to enjoy your evening." With a backward glance, the housekeeper exited the room, a smile on her lips.

Darcy picked up the bottle of champagne that had been left for them and poured a glass for Elizabeth. She, in turn, was filling his plate from the platters on the table. There were cold chicken and beef, several cheeses, fresh bread, still warm from the oven, and an assortment of fruits. There were also biscuits, small cakes, and a dish of syllabub.

Before they began to eat, Darcy raised his glass to offer a toast to his bride. "Elizabeth, from the moment I heard you laugh and saw your dark curls, I was lost to you. You haunted my dreams for many dark years, but meeting you again lifted the darkness from my life. Now my dreams will come true, for you shall be by my side the remainder of my life. I love you most ardently with the passing of each day."

Darcy touched his glass to hers, hearing the tinkle of the crystal. He watched as Elizabeth took a drink and then leaned to kiss her, tasting the champagne on her lips and tongue.

The couple talked and laughed as the meal progressed and took turns feeding one another. All of this was interspersed with kisses—some brief and others more passionate. As the meal drew to a close, Darcy quietly spoke, "Shall we retire, my love?" Elizabeth's face flushed, but she smiled softly at her new husband and nodded her assent.

Darcy stood and helped her from her chair. He gazed down at her for a brief moment. Slowly his hands traveled up her arms to rest upon her shoulders. The fingers of his right hand gently stroked the curls that lay there before sliding to the back of her neck. Darcy felt the tremor that ran through her as the back of his other hand gently brushed from her chin to her hairline. Then he leaned in and gently brushed his lips across hers. He followed this with a few more light kisses as she leaned into him. Stepping back, he offered her his arm to escort her to their room. Darcy could barely suppress the pleasure he felt to see the passion-drugged look in her eyes and the way she leaned into him as though her knees would no longer hold her upright.

Once in their sitting room with the door closed firmly behind them, Darcy swept her into his arms and kissed her with abandon. When they were both panting to regain their breath, he whispered, "Shall you need more than half an hour to prepare?" Still breathing heavily, Elizabeth shook her head. Darcy walked her to the door of her bedchamber and kissed her hand, opened the door, gently guided her through, and closed the door behind her. A smile on his lips, he crossed the room to his door and stepped inside to call for Chalmers.

Elizabeth collapsed against the door as it closed behind her. Her stomach was again all a flutter and her palms were damp. After kisses like she had just experienced, she could not imagine what more there could be. She saw Margot open the door to her dressing room and quickly moved across the room to change for bed. After washing thoroughly, she changed into the nightgown that was purchased for her wedding night and sat down before the mirror at the dressing table. Margot removed her jewelry and the pins from her hair. As she brushed out the curls, Elizabeth reached for her bottle of fragrance. She dabbed a bit behind her ears and on her wrists and, feeling very daring, also touched the scent to the valley between her breasts.

"I would recommend leaving your hair loose tonight, Mrs. Darcy, but I will braid it if you prefer."

"No, I prefer to leave it down tonight as well," replied Elizabeth with a last look in the mirror. Standing, Elizabeth turned to her maid. "I will ring for you in the morning when you are needed, Margot, but now you may retire for the night."

With a nod of her head and a whispered good night, Margot exited the dressing room into the hallway. She found Chalmers waiting for her, and together they made their way down the stairs to the servants' hall, where they joined Mrs. Buxton for a cup of tea before retiring.

Upon entering the sitting room, Elizabeth noted the lighted candles scattered about, bathing the room in their soft glow. However, her gaze was inexorably drawn to Darcy, who stood before the fireplace, staring into the flames, and his elbow on the mantle. He was dressed in a long silk dressing gown of deep blue trimmed with a black collar and cuffs. Her eyes wandered from his bare neck to his bare feet. She was still looking at his feet when she felt, more than saw, him turn towards her. She did not look up until she heard his sharply indrawn breath.

Blushing, she looked from his feet to take in the expression on his face. His eyes were wide and his jaw slightly slackened. The sight of her composed and reserved husband brought forth a giggle. Recovering himself at the sound of her laughter, he focused his eyes on hers. "I am overwhelmed, my love. I did not think it was possible for you to be more beautiful than you were as you joined me at the altar this morning, but I was wrong. You are breathtaking."

"Thank you, William."

"I am glad you left your hair free; I have long desired to see it. Your beautiful tresses are much longer than I expected," he said as he slowly crossed the room, stopping a few feet from her.

Darcy reached for her hands and drew her arms out to the side as he observed her intently. Her nightgown was made of the same ivory silk as her wedding gown. The silk clung to her figure, exposing all of her curves to Darcy's eager eyes. The bodice of the gown was trimmed with the same Alencon lace that graced her wedding gown. Over the gown she wore a sheer wrapper; the front edges, hem, and sleeves were trimmed with matching lace. Her dark curls tumbled past her shoulders, nearly reaching her waist. Darcy was mesmerized, and could not remove his gaze from his beautiful wife.

"Truly, my love, I have never seen a more wondrous sight!" Dropping one hand, he led her to the sofa before the fire, seating himself close beside her. Darcy leaned forward and picked up a package from the table and set it on Elizabeth's lap.

"What is this, William? You know there is no need for you to give me gifts."

"I know I do not have to, but I like to, so you shall just have to accustom yourself to receiving them. I derive great delight in finding gifts for my loved ones, and as you are now the most important and most loved person in my life, you shall just have to learn to like them." Darcy's teasing smile brought a smile to Elizabeth, as well.

"I must first get something before I can open this. Please wait one moment." Elizabeth set the gift back upon the table and disappeared into her bedchamber. She returned a moment later with a small wrapped package in her hand. Again seating herself on the sofa, Elizabeth handed Darcy the small package, then picked up the gift she had set on the table. "Should you like to go first, or shall I?" she asked with a small smile.

"Ladies first, of course."

Elizabeth untied the silk ribbon that was wrapped around the gift. She removed the paper and was left with a wooden box. Sliding the lid from the box, she found a beautiful collection of items for her dressing table. There was a brush, comb and mirror set made of silver and mother-of-pearl, as well as a pair of mother-of-pearl combs for her hair. There were also two beautiful cut crystal bottles with delicate crystal stoppers. Lastly, there was a small sealed bottle of perfume. "Oh, William, this is lovely. What is the fragrance?" she asked reaching for the bottle.

Staying her hand William said, "It is honeysuckle. It grows in profusion at Pemberley, and I have always been partial to the scent. I hope you will like it as well."

"I shall try it as soon as we arrive home." Elizabeth could see her reference to Pemberley as home caused great emotion in Darcy. As she watched, he leaned forward and placed a soft kiss on her lips, as a tremor shook his body. Not wanting him to become distracted just yet, she said, "It is your turn now."

Darcy slipped the light blue ribbon from the package and tucked it into the pocket of his robe. As he removed the paper, something white fell into his lap. Picking it up, Darcy saw that it was a handkerchief, embroidered with his initials surrounded by a laurel wreath. He then looked down to the book he held in his hand. "However did you come by this, Elizabeth? I did not think it was available yet!" Darcy ran his hand across the embossed leather cover and read the title, *An Interesting Account of the Voyages and Travels of Captains Lewis and Clarke, in the Years 1804-5, & 6.*

"One of Uncle Edward's contacts in America sent him two copies. He planned to give one to father, but I convinced him to let me purchase it from him as a gift for you."

"You could not have found anything I would more enjoy reading. I have been asking after it at Hatchard's, but they did not have any news of when it would be available. I shall treasure it always, my love."

Setting his book aside, he then removed the box from her hand and placed it on the table before the sofa. "Would you like a little more champagne?" he asked, picking up the bottle that had been sent up from the dining room after they departed. At her nod, he filled two glasses. Handing one to her, he leaned back beside her, placing his arm around her shoulders. For a moment, they sipped in silence, as they watched the flames dancing in the hearth.

Nervously anticipating what was to come, Elizabeth felt compelled to break the silence. "It was very kind of Mr. Stanhope to offer his home to us. From what I have seen, it is a lovely estate. Shall we be leaving early in the morning?"

"No, I thought perhaps to spend an additional night here."

"I should like that, though I am anxious to see Pemberley."

"You cannot know how it thrills me to hear you speak so excitedly of Pemberley. I am anxious for you to see *our* home and to explore its many beauties with you."

When Darcy had finished his champagne, he set the glass on the table and reached to take Elizabeth's from her hand, placing it next to his.

He again sat back and pulled her more firmly into his arms, kissing the top of her head. He was silent for a moment while he lightly ran his fingers up and down her arm. "How are you feeling this evening, my Elizabeth? Are you nervous?"

"A little," she admitted "but I am excited, as well. My aunt kindly explained what is to happen, but I do not know what to do, and I do not wish you to be disappointed." The words were uttered barely above a whisper.

Darcy lifted his head from hers and tilted her face up so that he could see her eyes. "Do you love me?"

"You know that I do!"

"Then you could never disappointment. Do you trust me, Elizabeth?"

"With all that I am, William."

"Then relax, my love, I want this to be an enjoyable experience for us both. So relax, trust me, and let me love you." The intensity of his look caused another little frisson to run down her spine as she nodded her assent.

William drew her back into his embrace and slowly lowered his head until their lips met in a gentle kiss. Deepening the kiss, her lips parted and his tongue gently entered her mouth. Soon her hands came up to the back of his neck and entwined in the curls that brushed his collar. Darcy was pleased to feel her relax in his embrace and to return the kiss with equal passion. Never breaking the kiss, Darcy lifted her into his arms and carried her into his bedchamber.

Darcy was drawn from a deep and peaceful sleep because of something tickling his nose. He twitched it a time or two, but the tickle was still there. Turning his head to the left, rather than relieving him, actually caused the tickle to become worse. Sighing as he was pulled further from his sleep, his senses were suddenly assaulted with the fragrance of lavender.

Knowing it to be Elizabeth's scent, his eyes slowly opened to discover her pressed tightly against his side. It was her untamed curls that were tickling his nose. A glance at the light coming in the windows showed that it was later than he would normally rise, but as he recalled how late into the night they had talked and made love, he was not surprised.

Darcy gently withdrew his arm from around Elizabeth's shoulders. He turned to his side and gazed contentedly at her beautiful face. A smile spread slowly across his features as he recalled Elizabeth's passionate response to her introduction to the joys of the marriage bed. She had been shy at first, but as she became more comfortable, she had followed his lead, matching his activities and passions with her own. Life with Elizabeth would be a joy, and he very much doubted he would ever be able to get enough of his beautiful, enticing wife.

As he lay lost in his thoughts of their wedding night, a sleepy voice said, "Good morning, my husband, what causes your smile?"

Darcy looked down to see her warm, chocolate eyes staring at him. Meeting her eyes with a look that left her in no doubt of his thoughts, Elizabeth blushed as a shy smile appeared upon her face. "I was thinking how wonderful it is to wake with you here in my arms, dearest, loveliest, Elizabeth. I know we have not yet discussed the matter, but I hope to wake this way every morning until I wake in heaven."

"I must agree that the comfort of your embrace is a most pleasant way to start the day. I am not sure I will be able to sleep without their reassuring presence."

"What would you like to do today, my love? I thought perhaps a walk in the gardens and a picnic lunch by the lake if that would please you."

"That sounds the perfect way to spend the day, William. We were cooped up in the carriage yesterday and will be so again tomorrow as we continue on to Pemberley. I would enjoy a day spent in the beauties of nature."

"Then I shall ring for the servants and request baths be drawn. Then we shall dine in our sitting room before we begin to wander the gardens. Will an hour be sufficient for you to make ready?"

"Certainly," said Elizabeth as she moved to the edge of the bed to rise. Darcy's arm reached out and pulled her close for a kiss before departing, but what was meant to be a quick kiss soon led to more.

It was another half hour before the servants were summoned. However, they had anticipated the master and mistress's desire for a bath, and the water was delivered shortly after they were called. Elizabeth was entering their joint sitting room as the breakfast tray arrived.

A short time later, with a shawl draped gently around Elizbeth's shoulders, the new couple was strolling the formal gardens hand-in-hand. They spoke about the plants they observed and the grounds of Pemberley. Darcy told her of the incomparable beauty to be found at their estate and of the many special places he wished to show her.

When they finished walking in the gardens, they moved to the music room for a time. Elizabeth played and sang for her husband—something he greatly enjoyed. After an hour or so, the housekeeper appeared in the doorway of the music room with a picnic hamper in hand. She handed the basket to Darcy and a blanket to Elizabeth and directed them towards the path that led to the lake. Again holding hands, they set off in the direction the servant's hand indicated. They walked round the lake until they reached the perfect spot along its banks. They were sheltered from the sun by the branches of a weeping willow tree that created a private bower for them. The weather was still too cool to enjoy dipping their toes into the water, but they enjoyed the reflection of the world around them in the smooth waters.

They shared a meal of cold chicken, bread, cheese, and fruit, as well as some biscuits, washed down with a bottle of wine. Darcy read to Elizabeth from a book by Voltaire. He was lying with his head in her lap, and her fingers gently stroked through his dark curls. His sonorous voice washed over her as she listened to his perfectly accented French.

Before long, the pleasure caused by her hands upon his head distracted Darcy from the words on the page before him. He set the book aside and sighed contentedly. "I hope to have the pleasure of spending many days with you in this delightful occupation as we enjoy the summer at Pemberley, my Elizabeth."

Elizabeth gave him a soft smile, a look of longing in her eyes. Darcy reached up his hand and drew her face down so that he could kiss her. Their lips brushed gently time after time before Darcy's passions overtook him. He pulled Elizabeth down beside him on the blanket, wrapping her tightly in his embrace, as he continued to kiss her. He began to move over her before he remembered their location. "Let us return to our room, my love, to rest before tea. I desire to hold you and love you more than I can do at the present."

When tea was served, again in their shared sitting room, their faces glowed from their recent exercise. Darcy watched as his wife poured out tea and prepared his cup as he preferred. Every movement she made was graceful, and his desire for her increased while he observed her in this small moment of daily life. The remainder of their day passed much as the previous evening had.

After a pleasant dinner and more time in the music room, the newlyweds spent another night of passion in each other's arms.

CHAPTER 7

FINALLY, THE DOORS of Netherfield closed behind the last departing guests. Not long after the Darcys had departed, those staying at Netherfield returned to the estate and made their preparations to journey back to London. They all wished to arrive before nightfall. The entryway was piled with luggage, and several carriages stood ready in the drive, waiting their turn to approach the entry and be loaded for departure.

Most of the visitors were going to town for the remainder of the season and then would move to their country estates for the warm summer months. As a result, they were traveling in small groups. The Matlocks, along with Richard, Georgiana, Anne, and Lady Penelope were among the first to depart. Due to Lady Catherine's most recent behavior, the earl planned to meet with the family solicitors to determine the best thing to be done to prevent Lady Catherine from causing further trouble. Once they were aware of all the details of Sir Lewis's will and their options for Lady Catherine, they would accompany Anne to Kent. During their sojourn, Georgiana would be joining the Gardiner family to further her acquaintance with her new sisters, Kitty and Mary.

The Darcys' friends from Derbyshire were the next to depart. They had enjoyed getting to know Elizabeth better and looked forward to seeing her upon their arrival in the north. Many of the ladies were eagerly anticipating their upcoming meetings and having Elizabeth join their circle of acquaintances.

Lord Wescott had offered to travel in tandem with Miss Pottsfield and her companion, offering them his protection upon the road. James Wescott had been very surprised to find himself drawn to the quiet, unassuming Miss Pottsfield. She was certainly not like the ladies of the ton—particularly his cousin, Lady Marjorie. During most of the quiet ride back to London as his carriage followed hers, he debated with himself the possibility of calling upon her. He knew that many in society would look down on him for courting, and perhaps marrying, the daughter of a tradesman. However, his opinion of the ladies of society was so low; they had never been much to his liking—except for making sport of them as he romanced first one and then another. He knew he had a reputation as a rake but was assured that many of society would forgive him that in order to gain a title. He wondered how a considerate young woman, such as Miss Pottsfield, would view his reputation. Would she ignore it for the title or expect more of him in the future? By the time the carriages reached London, he had made up his mind that he wanted to earn the regard of this young woman, just as Miss Elizabeth Bennet had earned his respect.

The last to depart were the Hursts and Mr. and Mrs. Albert Bingley. As they said their farewells, Jane received hugs and congratulations from her new sister and aunt. "I am so happy for you and Charles," said

Louisa. "I cannot think of anyone more perfect for Charles and feel quite fortunate to have such a kind and loving sister."

"You know not how much your words mean to me, Louisa," was Jane's shy reply. It still caused Jane pangs of discomfort that Charles was separated from his other sister because Miss Bingley could not accept their affection for each other.

As Louisa moved away, Barbara Bingley took her place. "My nephew chose very wisely when he selected you for his bride. We are delighted to have you join our family, dear Jane. Now be sure to visit us when you are looking for an estate later this year. There are other members of the family who are looking forward to making your acquaintance. I hope you both will be very happy."

The two couples moved to board their carriages. The Bingley carriage set off immediately, but Charles rushed to the Hurst carriage before it could pull away. Ducking his head in the open window, he reminded his family they would be searching for an estate and promised to advise them as soon as they decided on one. "If the timing works out, I hope you will consider joining us there for Christmas before going on to Pemberley." With that, he returned to where Jane stood on the steps and waved to his family until the carriage turned out of the drive.

Charles and Jane had no sooner entered the drawing room and closed the door behind them than he had Jane crushed to himself in a passionate embrace. Some time later, the couple, now seated on the sofa together and still in their embrace, was interrupted by a knock on the door. They jumped apart and quickly straightened their appearances before Bingley called out for the person to enter. Mrs. Dawson entered with the tea things, deposited the tray on the table nearest the sofa, and quickly departed, closing the door behind her. She stood briefly on the other side of the door as she heard their soft laughter. Smiling to herself, she moved to the kitchens to speak to the cook about the dinner Mr. Bingley requested. The servants had a quiet evening as the couple retired unusually early.

The party at Longbourn had just finished breakfast when a carriage pulled up before the door. Bingley stepped down and handed out his wife, and they made their way to the entrance. They reminded Mr. Bennet that they would be traveling on to Yorkshire after their stay in Bath to meet the rest of Bingley's family and then to Derbyshire to look for an estate. They expressed the hope of seeing Mr. Bennet at Pemberley after he took Lydia to school. Otherwise, they would see him when they returned at Michaelmas. After one more round of farewells, Bingley hurried Jane into their carriage, and with a wave, they set off on their honeymoon.

Not long after the Bingleys departed, the Gardiners prepared to return to London with Mary and Kitty in tow. There was much laughter and confusion with the children rushing about before being forced to be still in the carriage. Mr. Bennet was lending his carriage for the return trip to town. With the addition of his two daughters and their luggage, a second vehicle was required. The coachman would stay overnight and return the next day.

As the door closed behind his departing family, Mr. Bennet made his way to his library and settled in the comfortable chair behind his desk. He had barely seated himself before Mrs. Hill entered carrying a tray with a pot of coffee and a couple of the pastries remaining from breakfast. He smiled his thanks as she handed him a cup before leaving him to the peace and quiet of his library.

Mr. Bennet leaned back in his chair and thought over the events of the past week. There had certainly been a number of distresses that had to be dealt with, but as he reflected on the joy on his two eldest daughters' faces, he could not but be pleased with the happiness Mr. Bennet knew their futures would hold.

Setting his coffee cup aside, Mr. Bennet looked at the mail on his desk. He noted a large envelope whose return address read Winksley, Yorkshire, and quickly broke the seal. Mr. Bennet relaxed as he read the letter accepting Lydia into the Barrows School for Girls. He glanced through the list showing her studies and the list of items needed for school. Fortunately, the cost should not be too much for the estate to bear. He and his steward had instituted several of the changes that Darcy had recommended and hoped that the income this year would be higher than in past years. As the estate would now pass to Elizabeth, Mr. Bennet wanted very much to do his best for his family. He may be late in making this decision, but Thomas Bennet was determined that his family would no longer suffer from his oversight and lack of care.

Mr. Bennet thought for a moment about his need to meet with his wife and youngest daughter on the morrow. He was not looking forward to it, but Mr. Bennet planned what he would need to say to them and how he wished to deal with the situation. Once his decisions were made, Mr. Bennet poured himself a glass of port and settled back with his current book, enjoying the peace while it lasted.

On the morning after arriving in London, Lord Matlock set off early to meet with the solicitor for the Fitzwilliam and de Bourgh families. He had sent his requests to him before setting off for Hertfordshire and expected the man would have all the information they needed to find an effective solution to the problem that was Lady Catherine.

Several hours later the Earl returned home in a reflective state of mind. He had learned much about the late Sir Lewis's will and the future of the estate and the family. His anger at his sister grew as he realized the way she had kept the family in ignorance of a significant point in Sir Lewis's will. Lord Matlock immediately entered his study where he poured himself a glass of whiskey and downed it one gulp. When he was calm, the earl called his family and niece together and sat down to discuss with them what he had learned.

"Anne, my dear, what has your mother told you about your father's will and the estate?"

"Mother said the estate was hers until the end of her life, or until I married. However, she always pointed out that since I would marry Darcy and live at Pemberley that she would continue to care for it until her death."

"That explains why she desperately wanted you to marry Darcy, though she miscalculated if she thought he would allow her to run things without interference," muttered the earl.

"What do you mean by that, Father?" asked the colonel.

"Anne was to have inherited the estate last year, at which time Lady Catherine was to be forced to the dower house with only one thousand pounds per annum. In this way, he knew that her dowry would last the balance of her lifetime, and she would not be a continual draw against the estate," replied Lord Matlock. "Also, in the case of Anne's death before taking over the estate or marrying, then Rosings would pass to you, Richard."

Lady Matlock gasped. "Do you mean to say that there was no need for Richard to go off to war! How dare she risk his life that way?"

A grumble was heard coming from the viscount at Lady Catherine's blasé treatment of his brother's wellbeing.

"Now, now, Mother, calm down. I would only inherit in the event of Anne's death, something I hope is far in the future." Richard smiled at his cousin as he spoke.

"I hope so, as well, Richard, but whenever it may be, I know that I will not be able to manage the estate on my own nor to battle with my mother continually. Before we traveled to Hertfordshire, I met with Darcy's doctor, Mr. Sullivan. He spent a great deal of time talking to me about my health and gave me a thorough examination. The illness that weakened my heart will never improve. It could cause an attack at anytime, but undue stress or exertion will most likely bring about difficulties. As you have already survived two injuries in battle, perhaps you would consider resigning your commission and joining me at Rosings as co-owner. We can split all the profits equally. I could never need such a great income as the estate provides. Nor am I prepared to handle the demands of running the estate and dealing with my mother. Not to mention, it would be very lonely there by myself."

"It is not only the estate that provides you with income, Anne. Your father left several investments behind, as well. They were set up so that your mother could not access the funds and have been reinvested and earning a great deal of interest in the years since your father died. You could easily live on the interest from these investments without touching the money from the estate," Lord Matlock informed them.

"In that case, Richard, you could have the entire income from Rosings. That would allow you to marry, if you so wished," finished his cousin with a knowing look.

Richard's face reddened clear to the tips of his ears at her comment, but he acknowledged to himself the pleasure the idea gave him as Mary's peaceful countenance appeared to his mind's eye.

"Let us not get ahead of ourselves here," said Richard firmly. "However, I must admit I would be happy never to see a battlefield again. Do the terms of Sir Lewis' will allow for this co-ownership?"

"As the estate now legally belongs to Anne, and as she is offering the ownership to Sir Lewis' choice of heir, I do not see any difficulties with her decision," stated Lord Matlock firmly. "We can have the solicitors draw up whatever agreement you two wish."

"What say you, Richard: Will you accept my offer and help me return my father's estate to its former glory? Mother has let many things go, focusing her attention on her personal wishes, not necessarily what was best for Rosings and the tenants."

"I would be grateful and happy to accept your offer, Anne, but what shall we do about your mother?"

"We shall have the dower house prepared for her and move her into it immediately," was Lady Matlock's emphatic statement. Everyone laughed at her pronouncement.

"I believe we shall have the solicitors manage all of her accounts as well, so that she cannot overspend her allowance," remarked her brother with another chuckle.

"Well, before I travel to Kent, I must resign my commission, and I should like to return briefly to Hertfordshire to obtain Mr. Bennet's permission to court Miss Mary."

"You have shown her a great deal of attention since her arrival in town. Do you really need to court her longer?" His mother's encouraging expression made everyone laugh.

"I must spend time at the estate through the summer and harvest, but perhaps I could court her through the small season before we join the Darcys for Christmas. I believe they invited all the family for the holidays. Who knows, perhaps we could be married from Pemberley before the year's end."

"I believe, my dear son," said Lady Matlock as she gently placed her hand on her son's cheek, "that you have imagined this before. Otherwise, you are demonstrating why you were such a respected officer, for you certainly made a decisive plan rather quickly. A plan, I might add, of which I heartily approve."

Again, Richard blushed. "Thank you, Mother, for the compliment and your approval and support. They mean a great deal to me."

"Congratulations, Richard. I am glad you will no longer be facing the French. But, perhaps, you should get Miss Bennet's approval before you make wedding plans," said the Viscount with a laugh. "Who knows, she may say no to a jackanapes like you."

The family all laughed at Richard's look of dismay and settled in to finalize their plans to depart for Kent in two days time. Richard would join them after meeting with Mr. Bennet and Miss Mary Bennet. In fact, he sent an express to the gentleman asking to meet him midday the following day to discuss a matter of some importance.

Mr. Bennet was on the verge of retiring when an urgent knocking was heard at the front door. He stood outside his library door and listened as the messenger announced an express for Mr. Bennet. He said he was to await a reply. Mr. Bennet stepped forward and took the missive while Mrs. Hill led the young man to the kitchen for some food. Mr. Bennet worried what could be wrong to necessitate an express, so he quickly broke the seal and scanned the letter. As Mr. Bennet read, a look of confusion spread over his face. He returned to his desk and jotted off a quick reply. He took the message to the kitchen, and the messenger was soon on his way back to London.

CHAPTER 8

DARCY AND ELIZABETH departed The Elms with a happy glow. They thanked the housekeeper for her kind attentions. "You have done your master proud with the hospitality you showed us, Mrs. Buxton. I will be sure he knows of your excellent care when next I hear from him," Darcy informed her as he led Elizabeth to the carriage. Their second day of traveling was much like the previous one. Earlier, they had stopped at an inn for their evening meal. About an hour after leaving the inn, the carriage pulled off the main road onto a smaller one. They drove over a bridge onto what appeared to be an island in the middle on a slow moving river. The carriage stopped before the small building, and Darcy helped Elizabeth down. She stood taking in the surprising sight that met her eyes. In the center of the island, sheltered by ancient, large trees, stood a quaint cottage. It had a thatched roof and whitewashed walls. The door, shutters, and window boxes were a bright, cheery green. A multitude of rose bushes surrounded the cottage, their pink buds just beginning to appear, and bright yellow tulips filled the window boxes. Darcy led her to the door and opened it, stepping back to allow Elizabeth to enter first.

The interior of the cottage was clean and bright. The walls were a soft yellow with lace curtains at the windows. There was a stone fireplace before which sat two comfortable-looking wing-backed chairs in a blue striped fabric. There was a large canopy bed on the wall opposite the fireplace. The comforter on the bed had a white background with trailing vines of green decorated with little blue and yellow flowers while the same lace that covered the windows created a canopy above the bed. The dining set, wardrobe, bookcase, desk, and remaining items were made of rosewood. The far end of the large, open room had windows on three sides, and several easels sat there with an assortment of canvases in different sizes and various stages of completion. The picture the cottage presented both inside and out was one of charm and peacefulness.

"However did you find this delightful place, William? I imagine I could be happy here for the remainder of my life, so long as you are with me. What more could we need?"

"I am pleased you find it to your liking, my love, but it is ours only for the evening. And though I know you did not marry me for my money, please remember we do have a charming home awaiting us at the end of tomorrow's journey. I hope you shall be as pleased with it as you are with this place, my dear wife." Darcy cocked a brow at Elizabeth, and she could see how important it was to him that she like Pemberley.

Elizabeth had been so busy looking around that she failed to realize their trunks had been brought into the room, and the fire and several candles had been lit. However, Chalmers, Margot, and the carriage had all disappeared from sight. Elizabeth soon found herself in her husband's embrace. When they had to pause to recover their breath, Darcy took her hand and led her towards the bed. He stopped as they drew near and began to kiss her again, but this time, his roaming hands were creating a trail of fire everywhere he touched. It was not long before she realized that while she was distracted with his kisses, he had begun to undress her. She felt his hands move from her shoulders to the nape of her neck. Then she realized that he was slowly undoing the buttons down the back of her gown. Shyly she slid her hands down his shoulders to his forearms, before hesitantly beginning to unbutton his topcoat. They continued to slowly undress one another until there was nothing left to remove. Then Darcy again drew his beautiful bride into his arms and began to kiss her. As he deepened the kiss, he gently eased her down upon the bed. Elizabeth felt the soft mattress surrounding her, and when she opened her eyes, she saw his dark eyes staring back at her.

"Do not move," whispered Darcy. He straightened up and began blowing out the candles.

Elizabeth rose up onto her elbow to watch the enticing sight of her well-muscled, handsome husband in all of his masculine glory moving about the room. "I do not know if it is proper for me to say this or not, but you are far more perfect than any statue or painting I have ever before viewed. I knew that you were handsome, but the sight of your muscles as they move under your skin is quite intoxicating." Her face was red and the words no more than a whisper by the time she finished speaking.

Darcy paused to look down at his adoring wife. "Proper or not, you are more than welcome to say such things any time you wish," said Darcy with his dimpled smile. "I am happy that you find my body pleasing. And though I dreamed about loving you many times, not even my most realistic dreams prepared me for the beauty that was you, my love." So saying he kissed her again as he lowered himself down onto the bed.

Colonel Fitzwilliam was awakened by his batman shortly after dawn and given the messenger's letter. He moved to stand by the window and, shifting the curtain to permit more light into the room, read Mr. Bennet's reply to his express. He smiled to see the gentleman invited him to meet at noon and then to join him for luncheon.

He instructed his man to have a bath drawn for him in forty minutes before returning to the land of slumber. After breaking his fast with his family, Richard mounted his horse and set out for Longbourn. Fortunately, good weather accompanied him, and he was able to travel quickly. He arrived at Longbourn's front door five minutes before the appointed time. Mrs. Hill welcomed him and led him to Mr. Bennet's study.

His host directed him to a chair and offered him refreshment, which Richard refused. As Mr. Bennet sat behind his desk staring at him over the rim of his glasses, Richard's well-rehearsed speech was promptly forgotten.

After waiting several minutes for the officer to speak, a small smile began to play about the corners of Mr. Bennet's mouth. "I believe you requested to speak to me, Colonel Fitzwilliam. How may I assist you?"

Thomas Bennet watched as the normally confident man's mouth opened and closed several times without uttering a word. Finally, he could no longer conceal his humor, and a chuckle escaped him.

Hearing Mr. Bennet's laughter was enough to rally the colonel's senses. "Mr. Bennet, I wish to ask your permission to court your daughter, Miss Mary."

Though Mr. Bennet had suspected an attraction between the two, he was taken by surprise with the colonel's request. "I believed you married to the army, sir. To what purpose do you wish to court my daughter?"

"I have recently learned of a change in my circumstances which will allow me to have a home, wife, and family. I wish to court Miss Mary with the intention of winning her heart and making her my wife," came the colonel's confident reply.

"Just what is this change that will allow you to so well care for my daughter?"

"I am to be given the management and income of Rosings Park, in Kent."

"Lady Catherine's estate? Why on earth would she give it over to you? She appeared to be in good health and firm control of her estate. What has brought about this miraculous change?"

Mr. Bennet sat back in his chair, prepared to be entertained by the colonel's story, and he was not disappointed. He laughed at the plans being made for Lady Catherine; and at the conclusion of the colonel's explanation, Mr. Bennet agreed to the courtship.

"In that case, sir, may I make one additional request? I will be traveling to Kent to learn about managing the estate and remaining there through the harvest. May Miss Bennet and I write to one another? As soon as the harvest is through, I will return to town and assiduously court your daughter."

Mr. Bennet eyed the young man for some time as he considered Richard's request. He very much liked this young man and was pleased he would no longer have to face Napoleon's armies. Finally, Mr. Bennet replied, "I believe it will be acceptable for you to write. However, be forewarned that you should not write anything too personal, as I shall require that Mary read all your letters to her aunt as well as all her responses to you. Can you agree to these terms?"

"Quite happily, sir, and thank you."

"You are very welcome, young man. Now, I believe that Mrs. Hill has luncheon ready for us. Let us enjoy our meal before you must be back on the road to London."

After a delicious meal, the colonel prepared to depart Longbourn with a lighter heart than he had arrived. As he continued along the road to London, he looked forward to visiting with Mary on the morrow. He arrived in town in time to join his family for dinner and was delighted to deliver to them the news that he had obtained Mr. Bennet's approval.

The next morning the mood of the diners around the breakfast table at Matlock House was mixed. Richard was eager to visit Mary and ask for permission to court her. However, when he thought about resigning his commission, his feelings were somewhat more complicated. Richard had served in the army since the day after completing his studies at Cambridge. He had begun at the bottom and worked his way up, eventually earning the rank of colonel. He was fearless in battle, and his men adored him. Richard was also a good tactician and strategist, whose cool head on the battlefield kept both him and his men as safe as possible during wartime.

The other members of the group were somewhat subdued, for they knew they would have to deal with Lady Catherine and her antics. Georgiana was the exception, as she could not wait to move to the Gardiners to spend time with her new family. She planned to assist Susan in learning to play the pianoforte. She, Mary, and Kitty would have daily lessons from Mrs. Annesley and would also begin learning about how to run a household from Mrs. Gardiner.

When the meal concluded, Lord and Lady Matlock and Anne entered the largest of the Matlock coaches to begin their journey to Kent. Due to the early hour, Georgiana and Richard were required to wait for almost an hour before departing for the Gardiners' home. The servants did not know quite what to make of their behavior, as neither was able to settle for more than five minutes at a time before they were again pacing or wandering about the room. When the clock chimed half past nine, they both jumped up and rushed to the door, nearly colliding in the doorway.

With a laugh, Richard held out his arm, saying, "May I escort you to the carriage, Georgie?"

"I should be delighted, Cousin."

With another laugh, they were down the stairs, out the door, and entering the carriage headed for Cheapside.

The children had stationed themselves at the window to watch for the visitors. Susan was very excited that there would be another young lady in the house and looked forward to learning more from Miss Darcy. Edmund was quite unsettled that Miss Darcy would be staying with them. His infatuation had by no means ended, and he intended to show her how grown-up and gentlemanly he could be.

Finally, Hugh's voice was heard crying, "They are here!"

Kitty jumped up excitedly and moved to the window, watching as the colonel stepped down, then handed down Georgiana. Mary set aside the handkerchief she was working on and smoothed her dress with hands that shook just slightly. Mrs. Gardiner observed them all and tried to suppress her smile. A moment later, the housekeeper announced the visitors.

"Colonel Fitzwilliam, Miss Darcy, good morning."

"Good morning, Mrs. Gardiner. Thank you so much for allowing me to stay with you while my family is away." Georgiana curtseyed to her hostess.

"We are delighted to have you, Miss Darcy. Kitty, would you show Miss Darcy to her room?"

"Certainly, Aunt." Kitty took Georgiana by the hand, and with their heads close, giggling already, they left the room.

Richard just shook his head as he watched his normally shy cousin hurrying away.

Turning that smile on his hostess, Richard said, "I am so pleased to see her happy. Mrs. Gardiner, I wonder if I might have a word with Miss Bennet. I saw her father recently and have a message for her."

Mary looked at him with confusion, but Mrs. Gardiner gave him a knowing smile. "Will you be able to stay for luncheon, Colonel Fitzwilliam?"

"I should like that, ma'am."

"Well, you and Mary may have a few moments together while I inform my housekeeper about the addition to the meal. I shall leave the door open," Mrs. Gardiner said as she exited the room.

Richard moved to seat himself on the sofa beside Mary. "When did you see my father?" asked Mary quietly.

"Yesterday," came his unexpected reply. "Miss Mary, a surprising change in my fortunes necessitated my paying him a visit."

"You are not being sent back to battle are you?" The concern on her face was apparent.

"No. In fact, I shall be resigning my commission later today."

"Oh, thank goodness," said Mary, her look changing to one of relief.

"You see," Richard continued, "I have just learned I am the heir to Rosings Park." Mary's look of shock made him chuckle. "It is a long and complicated story which I will share at another time. However, as it means that I can now take on a wife and, hopefully, a family, I felt compelled to call on your father." Mary blushed becomingly at his words. "I needed his permission before I could ask if you would permit me to court you?"

"And did he give his permission?" Mary asked softly.

"He did, indeed. So, Miss Mary Bennet, will you permit me to court you for the purpose of becoming better acquainted and with the understanding that I hope someday to make you my wife?"

Mary could not believe what she was hearing. She looked at him with tear-filled eyes. "Are you in earnest, Colonel? We have known each other for such a short time."

"I am completely in earnest. You are quite a remarkable young woman, Miss Mary. You are intelligent, kind, peaceful, and loving. When I am near you, that peacefulness seems to fill me. After years of war, I long for a quiet, peaceful life. I do not believe I would find that with anyone else."

Her face aglow, she said, "I would be happy and honored to accept your courtship."

"There is one small hitch," Mary's face fell, so he rushed to continue, "but, I have made special arrangements with your father so that it will not delay our courtship."

"What is the difficulty?" came Mary's cautious voice.

"I must go immediately to Rosings after resigning my commission. I must learn about running the estate and be there for the harvest. I thought perhaps we could correspond while I am there, and your father has agreed. I will also return to London as often as possible, and we can begin our courtship in earnest for the little season before the holidays, if that meets with your approval.

Mary's relief was now apparent. "I should like that very much."

"Your father's only condition was that you must read all my letters to your aunt, as well as your responses."

"That was very kind of Papa, for one must usually be engaged before a correspondence may occur. I look forward to getting to know you better through our correspondence."

Mrs. Gardiner, who had overheard the last of this conversation, cleared her throat before reentering the room. They made light conversation until the other young ladies joined them.

As he road along to the barracks and his meeting with the general about resigning his commission, Richard kept a tight grip on the horse's reins. He could not quite fathom the turn his life had taken, nor could he believe his good fortune in having captured the affection of a wonderful young woman, or the he could actually marry and have a peaceful life together. For so many years, he had believed he would never have the joys of a home or family of his own, but now his future would be filled with love and peace.

Colonel Fitzwilliam knocked firmly on the door to the general's office. He entered at his commanding officer's call and smartly saluted.

Without looking up from the papers he was studying, the general said, "Ahh, Fitzwilliam. I was pleased to receive your message, as there is a matter I wished to discuss with you."

"Perhaps, General, I might be permitted to speak first. It may have an effect on your discussion."

Concerned at the tone of the colonel's voice, the general directed a hard look at the officer standing before him. "I see. What is it you needed to speak to me about?"

"I wished to inform you that I will be resigning my commission, effective immediately. I have recently learned of an inheritance and have been asked to take it up as soon as possible."

The general frowned. "I see. Is there anything I could do to convince you to delay this? The army, no, the Crown, has great need of you."

"I am sorry, General, but I would not wish to jeopardize my safety when I have such an opportunity before me. It would not be fair to my family or the young lady I am courting to place myself at risk when there is no longer a need for me to earn my support in such a way."

"A young lady, aye?" said the general with a smile.

"Yes, sir."

"Well, then, let me offer you my congratulations."

"Thank you, General."

"Perhaps you can still be of assistance, Colonel Fitzwilliam. Do you have someone in mind who wishes to purchase your commission? Perhaps that individual might be able to assist with the assignment I was planning for you."

"Yes, sir. There is a man in my outfit that has earned his way from foot soldier to the rank of sergeant, though I believe he is to receive a promotion to lieutenant after our last campaign. He has been saving to purchase a higher rank, and he is truly worthy. He is an excellent leader and someone I have been able to depend upon in time of need. In fact, while he has been on leave, he has been employed by my cousin, Fitzwilliam Darcy, for some private surveillance and protection work. I recommended six men to my cousin, Travers' assessment of the job was thorough and the recommendations he made excellent. They did an exceptional job, but their services are no longer needed and their leave will be up shortly. I planned to speak with him in a couple of days when he returns to town."

"Who is this man?" questioned the general thoughtfully.

"His name is George Travers."

"Do you honestly believe Travers has the skill and intelligence to advance to such a rank immediately?"

"I do, General."

"Well, then, bring him to me once he arrives in town. If I feel he is capable of filling your shoes, I will permit you to offer him your commission and may have an assignment for him. What of these other men who worked for your cousin? What is your opinion of their capabilities?"

"General, I recommended them for the purpose of guarding my cousin, his sister, and his betrothed, all of whom are very important to me. I was trusting them with their very lives and think highly of all of them."

"I see, and were their efforts successful?"

"Yes, sir."

"Good, good. How soon will you be in contact with Travers?"

"I believe he will return to town tomorrow or the next day."

"I will expect to see you here in my office in three days. Be here at ten o'clock sharp."

"Yes, sir, General." With a sharp salute, Fitzwilliam turned and left the general's office. He mounted his horse and turned it in the direction of the nearest express office. He dashed off a note to Travers, requesting that he meet him at Matlock House very early in the morning three days hence, then rode off quickly down the road to Kent. Richard knew he needed to be there to support his father as they confronted Lady Catherine, but he would have to return quickly to meet with the general.

As the carriage turned into the drive at Rosings, everyone shifted uncomfortably. During the journey, they discussed the best way to confront Lady Catherine, concluding that they would make it seem as returning Anne home was their sole purpose. After Richard arrived, their knowledge of Lady Catherine's misdeeds would be exposed.

When the carriage stopped before the entrance, everyone exchanged glances. The determination they felt was evident in their looks. Informing the butler they did not wish to be announced, they paused in the doorway to observe Lady Catherine before making their presence known. Her expression made it immediately obvious that Lady Catherine was anxious about something, as indicated by the steady drumming of her fingers on the arm of her throne-like chair.

"Good afternoon, Catherine," greeted the earl. At the unexpected sound of his voice, his sister jumped.

"Henry, what are you doing here? Anne, I am glad you have returned home where you belong. Why is Darcy not with you?"

"Darcy is on his wedding trip. Where else would you expect him to be?" Lord Matlock stared at his sister to see her reaction to this pronouncement. He did not miss the anger that appeared on her face.

When she spoke, the anger was also evident in her voice. "I held out hope that he would yet come to his senses and do his duty to Anne and the family." Her tone became more thoughtful, and the look that briefly crossed her face was speculative. "Perhaps he is not in his right mind? Henry, we should see that Darcy is examined by a doctor, so that we can ensure that his sister and his estate are protected as they should be. We would not wish for an interloper to assume control of such valuable assets should he be unbalanced."

"There is nothing wrong with Darcy, Catherine; you need not concern yourself."

She threw a disappointed look at her brother. "Where is Georgiana? She should have been brought to me for proper training before her coming out."

"Georgiana is with some of her new family in London. You need not concern yourself with her. Darcy does not plan to have her presented for at least two years."

"And, I shall happily help Elizabeth and him to prepare her when the time comes," offered Lady Matlock.

"Do not speak that harlot's name in my presence. She will be the ruination of our family.

Georgiana shall be fortunate to make a match at all with the dreadful connection Darcy has made. I am sure that he must be out of his mind to have accepted someone with such low connections. I shall summon my doctor, and we shall travel to Pemberley to examine him and – "

"You will do nothing of the kind, Catherine. He is on his honeymoon, and you are forbidden from disturbing him," Lord Matlock interrupted his sister. "Catherine, it has been a long day of travel, and we are tired. We brought Anne home to Rosings and plan to visit for a day or two. However, I do not wish to hear your malevolent thoughts about Darcy and his bride."

"You cannot tell me how I can or cannot speak in my own home," raged Lady Catherine.

"Catherine," interjected Lady Matlock, "could you please have your housekeeper prepare rooms for us and perhaps call for refreshments? It has indeed been a long day."

Lady Catherine bristled at being given instructions about the care of guests in her home, and with little grace, she finally summoned her housekeeper and issued the instructions.

Refreshments arrived shortly thereafter, and Lady Matlock deftly steered the conversation away from Darcy's marriage each time Lady Catherine attempted to comment on the matter. When the guests had finished their refreshments, they excused themselves to rest until dinner.

The evening meal and after dinner conversation was a tense time that required all the skills of Lord and Lady Matlock to prevent Lady Catherine from continuing her rant about Darcy and Elizabeth. Much earlier than they might have done so, the visitors were excusing themselves to retire for the evening. Lord and Lady Matlock had just started up Rosings' grand staircase when a knock at the door stopped their progress. Richard appeared tired as he crossed the threshold, but his parents were in no doubt of his success with the day's activities, for he could not quite suppress his smile.

Without greeting his aunt, Richard joined his parents as they climbed the stairs to their rooms. He followed them into the sitting room attached to their suite, and the smile grew larger.

"Well, son, I imagine your day proved fruitful?" asked his father as he exchanged a pleased glance with his wife.

"Indeed, it did. I am happy to announce that Miss Mary Bennet has accepted my request for a courtship!"

"I am so pleased for you, Richard," said his mother as she moved to embrace him. "I must remember to thank Darcy and Elizabeth. It seems that their felicity has encouraged both of my sons to find young ladies to marry. I can hardly wait to be a grandmother." Richard and the earl both laughed at the contented look on Lady Matlock's face.

"How did things go here?" the colonel asked.

"On the ride down, we decided not to discuss the matter until you joined us. Catherine has no idea we know of the trouble she tried to cause or that we are aware of the truth of Sir Lewis' will. We have spent our entire visit so far deflecting her complaints about Darcy's marriage. She went so far as to suggest he is not in his right mind, and that she and I should take control of Georgiana and his estate to protect them from any 'interlopers,'" his father said with a chuckle.

"I believe we should break our fast in the morning before confronting Catherine. I expect her to fight us at every turn, and it may be our only meal of the day," said Lady Matlock with a shake of her head.

"Well, then, if you will excuse me, I shall retire for the night. It was a very long ride. Am I in my usual room?"

"Yes, Richard," said Lady Matlock as she placed a kiss upon his cheek. "Good night, dear." Lord Matlock patted him on the back and wished him pleasant dreams, as Richard exited the room.

CHAPTER 9

AFTER A BLISSFUL night in the cottage on the island, Elizabeth and Darcy began the final leg of their journey home. They sat beside each other, Darcy's arm about his wife's shoulders. Each of them held a book, but Elizabeth's attention constantly wandered from the page to the changing scenery as the carriage continued its journey. The hills she observed were steeper, and large rock formations dotted the landscape. Fleecy white sheep filled many of the fields.

They stopped briefly for a midday meal, and Elizabeth's attentions were even more distracted upon the return to the carriage. Darcy had observed her throughout the ride, but he was not quite sure how to interpret her actions and waited patiently for her to speak.

Some time had passed before she asked her first question. "How soon shall we arrive at Pemberley, my love?"

"We should be there in time for tea."

"Oh, so soon?"

"I rather thought by your behavior as we traveled today that you were looking forward to arriving," said Darcy with a look of confusion on his face.

"I am looking forward to seeing my new home, but what if I cannot manage it properly?"

"My Lizzy, what would make you think such a thing? I have never met a more intelligent and capable woman. I expect you will be the best mistress Pemberley has ever had." He pulled her closer to him as he spoke, hugging her shoulders tightly.

"What if Mrs. Reynolds does not like me? I count on her to help me learn my responsibilities as mistress."

"Mrs. Reynolds will love you, just as Mrs. Trey does. I am sure the Darcy House housekeeper has already told her a great deal about you." Elizabeth's face paled at his suggestion. Darcy laughed at her expression as he continued. "Mrs. Trey has a great deal of respect for you, so you need not worry that she would have expressed any concerns to Mrs. Reynolds. More than likely, they are both delighted that Miss Bingley never managed to trap me into marriage and become mistress of the estate. In comparison, how could they not love you?"

Elizabeth lightly slapped his sleeve at his tease. "However, Mrs. Trey is not the only one to have written about you to her. Both Georgiana and I have written about you, as well. I know from the letters I received in return that she is very much looking forward to meeting you." At his words, Elizabeth felt her nerves slip away and excitement take their place. She snuggled closer to her husband and continued to observe the passing scenery.

A short time later, they were traversing the cobbled streets of Lambton. Darcy pointed out the bookshop, the dressmaker, the inn, and the church. As they exited the town, Darcy said, "We are only five miles from Pemberley, my dear wife. We shall be home very soon."

Elizabeth sat up straighter and brushed the wrinkles from her skirt. Then she reached across the carriage to the opposite seat. Picking up her bonnet, Elizabeth replaced it upon her curls. Then she put on her gloves and folded her hands in her lap as she observed the road, looking for landmarks along the way so that she might find her way back to the village alone sometime.

As last, they turned off the main road and passed through a large wrought iron gate set into stone columns. There was a dense wood on either side of the road that did not allow Elizabeth much view of the countryside. "How long is the drive, William?"

"More than two miles," was his calm reply.

Elizabeth gasped and turned to look at him, but her attention was quickly returned to the road as they cleared the woods and the road began a gentle climb. When they crested the hill, the carriage stopped, and Elizabeth gasped at the sight that met her eyes as she reached out her hand to the door to steady herself.

There, across the valley on another piece of rising ground sat the largest home she had ever seen. The light gray stone was the same used for the columns at the gated entrance, and it seemed to sparkle in the sunlight. Before the house were an expansive green lawn and a lake that reflected the house on its smooth surface. She caught a glimpse of gardens to the rear of the house before another wooded hill reared up behind the building. There was another complex of gray stone buildings off to the side of the estate that she assumed to be the stables.

As the carriage began to descend the drive towards the house, Elizabeth turned her gaze to her husband. "This is our home?"

"Yes, this is Pemberley. What do you think? Do you like it?"

"I cannot imagine anyone who would not like it. And for once, Miss Bingley did not exaggerate. It is the most beautiful estate I have ever seen." Darcy chuckled at her words. "I have never seen a place where nature has done a better job or where man has not made any awkward attempts at controlling his surrounds. Pemberley must surely be a small piece of heaven."

By this time the carriage was slowing to stop at the front entrance. Innumerable servants appeared to tumble out of the building. A footman quickly had the door opened and the step in place, as the remaining servants lined up along the stairs to greet their master and welcome their new mistress.

Darcy stepped down from the carriage and smiled in the direction of the servants, a surprising sight for most of them. Though always kind and pleasant, Mr. Darcy was known by his staff to be a reserved and quiet gentleman. Seeing such a smile upon his face was unusual. He extended his hand towards the carriage door, and the servants took a collective breath. From within came a small, delicate glove-clad hand; it was followed by a pair of small feet in kid boots peeking from beneath an aqua gown. Next came a straw bonnet decorated with ribbons of the same color, from which dark curls peeped. The lady's head was downcast, but at a word from the master, her warm, melodic laugh was heard, and she turned a beautiful face and enchanting smile up to look at her husband. They watched in further surprise as Darcy's smile grew and his dimples appeared, causing bright smiles to appear on the faces of his servants, as well.

Advancing toward the steps with Elizabeth on his arm, Darcy addressed his staff. "It gives me great pleasure to introduce to you your new mistress, Mrs. Elizabeth Darcy."

The housekeeper and butler exchanged looks as they watched the couple make their way up the stairs. Darcy introduced her to each of the servants lined up to greet them. Elizabeth took the time to repeat their names in turn and ask about their positions in the household. By the time she arrived at the top step, Mrs. Reynolds was twisting her hands together to keep herself in place. She had been delighted to see Darcy's smile and even more so to watch it grow as he interacted with his wife. However, the most delightful sight was the love that was evident in Mrs. Darcy's eyes. The young master had obviously found happiness, and she could not have been more pleased for him. He had known much sadness in his life, and she wanted so much to see that change. She now had complete confidence in what Mrs. Trey had told her of the new mistress.

"Elizabeth, this is our butler, Benton."

"It is a pleasure to meet you, madam," said the stately older gentleman with the dark hair showing a touch of gray at the temples and vivid green eyes.

"Now, my dear, allow me to introduce you to the present heart of our home. Elizabeth, this is Mrs. Reynolds, our housekeeper."

Elizabeth reached out and took the favored servant's hands in her own as she said, "I am so pleased to meet you, Mrs. Reynolds. I have heard such wonderful things from Mr. and Miss Darcy about you. I hope I can depend upon you to help me learn my responsibilities as the mistress of this beautiful estate."

"Indeed, Mrs. Darcy, I am very pleased to meet you, and all of us will be happy to help you get settled in here. We are delighted to have a mistress again."

"Thank you, Mrs. Reynolds. I look forward to knowing you better and to working with you to ensure my husband and family's comfort."

"It is a pleasure to have you home again safe, Mr. Darcy," said the housekeeper. "The water for baths has been prepared, and I will have tea sent to your sitting room whenever you are ready for it."

"Thank you, Mrs. Reynolds. Perhaps you could have the water sent up immediately and the tea in – " he turned to Elizabeth with a raised brow.

"I believe we shall be ready for tea in an hour," his wife responded

Turning back to the housekeeper, Darcy provided her with the information she sought. "As Mrs. Darcy said, serve the tea in an hour." Elizabeth's hand was still on his arm as he led her into the hall. Elizabeth stopped, looking about her in awe. Darcy helped her remove her spencer, then Elizabeth handed her gloves and bonnet to a waiting servant.

The remaining servants had followed the couple into the house to return to their responsibilities, but not without one last look at the new mistress before they quietly disappeared.

The hall was an expansive space with marble floors and dominated by a massive staircase. The rich mahogany was intricately carved with graceful spindles and a delicately curved rail that led upward. They mounted the stairs, at the top of which was a huge window that overlooked the terrace and formal gardens. They stopped for only a brief look before Darcy turned and led her up an additional flight of stairs. They turned to the right at the top of the stairs, and Darcy escorted her to the door at the end of the hallway.

Opening the door, they stepped into the sitting room that connected the bedchambers of the master suite. The wall opposite the door had a massive fireplace in the center, on either side of which was a set of French doors that opened onto a private terrace. Through the door, Elizabeth glimpsed some furnishings and several containers of flowers.

Turning her attentions to the room itself, she saw a large sofa before the fireplace that was flanked by a pair of comfy, oversized chairs. A table sat before the sofa on which was a large decorative box, a vase of spring flowers, and several books. Decorated in shades from deep hunter to the palest of greens, the room relayed a feeling of relaxing beneath the shade of a tree. In one corner were a dining table for two and a small sideboard. The other corner had a desk flanked by bookcases.

Elizabeth noted a door set into the center of each of the sidewalls of the room. "Where do the doors lead?"

Darcy directed her to the door on the right. Opening it, he waved her through with a bow and said, "This door leads to your bedchamber, my love. I hope you like the décor I chose for you. The furniture is the same my mother used, but I had everything else done especially for you." Elizabeth looked around the room. Several large windows let the bright sunshine into the room. The lower portion of the walls was painted in a soft shade of lavender, separated by moulding that ran around the room; the top half of the walls were covered with a cream striped paper painted with green vines and clusters of small purple flowers climbing from the moulding to the ceiling. A large poster bed dominated one wall. The bedding and hangings were in shades of lavender, green, and cream, matching the hangings at the windows. In one corner, a deep purple chaise rested with a small table beside it. Before the fireplace sat a small sofa covered in a print that matched the wall covering. There was also a pair of chairs in a soft green fabric and an escritoire stood near one of the windows. Several vases of white roses and lavender filled the room, giving off a heavenly fragrance.

William pulled Elizabeth through a door at the far end of the room that led to her dressing room. At one end, there was a tiled floor, where sat a small stove and a large copper bathtub. Surprisingly, there was also a chair that seemed to be fit with a chamber pot. Elizabeth looked at her husband, her eyebrow raised in question, but she did not ask him about the item. The other end of the room was taken up with racks for her clothes, as well as built-in drawers and shelves. There was a full-length mirror and a small wall mirror above the dressing table. Next to the dressing table was a large locked cabinet. There was another vase of flowers on the dressing table. It appeared that Margot had unpacked all of her many trunks, and a moment later, she stepped through a hidden door, followed by other servants carrying the water for her bath. Darcy and Elizabeth moved back into her bedroom to allow the servants room to complete their task.

"You chose all of this for me?"

"I believed I knew you well enough to choose something you would like. Was I successful?"

"Indeed, William, it is the loveliest room I have ever seen. Thank you, my sweet husband," said Elizabeth as she rose up on her toes to bestow a quick kiss upon her husband's lips. Darcy wrapped her in his arms and was about to deepen the kiss when he heard the clearing of a throat behind him. Darcy quickly dropped his hands.

"Excuse me, Mrs. Darcy, but your bath is ready," came Margot's softly accented voice.

Elizabeth leaned around Darcy's broad form, saying, "I shall be right there, Margot."

"Yes, madam." She stepped into the dressing room, closing the door behind her.

Darcy quickly gathered her back into his embrace and kissed her thoroughly. When he, at last, let go, her cheeks were flushed, and she was a bit wobbly. Darcy turned her towards her dressing room door, and, with a pat on her derriere, said, "I shall see you in our sitting room in an hour, my lovely wife," before striding from the room.

Elizabeth enjoyed a soak in her bath before being dressing in a pale yellow day gown. Margot arranged her hair with yellow ribbons entwined through the curls. As Elizabeth entered their shared sitting room, a servant was entering with the tea tray. As she took a seat on the sofa next to Darcy, he dismissed the girl with a thank you.

Elizabeth leaned forward to prepare the tea and pour for the two of them. She fixed his cup the way he liked before handing it to him. Without asking, she placed his favorite biscuits and some fresh fruit on a plate before handing that to him, as well. She then made a plate for herself before preparing her teacup.

They sat quietly for a few moments, enjoying their tea. Elizabeth was the one to break the silence. "What I have seen so far of the house is magnificent, William. Will we tour more of it today?"

"I thought we would save that for tomorrow when we would have more time and the daylight. Perhaps you would be content with a walk in the gardens after we finish our tea?"

"That would be lovely after a long day in the carriage," Elizabeth replied with a smile.

So it was that a short time later, he was leading her back down the main staircase and then down a hallway that led to a door onto the rear terrace. As she looked about, she could see several pieces of wrought iron furniture with plump cushions grouped for conversation. There was also a table surrounded by chairs that could easily seat twelve people. They crossed the terrace and continued down a broad set of steps onto the gravel path. On each side were flower beds bordered by low boxwoods, perfectly trimmed. In the center of these beds were various topiaries or statues surround by brightly blooming flowers. At the heart of the formal gardens was an octagonal fountain from which paths braced off in four directions. The happy couple made their way down the one to the right and then the left of the fountain. As they returned, again, to the fountain, Elizabeth made to head down the last path, which took them further from the house, but Darcy instead they turn back towards the terrace.

"Shall we not explore the last one, my love?" Elizabeth questioned.

"No, we must save that for another time, for at the end of that path are the steps that lead to the informal gardens. Knowing your love of nature, we shall need more time to explore in that direction. Instead, I shall show you my mother's private garden." He led her back to the terrace, and, this time, they descended some steps on the right end. From there they followed a flagstone walkway leading to a stone wall about ten feet high and nearly thirty-five feet on all sides. A stone arch in the center of one wall contained a wooden door. After retrieving the key from is coat pocket and unlocking the door, he pushed it open as he watched his wife's face.

Elizabeth gasped at the sight that met her eyes; within the walled garden, there was a riot of color. Flowers of every kind imaginable and some she had never seen filled the space. A huge tree sat in the center of the garden with a bench built around its thick trunk with soft green grass carpeting the ground. From a thick branch that reached almost to the back wall of the garden, a swing was suspended. There was not the order here that the formal gardens had, but much careful thought had been used when the plantings were designed. There were plants that bloomed in every season arranged by height, those tallest being against the wall. Turning in a circle, she noted that the wall with the door had climbing roses covering it.

Finally, Elizabeth stopped turning about and stared at her husband. "This is the most beautiful garden I have ever seen. No wonder it was your mother's favorite. I cannot imagine wishing to leave it."

"In spite of its splendor, I would certainly hope I could entice my beautiful new bride away from here," said Darcy with a laugh.

Blushing, she moved to his side. "Perhaps I should amend that to say, I should never wish to leave if you were here with me." She smiled provocatively up at Darcy. He needed no further encouragement and swept her up into a passionate embrace. Never breaking the kiss, he lifted her from the ground, carried her to the bench, and sat down with her in his lap. As the kiss intensified, he gently laid her back upon the bench, covering her with his body. Unfortunately, the curve of the bench made it impossible for his long form to fit and he rolled off onto the grass with Elizabeth still clutched in his embrace. Hitting the ground with a thump broke the kiss, and Elizabeth's glorious laugh filled the air.

"Perhaps, husband, we should bring a blanket for the grass with us next time we visit here."

In spite of his undignified position, Darcy could not help but join in her laughter as he heartily agreed with her. Elizabeth put her hand on the bench to aid her in rising to her feet before she offered her hand to her husband. Once on his feet, he kissed her gently before offering her his arm to lead her back to the house.

They returned with just enough time to change for dinner and then ate dinner in the family dining room. Darcy seated Elizabeth to his right and dismissed the servants after their meal arrived. They laughed and talked as they enjoyed their dinner. They moved to the music room briefly before retiring. As they reached their sitting room, Darcy said, "Would you care to join me in our sitting room when you have changed, my love?"

"That would be delightful, William," she replied as she turned towards her bedchamber. When she reappeared, she was wearing the gown she had worn on their wedding night, and, again, Darcy could not tear his gaze away from the stunningly beautiful sight. Smiling at his reaction, Elizabeth moved to the sofa and held her hand out to him to join her. When he sat down, she curled into his side.

"My love, I know that we have not yet discussed this, but I was wondering if you would consent to share a bed with me every night?"

"There is nowhere else I would rather be, but whose bed shall we share? Shall you show me your chamber and then allow me to choose?" He could not help but smile at her teasing expression.

"I should be pleased to show you my chamber and hope that you will consider staying there with me every night for the rest of our lives." Darcy pulled her up from the sofa and led her to the door opposite her bedchamber. Opening the door, she could see that the room was laid out much as hers was. By the light of the candles, the furniture appeared to be made of mahogany, and the furnishings were in shades of dark green and gold. Elizabeth wandered about the room, her fingers brushing across the surfaces as she went. On a table before the sofa sat a crystal decanter and two glasses. There was a bookcase where her escritoire stood, and she glanced at the titles. As she moved to the table beside the bed, she saw two books. Picking them up, she noticed that one was a book of poetry and the other, an account of the Battle of Trafalgar.

Darcy had stared intently at her as she moved about the room. He had long dreamed of her being here with him, and he could hardly comprehend that it was finally a reality. Walking around the bed to the right side, she slipped her robe off her shoulders and placed it on the end of the bed. Looking at him with passion in her eyes, Elizabeth spoke softly. "The room is much like its owner, and I feel at home here, just like I do in your arms."

That was all it took. Darcy stripped off his robe, exposing his muscular form to Elizabeth as he lifted her into his arms and placed her in the center of his big bed. He quickly settled himself beside her, and gathering her close, he began to kiss her as he again shared more of the joys of the marriage bed with his beautiful bride.

CHAPTER 10

HE COULD PUT it off no longer. Mr. Bennet knew that he must face his errant spouse and silly daughter. As he drove along the track in the farm wagon, he pondered how best to handle this difficult situation. Finally as the cart drew up before the dower house, Mr. Bennet had reached a decision. He stepped down from the wagon and was greeted by the guards that remained watching over his family.

"How have things been, Mr. Blake?"

"There has been very little noise since we have been here, sir. From what the others said, it was the same when they were on duty."

Mr. Bennet looked surprised at the information but said nothing. He moved to the door and withdrew a key from his pocket. Inserting it in the lock, he pushed the door open slightly. All seemed quiet as he cautiously entered, with Blake close behind him. He had just cleared the door when he heard a sound. Turning his head in the direction of the noise, he was just in time to step aside before a stool came down on his head, catching his shoulder instead. The impact caused him to lose his balance, stumbling further from the open door. Lydia rushed past her father and straight into the arms of Blake, who halted her progress. He picked the young lady up and threw her over his shoulder, as he locked the door. Then crossing the room, Blake, none too gently, deposited her in a chair in the parlor.

Standing over the girl, he addressed himself to Mr. Bennet. "Are you well, sir? Should a doctor be fetched?"

Blake could barely hear Mr. Bennet's answer as Mrs. Bennet was screaming at Lydia. "You foolish girl! You could have killed him! Where would we be if he died, and Mr. Collins took over? The others would not take care of either of us. We would be left to starve in the hedgerows!"

"At least I would not have to go to school!" cried an angry Lydia.

By this time, Mr. Bennet had recovered himself and moved to take a seat on the sofa across from his wife and daughter. Blake moved to stand at the door, his arms folded across his chest and his eyes focused on the women as they continued to bicker. "ENOUGH! I will have quiet!"

Mrs. Bennet glared at her husband but snapped her mouth shut and folded her arms across her chest. Lydia sniffed and subsided, as well.

"Mrs. Bennet, I wish to speak to Lydia. Please retire to your room."

"I will not. She is my dearest daughter, and I shall not allow you to determine her future without me."

"It is your future about which you should be concerned, madam." Mr. Bennet returned his wife's glare. "If you choose to stay, you are to remain silent, Mrs. Bennet. Do I make myself clear?" The fact that she was living this way reminded Mrs. Bennet that her husband meant what he said. With a huff, she flounced across the room and stared out the window, her back to her husband to announce her displeasure.

Turning his attention back to his daughter, Mr. Bennet considered her for several moments before speaking. "I had planned to release you today, Lydia, and return you to the main house, but your attempts to harm me give me pause to consider the sensibility of such an arrangement. I had hoped to spend time giving you some instruction before our journey to your school. I wanted to prepare you for the new experience."

"I do not want to go to school," Lydia pouted.

"Well, then, what is it you do want?" asked her father.

"I want to marry an officer and attend the endless array of parties and balls to which we would be invited."

"I see," mused Mr. Bennet. "You do realize that you would not be attending parties and balls all day every day, do you not? What do you expect you would do with the rest of your time?"

"I would shop and visit as I do now," came her flippant reply.

"Do you know what a soldier earns?"

Lydia was taken off guard and noted the smile tugging at the corners of her father's mouth, but was not sure of its cause. "No," came her terse reply, as her father's smile grew larger.

"Then you would be surprised to learn it is not much more than the total of the annual allowances of you, your mother, and your sisters combined. And from that amount he must pay for his uniforms and other expenses. It would not leave *any* funds for lace, ribbons, or dresses."

"Surely an officer would earn more!"

"I imagine most of Colonel Forster's rank and above earn more, but those like Lieutenant Denny would not make much more, and as you know, the militia officers are put up at the inn or sleep in tents in the field. Is that how you dream of living? Even if he could afford a room in which to keep you, you would have to do the cooking, cleaning, and sewing, as there would be no funds for servants or other extravagances. The girl you are now is not fit for more; in fact, you are not fit for that, as you know nothing about maintaining a home and the tasks involved. However, should you like to find an educated, well-to-do gentleman like your elder sisters, then you will need to obtain some education and accomplishments. If you still wish to marry an officer, you may stay here with your mother; otherwise, you will be leaving for school in three weeks. If you are going to school, there are things that we must do to prepare you."

Lydia looked doubtful at her father's words, and her bravado returned. "Who wants to marry someone as disagreeable as Mr. Darcy? Mr. Bingley would not care if I had a formal education. He married Jane, did he not, and she never went to school."

"You may recall that the congenial Mr. Bingley was no more pleased with the behavior of you and your mother than was Mr. Darcy." Recognizing that her father was correct, the first signs of doubt appeared on her face, as an indignant sniff came from her mother.

"Fine, then I shall go to school, but until I leave, I shall do as I please, visiting my friends and walking into Meryton every day."

"This is not a negotiation, Lydia," barked Mr. Bennet sternly.

"If you return to the house, you will be required to read and meet with me throughout the day to discuss your lessons. Furthermore, there will be no trips to Meryton and no visitors of any kind before your departure."

"I shall leave you now to make your decision, but I will visit after breakfast tomorrow. If you wish to return to the house with me, you shall have your trunk packed and ready to go."

As she heard the key turning in the lock, Mrs. Bennet turned from the window and screeched. "What about me? How long am I to be kept a prisoner in this miserable cottage?"

"Once Lydia makes her decision, I will consider what is to be done next. However, you will continue to live here until she has gone to school, and she will not be visiting. You will be permitted to say goodbye before her departure, but you will not be joining me at the main house until I have returned from delivering Lydia to school."

"You cannot keep me here! I am the mistress of Longbourn, and I have every right to live in the main house with my things around me!"

"You have no rights, madam, other than those I see fit to give you," came Mr. Bennet's stern reply, following which he walked from the house, locking the door behind him.

The next morning, Mr. Bennet took his time breaking his fast. As he was preparing to depart, his steward approached and asked for a word. When Mr. Bennet finished speaking to his steward, Mrs. Hill delivered the mail. He noted a letter from his brother, Edward Gardiner, and breaking the seal, he read Edward's short note stating they had arrived back home in safety. He expressed his pleasure at the opportunity to have Mary and Kitty with them and described what a good help they were with the children during the long carriage ride. He also encouraged his brother to hold firm in dealing with his wife and youngest daughter, promising to support him in any way they could.

With Gardiner's encouragement firmly in mind, Mr. Bennet, once again, took the wagon to the dower house. Blake was again there to greet him.

"How were things after I left yesterday?"

"There was a bit of shouting, sir. Miss Lydia was questioning her mother on her encouragement about the pursuit of officers if they could not support a wife. Mrs. Bennet did a lot of blustering, but she never had an answer that satisfied Miss Lydia."

"I see. What do you think her decision will be?"

"Well, I did hear a lot of thumping going on this morning. It might have been a trunk being dragged down the stairs," said Blake with a grin.

"I see. Do you think I will need to duck again this morning?"

"I do not believe so, Mr. Bennet."

He opened the door, pleasantly calling a good morning to the occupants of the cottage. Both of the ladies awaited him in the parlor. Lydia was attempting to sit still and looking anywhere but at her mother. Mrs. Bennet, on the other hand, was glaring at her daughter with an angry frown.

"I have returned for your answer, Lydia. Do you wish to remain here with your mother, or would you like to come back to Longbourn and prepare to go to school?"

"I will go to school, Papa."

"Very well. Is your trunk packed?"

"Yes, Papa."

Mr. Bennet stepped to the door and spoke to Blake. A moment or two later, he stepped inside to pick-up Lydia's trunk while the other guard kept an eye on Mrs. Bennet.

Without so much as a word to her mother, Lydia followed her trunk out to the carriage. Mr. Bennet looked after his daughter, then back to his wife. "You have nothing to say to your daughter? You will not see her for a few weeks."

"Why should I wish to speak to such an ungrateful child? How she can desert her dear mother . . . ," Mrs. Bennet's words trailed off as she stared at her husband.

"Perhaps she has begun to see the error of her ways. If so, she will hopefully find happiness for herself. You might review your own behavior for areas of improvement, if you, too, wish to find happiness."

Mr. Bennet exited the cottage and locked the door behind him. He heard a screech from inside and the sound of something breaking. Shaking his head, Thomas Bennet walked to the wagon and climbed up on the seat beside Lydia. Taking up the reins, the gentleman flapped them to get the horses moving and turned the cart in the direction of the manor house.

He stopped at the stables and assisted Lydia down from the carriage. The coachman came to take care of the horses as Mr. Hill approached the stables. He and the groom lifted the trunk from the wagon and returned it to Lydia's room.

Once in the house, Mr. Bennet turned to his daughter. "I asked Mrs. Hill to have water ready in case you wished to bathe. I will expect you to refresh yourself and unpack before joining me for lunch. Please do not dawdle. Also, bring your current sampler with you when you come down. After luncheon, we will begin your preparation.

Lydia nodded and slowly climbed the stairs to her room. When she appeared for the mid-day meal, she had bathed and washed her hair and was dressed in her favorite morning gown.

The meal was quiet as Lydia concentrated on her food while occasionally casting glances at her father. Mr. Bennet had finished his correspondence while waiting for Lydia and then spent his time determining what course her preparation would take. At the close of the meal, Mr. Bennet spoke.

"Please follow me to my study, Lydia."

"Yes, Papa."

He indicated a chair before his desk for her and moved to seat himself in his comfortable chair behind it. He sat quietly for a moment, and Lydia fidgeted under his gaze. Picking up a book from his desk, he held it out to her.

"Your lessons will begin with reading this book. Today, you will sit quietly in my study to do your reading. When you have completed the first chapter, we shall discuss what you have learned."

"I do not like to read, Papa," whined Lydia. Mr. Bennet fixed her with an unrelenting look. Finally, she said, "Yes, Papa," and reached out to take the book from his hand.

"Did you bring your sampler?"

"I forgot. Give me a moment, and I will go and find it."

"Hurry."

Lydia rushed from the room. Mr. Bennet heard her clambering up the stairs. He heard drawers being open and shut, doors creaking and being slammed. Then he heard his daughter rushing back down the stairs. The steps turned towards the parlor, and he could hear her muttering. Finally he heard her cry out.

"Ah ha!" Quick steps were heard coming towards the study. "Here it is, Papa."

Holding out the sampler, Mr. Bennet studied the picture carefully before handing it back to Lydia. "Take your book to the chair by the window and read for the next two hours. At the conclusion of that time, we will discuss what you have read. After that, you will spend time on your sampler. After dinner, we will read a poem together and discuss what it means. I will expect to see progress on the sampler each day, in addition to the reading that I assign you."

"Yes, Papa," came her sullen reply.

This schedule continued until the time of her departure. Occasionally, Mr. Bennet would add in different activities, such as sketching a vase of flowers or adding the sums in the household ledgers. There were frequent bouts of pouting on the part of Lydia, but Mr. Bennet held firm to his demands for her improved behavior and her attention to the studies he put before her.

On the day before her departure to school, Mr. Bennet took Lydia out to the dower house to say goodbye to her mother. Mrs. Bennet would still live there, but was no longer under guard. Mr. Bennet had thanked the gentlemen for their service and dismissed them on the day after removing Lydia. Mrs. Bennet received them with a decided lack of graciousness.

"Good afternoon, Mrs. Bennet. Lydia and I have come to share tea with you, as we shall be departing for her school in the morning."

"Humph, I expect you wish me to prepare it."

"I do expect you to set the proper example of a hostess for our daughter. It is one of many lessons she should have learned from you." The look that accompanied his words caused his wife to do as he had requested, though her muttering was easily heard by the others present. When she had prepared the tea and tray, she brought it back to the parlor and fixed cups for her husband and daughter.

After they had received their tea, Lydia handed her mother a box. "Mrs. Hill sent these for our tea." Before Mrs. Bennet could open the box, Lydia continued, "Mrs. Hill said they were your favorite, and there should be plenty left over after tea for you to enjoy."

"Please express my thanks to Mrs. Hill," said Mrs. Bennet tersely.

The conversation throughout the time they spent together was stilted at best. Finally, Mr. Bennet said it was time to depart. Lydia looked at her mother with tears shimmering in her eyes. "Goodbye, Mama. I will miss you."

"Then see that you write to me."

"I am scared, Mama."

Her words finally broke through her mother's apathy. Taking Lydia in her arms, she crooned, "There, there, my dear girl, everything will be well. It is so unfair of your father to send you away from me. You are my baby girl; you need your mother near." Mrs. Bennet cast a look of disgust at her husband as she held Lydia in her arms.

"I want to go Mama, but – "

Before Lydia could complete her sentence, Mrs. Bennet shoved her away, "You want to leave? How could you abandon me after all I have done for you?" Mrs. Bennet turned on her heel and marched through the door of her bedchamber, slamming it behind her.

Startled at her mother's words and action, Lydia stared at the closed door, while Mr. Bennet sadly shook his head. Putting his hand out towards the door, Mr. Bennet said, "Come, Lydia. We need to return to the house."

The young lady nearly ran from the cottage and climbed into the wagon unassisted. She spoke not a word on the ride home, but Mr. Bennet could hear her soft sniffs as they drove along. Upon arriving at the main house, Lydia hurried up the stairs to her room, where she threw herself down on the bed and cried. When she came down to dinner, Mr. Bennet could not help but notice her red eyes, which indicated the tears she had shed.

"Are you all packed for our trip?"

"Yes, Papa. There was not much on the list of items to bring."

"I believe we should retire very shortly after dinner as we must make an early start tomorrow. We have three long days of travel ahead of us."

"Yes, Papa. I am quite tired."

The carriage departed Longbourn at sunrise. Lydia, who did not like rising early, immediately returned to sleep as the carriage began rolling towards the junction with the Great North Road. Returning to their carriage following the midday meal, Mr. Bennet forced himself to have a difficult conversation with Lydia.

"Lydia, we must discuss one thing before you arrive at the school."

Hesitating because of the serious tone of his voice, Lydia said," Yes, Papa. What is it?"

"We must talk about your habit of taking things."

"When this issue was first brought up, you said you could not remember how long you had been taking things. Is that correct?"

"Yes, Papa."

"Do you always take what you want or have there been times when you did not take something you desired?"

"There are times I did not take an item I wanted."

"Can you remember what stopped you from taking an item?"

"I am not aware of a particular thing that made me hesitate," she responded. "Sometimes I just did not take an item.

"I must stress something that you may not wish to hear."

"I know that I must never take anything ever again, Papa."

"That is good, but do you clearly understand what could happen if you do take something while at school?"

"I believe I understood it when we spoke before the wedding."

"Would you explain it to me?" asked Mr. Bennet.

"If I take something, I risk being caught. If I am caught, I can go to jail."

"You do understand the basics, but I want to be sure you understand the details. Depending on the value of the items you take, you could face prison or, in the worse case scenario, you could be hanged. No one at school will be inclined to overlook the incident if they discover you with items belonging to them. You must control your compulsion. Also, you must learn to be more considerate of others and their feelings, if you wish to make friends. If you treat the people at school in the same haphazard way you have your sisters, you will find it difficult to make friends. I am certain you will grow and benefit from this time at school. But only you can make my belief into a reality. Your success or failure in school depends totally on you."

"I understand, Papa, and will do my very best to follow your instructions."

The remainder of the first day was passed in relative quiet, and the first night Lydia had ever spent at an inn was enjoyed in relative peace and comfort. Lydia found it enjoyable to dine in the public dining room for dinner, but Mr. Bennet was required to speak to her several times regarding her unacceptable, flirtatious behavior. After breaking their fast the next morning, they continued their travels in relative peace and comfort.

Late in the afternoon on the third day, the carriage arrived at Miss Bates School for Girls in Winksley, North Yorkshire. The building was made of a dark gray stone and surrounded on three sides by a thick forest. The groom who had traveled with them jumped down and placed the steps before opening the door. Mr. Bennet stepped down and handed out his daughter. Lydia looked up at her father with fear in her eyes. "What if they do not like me?"

"If you are the polite girl I know you can be, all will be well. If you are uncertain about how to behave in any situation, perhaps you might ask yourself how Jane or Lizzy would handle it." So saying, Mr. Bennet offered his arm to his daughter and led her inside to find the headmistress and get her room assignment.

Someone came to take her trunk to her room. She was required to say farewell to her father in the front hallway, as visitors were not permitted in the students' rooms. After receiving her father's hug, kiss to her forehead, and wishes for her success, she remained standing and watching until he was gone from her sight. A teacher positioned in the hall directed her to her room and told her she was to change into the uniform she found waiting for her. She would have time to unpack and was then to join the girls in the dining hall for a welcome and tea. Her feet feeling like lead, Lydia hesitantly made her way up the stairs to her assigned room.

CHAPTER 11

LORD WESCOTT HAD been back in town for a week now, and he was still pondering his decision regarding Miss Pottsfield. He had enjoyed her company when they stopped to break their journey on the return to London. They had talked briefly about the wedding—primarily how happy the Darcys appeared—before moving on to a host of other topics.

Thoughts of her had stayed with him in the intervening days. Lord Wescott felt he was ready to settle down and devote himself to his estate, and he wished for the companionship of a wife. James Wescott had never imagined marrying with any real affection for his spouse. He assumed he would end up with one of the shallow women of the ton who brought money and connections to the marriage. Now he wondered if he could have wealth and affection. How would someone like Miss Pottsfield be received? He did not have a family like the Fitzwilliams to support him. He was the last of his line. His only remaining relations were Lady Marjorie and her father, the earl. But as he thought on the matter, he realized that Mr. and Mrs. Darcy would certainly accept the young lady. The Matlocks had even included her in the engagement ball. Perhaps, a friendship with the Darcys would be enough for her acceptance.

Before making a final decision, he decided he would check out the next Almack's assembly. Hopefully, someone would catch his eye.

Lady Marjorie was growing more and more frustrated with each passing days. Her fury at the way things had gone at Darcy's engagement ball had overflowed for several days after the event. It was incomprehensible to her that anyone could prefer the little country mouse to herself. Lady Marjorie had better connections, more accomplishments, and far greater beauty than Miss Elizabeth Bennet could ever hope to possess. Darcy must be out of his senses not to see her greater worth. And then that miserable Caroline Bingley had tried to lay the blame at her door. She would ensure that the conniving wretch would pay for her treachery. But, perhaps, the greatest part of her anger was with her cousin. How could Wescott have betrayed her like that?

Upon arriving home from the engagement ball, she had informed the servants that she was not feeling well and would not be receiving visitors for a few days. As a consequence, Lady Marjorie had no idea that no one had attempted to visit.

Lady Marjorie saw little of her father during that time. She knew that he was home, but only because of the light that came from under his study door and the muttering she could hear within the room.

When she finally saw a notice in the papers hinting that there may be financial trouble for her family, Lady Marjorie decided it was time to return to society. There was an assembly at Almack's the next week; she would have to search out the next best candidate and quickly get him to propose. She sent a note around to her modiste, only to receive word the woman was too busy to complete an order on such short notice. Consequently, she sent a second to the modiste's top competition, sure that her title would gain her an appointment as the modiste would assume she wished to transfer her patronage. However, this, too, came back with a polite, but negative, reply. The modiste informed her that due to several last minute events planned for the end of the season, she did not have enough staff for her current orders and would be unable to handle any additional business at this time. Frustrated in her desires, Lady Marjorie called for her maid, and they began a search of her closet for the most spectacular outfit in her wardrobe. She needed to remind the ton of the status of her family and bring one of her many devotees up to scratch.

So it was that on the following Wednesday evening, Lady Marjorie exited her carriage before the doors of Almack's. Accompanying her was an elderly maiden aunt who served as her companion when her father was unavailable. Dismissing her coachman, she mounted the stairs to enter Almack's vaunted rooms. However, a liveried footman stopped her at the entrance.

"Forgive me, miss, but I was informed that your voucher has been rescinded, and you are no longer permitted to enter."

"How dare you block my entrance," cried Lady Marjorie. "Do you know who I am? I am the daughter of an aarl. You cannot keep me out!" Her voice had risen as her speech reach its end, and several of those near the entrance turned to observe the disturbance.

"Yes, miss, I am aware of your identity, and it is on the strict orders of Lady Jersey and Lady Cowper that your entrance is denied." Though a well-trained servant, he almost smirked at the young woman as he replied to her remarks. The guests, observing just beyond the footman's shoulder, did not bother to hide their smirks either, as they watched the arrogant woman be put in her place.

Cheeks flaming, Lady Marjorie raised her voice. "Who wishes to be admitted to a ramshackle place with dreadful refreshment that is run by woman lacking discernment? No one with sense would turn away the daughter of an earl!"

So saying, Lady Marjorie turned on her heel and stormed down the stairs, followed by her companion, who stood cowering at her side through the incident. As she descended the stairs, she noted one of her most ardent swains on his way up, but he turned his head away from her before she could speak, giving her the direct cut.

By the time they reached the street, her carriage was no longer in sight. She was about to hail a hackney when she realized she had no coins with which to pay for the ride. Turning to her aunt, she demanded any money the woman carried. "I have received no allowance from your father in several months. At present I am without funds."

Trying to decide what to do as her fury continued to mount, she failed to notice who stepped out of the coach that had just arrived at Almack's entrance. She was so lost in thought she did not hear what her companion was saying until she heard his hated name.

"Oh, sir, your arrival is most providential. Lady Marjorie has been refused admittance. We have dismissed the carriage and have not the money for a hackney. Please, Lord Wescott, could you take us home?"

Lady Marjorie had not told her aunt of her falling out with Wescott, so the elderly woman was surprised when her niece sharply rebuked her.

"Do not speak to that traitorous villain. My cousin turned on me. He is part of the reason I am denied entrance." If possible, the little woman became even smaller, wishing she could disappear altogether.

Marjorie stepped up to Wescott and, in the blink of an eye, slapped his face with all her strength. "Do not think I will ever forgive you, Wescott. I will ruin you for what you have done to me."

Wescott ignored Lady Marjorie, but, taking the elderly lady's hand, assisted her into the carriage and directed the driver to the Dalbert House. Before he could close the door, Lady Marjorie climbed into the carriage, as well. "I shall use you for transportation home, but I will never forget your betrayal!"

Wescott said nothing. He merely closed the door and told the driver to return for him in an hour. James Wescott stood watching the departing carriage. He felt sure there would be a red mark on his face, but he turned and mounted the steps to Almack's anyway. Wescott made his way to the refreshment table to retrieve a glass of the watered-down lemonade, then moved to a quiet spot to observe things as he drank. Eventually, he made his way around the room, joining in conversations here and there, as he looked over all the young ladies of the ton who were present. There were many who were quite lovely and many others who were quite well off, but there seemed to be a degree of artifice in each one with whom he spoke. A little over an hour later, when he observed the arrival of his carriage at the entrance, he was not disappointed to take his leave.

The next morning a notice of Lady Marjorie's debacle at Almack's was reported in the gossip column of London's largest paper. As he read of his daughter's disgrace at the desk in his study, Lord Dalbert made his decision.

A short time later, the sound of a gunshot woke Lady Marjorie from her troubled sleep. Coming fully awake, she heard shouting and the banging of doors, followed by an eerie calm. Within moments, a knock was heard at her bedroom door, and the butler asked for admission.

"I am sorry to inform you, Lady Marjorie, but it appears your father was cleaning his gun and must have had an accident. It discharged, my Lady, and your father was injured. He did not survive his injury."

Marjorie threw on a wrapper and rushed to her father's study. She rushed to his side and lifted his head from the desk. The first thing to catch her eye was her name in the gossip column. Quickly reading the account, she stepped away from her father and looked at him in disgust.

"You created this mess for us, Father, and now you take the coward's way out and leave me to repair the situation. Are all men as weak and undependable as you and Wescott?" She turned on her heel and walked from the room.

Four days after his evening at Almack's, Wescott saw Miss Pottsfield again when they bumped into each other on Bond Street. He was surprised by the strength of the pleasurable feelings he felt in seeing her again and realized how much he had missed her company in the days they had been apart.

"Miss Pottsfield, I wonder if you would be agreeable to my calling on you?"

"You, Lord Wescott, do something so mundane as calling on a young woman who is beneath you socially? Society will be shocked." Though she spoke in a serious tone, Lord Wescott, who was nervously observing the ground, missed the twinkle in her eyes.

"I have recently learned that character is far more important than social levels, so I care not what society will think." This time, as he spoke, he gazed steadily into her eyes. He was delighted to see the answer in her eyes before she spoke.

"I would be very pleased to receive your call, Lord Wescott." Evelyn reached into her reticule and produced a card with her address on it and handed it to him. "When should I expect you?"

"Would tomorrow at eleven be convenient?"

"I shall look forward to it, my Lord."

Lord Wescott offered to accompany her on the rest of her errands, but she explained that she had completed them, so he walked her to her carriage and handed her in. "Until tomorrow, Miss Pottsfield."

"Until tomorrow, Lord Wescott."

By the time James Wescott had returned to his London home, he was in a lighter mood than he could ever recall. Entering his study, he found the post had arrived. He was pleased to receive a note from his steward informing him that the requested changes had been implemented. The steward also commended him on his suggestions, stating he had recently learned something similar from another steward with whom he was acquainted.

He spent the afternoon working on business before attending a dinner hosted by some friends.

Lord Wescott arrived promptly at eleven the next morning. He attempted to control his nervousness as he paid his first real social call on a young woman, one in whom he held an interested, in any case. He was followed the butler to the entry of an attractively decorated drawing room where Miss Pottsfield, her mother, and her companion were all seated.

"Good morning, Miss Pottsfield, I hope I find you well this fine day." Evelyn rose to greet him, and he bowed over her hand.

"I am very well, thank you, Lord Wescott. Please allow me to introduce you to my mother, Mrs. Sarah Pottsfield." Mrs. Pottsfield rose, and the gentleman bowed over her hand, as well.

"It is a pleasure to meet you, Mrs. Pottsfield. It is also nice to see you again, Mrs. Morton," said Lord Wescott as he turned to Evelyn's companion. The companion greeted him politely and returned her attention to the needlework she held in her hands. Wescott took a chair near where Evelyn was seated and used all of his considerable charm and social skills, as he made an effort to converse comfortably with the ladies. Mrs. Pottsfield was even more reserved than her daughter and spoke very little. If the truth were told, she was a bit in awe of the fact that a titled gentleman was visiting her home and seemed to be interested in her daughter. Though she did not contribute much to the conversation, she smiled and laughed where appropriate, as she watched her daughter interact with a peer of the realm.

After the required half hour, Lord Wescott rose to depart. "May I call again in three days, Miss Pottsfield? Perhaps we could walk in Hyde Park?"

"I believe that will suit, my Lord. I shall look forward to our walk."

CHAPTER 12

IT WAS NOW mid-June. More than a month had passed since their wedding, and Darcy and Elizabeth had spent that time blissfully alone. However, their solitude was soon to be interrupted with a steady stream of visitors.

The sun was peeking through the closed curtains of the master chamber when Elizabeth opened her eyes. She could tell it was later than she usually rose, but they had enjoyed their last night of solitude making love until the wee hours of the morning. The Matlocks would be arriving sometime after luncheon to deliver Georgiana to Pemberley. They would stay for one night before going on to their estate.

As always, Darcy's arms were wrapped tightly around her, with her back pressed against his chest as they slept. Gently turning over so as not to disturb her husband, she gazed at his face, peaceful in slumber. She enjoyed watching him sleep. He looked younger and happy in the arms of Morpheus when the cares of the world fell away before the delights of his dreams. As she watched, her mind thought back on all the joys they had shared since arriving at Pemberley.

They had spent the first three days after their arrival in the master suite, being seen only by their personal servants when they called for meals or a bath. When they finally emerged, they passed their days touring the house and formal gardens. The servants, ever unobtrusive in the performance of their duties, frequently spoke of hearing laughter echoing from unused chambers or seeing the master and his bride emerge from a room blushing and slightly disheveled.

On the last day of their first week at Pemberley, Darcy took Elizabeth to visit the stables. They stopped and spoke to Darcy's horse, Aladdin's Treasure, affectionately known as Laddie. He was a large black Arabian with tremendous endurance and jumping abilities. Noting the stranger with his master, he neighed loudly and backed away from the entrance of the stall. Darcy spoke to the horse, and he cautiously moved within range of Darcy's long arms. He gave the horse a pat and spoke calmingly to him. Then Darcy placed a piece of apple in Elizabeth's palm and encouraged her to hold it out for the horse. Hesitantly, Elizabeth did as directly, and Laddie inched closer before nuzzling her palm to grab the bite of apple. When he finished, he again pushed his muzzle into her palm and rubbed it. Thus encouraged, Elizabeth raised her hand to rub the horse's neck, and Laddie whinnied in pleasure.

"I think he likes you," Darcy commented dryly. "He is rarely so easily pleased with the attentions of anyone but Jake and me."

"Who is Jake?" Elizabeth asked in confusion.

"He is the only one of the stable hands whom Laddie will allow to exercise or tend him in my absence. The majority of the others in the stables give Laddie a wide berth."

Darcy gave the horse a pat and steered Elizabeth to a stall three down from where Aladdin's Treasure stood. In this stall was a beautiful white horse. She was also an Arabian but was several hands smaller than Laddie and appeared to be quite gentle.

"Elizabeth, allow me to introduce you to Sheba. She will be your mount." He gave her another piece of apple, and she confidently held it out to the horse. After Sheba had taken the apple and Elizabeth had rubbed her neck, she turned to Darcy. "She is beautiful, William. Thank you for such a lovely gift. Now, all I need to do is learn how to ride," Elizabeth concluded with a teasing grin. Sheba, wishing to regain Elizabeth's attention, nudged her shoulder until she turned her gaze in the horse's direction. "All right, girl," said Elizabeth with a laugh, as she again reached out to rub the horse's neck and muzzle. "I shall be back to see you each day, but I must go for now." Sheba whinnied and shook her head as, with a last pat, Elizabeth and Darcy turned to depart.

Her riding lessons began the next week. As she descended the stairs in her habit, Darcy caught his breath. The black skirt was paired with a celestial blue jacket that had black collar, cuffs, and buttons. On her dark curls, she wore a low black top hat, sporting a feather and trailing ribbons in the same shade of blue. Mounted on her white horse, she would make a fetching sight. Darcy kissed her hand when she reached the bottom of the stairs and, tucking her arm in his, led her to the stables. Sheba was saddled and waiting for Elizabeth. As her rider approached, she gave a toss of her head and whinnied in greeting. Darcy opened the gate to the riding ring, and she entered, approaching Sheba with a pleasant greeting. After pointing out the things that Elizabeth should check before mounting her horse, he lifted her into the saddle. Elizabeth sat in the side saddle with a straight back and natural grace and took up the reins as Darcy instructed. With a gentle slap of the reins, Sheba began to walk around the ring. Elizabeth bounced a little in the saddle, but at Darcy's instruction, she was able to adjust her seat to be more secure. Darcy eyed her critically as she made two circles around the riding ring.

"Slap the reins again, Elizabeth, and increase her speed to a trot." Elizabeth did as instructed and began to bounce again with the increased pace before recalling Darcy's earlier instructions and again correcting her posture and seat. This time, they trotted around the ring three times. "Now pull back on the reins to slow her back to a walk," Darcy called. Elizabeth did as instructed and circled the ring a final time before bringing the horse to a stop before her husband.

With a delighted smile, Darcy reached up and lifted Elizabeth down from her mount. "You did very well, my Elizabeth. You shall be galloping across the estate with me in no time, and then we shall begin to explore some of Pemberley's natural beauty."

With a look of satisfaction and a pleased smile on her face, Elizabeth responded to his comment. "I look forward to doing so, my dear William. I enjoy every moment we can spend together."

So began the pattern for the next week. When they rose in the morning, they would walk through the formal gardens for some time before breaking their fast. Then they would each tend to their responsibilities. Darcy would answer his correspondence or meet with his steward, and Elizabeth began meeting with Mrs. Reynolds to learn her responsibilities as mistress of the estate. Then in the afternoon, they would spend some time in the stables until returning to the house to change for tea. They dined early, as neither cared for the hours kept in town, before spending some time in the music room or the library, then retiring to their chambers.

Elizabeth was pleased with the progress she was making in her riding lessons. She quickly advanced from a trot to a canter and then to a gallop. By midweek, they were traveling the length of the drive and back. Then on Friday, Darcy taught her how to manage her mount if it should be startled and rear up on its hind legs. After only two falls onto the loose sand in the riding ring, Elizabeth maintained her seat, and Darcy declared her ready for a longer excursion. She was pleased with his pronouncement, as she was very eager to see more of her new home.

Once Elizabeth had gaied a competency in the saddle, the pattern of the time together began to change. Each day after completing their work, Darcy and Elizabeth would ride out to see Darcy's favorite spots on the estate. With a picnic lunch stored in saddlebags, they would gallop away from the stables, always in a different direction. The first place he took her was to a high ridge that afforded a view of the entire estate. Elizabeth was mesmerized by the picture Pemberley presented. They visited a waterfall that created a small pool, beside which they picnicked and made love. They galloped across a wide field filled with wildflowers and stopped for their lunch beside the river that cut through one corner of the estate. Lastly, Darcy took her to his favorite spot of all. It was a sunny grove at the center of a dense stand of woodland. In the center of the grove was a large pool that was fed by an underground hot spring. They swam nude in the warm waters, enjoying the freedom found in this secluded spot.

After acquainting Elizabeth with some of the most beautiful locations on the extensive estate, the couple began to make visits to the tenants so that Elizabeth could meet those for whom she felt a great deal of responsibility. As they rode away from visiting with the Brown family at the end of their first day of visits, Elizabeth asked, "William, my father always held a small gathering for our tenants when the harvest was completed. Do you hold such a gathering for the tenants at Pemberley?"

"We do, indeed, Elizabeth. Why do you ask?"

"Well, as it is almost June, I believe I must begin planning if we are to uphold the tradition."

"Are you sure you wish to take on such a large undertaking so soon after arriving? After all, you are still learning about Pemberley yourself. I am sure Mrs. Reynolds and the other servants can handle it as they have in past years."

"William, I think it is important to take on this responsibility. They need to know that I am as concerned for their well-being as you are. They need to feel they can talk to me when they have troubles. If you do not object, I will speak with Mrs. Reynolds about what has been done in the past and then begin to make plans for this year's celebration."

"Please do not feel you must do this, but I am sure anything you plan will be enjoyable for all." Though he did not wish for Elizabeth to become overwhelmed by her responsibilities so early in their marriage, Darcy's heart swelled with pride that Elizabeth cared for their tenants as he did.

After meeting with Mrs. Reynolds, Elizabeth reviewed the records of the past harvest celebrations, reading the records in a journal maintained by Mrs. Reynolds. She also had journals that recorded all of the special events held at Pemberley, from Christmas celebrations and dinner parties to hunts and balls. Whenever Darcy came to the mistress' study, he would find Elizabeth pouring over old books and making notes on several sheets of paper. Though Darcy was extremely curious about the plans she was making, he asked no questions, for he did not want it to seem as if he doubted her abilities. However, he was frequently answering odd questions that she would make and then watch as she jotted his answers on one of her many papers.

The rustle of the silk sheets pulled Elizabeth from her memories of the past several weeks. As her gaze refocused, she saw William's soulful brown eyes staring into hers.

"Good morning, my love," said Darcy as he placed a gentle kiss upon her rosy lips. "You were deep in thought. What could be so important on this beautiful morning? Is something disturbing you?"

"No, William, I was merely daydreaming of the joys we have shared during the past weeks of solitude." Her face again held the far away look he had observed upon waking, and a small smile played about her lips. "Though I am anxious to see Georgiana again, I am sad to see our time together come to end. Soon we will have a houseful of guests."

"Yes. Though I, too, look forward to Georgie's return, I am not pleased that I shall have to share your attentions with others. This time together has exceeded all of the dreams I had for our life together. I shall miss your constant companionship and the freedom to love you whenever I wish." A rakish smile accompanied his words. "We shall have to use these last free hours to good effect," said Darcy as he pulled her close and loved her thoroughly.

It was nearing midday before they left their suite. They had dined in their sitting room after rising and had returned to bed for another bout of lovemaking before rising and dressing for the day. They separated briefly: Darcy to attend to any last minute work, and Elizabeth to make sure that all was in readiness for their guests.

Tea had just been brought to the sitting room when the couple heard the wheels of the arriving carriage stop before the entry to Pemberley. They quickly moved to greet their arriving family. Lord Matlock exited the carriage, first handing down Lady Matlock, then Georgiana. Georgiana rushed up the stairs and hurled herself into her brother's arms. Stumbling back a step from the unexpected weight of his sister practically leaping into his arms, Darcy regained his balance and wrapped his arms around her.

"I take it that you missed me, Georgie," he chuckled.

"Oh, yes, William! I have so much to tell you and Lizzy." As she spoke her sister's name, she struggled to remove herself from her brother's embrace and rushed to hug Elizabeth with equal enthusiasm. "Oh, Lizzy, I am so happy to see you here at Pemberley. At last, I have the sister I have always wanted!"

"We are glad to have you home, Georgiana," said Elizabeth with a laugh as she returned her new sister's hug.

By this time, Lord and Lady Matlock had reached the others. "Well, it is evident that married life agrees with the two of you," said Lord Matlock with a grin. "You are both glowing with happiness." He leaned in and kissed Elizabeth's cheek before clapping Darcy's shoulder.

"Indeed, Uncle. It far exceeds all of my expectations. If I had known how wonderful life with Elizabeth would be, I would have made an effort to search her out after our first brief acquaintance." Elizabeth, surprised by his words, was nonetheless pleased and gave him a glittering smile.

Lady Matlock gave Elizabeth a hug and kiss before turning to her nephew. Patting Darcy's cheek, she remarked, "I could not be happier for you both, my dears."

Darcy offered one arm each to his aunt and sister and led them to the drawing room where refreshments were waiting. Lord Matlock placed Elizabeth's hand on his arm and followed the others. Speaking louder than necessary, he leaned towards Elizabeth and said, "You let me know if Darcy fails to treat you properly, my dear, and I shall set him straight." Elizabeth's laughter floated on the air in reply to his Lordship's sally as they entered the house.

Once everyone was settled in the drawing room with a cup of tea, Georgiana began to rapidly convey to them all the things that she had done while in London. Laughing, Darcy said, "Slow down, Georgie; there is no need to rush. You have all the time you need to tell us of your many activities."

Taking a deep breath, she started again. She spoke of the time she spent staying with the Gardiners, about Mrs. Annesley's lessons she shared with Mary and Kitty. She talked of shopping, a concert they attended, and walks in the park. She spoke of teaching Susan to play the piano as well as the enjoyment she found playing with the Gardiners' children.

"Have you heard from Mary?" she asked, turning to Elizabeth.

"I believe there was a letter from her, but we have not taken time for any personal correspondence as of yet. We have been enjoying our honeymoon."

"Well, you must read it before I can say any more." Noting the smiles on the faces of the others in the room, she looked at Darcy, who shrugged in confusion.

"Well, then, as soon as you are all settled in your rooms, you may be sure I shall find and read Mary's letter."

They spoke of their travel, and then Darcy asked about the trip to Rosings.

A look of disgust on his face, Lord Matlock replied, "That is a tale for another time. I shall need a fortifying glass of brandy to recount what took place when we confronted Catherine."

Shortly, the guests departed for their rooms to rest and refresh themselves before dinner, and Elizabeth went immediately to her study to find the letter from Mary. She had settled in a comfortable chair to read it as Darcy entered the room. He stood watching the expression on her face as she read the letter. "Oh, this is wonderful news! Do you have a letter from Richard? If so, you must read it; then we can exchange letters!"

"What is so wonderful?"

"I believe that you should read Richard's letter before I say anything."

Darcy turned from the doorway to go to his study, Elizabeth following along. She seated herself in a chair before Darcy's desk as he looked through the stack of personal correspondence that awaited his response. When he found the letter, he seated himself behind the desk and began to read. Elizabeth watched as his face went from surprise to anger to pleasure. "I say, this is excellent news! I am delighted for both of them."

"I do not believe that Mary will want to marry from Longbourn. I wonder if she will marry from Gracechurch Street?" mused Elizabeth.

"She is welcome to marry from Pemberley if she would like, my love. I know you will wish to help with the planning," said Darcy with an indulgent smile.

"Thank you, William. I will be sure to mention it when I write to her. Husband, what was in Richard's letter that caused such a look of anger to appear on you face?"

"I believe you should read Richard's letter for yourself." Darcy handed the letter across the desk and watched as she read the words written there.

"How dare she abuse both her daughter and nephew in such a horrid way!" cried Elizabeth indignantly. As she glanced at Darcy, she noted his grim look as he nodded in agreement.

"I am more eager than ever to speak with Uncle about the events at Rosings," was Darcy's determined reply. "Shall we retire to rest before dinner, my love?" asked Darcy as he came around the desk, his hand extended to his wife.

"I believe a rest would be ideal," Elizabeth replied. Rising up on her toes she quickly kissed Darcy's lips before turning and darting from the room, calling over her shoulder, "If you can catch me, that is!"

Darcy raced after her, his long legs allowing him to quickly close the distance between them. Catching her, he swooped her up into his arms and carried her to their suite. The guests in the family wing could hear their laughter as they traversed the hall, causing pleased smiles to appear on the listeners' faces.

CHAPTER 13

GEORGIANA WAS THE first to arrive in the drawing room before dinner. She sat down to wait, but by the way her foot tapped a rhythm against the floor, her impatience was evident. Lord and Lady Matlock were the next to arrive. Georgiana jumped up and rushed towards the door, before realizing it is only her aunt and uncle. Returning her seat, her foot resumed its tapping.

"Georgiana," cautioned Lady Matlock, "I know that you are glad to be home with William and Elizabeth. However, you must remember that they are still newlyweds and will need some privacy. You cannot demand their attention every moment, dear."

"Yes, Aunt Rebecca," she replied with obvious frustration, "but it has been so long since I have seen them, and I have much to tell them."

"I am sure they are pleased with your return and will make time for you. I am just asking you to be respectful of their time. There is no need to tell them everything in one sitting. You shall have lots of time with them."

"Yes, Aunt."

Darcy and Elizabeth enter at that moment with flushed faces and happy smiles. Lord and Lady Matlock exchange knowing smiles as they greet the happy couple.

"It seems we are the last to arrive; I hope you will forgive us."

"Certainly, Darcy," replied Lord Matlock with a smile.

Before they could take a seat, Benton arrived to announce dinner. With Elizabeth still on his arm, Darcy offered his other arm to Georgiana and led the way to the dining room. He seated Elizabeth to his right and Georgiana to his left. Lord Matlock held the chair beside Georgiana for his wife before seating himself next to Elizabeth.

"I know you will forgive us for the informal seating arrangement, but it is only family, and I am not yet ready to have Elizabeth so far away from me." Again the older couple exchanged a happy smile. They could not be more pleased with the closeness the couple shared. It was a relief for them to know that Darcy had found such a wonderful partner with whom to share his life.

Georgiana managed to contain herself until the first course arrived, but as soon as the servants departed the room, Georgiana asked, "Did you read Mary's letter?"

"We did, and we are delighted for them. In fact, William has offered to allow Mary to marry from Pemberley." Lord Matlock coughed to cover the laugh that started, as he remembered his son's words regarding the advancement of his courtship. Lady Matlock brought her napkin to her lips to hide a smile of her own.

Recovering himself, Lord Matlock said, "I believe, Darcy, you should make the same offer to Richard, when next you write."

"I will, Uncle, if you believe it to be necessary."

"I believe he will be quite pleased with your thoughtfulness," replied the earl with a chuckle.

"Have you taken on any of the household responsibilities yet, Elizabeth?" asked Lady Matlock.

Before his wife could reply, Darcy proudly responded. "She has taken on a great many of them. Elizabeth has also met all of the tenants and insisted upon making the arrangements for the harvest celebration this year."

"I would be happy to assist you, Elizabeth, should you need it."

"Thank you, Aunt Rebecca, but I believe I have the plans well in hand. I am sure, with Georgiana's assistance, everything will be well." Georgiana's face lit up with pleasure at Elizabeth's remarks. "Perhaps you and Uncle Malcolm would join us for the celebration?"

"Have you decided upon a date Elizabeth?"

"William said everything should be completed by the first week in October, so I have decided on the first Saturday in October for the celebration. It shall begin at two in the afternoon."

"I will be sure that we plan our celebration for a different day, and we shall come that morning and plan to stay the night if that is acceptable."

"You know you are welcome at any time," said Elizabeth fondly. "Speaking of dates, have Jonathan and Penelope set a wedding date yet?"

"They have set the date for late October, just before the start of the little season," replied Lady Matlock. "Jonathan is handling the harvest this year, so that determined the date. They shall marry from London."

Looking at Elizabeth, Darcy said, "We will be in attendance, but we may stay in London for only a week or two. Having invited all of the family to

Pemberley for Christmas, we shall need to return and prepare for our guests. Elizabeth is used to large family gatherings for the holidays, and I want her to be comfortable her first Christmas away from her family."

"Thank you, William. Perhaps we could host a ball on the twenty-third?"

"I would be delighted to dance with you, my love, if you desire to host a ball. It can become a tradition."

"Will you also open the house for tours?" asked Aunt Rebecca.

"Perhaps next year. If all goes well with the holiday plans and the ball this year, I will feel confident enough to include tours of the house next Christmas," said Elizabeth with a laugh.

The remainder of the meal passed with pleasant conversation, and then everyone removed to the music room. Georgiana played several songs before retiring for the night. As she was leaving the room, Elizabeth called to her.

"Georgie, will you walk with me after luncheon tomorrow and tell me all about your stay at the Gardiners? I look forward to hearing about your time spent with my family."

Georgiana's face glowed with pleasure. "I would be happy to join you, Lizzy."

When her footsteps drifted away to nothing, Darcy spoke. "Shall we adjourn to my study so that you can tell us about your visit with Lady Catherine?"

"Do you have any of the excellent brandy I enjoyed on my last visit?"

"Yes, Uncle, I shall be happy to pour you a large snifter of it."

The four of them moved to the library, and Darcy poured wine for the ladies and brandy for his uncle and himself. He seated himself on the sofa pulling Lizzy close with his arm around her shoulders. His aunt and uncle could only smile at the way their reserved nephew flouted propriety within his family group.

"After Lizzy read her letter from Mary, I found one from Richard. Mary only mentioned that Richard had come into an inheritance. Richard, however, was much more forthcoming about his unexpected inheritance," remarked Darcy grimly.

"Has he resigned his commission yet?" asked Elizabeth.

Lord Matlock chuckled. "Yes, the minute Richard was informed about the inheritance, he wrote and requested a meeting with Mr. Bennet for the next day. The reply came in a timely fashion, and Richard was on the road to Hertfordshire early the next morning. After gaining Mr. Bennet's permission for courtship, he immediately returned to London. When he arrived home, Richard wrote to Mr. Gardiner, requesting a meeting in the morning, and to his commanding officer, requesting a meeting the same afternoon. He was delighted to gain Mary's acceptance of his courtship and spoke to the general that afternoon about resigning his commission. I think he said something about Travers buying it, though Richard didn't know if he would have the full amount saved. With his income from Rosings, he will be able to accept what the man has and allow him to pay the balance over time."

"Travers is a good fellow. I am sure he will do well as an officer," remarked Darcy. "So what happened when you arrived at Rosings?"

"Well, we planned to arrive just before tea time so that we could put off the discussion until Richard joined us. We told her we were just returning Anne to Rosings and planned to stay for a day or two. She was constantly berating you and Elizabeth, even going so far as to suggest you were not in your right mind and that we should take steps to protect Georgiana and Pemberley from undesirable influences."

"Humph," was heard from Elizabeth.

"She had the gall to suggest I was not in my right mind! She is certainly a more fitting candidate for Bedlam than I could ever be!"

A worried expression crossing her face, Elizabeth questioned, "She would not have the influence needed to have William committed would she?"

Darcy pulled her closer and kissed her forehead. "Do not worry, my love; there are many people who could vouch for my sanity, as well as all the family members who can call Lady Catherine's into question."

"That is a relief," Elizabeth sighed.

"So if these were her thoughts before she knew the purpose of your visit, how did she take your accusations?"

Rolling her eyes, Lady Matlock said, "With her usual bluster and threats. Fortunately, between Malcolm and Richard, they were able to make her see reason, or at least to stop her manipulations."

"I find that hard to believe," remarked Elizabeth.

"As do I" replied Darcy. "She will be plotting how to remove Elizabeth from my life. Do I need to hire a guard to protect her?"

"Calm down, Darcy. I do not believe you will have anything to worry over. Catherine was removed from Rosings to the dower house. She has a small monthly stipend and will not have the funds for extravagant plans. Furthermore, I did call her sanity into question based on her orders to Mr. Collins. She was disgusted to learn he had failed her and very surprised to find that he was now to be a missionary in Australia. To make matters worse, she was furious to discover she would no longer be able to select the candidates for the living. By the way, I was able to convince the bishop to keep the living within the gift of Rosings. I assured him that Anne and Richard would be far more selective and concerned that the candidate would be able to care for his parishioners than his predecessor. As I said, I questioned her sanity and told her that should any trouble befall you or Elizabeth, I would have her immediately committed to Bedlam." The earl wore a satisfied smile as he completed his tale.

"That is a relief, but, perhaps, it would not hurt to have her watched for a time. I would sleep better knowing that someone was aware of her actions."

"I do not think you need to take such a step, Darcy. Richard is currently in residence at Rosings, and I got the impression he has hired one or two of the men who served as guards for his staff. I believe that the men in question had completed their terms of service and, due to changes in their families, needed a less dangerous position that paid regularly to help in the support of their families. I am sure he will have someone keeping an eye on Catherine."

"Very well, Uncle, but I shall write to Richard and request that he send me regular reports on her actions."

They talked a bit more of the specifics and some of Lady Catherine's more outrageous remarks before retiring for the evening.

As Darcy and Elizabeth cuddled in the afterglow of their lovemaking, Elizabeth spoke. "I am so happy for Richard and Mary. I hope they shall be as happy as we are."

"I am sure they will be happy, but no one could be so happy as we are, my love." Darcy pulled her closer and kissed her face all over.

"Do you think we are safe from Lady Catherine's plotting?"

"No matter what she does, my love, I will keep you safe. You are far too important to my happiness; I would never let her harm you." And Darcy proceeded to show his wife just how devoted he was to her wellbeing.

After breaking their fast the next morning, Lord and Lady Matlock departed for their estate. Darcy and Elizabeth went to their respective studies to attend to business while Georgiana resumed her lessons with Mrs. Annesley. They met again over luncheon.

As they were finishing their meal, Darcy spoke. "Since you ladies have plans to walk this afternoon, I believe I shall ride out with Mr. Mills. There are a few problems with some of the structures on the estate. We need to review them and determine what work needs to be done and when it should be scheduled. Enjoy your walk, and I shall return in time for tea." Rising from the table, he kissed Georgiana's head and placed a lingering kiss on Elizabeth's lips. Today's outing would be the longest separation—in both distance and time—since their marriage. In spite of the importance of the issues he needed to discuss with his steward, he felt as if he left a piece of himself behind with his beloved wife.

After retrieving their bonnets, shawls, and gloves, Elizabeth and Georgiana began to walk the paths of the formal gardens.

"You mentioned you enjoyed your stay with the Gardiners, Georgie. What was the highlight of your visit?"

"I believe it was just being part of a large family. Mrs. Gardiner treated me no differently from Mary and Kitty. Though I had a room to myself, I enjoyed having them visit before bed each night to talk about the day's activities and our hopes for the future. And the children are such little dears. Did I tell you that Rachel's walking has greatly improved? She runs constantly, and it keeps her nurse on her toes. She is talking more, as well."

Elizabeth smiled at her description. "Has Hugh learned to feed the ducks without falling into the pond?"

"He has improved, but somehow he still manages to get his feet wet almost every time we stop by the pond in the park." Both girls laughed at the picture her words created.

"How does Susan fare with her piano lessons?"

"She is doing very well, for one so young. I believe she will prove to be more talented that I am, if she keeps up with her practice."

"Perhaps you could recommend a master who would be good with someone Susan's age? When did you have your first master?"

"I believe I was a year or two older than Susan, but she may be ready for that step. Should I write to Mrs. Gardiner and provide her with the recommendation?"

"Aunt Madeline would greatly appreciate any assistance you could provide," replied Elizabeth. "How did you enjoy your time with Mary and Kitty?"

"Kitty seems to have changed. She is still happy and outgoing, but it is tempered with more reserve than I remember her having when we first met. She loves helping with the children, and we both enjoy our art lessons. Mrs. Annesley took us to an art exhibit, and Kitty could speak of nothing else for days afterward. We are learning to paint with oils, and

Kitty has much more aptitude for it than I do. I prefer to work in watercolors."

"I am pleased to hear that Kitty is maturing and will look forward to her visit later in the summer. As I know Mary has no interest in art, what has she been doing with her time?"

"Actually, Mary has done some lovely still life pictures with charcoals, but she is dreadful at portraiture," said Georgiana with a laugh. "She is going to give landscapes a chance, but after Richard asked her for a courtship, she began to spend more time with Mrs. Gardiner learning about household management. When she is not otherwise occupied, she wears a dreamy expression on her face as though she is not seeing what is in front of her. If she is not careful, she will walk into a door or a wall." Elizabeth joined Georgiana in laughter.

"Perhaps when we go to town for Jonathan's wedding, I will take Mary and Kitty to Madame Colette's. They will both need a ballgown if we are having a ball. I believe we should purchase one for you, as well. You will be ten and seven by that time; it would be appropriate for you to attend the ball, though I do not believe you will be permitted to dance since you have not yet been presented."

"That would be wonderful!" exclaimed Georgiana. "Do you really think William would allow me to attend?"

"I do not see any reason he should not. It would be entirely proper to attend such an event in your home shire, particularly when your family is the host."

"Did Kitty have any word from Lydia? Papa is a rather indifferent correspondent. In fact, I rather expect him to appear at any time. I believe Lydia was to go to school sometime soon, and he said he would stop in to see Pemberley's library on his way home."

"I do hope I can see his face when you take him to the library for the first time." Again a chuckle escaped from Georgiana.

Laughing Elizabeth replied, "I will be sure you accompany us on the tour of the house so that you can enjoy his reaction. I must admit I am eager to see his expression myself."

"What do you think of Pemberley?"

"I think it is a piece of Heaven on Earth. I have enjoyed exploring all of the walking trails. William has succeeded in teaching me to ride and gifted me with Sheba, so I have also seen some of the more distant beauties of the estate."

They continued walking arm and arm, discussing whatever issues came to mind, until time for tea.

Elizabeth's prediction soon came to pass as Mr. Bennet arrived without notice on Pemberley's doorstep just two days later.

"Papa!" cried Elizabeth as she rushed into her father's arms. "I am so happy to see you. How was your journey? Is everything well at Longbourn?"

"Hello, my Lizzy. Can you not allow me in the door before the inquisition begins," replied Mr. Bennet with a chuckle. "Good to see you, Darcy," said Mr. Bennet as he noticed Darcy enter from down the hallway.

"How do you do, sir? We are pleased you could visit."

Elizabeth turned to Mrs. Reynolds to request that a room be prepared and tea sent to the blue drawing room. Tucking her arm into her father's, she led him in the direction of the drawing room. Seating herself next to her father on the sofa, she said, "Now you are seated, and refreshments will be here shortly. You must tell me all that has happened since our departure. I was disappointed not to receive a letter from you telling what happened after we left departure. How did things go with Mama and Lydia?"

"Impatient as ever, Lizzy, I see." Crossing her arms over her chest, she turned a stern eye on her father and waited for him to begin.

Laughing at her posture, he relented and began to speak of what had occurred. He laughingly told Elizabeth about his interview with Richard. Mr. Bennet outlined his discussion with Lydia about being the wife of a poor soldier and all it entailed before giving her the choice to move to the house and prepare to attend school or stay at the dower house with her mother if the life of a soldier's wife was her choice. Mr. Bennet spoke of her choosing school and the efforts to begin to educate her. He told Elizabeth and Darcy of Mrs. Bennet's continuing poor attitude and anger at her banishment and his dread of facing her upon his return. Lastly, her father told her of Lydia's leave-taking of her mother and Mrs. Bennet's anger that she would choose school and abandon her. He informed them of Lydia's concerns about fitting in at school.

"It was the first time I have ever seen her show a lack of confidence. I do hope she will be able to make the adjustment." His heartfelt concern for his youngest daughter was evident on his face. "She promised to write, and the school does make them write every other week. I am anxious to receive her first letter."

"You must inform us of what she says, as I am not sure she will write to me. She resents me for Mama's banishment and the fact that it was I who recommended that the girls go to school."

"I shall try to be a better correspondent, my dear Lizzy. She did make the decision to go to school for herself, and I believe that eventually she will grow from the experience. It is my greatest hope that she will appreciate the experience and improve her relationship with all those in her family."

Tea had arrived during their discussion, and Elizabeth had served her father and husband. Taking the opportunity to refresh their cups, she turned the conversation to the more complex issue—her mother.

"What of Mama?"

"I should prefer to put her from my mind for the present time and enjoy Pemberley's famed library, but I know that will not satisfy you, Lizzy. I have given the subject much thought. I plan to lay down some specific guidelines for your mother's return to the manor house. If she is unwilling to change, she may remain in the dower house permanently. If she agrees to try but fails to comply, I shall return her to the dower house." Mr. Bennet continued, "I will refuse her an allowance and notify all the shopkeepers they are not to extend her credit. All expenditures must be approved by me until such time as she proves she can be financially responsible. Gossip shall be forbidden and reading shall be required. Based on her behavior to her favorites, Jane and Lydia, I do not have much hope of Fanny improving her behavior."

Elizabeth did not like to see the defeated look on her father's face. "Try not to lose hope, Papa. I am sure you did not expect the changes you saw in Lydia. Perhaps all will turn out well with Mama, too."

"You sound more like Jane than my practical Lizzy," said Mr. Bennet with a chuckle. "I appreciate your encouragement, Elizabeth, but you need not worry. I am firm in my resolve to improve my family's situation—with or without their cooperation."

Elizabeth was pleased to see a look of determination replace the defeated look. "You have done so much good for us Papa. I hope that you know you have the love of all of your daughters."

"I do know that now and am sorry that I ignored such a precious gift for so long." Elizabeth patted her father's hand where it rested on the sofa between them. "Now, I believe I could do with a rest before we dine. For today, I shall be the perfect houseguest. However, I must have your promise to be introduced to the mythical library tomorrow."

"It is a promise, Papa. Now allow me to show you to your room." Upon standing, Elizabeth linked her arm through her father's again and led the way upstairs. Arriving at the door of the guestroom selected for him, Elizabeth hugged him tightly and placed a kiss on his cheek. She turned to depart, but, remembering something, turned again to her father. "We dine at six and shall gather in the same drawing room before the meal. Rest well, Papa."

"Thank you, Lizzy. I shall join you in time for dinner." She watched as her father entered his room, closing the door behind her before moving to find Georgiana. After notifying her sister about Mr. Bennet's arrival, she moved to the sitting room she shared with her husband. Sure enough, Darcy was waiting within. He opened his arms to Elizabeth, who rushed into his comforting embrace.

"Would you prefer to talk, my love, or to rest?"

"I would prefer the comfort of your arms, Will. There will be time to talk about my family's situation later." With that Darcy swept her up in his arms and carried her into his bedchamber.

CHAPTER 14

RICHARD LOOKED OUT over the fields of Rosings, watching the tenants working in the fields. The harvest was approaching and, according to his steward, the yields were expected to be above average. There had been much for him to learn, and he had been in constant correspondence with his father and brother. He was beginning to feel that he had a firm grasp on things, and as the harvest was a week away, he planned to take a trip to town for a few days to visit Mary. He had enjoyed the letters they shared during their time of separation, but he could not wait for her to be always by his side. He greatly admired Mary's common sense and felt she would be a good partner for him in all facets of his life. They had been courting for about two months now, mostly through correspondence, and he wondered if it was too soon to propose. He knew more about her through her letters than they could have learned through six months of courtship in the traditional manner. Deciding to discuss the issue with Anne when he returned to the house, he gave his mount a gentle nudge and moved in the direction of the next tenant's fields.

Returning to the house in time for tea, he knocked on the door of Anne's sitting room.

"Enter," came her soft voice.

"How are you feeling today, Anne?"

"I am well, Richard."

"Do you feel up to joining me in the drawing room for tea?"

"That would be lovely." Richard moved into the room and assisted Anne to stand before offering her his arm and escorting her to the drawing room. After seating his cousin, he rang the bell for the new housekeeper. When Mrs. Crawford appeared, Anne ordered tea for them. "How did the fields look?" she asked as Richard settled on the sofa opposite hers.

"Everything seems to be progressing very well. Mr. Rowley says that we should be ready to harvest in the next month or so. He also indicated we should expect bountiful yields. Much better than the past few seasons."

"I am sure that has a great deal to do with the care you have taken of the tenants since coming to Rosings Park, Richard. Mother never felt the need to recognize them or repair their homes. There was only so much Mr. Rowley could do without mother's cooperation."

"So she never held any harvest celebration?"

"Not that I can remember," Anne replied. "Do you think there would be time to arrange something? I could work with Mrs. Crawford and perhaps do something small this year."

"Are you sure it would not be too taxing for you?"

"As I shall only assist with the plans, I believe I can manage, Richard." Anne smiled sweetly, touched by his concern.

At that moment, the housekeeper returned with the tea tray. "Mrs. Crawford," said Anne, "in your previous post did you ever prepare any harvest festivities for the tenants?"

"Indeed, ma'am. I have assisted in organizing such events several times. Do you wish to plan something?"

"We expect to harvest in a month or so. Would that be a sufficient time to arrange a modest event?" asked Richard curiously.

The housekeeper thought for a moment. "In the past, the events have been large and out of doors with games and activities. I do not know if we have the time for that, or if it would be too strenuous for Miss de Bourgh, but we could host a buffet luncheon in the ballroom. Maybe provide each family with a small gift when they leave. Is that something that would be acceptable to you?"

Richard looked at Anne, and they both nodded. Turning back to the housekeeper, he said, "That sounds fine. Would you please work with Miss de Bourgh on the planning, but do not let her overtax her strength? Please let me know the cost as soon as you finish your making the necessary decision, and I will arrange for the funds to be available."

"I am at your disposal, miss," said Mrs. Crawford with a curtsey before exiting the room.

Anne poured tea for them both. After accepting his cup, Richard again spoke, "Anne, do you think that it is too soon for me to propose to Mary? I know that we have not seen much of each other, though I do plan to go to town tomorrow to visit with her for a few days. However, I have learned much of her through her letters, and I have known for some time that I wished to marry her."

A small smile playing around her lips, Anne looked at her cousin. "Where is the decisive colonel I have known for so long? What makes you hesitate?"

"It is just that she deserves the very best. I do not wish to deny her a proper courtship."

"Though I have not spent much time in Miss Mary's company, I do not think that the formalities or trappings of a courtship are as important to her as a meaningful connection to the man she loves. Even if you were to propose now, you still intended to take her about during the season, do you not?"

"Of course, I do. I wish to spend as much time with her as possible."

"If you do propose, when would you want to marry?"

"Well, William did invite all of us to spend Christmas at Pemberley. As both of our families are to be present, it would seem the perfect time to wed. In his most recent letter, Darcy congratulated me on the courtship and mentioned that Elizabeth planned to offer for Mary to wed from Pemberley, as she did not think Mary would wish to marry from Longbourn. I do not know if Mary has received Elizabeth's suggestion as of yet, but if I propose, we could discuss that option."

"Then I suggest you discuss Elizabeth's offer with Mary when you see her and make your decision based on her opinion of the offer. You should allow her enough time to purchase a trousseau and make preparations. Do you have a ring to give her?"

"I had not yet thought of that. I believe that mother has something set aside for my wife, but I do not know if it is a ring, nor would there be time to obtain it before I see Mary."

"As you are the heir to this estate, I would be delighted if you would look through the family jewels to see if there is a ring that you should like to give your intended."

"But, Anne, those jewels are yours," Richard protested.

"Richard, there are far more jewels than I could ever wear, not to mention that I rarely go anywhere where such accessories are needed. If you have finished your tea, let us go to the mistress's suite and look through them. I will assist you in finding something to give your lovely bride."

Richard offered his arm to Anne, and they made their way upstairs. He followed her through the mistress's chamber, stopping before a blank section of the dressing room wall. He watched as she pressed a hidden latch, and a portion of the wall sprang open like a door. Behind it, drawers were built in from the floor to half-way up the wall.

"My, my, are there other secrets like this one hidden in the walls of Rosings? I believe I shall have to do some exploring."

"Unless you particularly wish to explore, I would be happy to just show you the other secrets of Rosings," said Anne with a smile.

"I shall look forward to our adventure after the harvest celebration is over," Richard chuckled in reply.

Anne turned back to the drawers, opening first one and then another. Finally, she found the drawer she wanted. Turning to Richard, she said, "This drawer contains all of the rings that are not part of a particular jewelry set."

He stepped closer to Anne and began to peruse what was in the drawer. After carefully surveying the pieces, he lifted one from the drawer, holding it out for Anne's inspection.

"I think it suits Miss Mary perfectly," she replied. Opening another drawer, Anne pulled out an empty velvet sack. "You can store it in here for safe-keeping until you present it to your betrothed."

As Richard carefully put the ring in the bag, Anne closed the drawer and moved the section of wall back into place, listening for the click that indicated the latch closed properly.

Turning back to Richard, she said, "I believe I shall rest until we dine. Have a pleasant afternoon, Richard."

He escorted his cousin to her suite and took himself off to the study. He wrote out a note to the housekeeper at Matlock House, advising her of his arrival on the morrow, as well as one to Mary. Additionally, he sent a note to Mr. Gardiner asking if he would check the current performances, as he would like to take them all to the theater while he was in town. After arranging for the letters to be sent express, he focused his attention on the paperwork on his desk until time to dress for dinner.

Richard presented himself at the Gardiner residence in Gracechurch Street promptly at two the next afternoon. Mrs. Gardiner welcomed him in the drawing room where she sat with Kitty and Mary. After greeting the ladies, he took a seat next to Mary.

"How have things been going at Rosings Park, Mr. Fitzwilliam?" Mrs. Gardiner asked.

"Everything seems to be in hand, and my steward tells me that the harvest will be sometime in the next several weeks. Anne and Mrs. Crawford, the new housekeeper, are planning a small celebration for the tenants on the first Saturday in September. I hoped that your family might be able to attend and perhaps stay a day or two." Richard looked at Mary as he spoke but turned a hopeful glance towards Mrs. Gardiner.

"I will have to check with my husband. We should have returned from Derbyshire by then, but I am uncertain whether or not he will be able to take additional time off."

"I would enjoy having just you ladies and the children, if Mr. Gardiner's schedule did not permit him to accompany you. I would happily send an escort to ensure your safe arrival," offered Richard gallantly.

"Perhaps you could stay for dinner, and we could discuss it further this evening," invited Mrs. Gardiner.

"I should be delighted to stay. Thank you for the invitation."

Mary looked at Richard and remarked, "I thought you planned to retain Lady Catherine's staff, but you mentioned a new housekeeper."

"We did try to keep them, but they were far too accustomed to Lady Catherine's threats and abuse to refuse her admittance to the house. She was forever arriving uninvited and burdening Anne with her numerous complaints. I did not care for the effect her continuous tantrums were having on Anne's health. It became necessary to replace the butler and housekeeper. So far we have been quite pleased with their service and have not been bothered by Lady Catherine's intrusions. Anne seems much improved now that she no longer has daily contact with her mother."

"That is good news," said Mary. "I enjoyed meeting her and look forward to knowing her better."

"She has said the same about you, Miss Bennet."

Mary started when Richard addressed her as Miss Bennet. "I know I have technically been Miss Bennet for two months now, but I find it difficult to respond to the title. If my aunt does not have any objections, I should prefer that you continue to address me as Miss Mary as that is how we were first known to one another." Richard smiled at Mary before they both turned to see Mrs. Gardiner's reaction.

"I believe that would be acceptable when we are in the company of family. However, in public you must accustom yourself to Miss Bennet, Mary, dear."

"Yes, Aunt Madeline."

"Thank you, Mrs. Gardiner. Well, Miss Mary, Miss Kitty, as it is a lovely day and not too hot, would you care to walk in the park? We could bring the children if you wish, Mrs. Gardiner."

"That would be lovely, Mr. Fitzwilliam," said Mary with smile.

"I shall go and get the children ready. Kitty, perhaps you could fetch bonnets and gloves for you and Mary while I do so."

The two ladies left, and Richard and Mary had a few moments of privacy. "I found your last letter informative," said Mary softly. "I am pleased to hear that you enjoy your life as a gentleman farmer."

"I do find it very pleasant. There is something peaceful about an agrarian lifestyle, so very different from the ground of a battlefield."

"Do you still find yourself plagued by bad dreams?" Richard was pleased to note the care and concern in Mary's expression.

"It is improving every day. Though sometimes they return after having to do battle with my aunt." Richard's face wore a rueful grin.

Mary placed her hand on his arm and gave it a gentle squeeze. Richard covered her hand with his, holding it there until they heard footsteps indicating the others were ready to depart. Mary quickly withdrew her hand just before Kitty entered the room. She took the bonnet Kitty held out to her and placed in on her head before putting on her gloves. Mary then accepted the arm Richard held out for her and offered her other hand to Susan. Kitty followed, holding tightly to Hugh with Edmund by her side. The nursery maid trailed behind the group, carrying a bag of breadcrumbs to feed to the ducks.

As they approached the water, Richard and Mary stopped at a bench where they could talk quietly and observe the others. When the breadcrumbs were all gone, they returned to the house for tea. Over tea, Richard entertained the children with stories from his time training cavalrymen, mostly funny stories of falls and such.

When Mr. Gardiner arrived home, the children greeted their father before returning to the nursery to prepare for dinner.

"Good evening, Mr. Fitzwilliam," said Mr. Gardiner. "We are pleased that you could visit us. Will you be in town long?"

"I hope to stay for several days. Were you able to discover if there were any interesting offerings at the theater?"

"Yes, there is a production of *Cendrillon* that is reported to be very well done or a production of Shakespeare's *Antony and Cleopatra*. Do you ladies have a preference?"

"I take it we are going to the theater," remarked Mrs. Gardiner.

"Yes, I was planning to take you to a performance using my parents' box. Which performance would you like best, Miss Mary?"

"I assume *Cendrillon* is based on Mr. Perrault's story?"

Mr. Gardiner nodded. "Yes, it is performed as a comic opera in three acts."

"And you gentlemen do not mind attending an operatic performance of a children's fairy tale?" Mary asked with a hint of humor in her tone.

Mr. Gardiner blushed, but Richard gallantly replied, "I should enjoy seeing anything as long as you are with me, Miss Mary."

Now it was Mary's turn to blush, as Mr. and Mrs. Gardiner exchanged a pleased look.

"If anyone cares for my opinion. I should like to see *Cendrillon*," remarked Kitty in the silence that followed Mr. Fitzwilliam's remark.

"I should like to see *Cendrillon*, as well," came Mary's quiet reply.

"Then that is what we shall see. Which evening would be best for your family, Mrs. Gardiner?

"I believe two days hence would be perfect."

"Mr. Fitzwilliam," asked Kitty, "how many people does a box seat?"

"I believe there is room for eight, Miss Kitty. Why do you ask?"

"I wondered, since we are to see *Cendrillon*, do you think that Edmund and Susan might enjoy the performance? It is one of Susan's favorite stories, and she does love music so."

The other four occupants in the room looked at one another as if trying to decide how best to answer. Finally, Richard said, "I have no objection to the children's attendance if you believe they would enjoy the outing. They have always been well behaved in the past when I have been in company with them. The only concern might be the lateness of the hour and their ability to remain awake."

"My husband and I shall discuss the matter and decide between now and the evening of the performance if that is acceptable."

A short time later the housekeeper announced that dinner was served. Richard offered his arm to Mary to escort her into the dining room. Once they were seated, Richard asked, "Have you heard from the newlyweds recently?"

"I received a letter from Elizabeth a few days ago," answered Mary. "She spoke of her plans for Christmas when all the family is to be at Pemberley."

"Indeed," added Kitty with a touch of her former excitability, "there is to be a ball while we are there, and Lizzy said she will purchase ball gowns for Mary and me when they come to town in October for the viscount's wedding."

"I hope you will accompany me to the wedding, Miss Mary."

"I should be very pleased to do so, Mr. Fitzwilliam."

As dinner concluded, Mrs. Gardiner stood to lead the ladies into the drawing room so the men could enjoy a glass of port or brandy. Her departure was interrupted when Richard asked, "Mr. and Mrs. Gardiner, could I have a moment of your time?"

Mrs. Gardiner nodded, then turned to Mary and Kitty. "Please go ahead, girls. I will join you shortly."

When the young ladies left the dining room and the door closed after them, Mr. and Mrs. Gardiner, who now sat next to each other, looked at the suddenly nervous gentleman and waited for him to speak.

Richard cleared his throat and then rushed into speech. "Mrs. Gardiner, I was wondering if Miss Mary had mentioned any preference for where she would prefer to marry."

The married couple exchanged a look before she answered. "She told me Elizabeth offered to allow her to marry from Pemberley, if she did not wish to return to Longbourn. And, though she did not express a specific desire, she did say that she would prefer to marry away from Longbourn and her mother. Why do you ask, Mr. Fitzwilliam?"

"I would like your permission to propose to Miss Mary. After reading Darcy's letter, I thought that if we were to become engaged now, we could have the wedding at Pemberley when the family gathers for the holidays."

"Are you sure you are ready for an engagement, sir?" asked Mr. Gardiner.

"I have been ready since I asked for a courtship. I do still intend to come to town after the harvest and spend time squiring Miss Mary to events about town. However, I now wish to do so as an engaged couple."

"So are you asking permission to speak with Mary this evening?"

"I would like to do so, Mr. Gardiner, if it meets with the approval of you and your wife. I feel like I know Miss Mary very well from the letters we have exchanged. Our written correspondence has taught me far more than I could learn through polite conversation in a well-chaperoned drawing room. She is a remarkable young lady, and I would be honored to earn her affection and join my life with hers."

Mr. and Mrs. Gardiner shared another long, speaking look. Finally, Mr. Gardiner turned to the anxious gentleman before him and replied, "If you would like to use my study, I will send Mary to you. We will allow you ten minutes to make your proposal, and I will expect you to behave like a gentleman, sir."

"Of course, Mr. Gardiner, and thank you."

Richard bounded from his chair and quickly made his way to Mr. Gardiner's study. He left the door open and was pacing the floor when Mary arrived. She pushed the door almost closed and waited for him to notice her. When a minute passed and he had not looked up from his path across the carpet and back, Mary softly spoke, "You wished to see me, Mr. Fitzwilliam."

Richard stopped abruptly and turned in the direction of her voice. He noticed her tentative tone and the slight pink blush on her cheeks. Richard moved towards her and took both of Mary's hands in his. He led her to the sofa and seated himself closely beside her, still holding tightly to her hands. "My dear Miss Mary. I have something important I wish to ask you. Are you willing to hear me?"

"I should be pleased to hear anything you have to say, Mr. Fitzwilliam."

Richard slid onto one knee before the sofa, her hands still in his. "Mary, you are the most remarkable young woman I have ever known. You are lovely, brave, and kind, and possess a quiet strength that is quite admirable. I love you dearly and wondered if you would consent to be my wife and share life's adventures with me?"

Mary's blush increased and tears glistened in her eyes. "I love you as well, Richard, and would be honored to go through life at your side."

Releasing her left hand, he reached into his pocket, pulled out the ring, and gently placed it on her finger.

"It is stunning, Richard! You could not have given me anything I would like more than this lovely pearl."

Richard kissed the back of both her hands before turning them over to kiss the palm. Looking from her lips to her eyes, and back again, he asked, "May I kiss you, Mary?"

Blushing even more deeply, Mary could only nod. Richard stood and pulled her gently to her feet. He placed his rough hand against her soft cheek and leaned in, placing a tender kiss on her soft lips. Though Richard would have liked to deepen the kiss, he did not wish to scare his young betrothed. He withdrew, leaning his forehead against hers. As they stood thusly, he asked, "Shall we marry while at Pemberley for the holidays? However, if you prefer to marry from Longbourn or town, that would be acceptable to me, as well."

"I think a winter wedding at Pemberley would be wonderful. In her most recently letter, Lizzy offered to allow me to marry from Pemberley after learning of our courtship. I shall see if that is acceptable to her and ask her assistance in the planning."

Richard smiled widely. Then offering her his arm, asked, "Shall we go share the good news with your family?"

"I would like that very much. Oh, Richard, thank you."

"What for?"

"For loving me. I did not think anyone ever would."

"You are very easy to love. Those who cannot see it are fools."

Kitty was very excited for her sister when she heard the news. Mr. and Mrs. Gardiner also offered their congratulations. Then Mr. Gardiner called for a bottle of champagne to celebrate.

The next morning, the colonel again appeared in Gracechurch Street. He was to take Mary and Kitty for a walk in Hyde Park and then shopping. As they walked along the pathways of the park, Mary held the colonel's arm with Kitty walking slightly ahead of them. They spoke of their wedding and what they would both like to make the occasion special. The news of Richard's inheritance of Rosings Park had somehow reached the ears of the ton. As a consequence, he was approached several times by gentlemen and their daughters. The young women, who were not able to gain an introduction, smiled and batted their eyes in his direction. Richard could feel the tension in Mary as her grip on his arm tightened. He introduced her frequently, and those who met her wondered about the young woman whose arm he held so tightly.

Finally, Richard had reached the limit of his endurance. Calling to Kitty, he held out his arm for her and turned them back to where his carriage awaited. Mary walked silently beside him. As they entered the carriage, Richard made a noise indicative of his disgust. "Now I truly understand what Darcy was talking about," he muttered.

Mary looked at him in surprise. "I beg your pardon, Mr. Fitzwilliam."

Startled at her formal address, Richard looked closely at Mary. He knew she had been uncomfortable as they walked in the park, but he assumed it was because of the interruptions they were forced to endure. However, the look on her face was one of sadness and self-doubt. Trying to discern what she was thinking, he answered bluntly.

"Darcy always complained about being sought after like he was a prize bull. I used to laugh at the way the woman vied for his attentions. However, I find it disgusting that those same women we encountered in the park would not have paid me any attention two months ago when I was just Colonel Fitzwilliam, the second son of an earl. The only reason they are looking in my direction now is that they have heard about my eventual inheritance of Rosings Park. I shall owe Darcy an apology for all the times I laughed at him for complaining that too many women intruded upon him."

Though pleased at his words, Mary softly said, "Perhaps you should rethink our engagement. Anyone of those women can bring more to a marriage than I can."

"No, Mary, that is not true. What they possess—money and connections—have no value when not accompanied by a loving heart. Please, Mary, you saw me for the man I am when I was only Colonel Fitzwilliam. Nothing they possess could equal the love you hold for me. Please do not doubt my love for you, and please do not ever call me Mr. Fitzwilliam in that fashion again. I am your dear Richard, and you will always be my beloved Mary."

At his words, the tears spilled down Mary's cheeks. Kitty grasped her hand and gave it a squeeze as she looked out the window, giving the couple the privacy they needed.

A short time later, the carriage stopped before the teashop that was Lady Matlock's favorite. Richard handed the ladies down from the carriage and accompanied them inside. They quickly secured a table and ordered some tea and an assortment of pastries to share.

"Miss Bennet, I hope you do not mind, but I sent an express to your father early this morning requesting his approval for our engagement. As he is currently at Pemberley, I could not ride to Hertfordshire to obtain his blessing. As soon as I received his reply, I should like to send the announcement of our betrothal to the papers, if that meets with your approval."

When they had finished their refreshments, Richard offered an arm to each lady and directed them to the store on Bond Street that specialized in ladies' accessories. Mary and Kitty were both looking for some ribbons to compliment the gowns they would wear to the theater. Mary quickly made her selection, but Kitty was indecisive and frequently distracted.

"Oooh, Mary, look at this lovely fan."

Mary wandered over to where her sister stood and looked at the item she indicated. "Oh, Kitty, you are right. I think it is the loveliest fan I have ever seen." Richard, hearing Mary's remark, leaned over the ladies' shoulders to view the item.

"Miss Bennet, Miss Catherine, I believe we must leave shortly if we are to finish our errands and arrive at your aunt's in time for tea. I must also return home to prepare for your arrival for dinner. I am quite certain the housekeeper has everything well in hand, but it would not do for the host to be late," said Richard with a smile.

Mary moved to pay for her ribbons, as Kitty returned to the table to make her selection. Once both ladies were out of earshot, Richard spoke to a nearby clerk, requesting that he wrap the fan and send it to Matlock House along with the bill.

As he reached the front of the store, Mary and Kitty approached, each carrying a small package. Richard held the door open for them to pass through and they departed. They walked a short distance to the bookshop, so that Mary could look for some new music. After selecting several pieces, they returned to his waiting carriage, where he handed the ladies in and directed his coachman to Gracechurch Street.

Promptly at seven, the Gardiners' carriage pulled up before Matlock House. As Mr. Gardiner stepped down to assist the ladies, the front door opened, and Richard Fitzwilliam descended the steps. After Mr. Gardiner had helped Mrs. Gardiner down, Richard stepped forward and assisted Mary from the carriage. He placed her hand on his arm and turned to mount the stairs, and Mr. Gardiner followed with his wife and Kitty.

Once all had reached the front hall and were being attended by the servants, Richard said,

"Welcome! I am glad you could join me for dinner tonight. It is my pleasure to have an opportunity to host you."

"We thank you for the invitation," said Mrs. Gardiner politely.

"Dinner should be served shortly. Please join me in the drawing room while we wait." Richard extended his arm towards the room, and the ladies moved forward. He gently placed his hand on Mrs. Gardiner's arm, causing her to stop, as the others proceeded onward. "Mrs. Gardiner, I am not well versed on what gifts might be acceptable for a betrothed couple. Would it be permissible for me to give Miss Mary a fan that she admired on our shopping trip earlier today?"

"I think that would be acceptable, Mr. Fitzwilliam."

"Thank you, ma'am. I shall present it later this evening." Richard then offered his arm to Mrs. Gardiner, and they entered the room as the others were taking seats.

Richard seated himself beside Mary and turned to ask a question of the Gardiners. "I understand you will be traveling to Pemberley for a visit this summer. When will you depart?"

"We had originally planned to leave in ten days, but a business concern will delay our departure for two weeks. We will leave for the trip north just before the end of this month."

"And how long do you expect to be away?"

"We expect to take a week to journey northward, seeing some of the sights along the way. We will stay three weeks at Pemberley, and then another week to travel home. Since the children will be joining us, we cannot travel quite so far each day."

"I assume you will be taking two carriages for the trip?"

"We would like to, but I have not yet decided, as we only possess one coach. Darcy did offer to send one, but it would have to make two full round trips and that seems to be too much of an inconvenience."

"I am sure I could lend you one of the smaller ones that remain here if that would be of assistance to you?"

"That would be most helpful, but we would not wish to impose."

"Mr. Gardiner, we are already family and will be even closer after Mary and I wed. It would be no trouble for you to use one of the spare carriages. This time of year it sits here unused, as my family is at their seat in Matlock. You will return to town long before they have need of it. Please allow me to provide this convenience for you."

"Well, when you present the offer like that, it would be churlish of me to refuse."

"Just let me know the exact date of your departure, and I will have it arrive very early in the morning on that date."

"Thank you, Mr. Fitzwilliam. Having two carriages will certainly make the trip more comfortable for all."

The butler appeared and announced that dinner was ready. Richard offered one arm to his betrothed and the other to Mrs. Gardiner, then led the way to the dining room. Richard had asked the housekeeper to present three courses, and the ladies all noted that at least two of Mary's favorites were present during each course. The conversation over dinner was relaxed and happy and ranged over a variety of topics. After the meal, the gentlemen chose to remain with the ladies, and the entire party retired to the music room where Mary entertained them at the pianoforte with several songs.

As the party was preparing to leave, Mrs. Gardiner issued an invitation to Richard. "Mr. Fitzwilliam, please join us for an early meal tomorrow evening before the trip to the theater. I will save the dessert course for after the theater so that we might enjoy the evening more fully."

"I shall look forward to it. If the weather permits, I should like to walk with Miss Mary in the morning, but I have business to attend to in the afternoon."

"I shall look forward to our walk," said Mary shyly.

Richard escorted them to the carriage. Before handing Mary in, he took the opportunity to kiss her hand and whisper, "Until tomorrow, my dear."

After a pleasant walk with Mary in the morning, Richard spent several hours with his solicitor and banker, making some arrangements for the estate and entrusting a letter from Anne to them to handle for her. He was very surprised to learn from the solicitor that Anne had asked him to provide a home for her at Rosings until her death, as well as to be part of the family for all meals and special events held at the estate. The income from the investments her father left her would provide for all her other needs and personal expenses. She asked to have a slightly larger monthly allowance for her than her mother had provided for her. Richard was to receive all the income from the estate and to pay the estate expenses from that income. Any profit above that needed to run the estate was the property of Richard Fitzwilliam and his heirs.

He was astonished at her generosity. Rosings belonged to Anne until her death, and he did not feel it appropriate to be benefitting so greatly from what was rightfully hers.

"Are you sure you understood her directions correctly?" he questioned in concern.

"Allow me to read you a portion of her letter, sir," replied the solicitor. He pushed his spectacles further up his nose and picked up the letter, scanning it. When he found the section that he was looking for, he cleared his throat and began to read. "I am sure my cousin shall question this decision. Please assure him that I did increase my allowance and that my needs are simple. I am certain I can trust his generosity, should I ever have need of additional funds. I could also change this agreement at any time before my death, but know that it will not be necessary. Relax, Richard, this is what is best for all of us."

Richard could not help but chuckle at his cousin's words and, then, made no further reference to the matter.

Richard's carriage arrived promptly at half past five, and he was ushered into the drawing room where the Gardiners and their nieces were waiting.

"Good evening, Mr. and Mrs. Gardiner, Miss Mary, Miss Kitty."

"Good evening, Mr. Fitzwilliam," they all said.

He seated himself beside Mary and presented her with a small package whispering, "I intended to give this to you last night, but as we discussed your trip, it slipped my mind. I hope you will forgive the delay and accept this as a small token of my affection."

"Richard, you need not give me gifts," she whispered in return.

"I enjoy giving gifts and will do so whenever the mood strikes me," he whispered back with a laugh.

Having noted the gift in his hand when he arrived and recalling his request the day before, Mrs. Gardiner distracted her husband and Kitty as Richard made his presentation. However, Kitty had also seen the package and was curious as to what it contained.

Mary unwrapped the gift, setting the ribbon aside. She lifted the lid from the box and moved the paper to see the beautiful fan Kitty had pointed out the day before. "Oh, how lovely." She looked at Richard with bright eyes and a happy smile. "Thank you, Richard. How did you know I admired it?"

"I saw the look on your face, but knowing your practical nature, I knew you would not purchase it for yourself. It was my pleasure to purchase it for you."

She removed the fan from the box and opened it. The sticks were made of ivory, and there was a lovely picture painted on it showing a small pagoda and cherry trees in blossom.

"Mary, is that not the fan we saw yesterday?" asked her sister.

"It is, Kitty. It was a gift from Richard."

"It goes beautifully with the gown you have chosen for this evening."

Richard noted her attire for the first time. The gown was the same shade of pink as the blossoms on the fan and trimmed at the sleeves, neckline, waist, and hem in a darker pink ribbon. Her dark curls were swept up on the crown of her head with ribbons in both shades woven through them. "It does go beautifully, Mary, and you look beautiful tonight."

The group enjoyed a pleasant meal, at the conclusion of which Edmund and Susan joined them dressed to go to the theater. Susan sat beside Mary in the carriage with Richard across from her. She was busy watching out of the window the entire way to the theater. The children did not often go out to events held after dark, and Susan could not believe all the carriages, lights, and people. Entering the lobby, the little girl was struck silent by the sight of the gowns and the jewels adorning so many of the ladies. They went directly to their box and settled themselves. The children sat in the front row beside Kitty with their parents seated behind them. Mary and Richard sat behind Kitty. Susan and Edmund were enthralled by the crowds, as was Kitty, too, while they waited for the curtain to rise.

When the lights dimmed, all eyes turned to the stage. Seeing an opportunity, Richard reached over and clasped Mary's gloved hand, moving it to rest at the edge of her chair where he could hold it without being observed.

Tonight's performance was Mary's first opera, and, though she could not understand all the spoken words, the story was easily comprehended. Occasionally, a laugh or a sigh came from Susan as she watched her favorite story unfold. When the first intermission arrived and the lights came up, the words came bubbling from her like water from a spring.

"Oh, this is so much better than just hearing the story. From now on when someone reads this book to me, I shall close my eyes and see the story in my head. I can hardly wait to see the costumes for the ball!"

"Shall we promenade and obtain some lemonade during this intermission?" asked their host.

Everyone agreed, so with Mary on his arm, Richard led the way to the refreshment stand. They all retrieved their glasses, and Mr. and Mrs. Gardiner moved away with the children, leaving Kitty to chaperone. As they finished their beverages, Mary noted a pair of familiar faces coming towards them. "Look, Richard; it is Lord Wescott and Miss Pottsfield."

The other couple had seen them and moved to greet them. "Good evening, Fitzwilliam, Miss Bennet, Miss Catherine. How nice to see you." "You remember Miss Pottsfield, do you not?" asked Lord Wescott.

"It is a pleasure to see you again, Miss Pottsfield, Lord Wescott," said Mary.

"Good evening," said Kitty.

"Are you enjoying the performance?" asked Evelyn Pottsfield.

"It is wonderful," remarked Kitty enthusiastically.

"It is the first opera I have seen, and I am enjoying it immensely," agreed Mary.

"I had heard that the performance was very well done," said Lord Wescott, "and I must say I agree."

"It is a very good production," added Fitzwilliam.

"Have you heard from the Darcys recently?" asked Evelyn.

"Yes, we had a letter recently. Elizabeth spoke excitedly of our upcoming visit and the harvest celebration she was planning. She seems to be very happy in her new home."

"I would have to agree, based on the letters I have received," said Evelyn with a smile.

"They were very attached to each other, so I am not surprised that marriage agrees with them," said Lord Wescott, quietly adding, "I hope to be as happy myself sometime in the future." He looked at Miss Pottsfield as he spoke, and she blushed slightly, though her eyes sparkled with pleasure.

"I know that I shall be as happy very soon," added Fitzwilliam with a glance at Mary.

The bell rang to indicate the start of the second act. As the group parted, Miss Pottsfield said, "Please give Mr. and Mrs. Darcy my best when you visit."

"Please add my best wishes, as well," said Wescott with quiet sincerity.

"I will happily pass along your messages," replied Mary.

With final goodbyes, the party returned to their boxes. The Gardiners were already seated when Richard, Mary and Kitty arrived in the box. They quickly took their places for the second act. At its conclusion, Susan raved about the beautiful costumes and the dancing during the ball scene.

"What did you think, Edmund?" asked Richard.

"I would like it better with sword fighting or perhaps a dragon," said the young boy. The adults worked hard to suppress the laughter his comment engendered.

Suprisingly, both children stayed awake until the end of the play. However, by the time they arrived back in Gracechurch Street, they had succumbed to the lateness of the hour. Richard helped Mr. Gardiner carry the children to the nursery where their nurse changed them and put them to bed. Rejoining the ladies in the drawing room, the group enjoyed dessert and coffee.

As he prepared to return to Matlock House, Richard said, "I am afraid I must return to Rosings tomorrow. Please notify me when you plan to depart for the north, and I shall make arrangements for the additional carriage."

"I shall have Mary inform you in one of her letters," was Mr. Gardiner's response. "Mary, please walk our guest to the door."

Mary stood and walked with Richard into the hallway. "I wish you could stay longer," said Mary in hushed tones.

"So do I, but I will come back as often as I can."

"I know, but you shall be busy with your harvest before we go to Pemberley, and then we shall be away for a month."

"Yes, but hopefully you shall come to the harvest celebration at Rosings upon your return. It will give you a chance to see the house. You and Anne can discuss any changes you would like to have made to it in preparation for our wedding. Mary, will you grant me a kiss goodbye?"

Glancing towards the drawing room door, but seeing no one, she nodded and stepped closer, placing her hands gently against his chest. Richard's arms came around her, and he lowered his head until his lips met hers. He pulled her closer and deepened the kiss just a little. Before he could lose control, he broke the kiss and pulled her tightly against him, resting his cheek on her hair.

"Write to me soon, my dear Mary. Your letters warm my heart when I cannot be with you."

Drawing back slightly, she looked up at him and shyly said, "Your letters do the same for me. But now I shall have the feeling of being held in your arms and your kiss to dream of while we are apart."

Mary's words brought a huge grin to Richard's face. With a last kiss to each of her hands, he departed for home. He would be on the road to Rosings early in the morning.

CHAPTER 15

THOSE FIRST WEEKS at Miss Bates School for Girls were a miserable time for Lydia. She tried to be like her old self, but her exuberance was frowned on and earned her additional chores. When the way she had always behaved failed to get her the results to which she was accustomed, she withdrew and did not speak to anyone for the next week. Alone in her room one night, she had cried out her misery, but then recalled some of the things her father had said about trying to behave more like Jane and Lizzy. Lydia did not believe that she could be as serene as Jane; her feelings were just too intense for that. She also knew she did not have Lizzy's keen wit. She pondered what behaviors her sisters had in common, and she realized that they were both genuinely kind to everyone they met. They were also polite and listened to what others said rather than demand others' attentions. But was that enough? Would being kind, polite, and a good listener get Lydia the attention she sought? It was then she was struck by the truth; her sisters did not seek attention. They received attention because of the way they behaved. Mr. Bingley and Mr. Darcy felt drawn to her sisters by the way they acted, and both men preferred not to be in company with Lydia. Did she like Mr. Bingley and Mr. Darcy? Was that the kind of gentleman she wanted to attract? She also realized that Lizzy was happy and outgoing just like herself, only with better manners. Could she be herself and still be like her sisters? Throughout the sleepless night, she pondered these things, and by the time she drifted off to sleep she was determined to try.

Mr. Bennet had been at Pemberley for nearly two weeks—most of that time spent in the library. He had ridden out onto the estate with Darcy, Elizabeth, and Georgiana on a couple of occasions. He was delighted to see how accomplished a horsewoman Elizabeth had become, but then he always knew she would do well at any task to which she set her mind. He was very impressed with all that he saw and particularly the ease with which his dear Lizzy had adapted to her new home and station in life. Mr. Bennet could think of no one more deserving than she.

He had been away from Longbourn for some time now and knew he needed to return to attend to matters with Mrs. Bennet. However, he decided to remain a few more days so that he might see Jane and Mr. Bingley when they arrived at the end of the week.

Word arrived that a carriage had entering the park. Elizabeth could hardly contain her excitement. Finally, her dear Jane was to arrive! There was so much she wished to discuss with her sister. Elizabeth desired most earnestly to learn if Jane was as happy in her marriage as she was in hers.

Darcy and Elizabeth were waiting on the porch to greet the Bingleys when their carriage stopped before the door. Bingley had barely handed Jane down before the two ladies were crying out each other's names as they rushed to embrace each other. Darcy and Bingley stood back looking on the scene with amusement. Looking at Darcy with mischief in his eyes, Bingley cried Darcy's name and rushed forward, enveloping him in a bear hug and patting his back vigorously. Darcy reciprocated in good humor. Their louder voices finally got the attention of their wives, who laughingly observed them.

"I believe you have made your point, gentlemen," said Elizabeth with a grin.

The gentlemen broke apart, and Elizabeth moved to greet Charles, placing a kiss on his cheek. Darcy greeted Jane and offered his arm to lead her into the house. Bingley followed with Elizabeth on his arm. They went immediately to the drawing room for tea. The ladies, including Georgiana, were seated together on the sofa with the gentlemen in chairs across from them. Mr. Bennet sat to the side, observing the scene. Once everyone received tea and cakes, the conversation turned to the Bingleys travels.

"Everything we saw was very lovely, Lizzy. We visited the Pump Room at Bath and attended the assemblies there. They say the water is good for your health, but it tastes awful," said Jane with a laugh as Charles' face twisted in a grimace.

"You would indeed need to want a cure desperately if you could stomach the waters," her husband added.

"What did you think of the north country? Did you meet more of Charles' family?"

The Bingley's exchanged a look before Charles answered, "Indeed, I was able to introduce my dear Jane to all my family, and she was universally thought to be the sweetest woman they have ever met. Unfortunately, Caroline briefly intruded upon the gathering of my extended family, and she had nothing kind to say." Jane's eyes glistened with tears, but she quickly brushed them away. Darcy knew he would have to hear what Caroline said. He could not allow her to attempt to hurt Elizabeth again.

Not wishing to dwell on the subject of his sister, Charles quickly changed the direction of the conversation. "Darcy, has your steward had any luck in determining estates in the area that might be suitable for me to purchase?"

"Yes, we were lucky enough to learn of five that are available. I have the paperwork in my office. We can go over it and determine in which order you would like to see them. Then we can take day trips to visit each of them."

"That sounds wonderful, does it not, Jane?"

"Indeed. I do believe I will enjoy settling so near my dearest sister."

As they finished refreshments, Elizabeth had Mrs. Reynolds show the couple to their suite, as everyone chose to rest before dinner.

That evening after they dined, the ladies departed for the drawing room. The gentlemen remained over their port, but they were interrupted by the delivery of an express for Mr. Bennet. He excused himself to the library to read the letter. When the door closed behind him, Darcy looked at Bingley hesitantly.

"I do not wish to distress you by discussing this matter, but I must know what complaints your sister made when you saw her. I must be aware of her thinking so that I can ensure Elizabeth's safety."

"There was nothing new in her ranting, Darcy. She complained about the Bennet's low connections. She called Elizabeth a tart, who had used her arts and allurements to steal her betrothed from her and vowed to get her revenge. My aunt removed her from the party immediately, remaining in her home to ensure that Caroline did not return to cause more trouble. Her words had little effect on anyone, for Uncle Albert and Aunt Barbara had already told them so much about Jane and Elizabeth. They know of Caroline's grasping ways and did not take her words seriously. I do not believe you need worry." Darcy did not look convinced, but he let the matter drop.

They had just joined the ladies in the drawing room when Mr. Bennet came in holding the express he had received.

"I hope the letter did not bring bad news, Bennet," Darcy said with concern.

"Indeed not, but I must ask you, Lizzy, do you feel equal to preparing for a wedding along with all your other holiday activities?"

"What do you mean, Father? What wedding?"

"It seems that Mr. Fitzwilliam has proposed to Mary, and she accepted. They wish to marry from Pemberley when all the family is together for the holidays."

"Oh, how perfectl!" cried all three ladies at once.

"He certainly did not waste any time," said Darcy with a chuckle in which Bingley and Mr. Bennet joined him.

"Oh, perhaps we should go to town earlier than we planned so that we will have time to have Madame Colette prepare Mary's trousseau."

"We shall do whatever is needed, my love," said Darcy with an indulgent smile.

"You do plan to write with your approval immediately, Papa, do you not?" asked Jane.

"Do not worry yourselves; I shall respond immediately, even sending it by express rather than keep them waiting." Mr. Bennet was chuckling to himself when he turned to depart. "I shall be in the library should you have need of me."

"When you have finished your letter, sir," said Darcy, "please have a footman bring it to me, and I shall arrange for my messenger to deliver it." Mr. Bennet nodded and continued on his way.

As conversation in the drawing room continued, it became evident to the gentlemen that their presence was not needed. Accordingly, Darcy invited Bingley to play a round or two of billiards, and they departed without the notice of their wives and sisters. When a break in the conversation allowed Elizabeth to notice the men's absence, she wished good night to Georgiana and invited Jane to join her in her private sitting room. She rang for Mrs. Reynolds and asked for a tray of hot chocolate and biscuits to be delivered there.

Once comfortably ensconced in Elizabeth's sitting room, cups of cocoa in hand, the sisters talked late into the night about married life and the many changes they had experienced. It was quickly apparent to each that her dearest sister was incandescently happy and very much in love with her husband.

Mr. Bennet departed for Longbourn the next day, only slightly later than his express to Mr. Fitwilliam. He thought long and hard about his plans for dealing with his wife upon his return to his ancestral home. Thomas spent the first day after his arrival catching up on all the correspondence that had come during his absence. He was surprised to have already received a letter from Lydia. It spoke of her despair and loneliness. He questioned whether he had made the right choice, but knew that she was desperately in need of guidance and education, so he said a silent prayer for her improved spirits and circumstances. He immediately set about replying to his letter and had the groom take it to Meryton to post. After his correspondence was completed, he met with his steward to learn about the state of the estate and the preparations underway for the harvest. They spent the next day riding out over the estate, ensuring that everything continued as it should. Lastly, he met with Mr. Philips to revise his will.

Finally, he could delay no longer. Mr. Bennet mounted his horse and headed in the direction of the dower house. Upon arriving, he tied his horse to a nearby tree and, taking a deep breath, knocked on the door.

The maid opened the door and directed Mr. Bennet to the parlor where his wife sat.

"At last, you have returned. You have kept me waiting an inordinate amount of time."

"I am pleased to see you as well, Mrs. Bennet," was his dry response.

"You said you were taking Lydia to school and would return shortly, but you left me alone nearly a month! Obviously, you have no compassion for my needs or my poor nerves."

"With so much solitude and quiet, your nerves should have had nothing to disturb them, my dear. Did you perhaps go into Meryton during my absence and not find the welcome you thought to have?"

"How could I have gone to the village when you have not provided me a carriage?"

"It did not deter you when you accosted our daughters in the sweet shop."

"Do not speak to me of those disgraceful girls. This is all your Lizzy's fault, and she convinced my sweet Jane to treat me in so reprehensible a manner," said Mrs. Bennet with a sniff, her handkerchief fluttering.

"There is only one person to blame for your present situation, and it is not Elizabeth. You are responsible for the poor behavior you exhibited. It is that and that alone which led to your stay in the dower house, Mrs. Bennet."

"Am I to be left here to rot, Mr. Bennet?"

"What do you think should occur next, madam?"

"I demand you return me to my proper place as mistress of Longbourn, and expect you to force our ungrateful daughters to apologize to me."

"Have learned nothing during your time here?"

"I did not need to learn anything. It is our daughters who need to learn obedience to their mother and to respect my wishes."

"Do they not also deserve to have their wishes respected?"

"I have no notion of what you speak, Mr. Bennet." He heard another sniff from his wife.

"I have neither the time nor the patience to play games with you, wife. You know very well that you did not show respect for the wishes of our daughters regarding *their* wedding."

"They neither onc possess the knowledge of how such things should be done. I only wished to uphold my reputation as a hostess by arranging a wedding and wedding breakfast befitting the status of their husbands."

"Yet both gentlemen told you they would prefer a smaller more intimate event than you wished to plan, so your excuse will not do, Mrs. Bennet. Also, if our daughters were not prepared to plan such an event, then you have failed in your duties as their mother, for your primary responsibility is to teach them to manage homes of their own and to prepare just such events."

"I believe you need additional time to reflect upon your deficiencies as a mother. I shall leave you for now and return tomorrow to see if you can explain to me where you have failed." So saying, Mr. Bennet excused himself and departed, leaving a shocked and annoyed wife in his wake.

Mr. Bennet returned the next day to find that his wife was still abed at ten in the morning. He left word with the maid that he would call the next day. Mrs. Bennet's frustration grew as she was left to wait another day in her prison.

On the fourth day following his return, Mr. Bennet again arrived at the dower house in mid-morning. He was pleased to see that his wife had roused herself to be available when he called.

"You have had two days to think. Can you tell me, Mrs. Bennet, where you have erred in your instruction of our daughters?"

"There was no failure on my part. Our daughters were not attentive to the things I tried to teach them. Your Lizzy was particularly guilty of this, as she was forever rambling about the countryside in her unladylike manner."

"I believe it more likely they tried to be attentive, but you spent most of your time in frivolous gossip and directing them how to trap a husband than in providing the needed instruction," countered her husband.

"I am grateful Mrs. Gardiner was there to provide the lessons you failed to give Elizabeth and Jane. Now she is handling your responsibilities with Mary and Kitty, as well. It is fortunate we have such a charming and accomplished woman to step up and provide the needed guidance for our daughters."

"She is merely a tradesman's daughter and a tradesman's wife. I, as the Mistress of Longbourn, am far superior to Madeline," said Mrs. Bennet with derision.

"She may be a tradesman's daughter and wife, but she has been accepted among the first circles of society. Your behavior would be a disgrace to our family among those same circles."

"You dare to insult me, your wife, in such a despicable manner!"

"I speak only the truth. Unless and until you can improve your behavior, I promise you will not be attending any events hosted by our daughters or their relations. After the disgraceful way you treated our daughters, I would find it suprising if you heard from them, much less received any invitations," was Mr. Bennet's calm reply.

"They would not dare to disrespect me in such a manner, particularly not my dear Jane."

"They showed you respect at every turn; it was you who failed to display respect to them. Children love and obey because they are children. Our eldest daughters are grown women who have every right to be respected for themselves alone. I must admit that your continued unwillingness to recognize any fault in yourself makes me question the wisdom of allowing you to return to your position as Mistress of Longbourn."

"Do you plan to keep me prisoner here forever?" groused his aggrieved wife.

Mr. Bennet was silent for several minutes as he studied his wife. Eventually, he said, "I will allow you to return to the house, but there will be several changes, or you will find yourself returned to the dower house, permanently."

"What on earth could you possibly mean by changes?"

"I will no longer tolerate any loud speaking in my home. If you cannot speak in a proper tone of voice, you shall be removed. There is to be no screeching and wailing about your nerves nor taking to your bed. If you have a concern, I expect you to address me as a rational person in an appropriate tone of voice. Also, you will have no allowance for the next quarter. If your behavior improves, you shall receive it the following quarter, but only if there has been significant improvement in your behavior. Also, I will not tolerate your speaking ill of anyone—most particularly our children. You shall be required to spend at least two hours per day reading and improving your mind. It is not only our younger daughters who need improvement."

"How dare you –"

Mr. Bennet held up his hand to stop her remarks. "I am not finished. We will also be learning to live on less, so that I may put more aside for my daughters' schooling and the remaining girls' dowries. Do you think that you can manage to conduct yourself according to these guidelines?"

"How dare you treat me so, Mr. Bennet. I am your wife, and I expect to be given my due."

"You forget, madam, a wife must accede to her husband's wishes. If she does not, he may treat her any way he pleases. I have allowed you to rule our home for much too long, and it nearly brought disgrace upon our family when someone revealed your behavior and that of our youngest daughters to members of the ton. I can assure you that were I to take you to London and allow you to behave as you have in the past, it would bring shame to our family and our younger daughters would never be received by good families."

"Our neighbors have never found fault with my behavior. I think you are attempting to manipulate me, Mr. Bennet."

"I assure you, madam, I do no such thing. Now I shall ask you again. Can you conduct yourself properly and within the guidelines I have set?" When Mrs. Bennet did not answer immediately, Mr. Bennet asked, "Do you wish to remain here and think on it for another night?"

"Certainly not. I wish to come home immediately."

"Well, then I shall wait while you pack. However, bear in mind I shall allow you only one warning when your behavior slips, so I advise you to be ever mindful of the things I have said."

He picked up a book and began to read as he waited for his wife. He heard her start to screech for the maid, only to moderate her voice to something more appropriate. Mr. Bennet smiled slightly and prayed that his wife would strive to improve herself.

The first week or so back at Longbourn's manor house, Mrs. Bennet attempted to comply with her husband's wishes. If her voice began to rise in volume, a raised eyebrow from her husband was enough to make her modulate her speaking. She frequently started sentences that would cause her husband's disapproval but managed to stop herself before saying something unsuitable. She was angry the first time she heard Mrs. Hill turning Mrs. Philips away, but remained silent, venting her frustrations quietly in the privacy of her bedchamber. The first Sunday that she attended services with her husband, he arranged it so that they arrived at the last minute and rushed her out at the end of services before she could speak to anyone. It did not occur to Mrs. Bennet that none of her friends had approached her to ask after her health even after such a long absence.

The second week seemed to be easier for her than the first week, though she recited Mr. Bennet's rules as though they were a mantra. As they entered the third week, Mrs. Bennet approached her husband with the request for some new clothes. She said she needed something more befitting the mother-in-law of two such wealthy gentlemen.

"You will have to make do," said her husband. "As I mentioned, we are reducing our expenses at present to pay for our daughters' schooling. As you are not currently receiving company, you have no need of new clothes."

"But what will people think if they see Mr. Darcy's bride's mother in such unfashionable clothing?"

"As I said, you do not go out in company, so no one will see what you are wearing accept at church on Sunday."

Though annoyed with her husband's answer, Mrs. Bennet rather ungraciously allowed the subject to drop.

Several days later, as they were breaking their fast, Mrs. Bennet arrived in the dining room to see a stack of letters beside her husband's plate. In a rather annoyed voice, she said, "Must you read your business correspondence over breakfast, Mr. Bennet?"

"This is not business correspondence, my dear. These are my letters from our daughters."

"Are there no letters for me?" Mr. Bennet shook his head. "Not even from my dear Lydia?" asked Mrs. Bennet.

"You may recall that after demanding that Lydia write to you, you then expressed your displeasure with her desire to go to school. I am sure she is under the impression that you do not wish to

264 ∞ Linda Thompson

hear from her. Perhaps you should write to her and apologize for your behavior at her departure. Then she would realize you want to hear from her. However, I will need to read any letter that you send to her before it is sent, so please give it to me before it is sealed. I shall read it, seal it, and send it to Lydia."

"Why must you read my letters?" came Mrs. Bennet's indignant question.

"I must ensure that you are continuing to comply with my request and speaking only kindly and positive things to our daughter."

Mrs. Bennet sniffed in annoyance. "Well, since our daughters seem to have time to write to only one of their parents, what news do they share?"

"Kitty writes of having been to the opera and several other outings. She also speaks of enjoying her art lessons. The sketch she enclosed shows that her natural abilities are improving even more."

"What use is drawing? It will not help her to catch a husband. She should be using her time to attract some gentleman's attention."

"Kitty is too young to be married."

"But I will not have the funds to support myself, much less several unmarried daughters. You know Mary will never find a man who wants her."

"That is where you are wrong, Mrs. Bennet. Mary is currently engaged to Mr. Richard Fitzwilliam, the second son of the Earl of Matlock and the owner of Rosings Park in Kent."

"Whatever would the gentleman owner of a large estate want with such a staid and sober girl as Mary?"

"Mrs. Bennet, this is your first and only warning on this subject. I told you I will not allow you to speak disrespectfully of anyone, particularly our daughters."

"I was not speaking disrespectfully," she said defensively. "I was just surprised. Rosings Park, that name is familiar to me – " Mrs. Bennet's voice trailed off as she tried to remember where she had heard that name before. Finally, she cried, "Mr. Bennet, it is wrong of you to tease me so. Rosings Park belongs to Lady Catherine de Bourgh. Mr. Collins spoke endlessly of both his patroness and her estate often enough for me to know that."

"That was true, but it is no longer the case. Mr. Fitzwilliam now owns the estate and is engaged to our Mary."

"Well, then you shall have to give me funds to begin planning the wedding. There is much to do. Do you know when they wish to marry?"

"Yes, they will be marrying during the Christmas holidays at Pemberley."

"Oooh, we are going to Pemberley for Christmas! Perhaps I can forgive her for not permitting me to plan the wedding and wedding breakfast since I will get to see Pemberley."

"I am afraid you will not be in attendance. You are not welcome at Pemberley for the foreseeable future," remarked Mr. Bennet.

"What do you mean I am not welcome in my daughter's home?" screeched Mrs. Bennet.

"Mrs. Bennet this is your first and only warning about moderating the tone and volume of your voice. Why on earth would you expect to be welcomed in Mr. and Mrs. Darcy's home after the abominable way you treated them at your last meeting? Your significantly improved behavior will have to stand the test of time and a proper apology will need to be issued before you can even hope for such a thing. Perhaps, we should change the subject since discussion of our daughters does not seem to be something you can do within the boundaries I have set for you."

"No, I wish to hear of my beautiful Jane and my dear Lydia."

"Jane and Mr. Bennet are searching for an estate near Pemberley to purchase. I do not believe they will renew the lease on Netherfield Park." Mrs. Bennet frowned on hearing these words. She did not wish to have her daughter leave the neighborhood. Having her daughter as the mistress of the largest house in the neighborhood would increase her importance. "And what of Lydia?" she asked, the sound of annoyance in her quiet voice.

"After a difficult start, Lydia is beginning to enjoy her time at school. She writes that she is in frequent contact with her older sisters, trying to understand why the things you taught her are in direct conflict with what she is learning at school."

"What do you mean by that?" Mrs. Bennet demanded.

"The forward behavior you so encouraged is frowned upon by polite society. She is finding it difficult to understand why you would encourage her in behavior that is unacceptable and extremely forward."

"How else was I to ensure they all found husbands to support them and me?"

"It is not up to their husbands to support you. I will leave sufficient funds for you to live a moderate lifestyle without excessive extravagances," said Mr. Bennet firmly. "The economy we practice now will help you survive on the portion I leave you."

"I will not live moderately. I expect to be kept in high style just as my daughters are," Mrs. Bennet sniffed. "It is the least those ungrateful girls can do after all I have done for them."

"Mrs. Bennet, you had just spoken disrespectfully of our daughters again. I believe you shall return to the dower house for the remainder of your days."

"No, I shall do no such a thing. I shall go to my sister's. She will insist her husband make you keep me in my proper place." Mrs. Bennet pushed her chair back so far that it was upended as she stormed from the room. She took a bonnet from a hook by the door and took up a parasol that rested nearby before marching from the house.

She had not traveled far along the road towards Meryton when she came upon Lady Lucas and her daughters. She called out, "Lady Lucas, Oh, Lady Lucas," but the ladies did not look in her direction nor acknowledge her words, quickly turning down the lane to their home. Puzzled, Mrs. Bennet continued walking towards Meryton. A carriage carrying her friend Mrs. Goulding passed by, and though Mrs. Bennet waved at her friend, Mrs. Goulding lifted her nose in the air and turned her head away. Wondering at the lady's strange behavior, Mrs. Bennet continued walking. By the time she reached the village, she was tired and thirsty. Fanny stopped into the sweet shop, looking about for a table. Before she could find one, the owner, Mr. Brown, stepped towards her. Speaking quietly so as not to disturb his customers, Mr. Brown said, "I would ask you to leave, Mrs. Bennet. Your last visit was disgraceful and upsetting to my patrons. I do not want that to happen again. You will receive no service here."

Mrs. Bennet could not believe what she was hearing. She started to splutter, but Mr. Brown grasped her elbow firmly and guided her out of the shop, closing the door firmly behind her.

Mrs. Bennet stomped away from the shop in the direction of her sister's house. As she passed the mercantile, Mrs. Long was exiting.

"Oh, Mrs. Long, it is a pleasure to see you. How have you been? What is the latest news?" Mrs. Bennet was pleased to see her old friend, but that pleasure quickly faded as Mrs. Long gave her the direct cut and walked away.

Tears began to pool in her eyes, and Mrs. Bennet hurried towards the Philips' home as quickly as she could. When she reached the door to her sister's home, she knocked. Mrs. Philips opened the door but did not look pleased to see her sister.

"Dear sister, you shall not believe what has happened to me this morning." Mrs. Bennet moved as though to enter the house, but Mrs. Philips did not give way.

"I am sure that whatever has occurred was no less than you deserved, Fanny. I am ashamed of the way you behaved to Jane and Elizabeth, and I have no desire to see you until your behavior is much improved." With that, Mrs. Philips closed the door in her sister's face.

Her face flaming and her head down, Mrs. Bennet practically ran all the way back to Longbourn. When she entered the house, she saw her trunks sitting in the hallway. She looked up to see her husband coming from his study. For a brief moment, he felt sympathy for his wife, but it did not last long. "That hateful Lizzy. The ghastly treatment I received from the neighbors today is all her fault. I have been humiliated and cut by everyone I encountered this day, including my own sister. I shall never forgive her for the treatment I received. I shall see she is miser – " Mrs. Bennet's words trailed off as she clutched at her chest. Her eyes rolled up in her head, and she slumped to the floor.

Mr. Bennet called out for Mrs. Hill to send for Mr. Jones immediately as he rushed forward, kneeling at his wife's side. He placed his head upon her chest but did not hear a heartbeat. Then Mr. Bennet placed his cheek near her lips but could feel no breath upon his face. He lifted her in his arms and placed her on the sofa in the parlor. Mrs. Hill came rushing in with Mrs. Bennet's smelling salts in her hand. Mr. Bennet shook his head, halting her progress. The housekeeper stepped up beside the body and reached down for her mistress' wrist. Gripping it as the apothecary had taught her, she could find no pulse. Turning she exited the room, and when she returned, she closed Mrs. Bennet's eyes and covered her body with a sheet. She guided Mr. Bennet back to his study and returned to wait in the parlor for Mr. Jones to arrive.

CHAPTER 16

Upon Mr. Bennet's departure, Darcy and Bingley reviewed the information regarding the estates available for purchase. Where he had personal information, in addition to the documentation his steward provided, Darcy told Bingley everything he knew about the homes or the families that occupied them. Then over the next two weeks, the two couples visited all of the properties for sale. Two of them had been close enough to visit and return to Pemberley on the same day. The other two had been slightly further, and the estate agent had arranged for the housekeeper to put the couples up for the night.

After viewing all the properties, the couples reviewed all that they had learned. They took into account the condition of the land and house and any furnishings that would remain with them. They discussed the income potential and other opportunities nearby that might increase the income of the estate. In the end, Bingley and Jane decided to purchase Ashford Hills, which was only ten miles south of Lambton. The estate got its name from the ash trees that lined the drive to the manor house. The manor was built in the Georgiana style of the last century with limestone from the White Peaks but had been well maintained by the previous owners. The home had belonged to Peter Covington, a widower who died childless. His only remaining relations descended from his great grandfather's younger brother, who had struck out to make his fortune in the new world. As that branch of the family had risen to prominence in America, they had no need of the house. It was being sold with all the furnishings, livestock, and other items as part of the sale. However, because the family did not wish to be bothered with the property, it was being sold at an extremely good price. The estate was slightly larger than Netherfield Park and included a walnut grove, flocks of sheep, and filled tenant homes. The furnishings were of an older style but in good condition. A little paint and some new fabrics would make it a delightful place for the Bingley family and all its future generations.

Bingley and Darcy had just returned from the solicitor's office where they had signed the final papers making Ashford Hills the property of Charles Bingley. They were celebrating in the blue drawing room at Pemberley, when Benton, Pemberley's butler, entered the room carrying a letter on a silver tray.

"Pardon me, Mr. Darcy, this express just arrived."

Darcy took the letter from the tray as the butler bowed and departed the room. Looking at the sender's direction, a look of concern passed over his face. He made brief eye contact with others before breaking the seal. His eyes quickly scanned over the contents, while his hand unconsciously reached for his wife's.

"What is it, William? What has happened?" came Elizabeth's worried voice.

"The letter is from your father, dearest." Elizabeth's face paled. "Do not worry dearest; he is well. However, it seems your mother had a severe attack of apoplexy from which she did not recover."

"Please, may I read father's letter?"

"There is nothing much to report. Because of the warm weather they buried her the next day. Your father suggests a memorial service when next we are all together at Longbourn."

"What caused the attack," asked the gentle voice of Jane.

"Mr. Bennet does not give specifics," came Darcy's vague reply.

"William, please give me father's letter." Elizabeth realized when Darcy ignored her first request that there was something in the letter he did not wish her to know.

"Lizzy, my love, there is no need for you to read this. I have told you what it contains."

"Then humor me and allow me to read it for myself."

Darcy knew his wife would not relent, so he handed her the letter and increased his grip on her hand.

Jane moved to the seat beside Elizabeth so that she could read the letter for herself.

Though tears had gathered in her eyes as she read, Elizabeth's voice was calm, the undertone of hurt unmistakable, as she spoke. "I see to the end I was the cause of all the problems in mother's life. I had hoped she would learn and grow as my sisters are doing, but perhaps she was too set in her ways to consider changing."

Jane put her arms around her sister and hugged her tightly while Darcy brought Elizabeth's hand to his lips for a gentle kiss.

"Lizzy, you must not blame yourself for this. Mother was given an opportunity to improve, and she chose not to take it. For all her silliness, she was proud of her place in life as the mistress of Longbourn. That pride would not allow her to admit to errors, so she must always have someone to blame."

"Jane is right, dear sister. You have been gracious and understanding through all of your mother's mistreatment. Mrs. Bennet's death is not your fault." Bingley added his thoughts to those of his sweet wife.

"My love," said Darcy as he stared deeply into Elizabeth's eyes. "Your mother had ample opportunities to correct her behavior, but she saw only what she wanted to see. She was incapable of seeing her mistakes—much like Lady Catherine. They each chose to be isolated from the joys of their family. They are responsible for their behavior, not you."

"Thank you, all. I know that what you say is true, but it is still difficult to know that she was speaking ill of me at the time of her passing."

"Do you wish to travel to Longbourn for a memorial service?" Darcy asked those present. "We could fetch Lydia from school before doing so."

"Oh, poor Lydia! She was always mother's favorite. I wonder if father has contacted her. Perhaps we should travel to see her to ensure that she is handling the news well," worried Elizabeth.

"You and Jane should write to her, and I will send it express. I will have the express rider wait for her reply," offered Darcy. "We can be to her within a day if she desires our company or to return for the memorial service."

"But that leaves her comfortless for two or three days. I believe we should go straight to the school," was Elizabeth's anxious reply.

"If that is what will give you comfort, my love, then we shall leave at first light," said Darcy, as he pulled her tighter into his embrace, resting his cheek on her hair.

As Darcy lovingly held his wife, Jane rang the bell and asked that arrangements be made for them to travel early the next morning. They would stay only one night before returning to Pemberley. Mrs. Reynolds rushed to do as requested.

The dinner celebration of the purchase of Ashford Hills was somewhat subdued after Mr. Bennet's news, but Elizabeth made an effort to put off her self-pity, for she was delighted that her dearest Jane would be living so close to Pemberley. She reveled in the thought of how frequently they would all be in company with one another and the joy that would come from watching their children grow up together.

However, later as she lay in her husband's arms, she could not hold back the tears and the hurt. "What is wrong with me? Why could she not love me?" Darcy had no answer that would remove his wife's pain, but he held her close throughout the night and whispered words of love to her.

The Darcy carriage made good time on its way to Miss Bates' school in Winksley. The distance was great enough that the party had to spend a night on the road and made it to the school midday on their second day of travel. Darcy had sent an express to the headmistress explaining the situation and giving an approximate time for their arrival. They were shown immediately to the headmistress' sitting room, and Lydia's presence was requested.

Lydia had always been closer to Jane than to Elizabeth, so it was Jane who would speak for the group. When the door opened and Lydia entered the room, she rushed straight for her sisters.

She threw her arms around Jane, "Oh, Jane I am so happy to see you." However, rather than remain in the comfort of her eldest sister's arms, she moved to stand before Elizabeth. "Lizzy, I am very glad to see you, too. I am so sorry for the way I acted. I hope that you can one day forgive me for being so mean and selfish."

Elizabeth wrapped her arms around her youngest sister. "Of course, I forgive you. You are my dear sister, and I love you."

"I do not deserve your love or forgiveness, but I shall try to be worthy of it," said the young girl. Her humility was surprising to the visitors.

"Lydia," said Jane as she led her sister to a small settee. "When was the last letter you received from Papa?"

"I received one today, but I have not yet had a chance to read it," said the girl as she pulled it from her pocket.

"I believe you should read it now."

The serious tone of Jane's voice made Lydia anxious, so she broke the seal and read her father's letter. "Mama is dead," was the only comment she made.

Jane and Elizabeth looked at each other, an expression of perplexity on their faces. Finally, Jane said, "You are taking the news better than I would have expected. You have always been so close to Mama. We were afraid this news would be difficult for you to accept."

"Well, yes, I suppose it is sad, but I began to see Mama in a different light before leaving for school. She made it very clear that her love for us was conditional on doing what she wanted."

"What do you mean, Lydia?" Elizabeth questioned quietly.

Lydia explained what her mother had said when she told her she wanted to go to school. "I wanted a chance to grow into my best self, to learn to be more than the selfish, spoiled girl I had been before. Mama just wanted to keep me beside her so that she would have someone to order about and to whom she could complain. I realized that was all she had ever done. She never was happy with one of us when we made a decision contrary to her choice. My behavior, just like Mama's, was driving all of my sisters away. I may not have known how to show it well, but I love my sisters, and I did not wish to lose them. I guess that it was Mama's selfish voice that did not allow me to show them how I felt."

"Oh, Lydia, we love you, too!" cried Jane and Elizabeth almost as one. The sisters wrapped their arms around one another as tears began to fall. After several minutes had passed, Darcy cleared his throat, recalling the ladies to their surroundings.

"We are discussing going home for a memorial service for Mama," Jane remarked to Lydia. "We came to get you to join us."

"I thank you for your consideration and for making the long trip, but I would prefer to remain at school. I will make my peace with Mama the next time I am at Longbourn. I do not think you should make a special trip either. She would see it as her due and not appreciate that she was not deserving of your show of love and respect."

Jane and Elizabeth were startled by Lydia's remarks. "You do not wish to go home?" Elizabeth's voice was confused.

"No, I believe it would be best if I return to my studies. I wasted so much time following Mama's instructions and now have much still to learn, if I am to be as good a lady as you and Jane," was her simple reply.

The two couples exchanged looks and silently agreed to allow Lydia to make this decision on her own. Darcy excused himself and went to speak with the headmistress. He explained to her what had occurred and asked to be informed if Lydia later showed signs of distress. While he was speaking with the headmistress, Elizabeth shared the news of Mary's engagement and spoke of the upcoming holidays at Pemberley when the wedding would occur. She offered to send a coach and a maid to retrieve Lydia so that she could celebrate with the family, an offer Lydia was quick to accept.

After many expressions of affection and comments about writing, the two couples took their leave. They returned to the inn where they had spent the previous night and traveled on to Pemberley the next day.

Upon their arrival at Pemberley, a message from Mr. Gardiner was awaiting them. Darcy had sent an express to gain his opinion about the memorial. Mr. Gardiner, though saddened by his sister's demise, was unwilling to change the family's summer plans. He suggested they gather in the spring when those residing in Derbyshire made their way to London for the season.

Darcy spoke with Elizabeth, Jane, and Bingley and suggested that they make their way to Longbourn and meet the Gardiner party there before they all returned to Pemberley. He did not wish it to appear that the family was being disrespectful to Mrs. Bennet's memory. She did not necessarily deserve such attentions but reminded the others of the importance of showing proper respect, whether it was deserved or not.

Consequently, letters were dispatched to Gracechurch Street and Longbourn stating the plans to meet for the memorial on the third of August. Jane and Bingley set off two days after returning from the visit to Lydia. They were anxious to return to Netherfield and make the preparations for their move to Ashford Hills. Darcy and Elizabeth would follow in two weeks' time. They would stay at Netherfield with the Bingleys, leaving room for the Gardiner family at Longbourn.

CHAPTER 17

MICHAEL AMESBURY'S WEEKS back in England had been very busy. His father was gone and his older brother, Ralph, had stepped into the title of viscount. They had never gotten along very well, and now that Michael had amassed greater wealth than his brother possessed, he did not expect their rancor to end. The business matters that had required his attention after his long absence from England were finally completed. He had also been to White's once but had remained in the corner behind his newspaper listening to the latest gossip to understand what was happening in society. He had learned of the death and financial ruin of Earl Dalbert and wondered what had become of his childhood love, Lady Marjorie. For whatever reason, Majorie had preferred him to his older brother; in fact, as he recalled that was where the problems with his brother began.

His years in India had brought him great wealth, but he had also seen dreadful poverty, tragedy, and loss. After learning about the Earl of Dalbert's downfall, Michael made arrangments to purchase the earl's estate and townhouse. Tomorrow, before she was notified of the potential buyer, Michael planned to present himself to Marjorie and make her an offer of marriage, again.

When they were younger, Michael had proposed to Marjorie, believing she was the love of his life and certain she felt the same for him. Secretly Marjorie had scoffed at his proposal. As the daughter of an earl, she felt sure she could do better than a second son with little wealth. However, Marjorie had made her father's disapproval her excuse. Now, however, he was wealthy beyond his wildest dreams and was hopeful of her acceptance. When she agreed to the marriage, he would present her with her family homes as an engagement gift. She may not love him at present because of his lengthy absence, but Michael was sure they could recapture the love they once had.

At half past eleven the next morning, Michael Amesbury knocked at the door of Dalbert House. When it opened, he beheld a diminutive, elderly lady with white hair whom he recognized as Marjorie's aunt.

"Miss Vaughan, is it not?" Michael spoke politely, but no look of recognition appeared on the elderly woman's face. "It is Michael Amesbury. My family lived near Dalbcrt Hall."

A smile appeared on Miss Vaughan's face as she remembered the young boy that had followed Marjorie about in her youth. "My goodness! Michael Amesbury, it has been some time, has it not? Do come in."

Michael stepped into the hall and looked about, noting the lack of furniture and the paintings missing from the walls. "I have come to see Lady Marjorie if I might."

"Certainly, follow me. You can wait in the drawing room while I fetch Marjorie."

Michael stepped into the room she indicated and took up a place near the window. He waited for more than a quarter of an hour before he heard footsteps on the stairs. She swept into the room and did not see anyone. "I do not have time for games, Aunt. There is no one here."

"Actually, there is."

Marjorie turned in the direction of the slightly familiar voice, but the light from the window behind him kept his face in shadow. "Well, then state your business, I am quite busy today." The gentleman stepped into the light. Marjorie gasped as recognition struck. "Michael!"

"Hello, Marjorie."

"What are you doing here?"

"Is that any way to greet an old friend?"

"How long have you been back in England?"

"I returned several weeks ago. I received word of my father's passing and had achieved the goals I set for myself during my travels, so I decided to return home."

"What goals were those?"

"Will you not ask me to be seated?"

"Oh, yes, please," she waved her hand towards a pair of chairs. Once they were both seated Marjorie repeated her question. "What goals were those?"

"Why those you charged me with, of course."

"I do not recall charging you with goals or anything else."

"Do you not? I believe when you refused my proposal you told me that only great wealth would allow me to gain your father's approval for our marriage."

"Do not be ridiculous. We were but children then."

"You were ten and six and I a year older, but certainly old enough to know our minds. I had loved you for years, and you said you loved me as well."

"Did you come for a purpose? I have some things to attend to today."

Michael was a bit put off by Marjorie's attitude but realized that she was unaware that her future was about to be secure and her homes saved. Anyone would behave defensively living in her present circumstances. "Of course, I came with a purpose. I came to ask for your hand in marriage. As a wedding gift, I plan to purchase your estate and this townhouse so that you will not be forced to leave your home."

Marjorie's mouth gaped at the man before her, but her mind worked quickly. "But you have been gone for the last eight years. We hardly know each other anymore."

"You have never been far from my thoughts. I traveled great distances and worked hard to make myself acceptable to your father. If you had entirely forgotten me, you would have been married by now." Michael's voice held a wealth of emotion, as he stared at the woman he had loved for most of his life.

Marjorie wondered if she could tolerate him until she reached the altar. He had been a nuisance when they were children, following her everywhere, though she had enjoyed the way he would fall all over himself to please her, doing anything she asked. She looked down to compose her features. When she looked back up, her eyes were limpid, her cheeks gently flushed. When she spoke, her voice was tremulous.

"I never dreamed this would happen. You were gone so long. I feared you were dead. Michael, it would make me so happy to marry you."

Michael Amesbury's smile grew larger in his happiness. He had thought of nothing else over the past eight years. He swept Marjorie into his arms and kissed her with all the pent up passion he held for this woman he had loved since childhood.

Pulling back he looked into her face, "I do not wish to wait. I want to marry as soon as arrangements can be made."

"Michael, I shall need some time to have a wedding gown made and, though it embarrasses me to ask, I will need funds for the purchases I must make. If you are aware the estate and townhouse are for sale, you know my father has left our family's finances in a rather uncomfortable state. Things have been difficult of late." Marjorie looked down in embarrassment, but she was rapidly planning her revenge on both Caroline Bingley and Elizabeth Darcy.

Michael sat at his desk reviewing the marriage settlement for Marjorie. He was aware that James Wescott was her only living male relative and had made plans to meet him to sign the documents. As he was attending to his business, a knock came to the door of his hotel suite. When his valet opened the door, a footman presented him with the mail. He noted bills from the dressmaker, milliner, bootmaker, and several other shops. He had not realized how much would be necessary for a wedding. He would allow her to spend what she wished for the time being, but would insist that she manage not to overspend her generous pin money in the future.

As he stepped into White's, he heard the unwelcome voice of his brother. He looked about for Wescott but did not see him. Crossing the room towards a quiet corner table, he turned his head away to avoid his brother's notice, but to no avail.

"Well, well, little brother. How did a *cit* like you get into White's?"

"Ralph," he said shortly, "I believe the club is open to all gentlemen."

"But you are no longer a gentleman. You are a *cit*." Ralph put all the contempt he could manage in his drunken state into the insult. His hatred for his brother had not died during Michael's long absence from England.

"I am the son of a gentleman and soon to be a property owner. I do not know what more is required for being a gentleman. It cannot be good manners, as they allow you within these hallowed walls."

"Why, you – " Ralph attempted to rise from his seat, but he was a little the worse for drink.

"Amesbury, old friend! I am delighted to see you."

Michael turned to see James Wescott advancing on him. He held out his hand to his friend, and they clapped each other on the back in greeting.

"Wescott, I am happy to see you again. Thank you for meeting me! Ignoring his brother, now slumped in his chair, Michael led Wescott to the table he had spotted earlier.

"What have you been doing with yourself, Amesbury? It has been an age since I last saw you. I heard you were out of the country."

"Indeed, I have been in India for the last eight years. I needed a fortune to win the girl who owns my heart, but the usual careers for second sons do not offer such opportunities, so I had to search further afield."

The two men ordered a drink and discussed the happenings of the last few years.

"You are settling down?" asked Michael in surprise.

"I am. I am engaged to a delightful young woman. We met through some mutual friends."

"Is she one of the new crop of debutantes?"

"No, her father is in trade and extremely successful."

"Trade," said Michael in surprise.

"I have recently discovered the value of weighing people on their individual merits rather than on their social circle."

"Well, that is a surprise. Are you truly James Wescott?"

Wescott laughed. "Yes. However, you spending eight years laboring away for a fortune just to impress a woman is not the man I remember either."

"I have loved her all my life," said Michael earnestly. "I would do anything for her."

Wescott was disturbed by his friend's words. He easily recalled the adoration his friend felt for his cousin in their youth. "And who might this young woman be that you worked so hard to impress?"

"Why, Marjorie, of course. I have loved her since we were children."

"Have you seen her since returning to London?"

"I proposed a week ago. I asked to meet you to have you sign the marriage settlements for her."

"Does Marjorie know you are meeting with me?"

"I did not mention it to her, but as the only remaining male member of her family, who else would I speak to?"

"She has reached her majority and could sign for herself," remarked Wescott.

"I am aware of that. However, when I proposed to her the first time, she told me her father would never accept a second son with no fortune. I wanted to be sure that her family was aware I could support an earl's daughter in the style to which she was accustomed."

"That is very honorable of you, but you should know, Marjorie is not the girl you remember. In fact, we have had a difference of opinion recently, and she is no longer speaking to me."

"But you two have always seemed so close. What caused your misunderstanding?"

Wescott paused before speaking. He wanted to convey the truth without coloring the other man's opinion of his cousin. "Marjorie requested that I compromise an innocent young lady, so she could compromise the lady's betrothed and force him to marry her instead."

"That does not sound like Marjorie. Are you sure the young lady was innocent?"

"There is no question about it. However, as I came to realize her victim's worth, I could not accommodate my cousin's request. She is no longer speaking to me and has publicly claimed she will get her revenge."

"I am sure there must be more to it then you have said. I cannot imagine Marjorie acting so poorly."

"I will not try to convince you, but I would ask you to take your time before the wedding and get to know Marjorie again. Are you aware that her voucher to Almack's has been revoked? Lady Jersey and Lady Cowper both witnessed the exposure and downfall of Marjorie's plot against Miss Bennet."

Michael was startled to hear that her behavior could have been atrocious enough to cause such a consequence. It was hard for him to accept that the girl he loved could have changed so much. "The announcement has already been sent to the papers."

"Do you want me to sign the paperwork or would you prefer to delay for a few weeks?"

"I will let you know," said Michael thoughtfully.

CHAPTER 18

RICHARD RETURNED TO London to see Mary and the Gardiners off on their trip to Derbyshire. He had learned of the death of Mrs. Bennet and would accompany the family as far as Hertfordshire for the memorial service. Richard arrived a day or two early so that he could spend some additional time with Mary before their separation for a month. The staff at Matlock House was giving the carriage a thorough inspection before delivering it to the Gardiners.

In an attempt to spend as much time as possible in Mary's company, Richard accompanied Kitty and her for a walk in Hyde Park. It was a lovely summer day, if slightly warm, and the sky was a brilliant blue with fluffy clouds drifting lazily along. With Mary on one arm and Kitty on the other, they walked along, the ladies laughing at something Richard had said.

"I see the Bennet ladies have not learned that laughing in public is not accepted behavior in the first circles. What can one expect of country nobodies who are trying to force their way into circles where they do not belong?" Lady Marjorie sneered at the ladies in front of her. Mary regarded the woman angrily, while Kitty's eyes were wide with surprise. Before either of them could reply, Lady Marjorie continued, glaring at Kitty. "Have you lost your husband already, Mrs. Darcy? You were told you were unworthy of him; you should have stepped aside for your betters. Some of us would have known how to satisfy such a man as Mr. Darcy."

Kitty looked at the woman in shock. "I am not Mrs. – " she began.

Even though she knew she was not speaking to Mrs. Darcy, Lady Marjorie could not refrain from venting some of her anger upon the lookalike before her, so she reached out and smacked Kitty across her face. "Do not speak back to your betters."

Kitty's hand flew to her cheek where Lady Marjorie's handprint was already appearing.

"How dare you!" cried Mary.

"Marjorie!" cried Mr. Amesbury, appalled.

"I see you have not learned your lesson yet, Lady Marjorie." Richard's voice rang with anger and disdain. "Do I need to make mention of your disgraceful behavior to my mother and her friends. Do you like to have your name in the gossip pages even if the gossip reflects poorly on you? If that is the case, I will be happy to assist you with this." Mary tightened her hold on Richard's arm as he looked like he wished to strike the arrogant woman before them.

"Your pardon, ladies," said Michael Amesbury. "The sun must have caused her great distress. I have never seen Lady Marjorie behave so previously. I shall take her home immediately. Again, I ask your pardon." Michael took a firm grip on Marjorie's elbow and turned, walking rapidly away.

Mary released Richard's arm and moved next to her sister, wrapping an arm around Kitty's waist. "Are you well?" Mary asked in concern.

"Who was that?" asked Kitty, tears in her eyes and her chin trembling.

"That was Lady Marjorie."

"Oh!" was all Kitty said.

"Ladies, I believe we should return to the Gardiners' unless Kitty is feeling up to going to Gunter's for an ice."

Kitty looked at Mary and said, "How does my face look? Am I presentable to be seen at Gunter's? I would enjoy trying one of their ices."

Mary looked first at Kitty's cheek, then at Richard. "Perhaps we could just pick up a treat to take home with us," she suggested.

"I am sure we can do that," said Richard as he directed both ladies towards his waiting carriage.

Michael bundled Lady Marjorie into his carriage. "What on earth was that horrendous display?"

Surprised by Michael's anger, Lady Marjorie took a deep breath and allowed her eyes to fill with tears. She leaned her head upon his shoulder to conceal her expression as she spoke. "The Bennet sisters caused me a dreadful time during the season. They arranged things to embarrass me in front of several members of the ton."

Remembering Wescott had mentioned the name 'Bennet,' Michael asked, "What did they do?"

"They tried to arrange to have me compromised before a man to whom I felt a strong attachment for a time."

"If these young ladies are from the country, how do they have connections to members of the ton?"

"One of them managed to entrap Fitzwilliam Darcy into marriage. It was a disgrace for him."

"If it was a disgrace, then why were the young ladies in company with Mr. Darcy's cousin?"

"They seemed to have bewitched the entire family," complained Lady Marjorie spitefully.

"Well, no matter what happened, I shall expect that you behave better in the future."

Marjorie pouted prettily. "Why are you not defending me? Why would you take their side?"

"I am not taking anyone's side, Marjorie, but an earl's daughter should be above reproach."

Though she was seething with anger, Marjorie agreed that she would avoid such interactions in the future. As Michael directed the carriage toward Dalbert House, Marjorie asked that they go to Bond Street instead. "I need to pick up a few items," she said sweetly.

Amesbury gave the coachman the new direction. He reviewed in his mind what Wescott had told him and the behavior he had observed earlier today. Had Marjorie changed so much? Was she still the girl with whom he had fallen in love? It was disheartening to think that the woman who filled his thoughts for so many years was no longer someone he could admire. "How many items are you still in need of for your trousseau?"

"Oh, I have barely begun to shop," was her nonchalant response.

"Are you aware of how much you have already spent?"

"Oh, but I would not wish to appear poorly beside you when we debut in the ton." Anger and annoyance were evident in her tone.

"I had heard that the ton was none too happy with you at present."

"Oh, la, you know how quickly things change in the ton. My little mishap shall soon be forgotten. I am an earl's daughter, after all."

They arrived at the store Marjorie wished to visit. As she searched through the windows, a malicious look appeared on her face. Turning to her escort, she smiled, "I shall only be a moment, Michael. There is no need for you to attend me."

With that, she turned and swept into the store. Michael stepped closer to the windows and observed her progress. He noticed many of the denizens of the ton avoided looking at her. Michael Amesbury watched as she stopped briefly and looked about, then marched in the direction of a pleasant, modest-looking young woman. Seeing a look of apprehension cross the face of the young lady she approached, Michael entered the store and moved to stand behind Marjorie where he could overhear his betrothed.

"Ah, Miss Pottsfield," Majorie's voice dripped with disdain. "How surprised I was to see the announcement of your engagement to my cousin in the papers. You are aware of the fact that he is nearly broke and only marrying you for your money, are you not? Of course, coming from trade, you should count yourself fortunate he even deigned to notice you. You should not expect to be received by anyone of importance. I shall certainly never acknowledge you, and I am sure most others will follow my example."

Michael watched as the young woman drew herself up to her full height and smiled politely at the woman before her. "Lady Marjorie, I shall not find myself missing your company. I have many friends who shall fill my time. Nor do I believe your remarks about Lord Wescott. I am aware of his past and his reputation, for he has shared all of it with me. I am also aware that you are a spoiled, angry woman who does not hesitate to manipulate people for her own purposes. I believe, however, that after your display at the Darcys' engagement ball, you shall not find it so easy to do so in the future. Now if you will excuse me."

The young lady moved towards the front of the store to pay for her purchase. He watched as Marjorie's eyes followed the woman's progress. "You may feel secure now," she muttered, "but I shall ruin you and Wescott along with you." She turned abruptly and saw Michael standing just behind her.

"Michael, darling. I am so sorry; it took longer than I thought. Shall we go?" Lady Marjorie wrapped her arm about his and gave him a disarming smile, as she pulled him towards the waiting carriage.

Michael was silent on the drive to Dalbert House. He walked her to the door but declined her offer of tea. There was much on his mind, and he needed time to think away from her beguiling charms.

As he returned to his lodgings, he impulsively decided to stop at Matlock House to see Richard Fitzwilliam. They had a slight acquaintance from their Cambridge days. Richard was not in, but Michael left his card with a note that he needed to speak with him at his first opportunity.

Later that evening a knock was heard at the door of his suite. He opened it to find Richard Fitzwilliam.

"Colonel Fitzwilliam, I appreciate your coming to see me. Please come in and take a seat."

"Nice to see you, Amesbury. What can I do for you?" asked Richard as he sat in one of the chairs before the fire.

"I needed to speak with you regarding a matter of some concern. You may or may not be aware that I have known Lady Marjorie since childhood. I have cared for her for quite some time and upon my return to England, I sought her out and proposed to her. However, Wescott cautioned me that she is not the same girl I knew in my youth, and after what I have observed today, I am beginning to believe he may be correct. After leaving you and the young ladies in the park, I asked her what caused her behavior, and she claimed the Bennet sisters had embarrassed her in front of some key members of the ton. Would you please tell me what occurred?"

Richard looked about, and, seeing a decanter on a table by the wall, he brought two glasses and the decanter with him and set them on the table next to the chair Michael occupied. Sitting in the companion chair, Richard poured a drink for them both. After handing a glass to Amesbury, Richard settled back in his chair and told him about all of the encounters between Lady Marjorie and Darcy and Elizabeth. By the end of Richard's recitation, Michael's heart was heavy. Marjorie was not the woman he remembered. She was not the kind of woman with whom he could share his future.

"I believe I shall have to speak with Marjorie tomorrow. I can no longer marry her. I shall take the blame when I notify the papers, but I must end the engagement."

"I should warn you that she will not hesitate to blacken your name. She has done that to several rivals over the past few seasons. Though, because of her recent behavior, her words will not carry the same authority they might once have."

"If you would please extend my apologies to the young ladies we met this afternoon, I would count it as a great favor."

Richard agreed, and, after finishing his drink, he departed.

Elizabeth had worked very hard to ensure that all the plans were in place before their departure to Longbourn, for their guests would be returning with them. All the room assignments were made, the nursery prepared, the meals planned, activities, including a picnic with the neighbors, arranged. Elizabeth had found herself exhausted by the time she retired each night. Finally, the day of their departure arrived. When she woke on the first day of their travel, she found herself racing to the water closet to relieve her stomach of its contents. The feeling passed quickly, so Elizabeth readied herself for the day and did not speak to William about her stomach upset.

The first day of travel passed pleasantly. But on the second morning, Elizabeth's stomach was again upset. Darcy was concerned and questioned whether they should delay their trip a day or two so that Elizabeth could rest. Again her stomach settled quickly, and she was able to convince Darcy to continue their journey.

The final day of travel Elizabeth again dealt with a distressed stomach. Darcy was nearly beside himself with worry, but Elizabeth promised to speak with Mr. Jones if it continued. By the time the Darcys arrived at Netherfield Park, Darcy was rushing Elizabeth inside and up to their suite where he forced her to rest until time to go to Longbourn.

The cavalcade that included the Gardiners, Bennet sisters, Richard, and their servants set off for Longbourn. After a brief stop to change the horses, partake of refreshments, and allow the children to run about, they continued on their way, arriving in the afternoon. Mr. Bennet was delighted to see his daughters and happily greeted Mr. Fitzwilliam and the Gardiners. Mrs. Hill directed everyone to their rooms while they awaited the arrival of the Darcys and Bingleys for tea.

The memorial service for Mrs. Bennet was surprisingly well attended. When the neighbors came back to the house following the service, all of the ladies of the neighborhood offered sincere condolences and asked Elizabeth and Jane about married life. They also offered any assistance that Kitty or Mary might need when they were in residence at Longbourn. Many questioned the absence of Lydia and were surprised to learn she had chosen to stay at school.

When all the guests had departed, the family tried to recall pleasant memories of Mrs. Bennet. It was a happy time when each of the girls could recall at least one good memory of their mother.

"Girls, I must make a request of you."

"What is it Papa?" asked his eldest daughter, Jane.

"I do not wish you to wear mourning for your mother." There was a sharp intake of breath at his words. "Before you argue, please hear me out. None of you are residents of Meryton, and there are many special events planned over the next several months. Mourning is a sign of respect for the deceased. Aside from giving you life, your mother did nothing to earn your respect and certainly never showed you any, no offense intended, Gardiner. Her one goal in life was to have each of you settled in a good marriage. Mourning would only prevent much of that. Mary and Fitzwilliam would not be able to court and marry. Lizzy would have to cancel all of the plans she has prepared for your summer visit. I think the best way to show your mother respect after her death is to move forwarding in finding the lives she wanted you to have."

"I am sorry to say this about my sister, but I agree with your father girls. If you remained in Meryton, you would have to observe mourning or risk the censure of your neighbors. All of you will be away from the prying eyes. I know you will each mourn your mother in your hearts, I believe that will be sufficient."

The girls looked at one another and carefully examined the faces of both their father and uncle. Finally, Jane, as the eldest said, "If that is your wish, we shall comply." All of her sisters nodded in agreement.

The group dined at Netherfield that evening, and early the next morning a larger caravan of carriages departed for Pemberley with only Richard heading south for London.

Richard spent one night at Matlock House before continuing to Rosings. Perusing the paper as he broke his fast the next morning, a notice caught his eye.

Mr. Michael Amesbury is sad to report that he has released Lady Marjorie Dalbert from their engagement. The pair originally engaged themselves when the parties were much younger and was confirmed upon their recent reacquaintance. However, both parties realized that they had grown apart during their lengthy separation. Lady Marjorie is wished all the best going forward by Mr. Amesbury.

"I would like to have been a fly on the wall for that discussion," murmured Richard.

CHAPTER 19

LADY MARJORIE, THE daughter of Lord Dalbert, was too angry for words. Michael Amesbury, whose father was a mere viscount, had ended their engagement. He had said he could not accept her behavior towards others and that nothing could justify the ill-treatment he had seen her demonstrate. Michael had thrown her away as if she was of no importance. How dare he! But worse than that, he had stopped the purchase of the Dalbert homes. Lady Marjorie had recently received notification that the townhouse had been sold. She was required to remove herself from the premises in two days' time. She had nowhere to go. She could return to her father's estate as it had not yet sold, but how would she find a husband buried in the country? She still had a carriage to make the trip, but she no longer had any servants. They had begun deserting the family almost immediately upon her father's death. The servants had not been paid in some time and knew there would be no wages forthcoming. Marjorie could not go to Wescott. She could not forgive him for turning on her and would never be able to swallow her pride to ask for his help. Even if he offered help, she could never lower herself to accept.

Then a devious idea occurred to her. Marjorie remembered the rivalry between Michael and his elder brother, Ralph. She had known him since childhood, and he had hung about the edges of Marjorie's coterie since her debut. Marjorie felt she deserved better; he was only a viscount, after all. However, the family estate had always been prosperous and Marjorie felt sure she could manage him. She determined to convince Ralph she had broken things off with his younger brother because she had long had feelings for him. Ralph was known to be a bit the worse for drink most of the time, so he should be easy for Marjorie to convince. She moved to one of the few remaining pieces of furniture and wrote a quick note inviting Ralph for tea. Not long after having sent the note, it was returned with an acceptance of the invitation.

Marjorie prepared carefully, wearing one of the new dresses Michael had paid for as part of her trousseau. She felt a certain sense of irony and revenge as she set her trap. Marjorie had been waiting in the drawing room for more than ten minutes, and Ralph Amesbury had not arrived. Her temper was rising as she was kept waiting. Finally, her aunt admitted the gentleman. Pasting a smile on her face and, pushing down her temper, Marjorie greeted her guest.

"Ralph, how nice of you to come. It has been far too long since we have seen one another." Marjorie could smell the alcohol on his breath as he bent over her hand.

"Lady Marjorie, a pleasure," the viscount gave her a slightly wobbly bow.

She waved him to a seat and poured out tea for both of them. She allowed her visitor to take a few sips of his tea before asking, "Have you seen Michael recently? How is he taking my rejection?"

"Your rejection? From the item in the paper, I thought he had broken it off with you."

"Well, Michael has always been easy for me to manipulate. After all, I did not wish this broken engagement to taint my reputation."

Ralph Amesbury gave a disbelieving chortle, which he quickly converted to a cough as he noted the look of irritation crossing the lady's face. "Yes, you always could make Michael do anything you wished. Why did you agree to an engagement with the whelp?"

Tears filling her eyes, Lady Marjorie answered, "I thought it was my only way out of the mess my father left," softly adding, "and I wanted to stay close to you."

Ralph looked startled. "A way to stay close to me?"

"You mean you did not know I have been attracted to you since we were both young?"

"You ignored me when we were young," said the viscount skeptically.

"I was trying to make you jealous by paying attention to your younger brother. It was always you who drew me."

"Well, you could have fooled me!"

"Even when we were in town, you would stay close, but I could not get you as close as I wanted." A blush lighting her cheeks, Marjorie looked down to conceal the truth of her feelings. She glanced up through her lashes to observe his expression, and she had to fight the smile that wanted to appear.

Ralph knew how deep his brother's feelings for Marjorie were, and an evil thought occurred. Ralph went down on his knees before the lady seated across from him. Taking her hand in his, he spoke with urgency. "If only I had known your true feelings, I would have spoken sooner. Please, Marjorie, you must marry me. We can be so happy together. I will obtain a special license, and we can marry in a few days."

"But I must leave this house in just two days; repayment of father's debts required that the house to be sold, and I have received word I must vacate. Do you think we can marry so quickly? Where shall we live?"

"I shall have the townhouse opened immediately. I did not see the purpose of the expense when it was only me who would be residing there. I will leave immediately to take care of these matters, if you will only agree to marry me, Marjorie."

"Yes, Ralph, I shall marry you."

He attempted to draw her close and kiss her, but the lady played shy, turning her head away. "You have much to do, and there is no time to waste. We shall have all the time we need for such things."

Ralph was unhappy with her response, but he would only need to wait two days. He was no more in love with her than she was with him, in spite of what she said. However, the opportunity to rub his new wife in his brother's face was too great a temptation to resist. Ralph could be patient for such a delicious woman. With such a luscious wife at home, he could save the money he currently spent on courtesans and teach his wife how to please him. If she wished to have her pin money, she would keep him satisfied. If he were lucky, Marjorie would not give a thought to a settlement. Without one to protect her, she would be at his mercy. He gave a grim smile as he exited Dalbert House.

After three long days of travel, the caravan of carriages arrived at Pemberley. Mary and Kitty were awed by the size of the house. Mr. and Mrs. Gardiner were equally impressed, but they managed to conceal it better. The children stopped and stared at the largest house they had every seen. They had been relegated to the confines of a small carriage for three days and were thrilled with all they could see.

"This is bigger than the park near our house," cried Hugh, his eyes the size of saucers.

Darcy called to two of his footmen, Chaney and Fields, and asked them to take the children out on the lawn near the lake and watch over them as they played and enjoyed their freedom from the carriage. As the children followed the footmen, Mrs. Reynolds appeared with several maids to direct the guests to their rooms while the footmen assisted with the luggage.

The Gardiners and Bingleys were given suites in the guest wing. Mary and Kitty were in the family wing in the rooms on either side of Georgiana. The nursery was opened and cleaned so the children, their nurse, and their governess had rooms there. Darcy had also assigned two maids to assist with the children.

Edmund, Susan, Hugh, and even little Rachel played while the servants unpacked for the visitors. By the time that had been completed, the children had grown weary and were sent to the nursery for snack and to rest as the adults gathered for tea. Dinner that evening was a relaxed affair, and everyone retired early to recover from the days spent traveling.

Upon arising on their first morning back at Pemberley, Elizabeth was again sick, as she had been every day since leaving for Hertfordshire. She managed to convince Darcy that it was the stress of her mother's death that had caused her to feel unwell.

To placate him, she promised to contact the doctor should the illness continue after returning to Pemberley. Fortunately, Darcy had risen early and was hard at work in his study. After her stomach settled, Elizabeth rang for Margot. When the maid arrived, she asked her to request Mrs. Gardiner attend her. Elizabeth had a suspicion of what was wrong but wished to ask some questions of her aunt to confirm those suspicions.

It took only a few moments before Mrs. Gardiner knocked at the door of Elizabeth's sitting room.

"Lizzy, dear, the maid said you needed to see me. Is everything well?"

"I believe so, Aunt, but I need your advice about something."

"Of course, Lizzy, dear, what is it you need to know?

"What symptoms would I look for if I were with child?"

A large smile appeared on Mrs. Gardiner's face, but she calmed herself and answered the question. "There are many things that can indicate pregnancy. The first one is missing your courses. Do you remember when you last had them?"

After a moment of thought, Elizabeth said, "I do not think I have had one since the wedding."

"Did they occur before your wedding?" Lizzy nodded her head. "And you did not have your courses in June or July?" This time, Lizzy shook her head. "Other things to watch for include stomach upset first thing in the morning, though it can occur at other times of the day, tenderness in your breasts, and fatigue in the afternoon. Have you experienced any of these symptoms?"

Elizabeth nodded before saying, "I have been sick each morning since we left for Hertfordshire. I have also been unusually tired in the afternoons."

"Well, my dear Lizzy, I think you are, indeed, with child. However, the only way to be certain is when the quickening occurs."

"The quickening?"

"That will be the first time you feel the child move within you. It will be a fluttering feeling in your stomach."

"When does that take place?"

"About the end of your fourth month."

"So I am approximately . . . "

"I would say you are about three months pregnant."

"That means the quickening could be soon." A huge smile blossomed on Elizabeth's face. "I cannot wait to tell William." Her smile faltered. "Should I tell William?"

"What do you mean, Lizzy?"

"William's mother died in childbirth. I do not wish him to worry. How can I tell him when I know he will worry?"

"Lizzy, you are an active, healthy young woman; there is no reason for William to worry. Both your mother and your grandmother Gardiner delivered several times without difficulty."

"Do you think that will convince William not to worry?"

"Only you can decide that Elizabeth. However, if you wish to reduce the time he will worry, you can wait until you are certain of your condition."

"But he is already distressed about my sickness in the mornings. He is insisting I see the doctor."

"There are ways you can reduce the morning sickness. I suggest we ask Mrs. Reynolds and Margot to join us. They will be able to assist us in making this as easy for you as possible and to help reduce Darcy's reason to worry."

Lizzy rang the bell and when Margot appeared she asked her to fetch Mrs. Reynolds and for the two of them to join her and Mrs. Gardiner. A short time later, the two women entered the room, the housekeeper carrying a tray. "Here, Mrs. Darcy. I thought you would enjoy this as we spoke." She set the tray on the table by Elizabeth's chair.

"Mrs. Reynolds, my aunt thought you and Margot might be able to assist me with something."

"How may I help you, Mrs. Darcy?"

"I believe that I am with child, as I have been sick every morning for a week now. Mr. Darcy is already worrying about my health, and I do not want him to worry about my condition. I believe it would be wise not to tell him until I feel the quickening. Do you know of a way to prevent the illness I feel each morning so that he will not worry?"

"As I remember, the late Mrs. Darcy was also sick in the morning. She found if she had some dry toast and peppermint tea each morning before rising, it would settle her stomach. Margot mentioned you had been ill in the mornings, which is why I brought the tray for you." She nodded towards the tray and encouraged Elizabeth to sip some of the tea. "Margot can bring some in each morning and have it waiting on the table beside your bed for when you wake. Mr. Darcy may wonder about it, but if you are no longer sick in the morning, I doubt he will be too concerned."

"That sounds perfect, Mrs. Reynolds. I shall depend on you three ladies assisting me through this month with guests as we wait for the quickening. I know I can trust you to keep my secret until it is time to tell Mr. Darcy."

"Of course, Lizzy,"

"Certainly, madam."

"Yes, Mrs. Darcy. If you should find your stomach upset at other times, please let me know, and I will send you some peppermint tea. I will also speak with Cook about including some bland dishes with each meal, as sometimes certain foods and smells can also cause stomach discomfort in expectant mothers."

"Thank you, Mrs. Reynolds. As usual, I do not know what I would do without you."

"It is a privilege to help you, especially as we await the next generation of the Darcy family."

A short time later, Elizabeth joined the rest of her family in the breakfast room. "Good morning, Mary, Kitty. Did you sleep well? I hope you found your rooms comfortable." Elizabeth filled her plate from the sideboard and seated herself as she spoke.

"Good morning, Lizzy," responded Kitty. "I do not think I have ever slept in a more comfortable bed nor seen a more beautiful room. I noticed the gardens from my window and look forward to sketching many of the sights of Pemberley."

"I, too, slept well and appreciated the lovely room. I look forward to learning from you while I am here, as I will soon be the mistress of Rosings Park."

"You are more than welcome to join me in the mornings when I deal with household matters, Mary. However, I hope you shall also relax and enjoy your visit. We have a dinner party planned one evening and an al fresco meal on another occasion. We can also travel into Lambton to shop, and there are several mounts in the stables for those who wish to ride or learn to do so. I cannot wait to introduce you to Sheba."

"Can we see the horses soon, Lizzy?" asked Hugh. "Can I go for a ride?"

A large smile appeared on Elizabeth's face. "I believe that Mr. Darcy has recently acquired three ponies for some special visitors we are having." Cheers of delight greeted her statement!

"Then after I have met with Mrs. Reynolds, how would you like to go to the stables and meet the ponies?"

"Yeah!" cried three little voices.

"Good morning. This seems like a happy group," said Darcy as he entered the dining room. "I am sorry I am late. What has caused all this excitement?"

"Lizzy said we could see the ponies," said Susan.

"And when is this to happen?"

"As soon as she meets with someone," said Edmund.

Darcy smiled at Elizabeth as he said, "I do hope I shall be allowed to join you on this exciting expedition."

"We would not think of going without you," said Elizabeth, returning his smile.

"Perhaps we should do more than just visit. Perhaps Edmund, Susan, and Hugh would like to go for a quick ride."

"Could we, Mama, Papa?" chorused three voices.

Mr. and Mrs. Gardiner looked at one another before answering. "I believe if you go up to the nursery, you shall each find a riding outfit waiting for you," responded their father. The children quickly finished their meal and politely asked to be excused. All of the adults at the table watched with smiles as the children rushed from the dining room.

As Elizabeth finished her meal, she said, "Mary, would you care to join me to meet with Mrs. Reynolds?"

"Yes, thank you." The ladies excused themselves, as did Darcy. As he left the room, he said, "Shall we meet in the foyer in an hour to visit the stables?" The others agreed, and everyone went about their work or prepared for the outing.

When the family was again gathered in the hallway, smiles were on the faces of all the adults. Edmund and Hugh were both dressed in tan breeches, dark brown coats, boots, and top hats. Susan was wearing a deep pink riding habit with black boots and a low top hat that had a matching pink ribbon around it.

Darcy offered his arm to Susan, and the boys took Elizabeth's hands as they all headed for the stables. As they entered the stable complex, Darcy walked to the stall housing his horse. Spying a piece of apple Darcy held out, the horse walked forward and took it from Darcy's hand. As the horse ate the apple, Darcy said, "This is my horse, Aladdin's Treasure. I call him Laddie." The children were awed by the big black horse. Next, Darcy led them to the stall housing Sheba. "This is Elizabeth's horse, Sheba." This horse was not so intimidating as Darcy's big one. Elizabeth stepped up to the stall, and Sheba nudged her shoulder. She patted the horse and spoke sweetly to her, holding the other piece of the apple out to the horse.

"Now there are some special friends waiting to meet you," said Darcy. He led them down the center of the stables and out into a ring at the end. There, tied to the rail, were three Welsh ponies. Darcy stepped to the first one, a buckskin, and said, "Edmund, this is Applejack." Edmund walked to where Darcy stood. Darcy handed him a piece of the apple and showed him how to hold his hand. Applejack took the apple from Edmund's palm, and then Edmund reached out to pat the pony's neck. A groom replaced Darcy and stood with Edmund as he got to know his pony.

Moving to the second pony, a dapple gray, Darcy called to Susan. Repeating what he had done before, he introduced Susan to Diamond Star. Darcy was, again, replaced by a groom, and he and Hugh moved to the last pony, a chestnut. He gave Hugh a piece of apple and introduced him to Cinnamon. He waited several minutes as the children became familiar with their mounts.

Then the groom with Edmund showed him how to mount the horse. Once Edmund was in the saddle, the groom untied the horse and began to lead him around the ring. Darcy called to him to sit with his back straight. The second groom led Susan's pony to the mounting block, as Elizabeth explained to her how to mount the child-size side saddle. The pink of her habit against the gray pony made a striking sight. Once Susan was properly settled in her saddle, the groom began to lead the animal around the ring. Lastly, they watched as Hugh tried to mount as his brother had. However, his little legs could not quite manage it, so Darcy gave him a leg up as Hugh swung his other leg over the pony's back. He showed Hugh where to hold on as the groom began to lead the pony around the ring.

The others stepped out of the ring and watched as the children were led around. Elizabeth stepped up on the bottom rung of the fence to better see the children. Darcy stood behind her and placed his arms on the fence on either side of his wife. "I cannot wait until we are watching our children learn to ride," he whispered in his wife's ear. Though Darcy could not see it, Elizabeth could not contain her smile at his words.

After watching the children for a quarter of an hour, Elizabeth asked the ladies if they would like to walk in the gardens with her before returning to the house for luncheon. All but Mrs. Gardiner joined

Elizabeth, as she preferring instead to watch her children's first ride. The ladies moved off in the direction of the gardens. They walked all the paths of the formal gardens and Georgiana showed them the hedge maze, but they did not have time today to attempt to learn its secrets.

After a pleasant luncheon, everyone retired to quieter activities. Hugh and Rachel napped, and the older children had lessons, though they too appeared a bit tired from the morning's activities. The young ladies retired to the music room, and the couples settled in a drawing room for conversation.

The afternoon included a tour of the house led by Mrs. Reynolds, a quiet tea, and a pleasant dinner. At the end of the day, everyone retired, well pleased with their first full day at Pemberley!

Two days after departing Dalbert House, Ralph Amesbury and Lady Marjorie Dalbert stood before the rector at St. George's church and exchanged vows. One of his friends stood beside him as a witness and Miss Vaughan, Marjorie's aunt, was her witness. After the service was completed and the register signed, they proceeded to the Amesbury townhouse. The only rooms prepared for habitation were the main drawing room, dining room, and master's and mistress' suites. Marjorie was not impressed with what she saw and looked forward to spending her husband's money to make improvements to the house. This desire would be thwarted when she later discovered that her husband's neglect had reduced the productivity of his estate and, consequently, his income. After a small meal, Ralph practically dragged his wife to the mistress chambers where, with no thought for her comfort or pleasure, he consummated their union.

The next day the following notice appeared in the paper:

Ralph Amesbury, Viscount Barlow, wed Lady
Marjorie Dalbert
at St. George's London yesterday.

After reading the notice of the marriage, Michael Amesbury shook his head sadly. The behavior Lady Marjorie had exhibited had done much to kill the affection Michael felt for her. Consequently this notice did not have the effect its principal parties desired. Michael saw it for what it was, each of them attempting to exact some sort of revenge upon him. Well, they could have each other. In fact, he thought them quite well suited.

Putting the paper aside, Michael left for a meeting with his solicitor. He had found a different townhouse to purchase and was to sign the final papers today. The house was on Park Lane and would be a fine place to begin his new life.

Across town, in an elegant townhouse where the wealthiest merchants lived, a difficult interview was taking place.

"I understand you wish to speak to me, Lord Wescott,' said the gentleman seated behind the desk, an almost grim expression on his face.

More nervous than he could ever remember being, Lord Wescott cleared his throat, wishing he had a glass of brandy to help ease the dryness and steady his nerves. Since there was none at hand, he took a deep breath and spoke. "Mr. Pottsfield, I wished to ask your permission and blessing to marry your daughter. Miss Evelyn is the finest young woman of my acquaintance, and I love her."

Mr. Pottsfield was pleased with the words the young man spoke, but would not grant his permission without expressing his concerns. He had known little of the man who requested a courtship with his only daughter; he had, in fact, been overwhelmed that a peer of the realm was making such a request. After the courtship had begun, he had James Wescott thoroughly investigated, and he was concerned with what he found.

"Lord Wescott, I must say I have some concerns about granting my approval. Since you requested to court my daughter, I have tried to learn more of you and have heard many things about your past behavior that cause me concern. I do not wish to give her to someone who may break her heart."

"Mr. Pottsfield, you have no reason for concern. I admit there are many things I have done in the past of which I am not proud, but I am no longer that man. My past experience was clouded by the behavior of my cousin and most of the young women I met in the ton. Recently my eyes have been opened to the fact that not all women are shallow, grasping, and mercenary. I admit to being surprised by the realization, but I am very grateful for the lesson, for it has brought me the blessing of your daughter's love."

"I promise you, sir, you will have no reason for concern if you grant me Miss Evelyn's hand. I will love and cherish her for the rest of my life."

The unquestionable honesty and earnestness of Lord Wescott's words were a balm to Mr. Pottsfield's troubled spirits.

"Very well, Lord Wescott, you have my permission to marry Evelyn and my blessing. I hope I shall never have cause to regret my decision."

"Sir, if you had me investigated, then you know that my estate has not been as productive as it could have been in the past. My father did not manage things as he should, and the house and land are in need of improvement. I have taken several steps to maximize the estate's productivity. I believe we will see, at least, a thousand pounds increase over last year. When it is producing at its optimum level, it should bring in about seven thousand pounds per year."

"I expect there will be gossip from those who are familiar with my past behavior. You may hear it said that I am only marrying Evelyn for her large dowry. I want you to know that is not true. I do wish to use a portion of the dowry to make improvements for our home, but I shall include in the marriage settlement that she is to retain her full dowry in the event I predecease her. Please understand that I am serious when I say Evelyn's care and happiness are of paramount importance to me and always will be."

"Thank you, Lord Wescott. You have put my mind at ease. Perhaps there are some ways in which I can be of assistance to the two of you."

"That is kind of you, sir, but I believe we shall be able to manage on our own. I need to prove this to myself as much as to you."

"You should know that I gave serious consideration to refusing you this interview, but Evelyn spoke very highly of you and of the improvements you had made in your life. I am relieved to find that your words agree with what she has said of you." Mr. Pottsfield stood and extended his hand to the young man who now stood before him. As the men shook hands, the gentleman said, "Shall we go and tell the ladies of the good news?"

"That would make me very happy, Mr. Pottsfield."

CHAPTER 20

THE FAMILY MEMBERS gathered at Pemberley enjoyed every moment of their time together. The children, as well as Mary and Kitty, all learned to ride, so they could enjoy traveling around the estate together, and picnicking at the most scenic spots Pemberley had to offer, save for their lovely grove. Darcy would share that secret place with no one but his beloved Lizzy.

On occasion, Bingley and Mr. Gardiner rode out with William when he attended to estate business; though frequently, Mr. Gardiner could be found at one of Pemberley's many streams, fishing for several hours each day. Fishing was a pastime, he was unable to enjoy much, residing, as he did, in the city, and Mr. Gardiner was an avid angler. Edmund and Hugh accompanied their father fishing one morning, but Hugh's first catch was more than the young boy could handle, and he was pulled into the stream before his father could grab him. Fortunately, the water had been relatively shallow, and Hugh had dropped the pole before the fish could pull him further into the stream. After that, the young boy was left behind when the others went fishing, though it did give Hugh the best tale of the 'fish that got away' to tell.

Elizabeth invited her new friends from Derbyshire for tea one afternoon, eager to introduce them to her beloved family members. The occasion was filled with intelligent conversation, witty repartee, and a smidgen of local gossip, and all in attendance reveled in the experience. As a result, the local ladies invited the women of Pemberley to a tea each week during the month the guests would reside at Pemberley. Consequently, on Wednesday of each of the succeeding weeks, Pemberley's female contingent traveled to visit Elizabeth's dearest friends, going first to the home of Helena Whitman. The next week they visited Margaret Hughes, and, finally, they joined Chloe Westingham for tea at her home. These visits were the first of many Elizabeth enjoyed in the homes of her friends. Even after her family's visit ended, the ladies enjoyed time with one another at least weekly.

Two weeks after their family arrived, Elizabeth hosted her first dinner and dance as a married woman. She had poured over the books from Mrs. Reynolds, which detailed past events held at Pemberley before making her plans. When the evening finally arrived, Elizabeth found herself anxious, convinced she had forgotten something and would embarrass her dear husband. Dressed in a new gown of bronze green with a sheer overskirt in the same shade, short puffed sleeves, and a low, square décolletage, Elizabeth looked truly elegant. With this, she wore her wedding jewelry, and the jeweled pins Darcy had given her decorated her stylish curls.

Coming into his wife's dressing room to escort her downstairs, Darcy stopped and allowed his gaze to wander over the sight before him, lingering on the swell of her bosom revealed by the décolletage of her gown. "My love, you are beautiful. Many ladies could learn something from the simple elegance of your attire."

"Thank you, dear husband. I adore the way you look in your formal attire, as well."

As he offered his arm, Darcy asked, "Are you ready to greet our first guests? I uderstand the Matlock carriage has entered the park."

"It will be lovely to see our aunt and uncle again."

The couple arrived in the hall just as the earl and countess, along with Lady Julia, were admitted. "Aunt Rebecca, Uncle Henry, we are delighted you could join us this evening," said Elizabeth as she moved to welcome the new arrivals.

"Elizabeth, you look lovely, my dear. Thank you for including us. I am very pleased to be able to watch your triumph this evening," replied Lady Matlock as the ladies exchanged kisses.

"As usual, my wife is correct. You look quite handsome tonight." The Earl of Matlock kissed his niece's hand before leaning in to kiss her cheek, as well.

"You are ever the charmer, Uncle Malcolm," remarked Elizabeth with a laugh.

Finally, Julia got her chance to greet her cousins, giving Elizabeth a kiss and receiving a kiss to her hand from Darcy. "Oh, I have missed you, Lizzy! I am delighted to have the opportunity to visit Pemberley tonight. How do you like it?"

"I love being here. I cannot imagine a more beautiful or perfect place to live. Sometimes I feel like it was created especially for me," Elizabeth replied with her lilting laugh.

The group moved into the drawing room where the other family members gathered.

"Mary, dear," said Lady Matlock as she stepped forward to greet her soon to be daughter-in-law. I am delighted to have the opportunity to see you and tell you how delighted we were to hear of your engagement."

"It is a pleasure to see you again, as well, Lady Matlock."

"Now none of that. You must call me Lady Rebecca, and hopefully you will feel comfortable enough to call me mother in the not too distant future."

"I believe I would like that very much. You treat me more like a daughter than my mother ever has." Lady Matlock patted Mary's cheek as she returned the girl's timid smile.

"Have you begun making plans for the wedding? Is there anything I can do to help?"

"Since you are planning to stay overnight, Lady Rebecca, Elizabeth and I thought we could begin making plans tomorrow, so we could have your participation in the planning."

The Matlocks greeted the others in the room before settling themselves to enjoy the conversation, as they awaited the arrival of the other guests. They did not have long to wait, as those who had received invitations to tonight's event were eager to attend the first dinner held at Pemberley in many years. The guest list included their close friends from the neighborhood, as well as all the other prominent families.

Darcy and Elizabeth remained in the hallway until all their guests had arrived. Most of the guests greeted Elizabeth with genuine welcome. However, she could not fail to note the number of young women whose greetings were somewhat reserved, or even downright cold, nor how those same young women were gathered in a group frequently casting looks in Elizabeth's direction. She smiled disarmingly in return whenever she caught the eye of one of the young ladies. When Darcy saw the smile, he could not help but ask its cause.

"I believe I am the topic of conversation for all the disappointed young ladies of Derbyshire," she said with a laugh.

"I cannot believe there are very many. I did not often participate in Derbyshire society, especially after my father's death."

"I am sure that lack of participation only made you more desirable, my love." A light laugh accompanied her words.

"You know that is my favorite sound in the world. You really should not tempt me so, or I may be forced to kiss you in front of all our neighbors."

"I will restrain myself, then, as I would not wish to scandalize all our neighbors upon our first meeting." However, another soft laugh escaped her as she spoke, causing Darcy to slip his arm around her waist and pull her close to his side as he placed a kiss on her temple. Elizabeth blushed brightly, which caused a deep, resonant chuckle to escape from her husband.

Once all the guests had arrived, the couple began making their way around the room to speak at more length with their guests. They had not managed to complete their circuit before Benton announced dinner. Darcy offered his arm to the Marchioness of Redvale and led the way to the dining room. Elizabeth followed on the arm of the marquess. He seated Elizabeth at the foot of the table and took his place on her right. Elizabeth glanced up to see a frown on her husband's face. She gave him a bright, encouraging smile, knowing he frowned because of the distance separating them at the table. Tonight's dinner was the first time they had not been seated side-by-side since their marriage.

Seated to Elizabeth's left was Uncle Henry, the Earl of Matlock. As the two highest-ranking gentlemen in attendance, it was their right to be placed beside the hostess. With two such congenial dinner partners, Elizabeth's intelligence and sparkling wit made for lively conversation at her end of the table. Darcy sat between the Marchioness of Redvale and his aunt. As a consequence, he was able to relax and enjoy the evening. No one in attendance missed the adoring glances Darcy frequently directed to his wife. It left no one in doubt that Darcy and Elizabeth married for love.

Following the delicious, four-course meal, everyone removed to the ballroom for dancing. Darcy had hired the local musicians to provide music for those who wished to dance. Gold and white striped settees and gold and deep green brocade chairs placed in comfortable groupings for conversation ringed the dance floor. A small table filled with fruits, cheeses, and desserts sat in one corner of the room with a table of beverages nearby. The doors to the terrace were open to allow the breeze to cool the room. Glass cylinders in various shapes held candles and were spaced along the terrace rail, and lanterns, in similar styles, hung from the branches of the nearby trees, lighting the area with a golden glow. Also, torches lined the paths of the formal gardens just off the terrace. As on the dining room table, vases of lilacs and yellow roses decorated the tables around the ballroom, filling the room with their delicate fragrance.

Darcy and Elizabeth danced the opening dance, before beginning to circulate around the room, visiting with all their guests. Darcy had stopped to speak with a friend as Elizabeth came upon Lady Matlock, Lady Redvale, and the elder Mrs. Whitman. The ladies each complimented Elizabeth on the arrangements for the evening.

"This has been a delightful evening, Mrs. Darcy," remarked Lady Redvale. "It is comparable to any event I ever attended at Pemberley which Lady Anne hosted."

"My thanks, Lady Redvale. That is a marvelous compliment." Elizabeth blushed at the praise.

"Indeed, Mrs. Darcy, it has been an exceptional evening."

"I agree, Elizabeth; you have done very well, my dear niece."

"I am grateful for your words and pleased to know I have represented the Darcy family so well."

"I expect that you will soon be the leading light in Derbyshire, Mrs. Darcy," added Lady Redvale. "I look forward to seeing you shine among the ton next season."

Several of the disappointed young ladies, among them Fredrica Poole and Laura Parkington, were standing nearby and found it disappointing to hear such well-respected ladies' easy acceptance for the upstart Mrs. Darcy. "Such countrified flower choices as lilacs shall certainly not impress the ton," said Laura Parkington in a carrying voice. Some of the young ladies around her tittered while others shook their heads slightly and looked embarrassed for their friend.

Casting a stern look at the young lady who had insulted her hostess, Lady Redvale said, "That only proves you are not yet ready to manage a household, Miss Parkington. A good hostess knows to use what is in season and to make the most of what nature provides in abundance. Mrs. Darcy chose beautiful colors, ones that also provided a light fragrance that could counteract the smell of an overheated crowd of people."

"You should also know that a disgruntled female is not one people wish to be around," added Lady Matlock.

Mrs. Whitman added her opinion as well. "Your mother would be very disappointed in your rude and jealous behavior. She taught you better."

"Indeed, she did," came the voice of Miss Parkington's brother. Laura jerked in the direction of the voice to see Michael standing next to Mr. Darcy. Laura's face flushed as she noted the scowl on her host's face and wondered how much he had heard.

"I beg your pardon, Mrs. Darcy," muttered the young woman, her eyes firmly on the floor.

"We have all said and done things we wish we had not. You must learn a little of my philosophy, Miss Parkington."

Her color high and her fists clenched at her sides, the girl asked the obvious question. "And what is that, Mrs. Darcy?"

Before Elizabeth could reply Darcy's voice was heard saying, "Remember the past only as it gives you pleasure. It is a good philosophy, Miss Parkington. I am sure my gracious wife would be willing to overlook your past attitude." As he spoke, Darcy had moved closer to Elizabeth, and his hand now rested on the small of her back. She smiled up at her husband and leaned into his shoulder. He looked back at her with the small smile on his lips reserved only for his beloved wife.

Michael Parkington, unhappy with the quality of his sister's apology, spoke. "I believe that Laura and I must be leaving. I hope that it is a headache which prompts her poor behavior."

"I do hope you headache improves, Miss Parkington and that you are recovered in time for the picnic we have planned."

"Thank you for the well wishes and invitation. Good night, Mr. and Mrs. Darcy," said the subdued young woman as her brother led her out of the ballroom.

"I pray by the time we return to town next season, the disappointed young ladies will have all found a new target for their hopes," said Elizabeth with a soft laugh, which was joined by those standing with her.

The last dance of the evening was a waltz, and Darcy was thrilled to hold his wife in his arms as he whirled her around Pemberley's ballroom. It was the embodiment of so many of his dreams. He could not imagine anything more perfect. As the Darcys said farewell to their guests, the other members of the household retired.

The residents of Pemberley rose later than usual the morning after the dinner. After a leisurely breakfast, the gentlemen headed for the stream to enjoy some fishing, while the ladies adjourned to the family sitting room to begin planning for Mary and Richard's wedding.

"Have you given any thought to what you wish, Mary? What color would you like your gown to be? That may help us decide on what type of flowers to use. Or have you thought of what you would like to serve at the wedding breakfast?"

"The only decision I have made is that I should like you, Kitty, to stand beside me one that day."

"Oh, Mary, I would be honored to do so. Thank you so much," cried Kitty as she moved to hug her sister. The elder Bennet sisters and Mrs. Gardiner looked on with tears in their eyes at the bond that had developed between the younger girls.

"Well, that checks one item off our list," said Elizabeth with a laugh.

"Since it is to be a Christmas wedding, I thought about wearing a gown of gold, but I also love the color green."

"With your coloring, I think either would be lovely, Mary," said Lady Matlock."

"And we could decorate everything with evergreens and red roses tied with gold ribbons," suggested Georgiana.

"What color would my dress be?" asked Kitty.

"With your coloring, a rich red might would look lovely," replied Elizabeth. "Would that be appropriate, Aunt Rebecca?"

"Though such colors are usually only worn by matrons, I believe it would be acceptable for this joyous occasion," came the countess' answer.

"Mary, please be sure to see Madame Colette upon your return to London. William and I wish to purchase your trousseau for you. Just have her send the bills to Darcy House, and we will arrange for payment when we arrive for the viscount's wedding.

"Lizzy how can I – " began Mary, but the countess interrupted.

"That will not be necessary, Lizzy. Richard is aware that Darcy and Bingley paid for your trousseaus, and he wishes to pay for Mary's. He would also like to review the settlement with Darcy when you come to London in October, before presenting it to Mr. Bennet."

Mary's eyes glistened with tears. "Are you certain it will not place too much strain on Richard, Lady Rebecca?"

"No, my dear, there is no need for concern. The arrangement he and Anne have with regards to Rosings gives him a secure and prosperous future. Having you by his side will make things perfect."

"Thank you, mother," said Mary softly as the tears trickled down her cheeks. Lady Matlock's eyes teared up as well, as she pulled her future daughter close in a comforting hug.

The conversation continued until time for the mid-day meal, and the ladies were pleased that the plans were well in hand.

The Matlocks stayed one additional night before returning to their estate. The next week the guests experienced more of the enjoyments Pemberley had to offer. With only three days before her family was scheduled to depart, the picnic Elizabeth planned was held. Not only were the local gentry and their families invited but also many of Mrs. Gardiner's friends from Lambton.

A tent was set up on the lawn to shade the tables laden with food. For the guests, blankets and pillows were spread about on the grass, as well as a second tent with tables for the older members of the company. Games were set up on the lawn for the children, including races, hoops, and the equipment for bilbocatch and graces. For the adults, there were bowls, pall mall, battledore and shuttlecock, archery, and cricket equipment.

The sound of children's laughter floated on the air. There were three-legged races and games of tag and catch. They ran and played until hunger or thirst overtook them, at which point they were observed sneaking food from the buffet table, or begging their mothers to fix them a plate or fetch them a beverage.

They would eat so quickly many a mother was left wondering if they had even chewed the food before returning to their play.

To tell the truth, the adults, or, more precisely, the men, behaved much like children, as well. An intense game of cricket began once all of the guests had arrived. For a while, the ladies cheered on the gentlemen, but as the match dragged on, many of them moved to the area designated for archery to demonstrate their skill. When the cricket match ended, the gentlemen made their way towards the kegs of small beer before moving to fill their plates at the buffet tables. The women soon joined them at the buffet, and everyone searched for a comfortable place to relax and enjoy the meal. Young couples separated into small groups and seated themselves upon the blankets spread about the lawn. The ladies were dressed in an array of pastel colors and wore large hats or carried parasols to protect themselves from the sun. They looked like a bouquet of brightly colored flowers. Many of the ladies held parasols in one hand white eating with the other. Servants, carrying pitchers, moved among the guests, offering to refill drinks and fetch additional delicacies for the guests.

As the sun was setting, the guests gathered their families and thanked their hosts before making their way home. Many parents were observed carrying their youngest children as they departed, for the children had played until they dropped from exhaustion. All were heard expressing their delight with the day as they departed.

Everyone at Pemberley enjoyed the remaining days of their visit indulging in their favorite leisure activities. The adults were content to relax and enjoy one another's company before their upcoming separation. However, the children were desirous of spending more time with the ponies before they departed. Darcy entrusted them to his most competent groomsmen and sent them out to the stables for a portion of each day. In the mornings, Mr. Gardiner and Charles would visit the trout stream for some fishing. The ladies discussed the upcoming wedding and made plans for meeting again in London.

On the morning her family was to depart for London, Elizabeth awoke to a settled stomach. She lay still pondering the delightful feeling only to be startled by another sensation. The fluttering in her stomach was brief, causing her to wonder if she had imagined it. Elizabeth lay still pondering if it could be the confirmation for which she waited. She did not have long to wait before the strange fluttering was repeated. Her smile grew, and she could not wait to share the wonderful news with her husband.

Elizabeth rolled onto her side and looked at her sleeping spouse. She loved the opportunity to observe him as he slept. His face was relaxed, and he appeared much younger. Elizabeth reached out and pushed back the curl that always fell across his forehead. At her slight touch, his lips lifted in a smile, and she heard him breathe her name. "Lizzy." The sound was as soft and gentle as a caress. Elizabeth returned her eyes to his face and saw his dark eyes looking back at her.

"Your gentle touch is a delightful way to awaken, my love."

"I must agree, for I have enjoyed it when you woke me in a similar manner."

"Do you have a busy day today, my husband?"

"I shall, of course, be here until our guests have departed, but then I must check on a few issues about the estate. Why do you ask?"

"I have some news I wish to share, and I am trying to determine the best time to do so."

"You have my undivided attention at this moment, my love. I should be pleased to hear anything you wish to tell me."

"We are to have another visitor sometime after the first of the year."

"Who is this visitor, and how long do they intend to stay?"

"The length of the visit will be very long, indeed." Darcy looked puzzled.

"And, who might this visitor be who plans an extended stay with us? I do hope it is someone whose company I enjoy."

"I believe you will, as the visitor shall be our first child."

Darcy's eyes widened, and his jaw fell slack. Elizabeth watched as numerous emotions crossed her husband's face. As she saw fear, she felt her heart clench, but it was quickly replaced by overwhelming joy. "A child, my love, are you certain?"

Elizabeth nodded her head as she again watched emotions fly swiftly across Darcy's visage. "Is that why you were sick in the mornings? Are you well now? Should I send for the doctor? Do you know when the child is due? We must arrange for the midwife to move in with us."

Elizabeth laughed at his reaction and answered the many questions he had put to her. "Yes, yes, no, early February, and it is much too soon for that. Are you happy, dearest William?"

"How could I not be? The product of our love is growing inside of you!"

"I am very pleased this occurred today," said his wife. "Would you mind if we shared the news with our family before they depart?"

"I can think of nothing I should like better. I will also have to write to Uncle Malcolm and Richard."

"Yes, and I shall write to Papa and Lydia."

"You are positive about your condition?" Darcy questioned.

"I am, William, I felt the quickening this morning. That is the sign I was told to watch for to confirm my pregnancy."

Darcy wrapped his arms around his wife and pulled her close, kissing her quite passionately. His affection for his wife naturally moved to a greater display of his love for her. He was startled when Elizabeth placed her hand against his chest pushing him further away. With a look of concern on his face, he said, "May I no longer love you, my Lizzy?"

"I have no objections to you loving me at any time, dear William, but I believe we must wait until our guests have departed. We must dress if we are to join our family at breakfast before they go."

"Then save time for me later today, for I intend to love you thoroughly, so that you understand how delighted I am with the gift you are giving me."

Half an hour later, Darcy and Elizabeth joined the others in the dining room. Mrs. Gardiner noted their smiles and wondered if there was to be an announcement.

"Good morning, everyone," said Darcy with the largest smile anyone had ever seen upon his face.

"You look unusually happy this morning, William. Are you eager to see the last of us?" teased Mr. Gardiner.

"Not at all. We are always delighted to spend time with our loved ones. It is just that my darling wife has given me the most excellent news this morning."

"What news would that be, Brother?"

"Shortly after the first of the year, I am to be a father!" If possible Darcy's smile grew larger as he completed his announcement.

Pandemonium reigned in the dining room, as all those present jumped up and moved to congratulate the couple, everyone talking over each other to be heard.

"Oh, I shall be an aunt!" cried Kitty.

"As will I," said Georgiana.

"Congratulations, William, Lizzy. I am very happy for you. And Lizzy, should the wedding plans be too much for you, you must let me know. I would not wish to cause you undue stress or strain at such an important time."

"You need not worry, Mary. The plans are well underway, and I am sure my devoted husband and dedicated staff shall ensure I not overtax myself," replied Elizabeth with a smile.

Next she received the congratulations of her aunt and uncle, with Mrs. Gardiner encouraging Elizabeth to write with any questions she may have. Perhaps the children and I will have to remain after the holidays," suggested Mrs. Gardiner. "That is if it would give you comfort to have me with you during that time, Lizzy."

"It would, indeed, comfort me to have you close, dear Aunt Madeline."

When the congratulations concluded, everyone returned to their seats at the table to finish their meals. The excited conversation continued throughout breakfast. As those who would be departing retired to their rooms for the final preparations, Darcy and Elizabeth had Benton and Mrs. Reynolds gather as much staff as they could before making their announcement about the arrival of the next generation of Darcys. The staff was equally exuberant in the expressions of pleasure as the family had been.

Far too quickly, the Gardiners and their children, with Mary and Kitty in tow, returned to the front hall to make their departure. The Bingleys planned to depart for London, as well. They wished to make some purchases for their new home. They had traveled to Ashford Hills several times over the past month to take measurements, discuss colors, and determine what updates needed attention first.

There were hugs, expressions of thanks, and requests to write from all present. Darcy and Elizabeth escorted their guests out to their carriages, remaining on the steps to wave until the carriages were out of sight.

As they turned toward the house, Darcy put his arm around Elizabeth and pulled her close to his side. "I believe, my love, we have a delayed celebration to attend." He waggled his eyebrows at her as his fingers tickled her side. Elizabeth giggled at his relentless tickling and twisted away from him to race inside and up the stairs, her laughter floating on the air behind her. Her husband was in quick pursuit.

CHAPTER 21

CAROLINE BINGLEY SAT in the window seat of her room, wallowing in the anger she felt for Elizabeth Bennet. It had continued to grow every day of her banishment to the home of her Aunt Horatia. Her elderly aunt was a teetotaling gorgon. She was a spinster who had been far too strong willed to allow a man to control her. She was strict and did not like the ridiculous rules and behaviors of society. Caroline was certain life in her aunt's home was worse than any prison could possibly be. She passed the endless days imagining hundreds of scenarios whereby she would get her revenge on that country nobody, Eliza Bennet. Caroline determined to find a way to get away from her aunt and get her revenge if it was the last things she did.

Regular letters from Charles to Aunt Horatia were received. Charles had married Jane Bennet, his angel, just as planned. Unfortunately, while he resided at Netherfield, visiting him would not allow Caroline to achieve her desired goal. And he never mentioned the Darcys in his correspondence to his aunt. Knowing she would never be invited to her brother's home, she would have to find some other way to achieve her desires.

Caroline always read the society column of her aunt's paper. She had read of Lady Marjorie being turned away from Almack's and had laughed over the notice for several days. Caroline had also fumed upon reading of the lady's engagement to the unknown Michael Amesbury, hoping the woman was forced to accept a tradesman or some other equally low gentleman. At her discovery of the broken engagement, Caroline enjoyed a sense of exultation at her false friend's downfall. Then, just a short time later Caroline read the wedding notice of Lady Marjorie and a viscount. She assumed Lady Marjorie's rank had allowed her to return to the ton while she was still banished to the wilds of Yorkshire to reside with her dragon of an aunt. Caroline's fury grew and her desire to revenge herself upon the woman responsible grew exponentially.

Having remained in her room as long as she could tolerate, she was forced to face her aunt and endure her tiresome company. As Caroline walked into the room, she recognized her brother's familiar handwriting on the letter her aunt was reading.

"What news does Charles send today?" Caroline asked with disdain in her voice.

"Your brother has purchased an estate named Ashford Hills. It is ten miles south of someplace called Lambton."

At the mention of Lambton, Caroline's interest was piqued. Lambton was but five miles from Pemberley. "When does Charles expect to take possession of his new estate?"

Her aunt continued to read, looking for the information that Caroline wished to know. "It appears he will take possession mid-September, but will only be there for a short time before journeying to

London with friends to attend the wedding of some viscount. They expect to return by the end of October."

Caroline was thrilled with the news her aunt provided. It was a safe assumption to imagine the friends were the Darcys, and the wedding would be that of the Earl of Matlock's eldest son. With this information, a plan began to form in Caroline's mind. She had several weeks in which to refine her plan and ensure her success. Though she wished to return to her room to plot her revenge, she determined to remain with her aunt in case there was further helpful information to be learned.

The Gardiners were back in London for only a day before Mary, Kitty, Mrs. Gardiner, and the children set off on the short ride to Rosings. Their return trip from Pemberley to London had been unremarkable. Other than the frequent stops to change horses and the need to keep the children entertained on the long ride, it was accomplished easily. They had passed some of the time talking about the many events and activities they had enjoyed at Pemberley.

As the carriage drew closer to Rosings, Mary grew more excited and a little bit anxious. She had not received much notice from her mother and very little training about running a home. She was grateful for the time Mrs. Hill spent instructing Kitty and her, as well as the time she had spent observing her Aunt Gardiner and Elizabeth as they went about their daily responsibilities.

Finally, the carriage turned onto the drive leading to Rosings. They passed the Hunsford parsonage that had belonged to Mr. Collins. Mary observed that it was a lovely cottage, one that was on the large side. She wondered about the new parson Richard mentioned how held the living. Then the great house came into view. Rosings was not so large as Pemberley, but the style was far more ornate. The carriage drew to a halt at the front entrance, and a footman quickly set the steps and helped the passengers to descend from the vehicle. The front door opened, and Richard and Anne appeared to greet their guests.

"Mary!" cried her intended as he rushed forward to pick her up and swing her about before setting her back on her feet. "You were gone for much too long," he almost pouted. "I shall not allow that to happen again. Two weeks is too long. A month was almost unbearable!"

Mary was laughing as Richard set her back on her feet. "I missed you, as well." Her warm smile and soft look were a balm to Richard's lonely heart.

"Mrs. Gardiner, Miss Bennet, Miss Catherine, it is a pleasure to welcome you to Rosings." They acknowledged the greeting of Miss de Bourgh.

"We thank you for your kind invitation," replied Mrs. Gardiner.

"And who might these charming guests be?" asked Anne as she looked at the children.

"Miss de Bourgh, allow me to present my children. This is Edmund, Susan, Hugh, and Rachel," said their mother, indicating each child in turn.

With Mary's hand tucked into his arm and his other hand holding it in place, Richard said, "Please do come in. Anne has called for refreshments for everyone." The group all trooped into the house.

The hallway at Rosings was nothing like that at Pemberley. Dark paneled walls and suits of armor filled the space. Hugh's eyes grew wide at the sight, and Susan reached for Mary's hand.

"I see that Rosings is decorated in a much different style from Pemberley," remarked Mrs. Gardiner with a smile.

Both Richard and Anne smiled, as well. "Indeed, my mother designed all in the house to intimidate visitors and remind them of their *proper* place."

"Their place according to Aunt Catherine, that is," continued Richard.

"While you are here, Miss Bennet, I thought perhaps we could look through some fabric samples and paint colors. I did not wish to make changes to the house without your input, as it will soon be your home," said Anne.

"That is very thoughtful of you, Miss de Bourgh. However, Rosings belongs to you; do you not wish to make the decisions?"

"No, indeed, but I should enjoy working on it together."

"Then I should be delighted to assist you," said Mary with a shy smile.

Consequently, as Richard entertained the children and Mrs. Gardiner explored the gardens after luncheon, Mary and Anne sat in the main drawing room and made selections for the updating of Pemberley.

They were thus engaged, having recently been joined by Kitty and Mrs. Gardiner, when Lady Catherine burst into the drawing room. "Mother, you are not supposed to be here without an invitation," said Anne in an annoyed voice.

"So I am to be kept from all visitors to my home, as well as from the house that has been mine these last nearly thirty years!"

"You are, Mother, for it is no longer your home. Whom Richard and I invite to visit is none of your concern."

Ignoring her daughter, Lady Catherine moved in the direction of the largest chair in the room. Her 'throne' had been removed from the room immediately upon her being ousted from the main house. In fact, Anne and Richard had allowed her to take it with her to the dower house.

"Introduce me to your guests, Anne. You have never entertained before, and I am sure you need my instruction."

Knowing that her mother would not depart without gaining her way, Anne reluctantly made the introductions. "Mother, this is Mrs. Gardiner, Miss Mary Bennet, and Miss Katherine Bennet."

"Anne, what are you thinking allowing those upstart Bennets into Rosings?"

Mary bristled at Lady Catherine's words while Kitty seemed to shrink in upon herself and edge closer to her aunt for protection.

It was at this point that Richard returned. He had taken the children to the nursery for a snack and was just entering the drawing room as his aunt made the derogatory words about his betrothed.

"Not only are the Bennets and Mrs. Gardiner, who is their aunt from London, -- "

"Not the tradesman's wife!" interrupted Lady Catherine, scandalized.

Richard cast a harsh glare at his aunt, ignoring her interruption.

"As I was saying, not only are the ladies welcome at Rosings, Miss Mary Bennet will soon be its new mistress."

Again, Lady Catherine interrupted. "A Bennet is no more fit to be mistress of Rosings than her upstart sister is to be the mistress of Pemberley. This is not to be borne!"

"ENOUGH!" cried Richard in a voice that made his aunt jump.

"You shall apologize to my betrothed and her family this minute, Aunt, and then you shall leave, as you were not invited to visit at this time. In fact, I should like to know how you gained entrance. The staff has orders not to admit you unless we have notified them of your invitation."

"I did not bother to knock. Rosings is my home, so I walked right in."

"Rosings is no longer your home, as you well know. Now apologize and leave under your own power, or I shall have the footmen throw you out. I will also ensure there is no way you can walk in on your own again. Now permit me to escort you to the door, Aunt."

"I do not wish to leave. I shall stay for tea."

"No, you shall not, Aunt. Anne and I have guests to entertain today, and your unpleasantness is not the impression we wish our guests to obtain of Rosings."

Richard's defense of her and her relatives allowed Mary's anger to wane. In fact, a small smile played about her lips at the way he managed the arrogant, demanding woman.

When Lady Catherine made no move to do as her nephew had requested, Richard pulled the bell for the butler. Upon Egerton's appearing in the doorway to the drawing room, Richard petitioned, "Please have two large footmen come immediately to remove my aunt from the house, then return so that we might speak.

"Yes, sir," said the butler before making a stately exit, though he reappeared quickly with the requested servants. Richard instructed the footmen to escort his aunt from the room. The men stepped up on either side of the lady's chair. They waited only a few seconds before taking hold of the Lady Catherine's upper arm and lifting her from her seat. In fact, her feet did not touch the floor until she was set down on the front steps and the door was closed firmly behind her, cutting off the squawks of the elderly lady.

Richard then directed his attention to his butler. "Lady Catherine informed me that she was able to walk in today undetected. Please ensure that someone is always on duty in the hallway. If someone cannot be there, please ensure that the door is locked to prevent anyone from entering uninvited."

"Yes, sir. I shall see to it immediately." Egerton bowed and exited the room.

Laughing heartily Richard remarked, "That was not the welcome to Rosings I desired for you, Mary. I do hope that my aunt's presence so close to our home shall not cause you to reconsider your acceptance of my proposal." Mary noted that in spite of the laughter in his voice, there was a look of concern in his eyes.

"Of course not, Richard. You forget I have lived with a disagreeable parent for many years. Your aunt may be blustery and domineering, but she does have some sense, a quality my mother lacked. I am sure if we continue to be firm with her, to treat her just like a child, she will learn what is acceptable and what is not." Mary gave her betrothed a soft smile as she answered. She was glad to see the concern leave his eyes.

"You have greater faith in my mother than I have," said Anne de Bourgh. "I hope you have the patience to repeat yourself countless times, Miss Bennet, for I am sure it shall be necessary." A small smile graced Anne's face as she spoke, and the smile grew as she and Mary shared a look.

"Perhaps she will be so disgusted that a Bennet is in charge, she will stay away for fear of contamination," laughed Mary.

The next day was the day for Rosings' harvest celebration. The harvest had been very successful as the weather had cooperated throughout the growing season. The yields were higher than last year's, and Richard and the steward, Mr. Rowley, had already determined what needed to be done to each of the fields to ensure they were at their most productive for next year.

Having been introduced to Mrs. Crawford the previous day, Mary offered her assistance to her today in the last minute preparations for the tenant gathering. Mrs. Crawford was pleased with the young lady and felt having Miss Bennet as a mistress to the estate would not be a hardship.

Finally, it was time for the celebration. The tenants began to arrive at the ballroom doors where Anne, Richard, and Mary waiting to welcome them. Anne and Richard had insisted that Mary join them, as she would be the mistress of the house by the time of the next harvest. Mrs. Gardiner and Kitty assisted at the tables which held activities for the children. There was a long banquet table laden with food along one wall of the ballroom. Smaller tables were set up around the room where the guests could sit to partake of the meal. Once everyone had arrived, Richard addressed the tenants and their families.

"We are very pleased to welcome you to Rosings today for our first harvest festival in many years. We know that your efforts make Rosings the great estate that it is, and we are very grateful for the work you do on behalf of our family and yours. Please enjoy the food and drink prepared for you. There are activities for the children at a table at the far end of the ballroom. Again, please accept the thanks of Miss de Bourgh, myself, and my betrothed, Miss Bennet, for all your support of the place we all call home. Enjoy, and please do not leave without collecting the small gifts we have prepared for you."

Generous applause greeted Richard's words and allowed the tenants to relax and enjoy the event. To ensure that Lady Catherine did not interrupt the special event, two footmen had been dispatched to watch over the doors of the dower house to guarantee Rosings' former mistress did not disrupt the proceedings.

Mary was again part of the farewells and the distribution of the gifts for the tenant families. There was evident pleasure on the part of the tenants to finally be recognized for their efforts. They were delighted to have Lady Catherine no longer in charge of the estate and expected the future of the Rosings, as well as their ties to it, would be much happier.

On the last day of the visit to Rosings Park, the family attended church. Mary was very impressed with the new pastor. He seemed pleasant and intelligent, and the sermon he delivered was both uplifting and thought-provoking.

Overall Mary was delighted with her first visit to her new home. She had enjoyed the time with Anne in determining a new look for the ostentatious house. She looked forward to seeing the changes that would occur before her next visit. Mary was also thrilled with the way Richard had interacted with her young cousins. He had played ball and tag with the children out on the grounds of Rosings. Richard had also taken all of the children up before him on his horse and shown them around their cousin Mary's new home. With Mrs. Gardiner's permission, he even taught some of the basics of fencing to Edmund. Mary was enthralled to dream about what a wonderful, attentive father he would make.

Now that the harvest was completed, Richard would soon join them in London, staying at Matlock House. "I should be arriving in London on Friday. That will allow me to wrap up things here. I should be able to deal with any new issues that arise via post with the steward, so I will happily escort you all around the town."

"Will Miss de Bourgh be joining you?"

"I have not yet convinced her to come to enjoy some of the delights of London, but I feel certain I shall have her beside me when we arrive in town. I heard from Mother that you will soon be shopping for your trousseau. I do hope it shall not require so much of your time that I shall not be able to enjoy your company."

"Indeed not. I am not a big shopper, though I do look forward to purchasing my wedding gown. Lizzy, Lady Rebecca, Aunt Gardiner, and I completed most of the wedding plans while we were visiting Pemberley. Other than my trousseau, there is not much for me to do. I will write the invitations as the day draws closer. Are you sure there is no one outside the family you wish to invite?"

"Only a few friends from my army days and a few from my university days."

"Please be sure to provide me with the names and addresses of those you want to include."

"I shall provide it as you write the invitations as it will allow me to sit with you as you do this important task for our wedding."

"That sounds lovely, Richard."

When the time to depart at last arrived, Mary was sad to again be separated from her love, but Richard promised to present himself at Gracechurch Street within hours of arriving in town. He escorted her to the carriage, handing in all of the ladies. Mary was the last to enter the carriage, and he left her with a lingering kiss upon the back of her delicate hand.

The morning after her family departed, Elizabeth found the opportunity to write to her father and sister, Lydia. She sat at her desk in her cozy study and penned the letters on the personalized stationary Darcy had purchased for her. He had also given her a new seal that displayed her initials entwined with the top of the family seal. Completing her task, she moved towards Darcy's study.

"William, have you finished your letters? I thought perhaps we could take them into Lambton and have them posted. I also wished to visit the draper's shop. I thought to purchase some cloth, so I might begin making clothes for our little one."

Looking up, Darcy smiled at his lovely wife. "That sounds like a pleasant outing, my love. Perhaps we should visit the nursery to see what other items we will need to purchase before the babe's arrival."

"I believe there will be time for that another day, William. I know you have work to do about the estate as the harvest approaches."

Darcy nodded at the truth of her statement. "Allow me to call for the curricle, and we shall take a trip to the village. I shall drop you at the draper's, then have the letters posted before returning to you."

"That sounds like a perfect plan. I shall be ready to depart by the time the carriage is ready." Elizabeth turned and mounted the stairs, returning quickly with her bonnet, pelisse, and gloves. Darcy was awaiting her in the hall and escorted her out to the curricle, assisting her into the vehicle.

The azure sky and light breeze added to the multi-colored leaves on the trees made for a lovely day. Darcy stopped before the drapers shop and helped Elizabeth from the carriage. He walked forward, opening the door to the shop for her. "I shall return shortly, Mrs. Darcy," said her husband with a loving smile.

"I shall be eagerly awaiting your return, Mr. Darcy." Darcy was delighted with the look in her eyes as she spoke.

"Welcome, Mrs. Darcy. How may I assist you today?"

"I wish to look at some fabrics and items to make gowns for a baby. I also wonder if you have some samples of paint colors, wall hangings, and fabrics for window treatments that I might take with me."

"What rooms do you wish to redo, Mrs. Darcy, so that I might know the best samples to send with you?" asked the proprietor.

Having observed one of the biggest gossips in Lambton in a back corner of the store, Elizabeth quietly replied. "We need to refresh the nursery."

"My congratulations to both you and Mr. Darcy."

"Thank you, Mr. Poole."

After directing his esteemed client to the area of the shop where she would find the fabrics she was looking for, Mr. Poole went into the back of the shop to gather the samples she requested. Before he returned, Darcy arrived back to the shop, standing next to his wife to hold her selections. She purchased some soft flannel in several pastel colors, some cutwork lace, and ribbons to use to trim some of the gowns, as well as threads for embroidery and yarn for knitting.

Darcy carried everything to the counter at the front of the shop and set the items down while Elizabeth looked at patterns for gowns, caps, and other baby items. Selecting the styles she liked, Elizabeth brought them to the counter, and Mr. Poole cut what was needed and wrapped the items. Darcy carried their purchase from the shop, setting it on the floor of the curricle at Elizabeth's feet. Then he helped his wife into the carriage, and they headed for Pemberley.

When they arrived home, Darcy carried the items into Elizabeth's study as requested before making his way upstairs to change. After dining with Elizabeth, he rode out to meet his steward and oversee the harvest. Elizabeth sent all of the fabrics to be laundered, then picked up the yarn and began to knit a blanket for the baby.

A few days later, Darcy sought out his wife as she was cutting out a gown from the recently purchased fabric. "My love, it seems there is another event we must attend while we are in London."

"Are you speaking of the wedding of Lord Wescott and Evelyn Pottsfield?"

"I am, but as I just opened the invitation, how could you possibly know?"

"Evelyn wrote to me when they set the date. As we were not in town she wished to be sure I was aware of the event and hoped that we might be able to attend."

"I must admit the thought of Wescott settling down with a young woman for whom he holds true has affection is not something I ever expected to see."

"Is it not heartening to realize there are some people in the world who can grow and change for the better? We have encountered so many who cannot, I have hope for the future of mankind," said Elizabeth with a smile. "I also appreciate the way you have allowed your good opinion to be regained." Elizabeth cast a saucy smile at her husband.

"Shall I leave this with you to send our reply, my dear?"

"I shall be happy to attend to it, William. By the way, my love, I believe I shall have to see Madame Colette to have some new gowns made. Those that I have are becoming quite snug, and the décolletage on some has become almost indecent."

"I have noticed and enjoyed it very much," said Darcy with a roguish smile. "However, I shall happily attend you to the modiste, my love. I would prefer no others see this delightful view."

Noting the passionate look that had appeared in her husband's eyes, Elizabeth immediately spoke so as to redirect his thoughts. "I wonder if she might have time to make a new gown for me before the wedding."

"Perhaps you could write to her and send your altered measurements. That way, she could have some items ready for fitting upon our arrival in town."

"That is an excellent suggestion, William. I shall have the Pemberley seamstress take my measurements and send them off tomorrow."

Darcy leaned down and bestowed a loving kiss upon his wife. "How are the plans for the harvest festival coming, Elizabeth? Is there anything with which I can assist you?"

"No, William. I believe the preparations are well in hand. How soon after the festival shall we be able to leave for London?"

"We could depart the next day, unless that will be too taxing for you, my love."

"I am sure that I can manage to ride in a carriage without too much difficulty, provided you will allow me to rest upon your shoulder," Elizabeth answered with a smirk.

"I will be more than happy to serve as your pillow, dear wife. Then I will send out the notices to the inns to prepare for our arrival."

The rest of September passed with Elizabeth finalizing the details for the harvest celebration and busily making clothes for the baby. The parents-to-be happily explored the nursery one morning, as well.

Elizabeth loved the light and airy room. It had two fireplaces to insure the baby was protected from the risks that accompanied the extremely cold air of a Derbyshire winter. Much of the furniture was still in excellent condition, so they decided to have the pieces cleaned and revarnished. Elizabeth was particularly pleased with the comfortable rocker she found in the room. The size was a perfect fit for Elizabeth. They looked at the paint samples and selected two colors for the walls. They also found a delightful fabric that would compliment both the wall colors.

After completing the inspection of the nursery, Elizabeth met with Mrs. Reynolds, explaining what they wished to have done in the nursery and asking her to arrange for the work to be done while they were in London. Mrs. Reynolds noted the colors and fabric to be ordered. She would have the seamstress measure for the draperies and begin work on them when the fabric was received.

The day of the harvest celebration arrived. Elizabeth had flittered about the previous day double checking all of the details. To Elizabeth's eye, the skies appeared menacing, but Darcy assured her the weather would hold, and rain would not interrupt the celebration. The arrangements for the harvest celebration were almost identical to the picnic they had hosted in August. The tables were decorated with the beautiful bounties of nature. As each family arrived, Elizabeth was presented with a small wrapped gift. Word of the arrival of the next generation of Darcys had made its way throughout Pemberley, bringing joy to all those who heard the news. The tenants were encouraged to know that the Darcy family would remain at the estate for many more years.

CHAPTER 22

MARY FOUND THAT London held many delights when explored in the proper company. Richard had taken her to the theater, to an art exhibition, and to two musical evenings. They had also attended several dinners and three balls. She had spent many afternoons shopping with Lady Rebecca, Lady Julia, Miss de Bourgh, her Aunt Gardiner, and Kitty. Mary was delighted with the fabric she found for her wedding gown as well as the design for the gown that Madame Colette had created for the occasion.

Today was Elizabeth's turn to visit the modiste. Madame was fitting her sister with two gowns for the upcoming weddings, as well as several other dresses for her use while in London. She also received the commission to prepare a large quantity of winter clothing that would accommodate Elizabeth's ever-growing figure. Elizabeth was delighted with the designs, as they were fashioned in such a way as to grow with her expanding body. Madame promised to have another dozen day dresses ready to take with them upon their return to Pemberley. In addition, she would be shipping more dresses for day and evening wear, as well as something special for the Darcy Christmas ball and another for Mary's wedding.

Darcy also took her to the furrier for a fur-lined winter cloak, as well as a fur trimmed hat and matching muff. There was a need to visit the shoemaker for warmer winter footwear and boots in which she could tramp through the thick snows common to Derbyshire.

On their third night in town, they dined with the Fitzwilliams.

"Welcome, Darcy, Elizabeth. We are delighted you could make the journey to join us. Elizabeth, you are positively glowing. When we heard the news of the heir to Pemberley, we were afraid Darcy would forbid you to travel," said Lord Matlock.

"He did express his concern most determinedly. However, Dr. Elliott and I were able to convince him that I was perfectly healthy and should not have any adverse effects from the travel. I am sure this will be our last visit to London for many months."

"Well, we are so pleased you are here. You are looking well, Elizabeth. How are you feeling?" asked Lady Matlock.

"Other than being perpetually tired, I feel wonderful. I seem to be growing daily, but I am anxious for the time to come that I can hold my child in my arms."

They moved towards the drawing room where the rest of the family waited. Elizabeth was excited to see Penelope and moved forward to greet her.

"Penelope, dear, I am so happy to see you. Are all the preparations for the wedding well in hand? Is there anything I can do to assist you?"

"Elizabeth, you look superb. No, there is nothing you can do, but I am so pleased you will be able to attend."

"You and Jonathan will be joining the family at Pemberley for Christmas, will you not?"

"Indeed, we are very much looking forward to it. Jonathan has suffered greatly from Richard's teasing in the last several weeks. He is looking forward to getting in some teasing of his own in prior to Richard's wedding." The two women laughed.

Elizabeth then moved on to her sister to greet her. She stood with Lady Julia in animated conversation. Richard was at her side a frown on his face, and Elizabeth could see that Darcy was fighting to keep his grin hidden. As she drew closer, she could hear Lady Julia's words."

"So there is Richard; his horse has thrown him; he landed in a briar patch, and, as he fights his way free, he tears a big hole in the seat of his britches. He had to walk all the way back to the house with his hands covering his posterior." Julia was laughing so hard that tears trickled down her cheeks, and Darcy lost his battle as a huge grin appeared on his face.

Mary, a smile of her own on her face, patted her betrothed's arm and cast a mischievous look at the approaching Elizabeth as she said, "I guess that means our children shall behave much like Lizzy, so I shall know how to act." This made everyone involved laugh, including Elizabeth, who felt the need to defend herself.

"Yes, I did have my share of adventures as a child, but life is much more fun lived in the beautiful outdoors than the rigid behavior expected of young women indoors."

"I assume that means I should prepare for our children to test their boundaries and my patience," said Darcy with a raised eyebrow.

"Would you have me any other way, my dear husband?"

"Absolutely not!" Darcy's grin was in evidence as he continued. "I very much hope for a daughter who is the spitting image of her beautiful mother, complete with her sense of adventure. It will allow me to see what you were like as a child, my love." Darcy put his arm around his wife's waist and pulled her close to his side, glancing deeply into her sparkling eyes.

The Darcys enjoyed the evening visiting with their family and looked forward to the upcoming wedding.

Two days later, the Darcys, Bingleys, and Richard Fitzwilliam were dining with the Gardiners. They had barely entered the parlor when Hugh, a big smile on his face, ran to meet Darcy. He stopped a foot from Darcy's tall form, leaning to look behind the new arrivals.

"Where is Cinnamon? Did you leave him outside?"

The adults all chuckled, as Darcy kneeled down to look his young cousin in the eye. "I am afraid that Cinnamon was required to remain at Pemberley," Hugh's face fell, but it quickly regained its look of expectation as Darcy continued speaking, "but if the weather cooperates, perhaps you may ride some when you come to Pemberley for Christmas."

"Was Diamond Star happy when you left?"

"She was," said Elizabeth. "We made sure to visit them before departing and fed each of the ponies an apple."

"Will you please give her another one when you return and tell her I miss her?" Susan asked politely.

"Of course," replied Elizabeth.

"I believe they miss you too," added Darcy. "I am sure they will be happy to see you when you are next at Pemberley."

The children all looked pleased to hear this news.

After dinner, as the ladies visited while the gentlemen enjoyed a glass of port, Elizabeth turned to her aunt, asking. "Have you decided when you will arrive at Pemberley for the holidays?"

"We hope to arrive on the twenty-second. That way we shall be there for the ball, and we will be able to stay until after Twelfth Night."

"Oh that will be lovely, but I worry that it will not be enough time for Mary to ensure that everything for the wedding is to her satisfaction."

"Kitty and I decided to travel with Papa, and we shall arrive the first week of December. He wished to have time to rest before traveling again to retrieve Lydia from school."

"I may accompany him to fetch Lydia. I am anxious to see if she is as changed as she seems from her letters," added Kitty.

"I believe you will be pleasantly surprised, Kitty. I was very impressed with her behavior when we traveled to inform her about Mama's death. She finally seems to have matured, though she was angered and hurt by Mama's behavior before she departed for school. It was difficult for her to realize that Mama's love was conditional—even to the child she openly spoke of as her favorite. I believe we may need to help her to forgive Mama even if she cannot forget her final actions."

They were joined by the gentlemen shortly thereafter and decided to enjoy a night at the theater the next evening. That would give them a day of rest before the wedding of Viscount Gilchrist and Lady Penelope.

The night at the theater, which included Kitty and Georgiana, was quite eventful. As it was the beginning of the little season and with the wedding of the heir to an earldom would be taking place, most members of the ton were in the city, and it seemed that all of them were at the theater. The performance that evening was *Othello*, which seemed appropriate as the events of the evening unfolded.

With the crowds, the party was almost late arriving at the theater and rushed to their box just in time for the start of the performance. The drama unfolding on stage was nothing compared to what occurred during the first intermission. Darcy, Georgiana, Richard and the Bennet sisters, except for Jane, departed the box for refreshments and soon encountered Michael Amesbury. He was introduced to Elizabeth and Georgiana, who were the only ones present with whom he was not acquainted. As the group stood speaking and enjoying the punch the gentlemen obtained, a sneering voice was heard.

"Well, well what have we here? I still find it astounding that the premier bachelor on the London scene could fall so low as to marry a country nobody. And it appears to be catching, as even the son of an earl is soon to be joined to another from the same family."

Those whose backs were to Lady Marjorie stiffened, and Kitty stepped closer to Michael, beside whom she stood.

Darcy, Elizabeth, and Richard looked the lady over, ignoring her companion completely, before giving her the cut directly. They turned back to the others of their party, continuing the conversation as if no interruption had occurred. Mary, at Richard's side, was focused on comforting Georgiana, who stood next to her, while Kitty was now halfway hidden behind Mr. Amesbury.

"Ignore this group, Marjorie," slurred Viscount Amesbury. "They are two of your castoffs; you need not pay them any attention. Good evening, little brother," sneered the viscount, "as you see, yet again, I have bested you! This time by marrying the woman you have always loved."

"It appears you have been misled, Brother. I tried to be a gentleman in my notice, but clearly Lady Marjorie does not feel she must follow the rules of polite society. I found it necessary to break off the engagement because your wife has become the epitome of what I dislike in the women of the ton. I could never tolerate her boorish behavior, let alone love her. You are welcome to Lady Marjorie." The dismissive tone of Michael's voice angered the couple.

Darcy refused to acknowledge the intruders, but Richard, out of patience, turned and, in a cold, clipped voice, said, "If you would excuse us." Turning to Mary and Georgiana, he offered each an arm and moved away from Viscount and Lady Amesbury. Michael offered his arm to Kitty and followed them, with Darcy and Elizabeth quickly joining them. They had not gone far when the Viscount's voice rang out.

"How dare you insult my wife and me in such a fashion! I am a peer of the realm! You are nothing compared to me!"

Those standing nearby could not help but notice the confrontation. However, with the loud words of the viscount, everyone went silent and turned to watch the scene playing out in front of them.

"You will pay for this insult. I challenge you to a duel!"

Richard, choosing to believe the challenge was directed at him, turned. He felt Mary pull at his arm, so he turned to give her a reassuring glance. "Amesbury, due to your rather inebriated state, I will allow you to withdraw that remark." The deadly look in his eyes caused the viscount to falter. He glanced at the other gentlemen in the party and saw similar looks in their eyes. Inebriated though he might be, the viscount was well aware of both Fitzwilliam's and Darcy's reputations with both sword and pistol. He also knew that the only times he had ever defeated his brother in competition was when brute force was involved, an option not available in dueling.

"You are correct, gentlemen, that is the alcohol speaking. Good evening." So saying, the Viscount Amesbury took Lady Marjorie's arm and turned, hurrying away. They had not gone but two steps when they heard Lady Marjorie's low voice calling her husband a coward. With a furious glare at his wife, he grasped her upper arm in a fierce grip and practically dragged her away. They went down the stairs and exited the theater, where they hailed a hackney and returned to their townhouse. The viscount forcefully demonstrated to his wife his displeasure with her words.

As Michael watched his brother and the woman he once loved rush away, he became conscious that the young lady on his arm was trembling. "Miss Katherine, are you well?"

"Y – y – yes," she stammered.

Looking down at her wide brown eyes, flecked with gold, he noticed her fear. "Please allow me to escort you back to your box. Or would you prefer a glass of wine first?"

"I should like to go back to the box, please." Her sweet voice held a tremor, so he directed her to the Darcy box as quickly as possible. He helped her to her seat and returned to procure a glass of wine for her just as the bell announcing the resumption of the performance rang.

Michael could not help but notice the murmurs and looks directed at the Darcy party after the confrontation. He could only imagine what the gossip would be on the morrow. Michael arrived in the box just as the others were settling into their seats. He handed the glass to Kitty, saying he would return to check on her at the next intermission. Before he could return to his own box, Darcy offered, "Will you not join us for the remainder of the performance?" Michael accepted and took a seat behind Kitty.

During the second intermission, only the gentlemen left the box. They were returning with drinks for the ladies when the Duke of Devonshire approached them. Darcy and Fitzwilliam were both familiar with the Duke, for his estates were in Derbyshire.

"Good evening, Your Grace," said Darcy with a bow.

"Your Grace," said Fitzwilliam, as he too bowed.

"Will you introduce me to your friend?" asked the duke.

"This is my brother, Charles Bingley and a family friend, Michael Amesbury." The gentlemen both bowed and acknowledged the introduction.

Raising his voice slightly, the Duke remarked, "Nasty business that earlier. You gentlemen handled a difficult situation most impressively. Now, Darcy, I know that you have recently married. I am sorry I have not yet had the chance to meet your wife. May I please be introduced to her?"

"Certainly, Your Grace."

The men entered the Darcy box and set the drinks on a small table inside the door. At the men's entrance, Georgiana rose as she recognized the Duke, so the other ladies rose as well.

Stepping up next to his wife, Darcy placed his hand on the small of her back. "Your Grace, allow me to present my wife, Elizabeth Darcy. My love, this is His Grace, the Duke of Devonshire."

Elizabeth curtsied, and the duke reached for her hand, bowing over it and bestowing a kiss upon the back. "It is a great pleasure to meet you, Your Grace."

"The pleasure is mine, Mrs. Darcy." Elizabeth gave the duke a dazzling smile. "And will you introduce me to your companions?"

"These are my sisters, Your Grace." Indicating Jane, she said, "This is my elder sister, Jane, Mrs. Bingley. Then we have my next younger sister, Miss Mary Bennet, who is betrothed to Mr. Fitzwilliam, and then my sister Miss Katherine Bennet. I assume you know my sister, Miss Georgiana Darcy."

"I have never before seen a family with so many lovely young ladies. You brighten the theater with your beauty, ladies," said the duke as he bowed over each of the ladies' hands.

The duke stayed but a moment longer. As he departed, he remarked, "It is a great pleasure to have met you. I looked forward to seeing you at Viscount Gilchrist's wedding."

The remainder of the evening passed without incident. Those in the Darcy box concentrated on the performance, though many in attendance had their attention focused on the box containing the Darcy party rather than the stage. As the group departed the theater, Michael Amesbury escorted Miss Katherine Bennet to their carriage. He assisted her into the vehicle and turned to depart but paused as Darcy extended his hand. "My thanks for your kindness to my sister, Amesbury. It was good of you to offer your assistance."

"I am only sorry that the unpleasantness was caused by those I must call family," he said with a sheepish look.

Darcy laughed and clapped his shoulder, "All of us present have had to deal with an obstreperous relation. Think nothing of it."

Before Darcy could step in, Lizzy leaned out the open carriage door. "Mr. Amesbury, would you please join us for tea tomorrow afternoon at three?"

"It would be my pleasure, Mrs. Darcy. Until tomorrow." His eyes slid quickly towards Kitty as he responded.

The Bingley carriage that contained the Bingleys, along with Mary and Richard, had already pulled away from the theater. As the Darcy carriage moved away from the curb, Elizabeth remarked, "I do not know whether the most drama appeared on the stage or in other parts of the theater this evening." The laugh in her voice eased the tension that had remained since the incident with Lord and Lady Amesbury.

"Are there many people in society like that?" Kitty asked. Her voice displayed the discomfort she had experienced.

"You know there are difficult people in all walks of life, Kitty. Those in society are just better dressed and often possess an undeserved feeling of superiority or entitlement." Elizabeth tried to make light of the situation. "Kitty, you seemed almost frightened of Lady Marjorie when you saw her. Have you met her before?"

Her face flushed at the question, but with her eyes on her lap, she related her experience with Lady Marjorie in the park.

Elizabeth and Georgiana both expressed their sympathy, and Darcy turned to gaze out the window to hide his anger at the woman.

In the other carriage, the evening's events were also being discussed. "Richard, I was so worried when I heard that man challenge you to a duel."

"You need not have worried, my dear. As I said, it is not the act of a gentleman to accept such words from someone who is obviously impaired. But even had a duel been necessary, I would have easily won. Ralph Amesbury has no skill with either pistol or sword."

"That is hardly a relief, Richard," cried Mary.

He grabbed her hand and kissed it. "I shall do my very best to avoid ever being involved in a duel, my dear. You have my word as a gentleman."

Mary could not help but smile at his answer as she leaned her head against his shoulder. "Thank you, Richard, I appreciate that, for I could not bear to lose you."

He kissed the top of her head and sighed in satisfaction.

Bingley's carriage dropped Richard at Matlock House before returning to Darcy House. Mary and Kitty were staying there during the Darcy's short time in town.

Most of the family was gathered together around the breakfast table the next morning when Elizabeth entered the dining room. The late night and the emotional toll had left her exhausted. Darcy was in his place at the head of the table with the newspaper spread beside him.

He looked up as she entered. "Good morning, my love. Did you sleep well?"

"Yes, thank you, William. I feel well rested."

The others present offered their greetings, as Elizabeth filled a plate from the sideboard. As she took her seat, Darcy cleared his throat. "I believe there is something all of you will be interested in hearing." Clearing his throat, again, he began to read an item from the paper.

'Theatergoers last evening were treated to two dramas. There was an excellent performance of Shakespeare's Othello played out on the stage. Perhaps the more dramatic performance of the evening played out in the upper lobby when the disgraced Lady M., recently married to Viscount R.A., felt the need to further embarrass herself by forcing her attentions on Mr. and Mrs. D., recently returned from their estate, P., in Derbyshire.

Lady M. and Viscount A. flung insults that met with a direct cut from several members of the party, including the viscount's brother. The viscount, in his cups as usual, was foolish enough to issue a challenge to the former Col. R. F., which he quickly withdrew. The newlyweds were seen fleeing the theater in disgrace. The ridiculous behavior leaves this reporter to wonder if either possesses any sense. It appears jealousy of his younger brother was behind the viscount's recent wedding to the already disgraced Lady M. For a man whose behavior often borders the unacceptable, his recent marriage and unseemly display last night will soon make him as unwelcome as his wife in society. This reporter has to wonder if either of them has the intelligence to withdraw gracefully or will society be required to make their opinion of the couple more obvious. This report must also confess to admiration for the entire D. party and Mr. M. A. for their gracious handling of an unnecessary melodrama. I cannot end without mentioning the attention the group received from the D. of D., who seemed taken with the bevy of lovely women ensconced in the Darcy box last evening.'

Many at the Darcy table look relieved at the words they heard. All of the focus in the gossip notice was on Lady Marjorie and the viscount with only a compliment paid to the Darcy family rather than vicious speculations.

In the homes of the Fitzwilliam and Gardiner families, as well as that of Michael Amesbury, similar feelings of relief and pleasure were experienced as those felt in the Darcy home. In fact, across town, most of the ton agreed with the reporter's comments.

However, in the home of Viscount Amesbury, the feelings were very different. Lady Marjorie was furious to again be portrayed as persona non grata in society. The viscount, feeling her behavior to be the cause of the poor comments about him, handily showed his wife his displeasure. Their carriage was seen departing London that afternoon on the Great North Road. Speculation is that the Amesburys have decided to retire to the country for a time.

Michael Amesbury arrived at Darcy House promptly at the appointed time. He had enjoyed the feeling of protectiveness he experienced the previous evening. Miss Katherine Bennet had lovely eyes, and her sweet disposition was starkly in contrast to that of the woman he thought he loved.

Treywick showed him into the drawing room where the family waited to receive him.

"Mr. Amesbury," the butler announced in his dignified manner.

Those present rose and bowed or curtsied to the newcomer.

"Welcome to Darcy House, Mr. Amesbury," said Elizabeth graciously.

"I thank you for inviting me, Mrs. Darcy. It is a pleasure to be in the company of you and your family again."

"Please be seated." He noticed an empty chair next to the sofa on which Kitty sat and moved to take it.

Kitty, whose spirits were much recovered, turned to him as he took his seat. "Mr. Amesbury, please allow me to thank you for your assistance last night. It was very kind of you. I am sorry to have been so distressed that I failed to express my thanks then."

"You need not apologize, Miss Katherine. Your distress was perfectly understandable after your initial encounter with the lady. I was pleased I was at hand to help you." He smiled brightly at Kitty. She, in turn, blushed and returned to him a shy smile.

At that moment, Mrs. Trey entered, carrying the tea tray and followed by another maid whose tray contained fruit, pastries, and the like. Elizabeth prepared and served the tea. As the refreshments passed among the guests, Elizabeth began the conversation.

"My cousin Richard was telling me that you have recently returned from an extended stay in India. I have read much about the country. Tell me, what were your impressions?"

Michael spoke about the varied natural beauty of the country, the exotic foods, and smells, and the colorful saris worn by the women. He told them of the extremes in the weather and the sad state of poverty in which most of the natives lived. His story about riding an elephant caused the eyes of the young girls to widen in astonishment, so he mentioned the other animals he had encountered, including monkeys, snakes, and a tiger.

"Was your time there merely one of pleasure?" asked Kitty.

"No, as a second son, I traveled to India in hopes of making my fortune. At the time, I believed it was necessary to impress someone. With a small inheritance from my maternal grandmother, I purchased some land that was rich in spice production, as well as some mining interests. In one of the mines, diamonds were found. I kept the largest stone I discovered and plan to have it made into jewelry for my wife someday when I find her. I sold several unusually large stones to a Russian I met whose family crafted jewelry for the Czars. Not wishing to remain to oversee the operation of the mine, I sold it, recouping my original investment and making some profit. The spice fields I acquired have been left in reliable hands. I receive regular reports on the growth and production levels. I have been looking for a reputable importer to work with, and my solicitor suggested I speak to a man by the name of Gardiner to arrange for the importation of the spices I grow."

"Edward Gardiner?" Darcy asked.

"Indeed, do you know him?"

"Quite well. I am involved with him in a few interests, as is Bingley. He is an excellent businessman. He also happens to be the Misses Bennets' uncle. "

"My sister and I reside with my uncle when the Darcys are not in town," said Kitty quietly.

"Perhaps I could call on you there sometime, Miss Katherine."

"I would enjoy that, Mr. Amesbury." The others in the room paid close attention to this exchange.

An hour passed far too quickly to those present, who had all enjoyed the pleasant company and conversation.

"I thank you for the invitation to tea, Mrs. Darcy. It has been a lovely afternoon." He spoke to Elizabeth, but his eyes briefly slid to Kitty as he said the word lovely, causing the young lady to blush.

"Perhaps you would allow me to host all of you for dinner at the Clarendon to make up for the uncalled for bad behavior of my family. Would two nights hence be acceptable?"

Darcy looked at Elizabeth, then to Richard. Receiving a silent acceptance from both of them, he replied. "We would be delighted to join you."

"Good, good. I shall make the reservation and notify you of the time," replied Michael.

"Mr. Amesbury, might I share a bit of my philosophy with you?"

"Of course, Mrs. Darcy."

"I suggest you remember the past only as it brings you pleasure. It is not up to you to apologize for the poor behavior of others. We are pleased to accept your invitation solely on our enjoyment of your company."

"Based on my past with my brother and his wife, I believe that is a wise philosophy, madam. Well, then, let us say I wish to host you for the pleasure of your company."

"As my husband said, we would be delighted to join you for the evening."

Michael stood and bowed to the room. He took Elizabeth's hand and bowed over it. "Again, thank you for a pleasant afternoon, Mrs. Darcy. Good day, everyone, I look forward to our evening out." He smiled gently at Kitty as he spoke.

CHAPTER 23

DARCY HOUSE WAS bustling early as its many occupants busily prepared to attend the wedding of Viscount Gilchrist, Jonathan Fitzwilliam, and Lady Penelope Caswell, daughter of the Earl of Barrington. Richard would be standing up with his brother and Lady Penelope's younger sister would be her witness.

The wedding was scheduled for ten o'clock at St. George's Church in Hanover Square. Both the Fitzwilliam and Darcy families had long been members of this parish. The church itself was a lovely building. The vaulted barrel ceiling and *bas relief* décor were trimmed in gold leaf, highlighting the beauty of the structure. Its many stained-glass windows blanketed the interior in delicate colors as the weak autumn sun came through the windows. The interior was filled with bouquets of fall flowers. It was a dazzling setting for the heir to an earldom and the daughter of an earl.

Those of the Darcy party were seated in the second row behind Lady Matlock. The church was filled with a refined selection of the cream of London society. The handsome groom stood at the altar in a dark blue suit and a gold brocade waistcoat with his brother beside him in charcoal gray suit and burgundy waistcoat. The bride's attendant wore a dress of deep burgundy, while the bride appeared in a gown of deep gold trimmed in gold lace and a wedding bonnet trimmed with the same lace. Both carried a bouquet of beautiful fall flowers.

The wedding ceremony was just like any other as the words of the rector washed over the congregation. Darcy reached for Elizabeth's hand and entwined her fingers with his. Each of them was caught up in the remembrance of their wedding day. The Bingleys had similar feelings, and Mary's eyes were focused on Richard as he stood next to his brother. When the service ended and the register had been signed, the bride and groom departed for the wedding breakfast at Barrington House.

The wedding breakfast was a magnificent affair, which would be the talk of London for weeks to come. The attendance at the wedding and breakfast had been very select members of the ton. This evening, Matlock House would host a wedding ball. It was expected to be the event of the year. The Darcy party was among the last to leave the wedding breakfast. They returned to Darcy House, where Darcy insisted his wife rest for several hours before attending the ball that evening. The gown Madame Colette fashioned for the wedding ball was of dark green silk, embroidered with gold thread in a leaf pattern. With the gown she wore a set of topaz jewelry in a delicate gold filigree setting. Her upswept hair sported the gold combs Darcy had gifted her last Christmas and hairpins studded with topaz stones.

Kitty was very excited to have been invited to the ball. It was her first big London ball. Elizabeth had bought her a ball gown for the occasion that she could also wear for the ball at Pemberley. The gown was ivory satin trimmed in emerald green with an embroidered trailing green vine pattern decorating the neckline and hem of the gown. She wore a delicate chain from which hung a small square emerald and matching earbobs. They had been a gift from Darcy and Elizabeth for her seven and tenth birthday the previous month. She wore her dark curls upswept in a complicated pattern of braids with matching ribbon incorporated in them. A lone curl hung down caressing her shoulder.

The Darcy carriage was one of the first to arrive. As she had not yet made her debut, Kitty would not permitted to dance with gentleman who were not family, but that did not concern her, she was just delighted to be in attendance and to take in the splendor of a London ball. She had made a sketch of the church and wedding from memory to send to Lydia and would include as much detail as she could of the fashions she observed this night.

The Darcys danced the opening dance and then returned to stand near the seats occupied by Kitty, Georgiana, and Mrs. Annesley. Both young ladies danced with Darcy, Richard, and Bingley as well as Lord Matlock. They were content to sit and observe for the time being. Originally they were to have been presented next spring, but the fact that Elizabeth was with child now put that in question unless someone else volunteered to accept that responsibility.

After the supper break, Mrs. Annesley escorted the young ladies back to Darcy House in the Darcy carriage, accompanied by four footmen. Kitty and Georgiana snuggled into the sofa before the fire in Georgiana's sitting room, discussing the evening until they could no longer keep their eyes open. They were both fast asleep when the remainder of the family returned home from the ball in the wee hours of the morning.

It was a lazy morning at Darcy House as many of the occupants had been at the wedding ball. The first to rise were Kitty and Georgiana, and they were again busily chattering about all they observed the previous evening. In the master's chambers, Darcy quietly observed his lovely wife sleeping. Elizabeth had been so exhausted he had practically had to carry her to their room the previous evening. When he felt her begin to stir, he gently brushed the hair from her face, so that he could see her eyes. It was not long before her lashes began to flutter and her eyes slowly opened. The warmth of her expression and the seductive smile, which slowly spread across her luscious lips, caused an instant reaction in his body. "Good morning, my sweet William." Her sleep-husky voice only increased his desire for her.

"Good morning, my love." Darcy leaned forward to kiss her forehead, her eyelids, her cheeks, her nose, and finally kissed her lips slowly and deeply.

"I wish we could stay here all day," murmured Elizabeth as she stretched, arching her back which brought her into closer contact with his chest.

"I am happy to oblige my beautiful wife."

"If we did not have a houseful of guests, I would refuse to move from the comfort and warmth of your embrace."

"I am sure our guests will not be about so early. Let us enjoy some time together. Even should they awaken, they can manage without us for a little while.

Darcy tightened his embrace and drew his wife closer to his chest as he kissed her lips with unrestrained passion.

They loved slowly, and an hour later, Elizabeth was once again in the arms of Morpheus. Darcy gently eased his large body away from his wife and slipped from the bed, disappearing into his dressing room. Thirty minutes later he walked into the breakfast room and found most of the family at the breakfast table.

"Where are Georgiana and Kitty?"

"I believe they have already dined and can be found in the library. Kitty wished to write to Lydia about last evening. They hoped a walk in the park might be possible later in the day," Mary informed him.

"Where is Lizzy?" asked Jane.

"Though she wished to rise to attend to our guests, I convinced her to rest longer." The slight smile on his face indicated to Jane and Bingley what method was implored to convince her. "I suggest we all enjoy a leisurely morning and perhaps take that walk after Elizabeth joins us."

As a result, when everyone had finished their meal they departed to their preferred activities.

Jane and Bingley descended from their carriage and presented themselves at the door of Hursts' townhouse. Shown into the drawing room, they found Hurst and Louisa seated next to one another on the sofa.

"Bingley, Jane! How wonderful to see you!" The enthusiasm in Mr. Hurst's greeting was quite unusual.

"Good to see you too, Hurst." Bingley put out his hand to his brother, only to have Hurst grab it and pull him into a bear hug.

Hurst moved to Jane and lifted her hand to his lips to kiss it. "You see to be in exceptional spirits, Gilbert."

Louisa had not stood to greet the guests but reminded her husband to allow their visitors to take seats. In a jolly manner, quite unusual for the gentleman, Hurst ushered Bingley and Jane to the sofa across from the one where Louisa sat before returning to sit beside his wife.

"So how was your visit to your family, Hurst?"

"It was the best visit we have had," answered Louisa. "Caroline's absence made a huge difference in the atmosphere. It was truly a very pleasant experience."

"I am glad to hear things have improved for you without her presence," said Bingley earnestly.

"The Darcys asked me to find out if you planned to join us at Pemberley for the holidays. You did receive their invitation, did you not?"

"Yes, we did, but I am afraid we shall not be able to join them. We must stay in London this winter."

"What keeps you in town?" questioned Bingley.

"We will become parents in early November," was Hurst's proud response. Louisa shifted her position, and her protruding stomach was very visible.

Jane and Bingley both stood to offer their congratulations. Bingley pumped Hurst's hand enthusiastically, as Jane seated herself next to her sister, hugging her.

"Why did you not tell us?" asked Bingley with a puzzled expression.

The couple, who had been married for seven years, shared a look before Louisa spoke. "I did not wish to raise anyone's expectations—particularly my own."

Jane and Bingley looked confused. "This is the first time Louisa has been able to carry the child past the first three months."

Looking even more confused, Bingley said, "How many other times have there been?"

"Three," said Louisa with tears shimmering in her eyes. The quickening occurring just before the

Darcys' engagement ball, but even though things seemed to be going well, I was afraid to believe all would end well. Gilbert insisted we return to town, and we will stay here for the delivery."

"I want her to be near the very best medical care to available," confirmed the proud father-to-be.

"We are so happy for you. It must be something in the air, for Mrs. Darcy is with child as well. I believe they are due in early February."

"Oh please give Elizabeth my best wishes," Louisa said to Jane.

"Of course I will."

"Perhaps in the spring when the weather is warmer, you could visit Ashford Hills," offered Charles.

"You will not be coming to London for the season?" questioned Hurst.

Charles looked and Jane and she nodded slightly. "We are not certain yet, so please do not say anything, but we believe we may become new parents in early April. It is too soon to have felt the quickening, but many of the signs are there."

A new round of exuberant congratulations took place. Louisa called for tea, and the couples enjoyed a pleasant hour together.

By the time the Bingleys returned to Darcy House, Elizabeth had risen. They asked to be excused from the walk, and the remainder of the party prepared to exit the house. They walked the short distance to the entrance of the park and began down their favorite path. They walked to the lake to view the ducks, then wandered along the various walks for some time. As they were returning to Darcy House, Darcy leaned down to his wife and whispered. "This walk will always be dear to my heart. It was here that Wickham attempted to abscond with Georgie and you came to her rescue. As dreadful as his actions were, it is what brought you to my attention. Now with you as my wife and a child on the way, my life is more wonderful than I could have ever dreamed."

"I have always felt that way as well. I am glad I was able to assist Georgiana and grateful that you noticed me." Elizabeth leaned her head against Darcy's shoulder as they completed their walk.

Entering Darcy House, Treywick announced, "A note was delivered for you, sir. I placed it on your desk.

"Thank you, Treywick."

Darcy walked down the hall to the study door, as the others settled in the drawing room and Elizabeth rang for tea. Darcy and the refreshments arrived in the drawing room simultaneously.

"Was it anything urgent, my dear?"

"No Lizzy. The note was from Mr. Amesbury. We are to meet him at The Clarendon at seven. He has arranged for a private dining room and special menu for the evening."

As Darcy finished speaking, Jane and Bingley joined them in the drawing room. Elizabeth poured them each a cup of tea and relayed the message about the outing the next day.

"We visited with the Hursts this morning," said Jane. "Unfortunately, they will be unable to join us for the holidays."

"I hope there is no problem," remarked Elizabeth.

"Indeed not. However, Louisa is expecting their first child in early November. I hope you do not mind, but we shared your news with them, Lizzy. They sent you their congratulations."

"I do no mind in the least. I am delighted for Louisa. How is she feeling? Is everything going well?"

"They are cautiously optimistic as they have experienced loss in the past."

"Oh, I am sorry to hear that," said Mary.

"We invited them to visit in April," Bingley added.

"You do not plan to visit London for the season?" asked Darcy, surprised.

"I do not think it will be possible," was Jane's quiet reply.

The two married couples exchanged looks and an understanding was achieved. Large smiles appeared on all their faces, leaving the others to wonder.

As the Darcy carriage traversed the streets of London to the Clarendon Hotel, Kitty Bennet was filled with a sense of excitement, mixed with a large dose of nerves. Each time she had encountered Michael Amesbury, she had felt a flutter deep inside. She paid no notice to the feeling when they first met because of the beautiful woman on his arm.

During their meeting at the theater, Mr. Amesbury had protected her and shown her some specific attention. He was a handsome man. His blond curls and blue eyes were both accented by the dark tan of his skin. He was not so tall as Mr. Darcy, but his chest was broad and his arm muscles, well developed. He had an air of confidence about him that was both attractive and comforting. Mr. Amesbury appeared to be focused and willing to work hard to obtain his goals. He was polite and charming, but certainly such a man would not be interested in young Kitty Bennet from a small estate in insignificant Hertfordshire.

It was with this disheartening thought that the carriage arrived at its destination. The Clarendon Hotel was a glittering sight. There were liveried footman waiting to assist guests from their carriages and additional ones waiting to open the hotel doors to those arriving. Darcy stepped out and handed down his wife. The footman then moved forward to assist Georgiana and Kitty.

Waiting in the lobby, was a young boy in full Indian garb, complete with a turban. He bowed to Darcy and said, "Mr. Darcy?" At Darcy's nod the young boy pressed his palms together and bowed to Darcy. "If you will follow me, sir, I will guide you to the private room that has been arranged for this evening. Darcy nodded again, and the boy bowed once more before turning to guide them.

They went through the main dining room to the far side where glass French door's opened into a small dining room. The room was a soft green color, the walls lined with gleaming sconces from which beeswax tapers filled the room with their soft glow. A small chandelier hung above the rich mahogany dining table. The polish on the matching chairs and twin sideboards glistened. There was also an elegant marble fireplace. The table was set with the whitest of linens, exquisite china, sparkling silver, and glimmering crystal. An elaborate centerpiece of flowers and fruits dominated the table, interspersed with beeswax tapers.

Michael Amesbury stood just inside the door and graciously welcomed his guests. Michael seated Kitty to his right and Elizabeth to his left. It was not lost on anyone in attendance that the gentleman was attracted to Katherine Bennet. Beside Elizabeth sat Darcy, Jane, and Bingley. Beside Kitty were Richard, Mary and Georgiana.

"I am delighted you were able to join me this evening. I took the liberty of ordering one of the French chef's special menus. I hope you will enjoy his selections.

A tureen was removed from the sideboard, and the soup course was served. As that was cleared away an army of servants carrying trays bearing silver covered dishes appeared in the dining room. The first course was filled with dishes, many of which the diners had never before experienced. Course after course appeared and the diners sampled as many of the dishes as they could. Each course of the meal was accompanied by a different wine, and as the last dishes were removed from the table, coffee, tea, port, and brandy were brought in.

Throughout the meal, the conversation flowed freely. The placement of Elizabeth, Richard, and Bingley ensured that the room did not lack for liveliness. As the host, Michael first addressed himself to Elizabeth.

"Have you and Mr. Darcy been married for long, Mrs. Darcy?"

"We were married in early May, and it has been like an endless honeymoon."

"How very fortunate you are. Not many of our society may claim such joy. From observation, I would assume it is a love match rather than an arranged one."

"Indeed, it is rather a romantic tale. My husband saw me once briefly in Hyde Park as I assisted Miss Darcy, who was unwell. He came with Mr. Bingley to advise him about estate management when Mr. Bingley leased his first estate. That estate just happened to border my father's estate. We met again at the local assembly where he recognized me. From there, the adventure and excitement began," said Elizabeth with her warm laugh.

Darcy turned at the sound of his wife's sweet laugh and could not help but smile at her.

After a bit more conversation with Elizabeth, Michael turned to Kitty. "Miss Katherine, when I visited Darcy House for tea, the conversation seemed to revolve around my adventures in India. I wish to know more about you." He smiled warmly at her.

"What is it you would like to know, Mr. Amesbury?"

"Do you have any other siblings, besides those who are with us?"

"I do have a younger sister, Lydia. She is currently in school in the north."

"You have no brothers?"

"No, we do not. Our estate was entailed to a distant cousin of my father's, but he recently accepted a position as a missionary in Austrailia and made my sister, Elizabeth, his heir."

"How unusual that he would make a female his heir."

"I thought it unusual as well, especially as he wished to marry Lizzy, but Mr. Darcy was the first to request her hand."

Michael was charmed with her naïve answer. "You said you are residing with the Gardiners while you are in London. Will you be returning to Hertfordshire soon."

"No, I will remain in London until our family travels to Pemberley for Christmas. Mary and Mr. Fitzwilliam will be married during our visit there."

"That will then make you Miss Bennet, will it not?"

"I suppose it will, but I had not given it much thought."

"You will make a lovely Miss Bennet." Kitty blushed at his words. "Have you been presented in London yet, Miss Katherine?"

"No, I have not. Miss Darcy and I were to be presented in the spring, but our debut may have to be postponed."

"Why is that?" Michael questioned.

"It is unlikely the Darcy's will be in town in the spring as they will become new parents in early February. There has been some talk of Lady Matlock overseeing our debut season, but nothing has yet been decided."

"Then I shall pray for the situation to be resolved without delay to your presentation and hope to encounter you frequently when the season begins." Again, he smiled at Kitty.

"It would be a pleasure to meet with a friend upon occasion. I must admit that I am somewhat nervous about making my debut."

"A lovely and delightful young woman, such as you, should have no difficulties. I expect you shall take the ton by storm."

"I once thought it would be an exciting adventure to attend balls and parties every night, dancing until I wore out my shoes, but I do not believe the reality is quite what I imagined."

"What do you mean, Miss Bennet?"

"In the small community where I grew up, the society was much different from what I have experienced in London. I am not sure I can explain it well. Those I have met in town are all more concerned with outdoing one another than with being neighborly. Though there are always those who wish to stir up trouble, there is a sense of community or connection that exists in small towns, which is sadly lacking in the city. Perhaps I have just matured. I no longer think that the whirl of society is what I want from life. I would like to have a kind and loving marriage like I have observed with my elder sisters, a home and family of my own, and the opportunity to devote my time to the things that are important to me, including my art."

"You are fond of art?"

"Oh, yes! I enjoy it above all things."

"Have you been studying with the masters for very long?"

"Only for the last few months, since coming to London. My younger sister used to make fun of me for my attempts at sketching, but Mary has been very supportive of me and once they saw some of my sketches, my older sisters have also encouraged and supported me. Lizzy and William were the ones to arrange my lessons with a master."

"I should enjoy seeing some of your work," Michael replied.

"There is a piece at Darcy House. I would be happy to show it to you the next time you visit."

"Then I shall hope to be invited soon." Michael directed another warm smile upon Kitty.

The conversation around the table continued throughout the several courses of the dinner, with Michael and Kitty often talking exclusively to each other. At last the dessert course was presented. It was a castle, complete with turrets, constructed of cream filled profiterole and sugar strings. It was a sight to behold and drew applause from the diners.

As the evening concluded, Michael accompanied his guests to their carriages. "Mr. Amesbury," said Elizabeth, "thank you for a lovely evening. The meal was superb and the dessert a work of art. It was so beautiful, I felt guilty eating it." Everyone laughed in agreement.

"My wife is correct, Amesbury. It was a delightful evening; we thank you for the invitation."

"It was my pleasure to entertain you. I look forward to seeing you tomorrow at Lord Wescott's wedding." Bingley and Richard helped their ladies into the Bingley carriage. Darcy helped Elizabeth and Georgiana to enter. When he turned to assist Kitty, Michael Amesbury already had her hand in his and was preparing to hand her in. He bowed over her hand before releasing it. With a nod and bow to Darcy, Michael stood back as Darcy stepped into the carriage then stood waving at his departing guests until the carriage was out of sight.

Entering the townhouse of Lord Wescott, the Darcy party waited their turn to greet the bride and groom before moving into the dining room for the wedding breakfast. They appeared to be among the last guests to arrive, so they were afforded more of an opportunity to speak with the newlyweds.

Darcy was the first of the group to approach the couple. "Congratulations, Wescott! We are very pleased for you both. We wish you every happiness."

"We do, indeed," added Elizabeth. She presented her hand to Wescott, who bowed over it, giving it a slight squeeze.

"We are extremely pleased that you could be here with us this day. We greatly appreciate your friendship and support."

"We are delighted to share such a special occasion with you. You make a truly beautiful bride, Evelyn," said Elizabeth as she grabbed her friend's hands and leaned in to kiss both of her cheeks. "Will you be taking a wedding trip?"

"No, we wish to return to our estate. There are some updates and improvements to be made."

"Yes," added Wescott, "the harvest was very successful. We plan to invest some of the funds and use some to make some of the needed improvements. I must thank you again Darcy for you suggestions and support as I attempted to turn the estate's productivity around and return my family home to what it once was."

"Think nothing of it, Wescott. It is what friends do for one another. Though it is not something I ever expected, I am pleased to be able to count you among my friends." Both gentlemen chuckled. "Perhaps you would wish to visit us at Pemberley next summer."

"We would enjoy having you visit, and you will be able to meet our newest family member," added Elizabeth.

"Please accept our congratulations, and you may count on it then," replied Evelyn after sharing a look with her new husband. "I do wish I would have your support during my first season, Elizabeth, but I certainly understand the reason it is not possible."

"May I make a suggestion?" Evelyn nodded. "Be yourself and lean on one another for support when you encounter those who wish to question your worthiness to join their society."

Wescott put his arm around his wife's waist, giving a gentle squeeze. "I will do my very best to support her and protect her. Evelyn is very precious to me." She looked up into her husband's eyes, a loving expression on her face that reached the depths of her eyes. The smile on her face gave her an ethereal beauty. Before Darcy and Elizabeth moved away, Wescott felt compelled to add, "Thank you for showing me that love and real happiness were possible in our society." The earnest sincerity in his words could not be doubted. Both Darcys inclined their heads and smiled at the couple.

The rest of the group offered their congratulations to the bride and groom before following the line of guests entering the dining room. As they looked for their places at the table, Elizabeth and Darcy found themselves seated near the bride and groom. Georgiana and the Fitzwilliams were not far away. A bit further down the table Richard, Mary and

Kitty found themselves seated next to Michael Amesbury.

"This is a pleasant surprise," remarked Richard incredulously.

"Not quite," remarked Michael with a laugh. "Having been acquainted with Wescott since childhood, I requested that he seat me near your party."

Michael held the chair for Kitty to be seated. As he took his place beside her, he asked, "Did you enjoy the wedding, Miss Katherine?"

"It was very lovely. Miss Pottsfield made a beautiful bride, did she not?"

"Indeed she did. I believe Wescott was very fortunate to find such a captivating young lady to make his wife. Lady Wescott seems polite, wise, and very pleasant."

"She is all of those things. I had the opportunity to meet her when she attended Lizzy's wedding to Mr. Darcy. Both she and Lord Wescott were guests. In fact, I believe Lizzy was responsible for introducing them to each other."

"It seems Mrs. Darcy has a knack for bringing people together, either that or a magic touch," Amesbury said with a smile. "How are your wedding plans coming, Fitzwilliam?"

"I have been leaving the plans to Miss Bennet. She has promised to inform me where and when to show up. That is all I care about and, of course, for her to be there." Fitzwilliam cast a loving glance at his future wife, who blushed and smiled in return.

Everyone looked to Mary for the answer to Mr. Amesbury's question. "All the plans are well in hand. It was very kind of William and Elizabeth to offer us the use of Pemberley's chapel for the wedding. Neither of us wanted a large society wedding. I do worry about putting too much work on Elizabeth, though, as her condition will be quite advanced by then. The baby is due in early February."

"There is no need to worry, Mary," said Richard. "Neither Darcy nor Mrs. Reynolds will allow her to overdo. All the rest of the family will, also, be there, so she will have plenty of assistance." Mary looked reassured.

Mr. and Mrs. Pottsfield had spared no expense to arrange a stupendous wedding breakfast. They wished to ensure their daughter was presented in the best possible light to the many members of her new society. They had hired a French chef to plan the menu and oversea the meal and a popular string quartet to play during the breakfast.

When the time came for the toasts, Mr. Pottsfield stood to offer the first one. "To Evelyn and James, may the life they forge together be the happy beginning of a brave new world."

Many in the room recognized the lines between peers and wealthy merchants were blurring. Some would fight the change every step of the way, but the smarter members of the ton knew that diversifying and broadening their investments would be what kept their wealth growing in the future. There were no remaining members of Lord Wescott's family to offer a toast, so Michael Amesbury, who stood up with James Wescott, next rose to his feet. "It has been my good fortune of late to encounter many couples who have married for a deep and abiding love. James and Evelyn are one of those couples. May the love they share today grow throughout the years, and may they be an inspiration to those of us not yet so blessed."

This toast was almost as controversial as the first. Many in the older generation did not approve of this newfangled habit of marrying for affection rather than money and connection. In some families, the desire to set aside money and status for love was causing considerable upheaval.

The wedding breakfast continued pleasantly for several hours. The Darcy family departed soon after the bride and groom left the event. So far their time in London had been quite busy. I believe all of them looked forward to spending the remainder of the day in quiet activities and rest.

The Hursts were invited to tea at Darcy House one afternoon following the wedding. When the pleasantries had been exchanged, Elizabeth, Louisa and Jane were observed with their heads close together rapidly talking about the many changes they were experiencing with approaching motherhood. Their husbands were seen observing them with tender looks and proud smiles. During their remaining days in town, Darcy and Elizabeth did a little more shopping for the nursery, including, of course, a selection of children's books and picked up the remaining items of Elizabeth's winter wardrobe. They also took in a new art exhibit before retiring to Pemberley for the holidays.

CHAPTER 24

THE JOURNEY FROM London to Ashford Hills had been a difficult one. Rain had clogged the roads, turning them into a muddy morass. It had taken them four days just to reach the Bingley estate. Elizabeth did not feel her body could handle another moment in a carriage, so they decided to spend a few days with the Bingleys before covering the last ten miles that would take them to Pemberley.

The drawing room they entered had been updated while they were in London. The soft blue and gold gave the room a calm, elegant feel that was just what the weary travelers needed. They looked the room over as they waited for the refreshments to arrive. As they settled into the newly upholstered furniture, the housekeeper appeared with the tea tray. She was followed by a maid, with a second tray piled with scones, biscuits, and other offerings to sate the travelers' hunger.

Jane had just finished pouring tea for everyone when into the room swept Caroline Bingley.

"Charles, Jane, how lovely to see you. What a quaint little estate you have here."

All of those in the drawing room stared at the newcomer as if she had two heads. Darcy moved closer to Elizabeth and gripped her hand tightly.

"Caroline! What the devil are you doing here?"

"I missed you, Charles. It is lonely at Aunt Horatia's. With the holidays approaching, is it so surprising that I would wish to spend time with my family."

"Based on your last words to me, I find your sentiments hard to believe."

Darcy stood up and gathered Elizabeth close to his side. "I believe that we should be leaving, Charles." There was a hard edge to his voice, and he glared at Caroline.

Hearing the voice of the man she desired above all others, she turned her possessive gaze on Darcy. "Why Mr. Darcy, how lovely to see you and Miss Darcy." Failing to note his glare she took a step towards him, her hand extended. He, in turn, stepped back, pushing Elizabeth and Georgiana slightly behind him.

"Why, Miss Eliza, you are here as well." Caroline looked her rival over from head to toe. She smirked to notice that the chit had gained quite a bit of weight in the short time of her marriage.

"Her name is Mrs. Darcy, and do not dare to address her or me ever again."

Jane looked pleadingly at her husband when Darcy said they would depart immediately. He understood his wife's desire and said, "That will not be necessary Darcy." He rang for the housekeeper. "Mrs. Greenwood, please show the Darcys and Miss Georgiana to the rooms prepared for them and then return here immediately afterward."

"Certainly, Mr. Bingley." In the months since the Bingleys took residence, Mrs. Greenwood could not remember ever seeing her employer in a bad temper.

Turning to his guests, he said, "Go and rest in your rooms. I will deal with sending Caroline on her way." Bingley heard his sister's indrawn breath and turned a quelling look on her to prevent her from speaking further.

"Yes, William, Lizzy, please do not leave. It might be detrimental to Lizzy's health to continue traveling today."

Elizabeth looked at her husband. He could see that she did not wish to be in the presence of Caroline Bingley any more than he did, but her exhaustion and discomfort were also easily discerned by her loving spouse. Nodding to Bingley and Jane, Darcy directed Elizabeth from the room, giving a wide berth to Miss Bingley.

"Why would it be detrimental to Miss Eliza to travel? Is she dying?" asked Miss Bingley, delight in her tone.

Jane looked aghast at her sister-in-law's words, while Bingley said, "Of course not. She is with child and due not long after the first of the year." At his words, Jane's cast a brief, disapproving look at her husband before turning to observe her sister-in-law's reaction. What she saw caused a chill to travel down her spine.

"Sit down, Caroline," Bingley ordered.

She gave her brother a sour look. "Are you not pleased to see me, Charles?"

"No. I told you when you left London that I wished to have nothing further to do with you. I have not had any contact with you in that time, so what made you think I would desire to see you."

"I could not believe that you were serious, Charles. Father and Mother would be very disappointed in you for the reprehensible way you have treated me."

"No, Caroline, any disappointment they might feel would be for the outlandish and demeaning behavior you exhibited in London. Your actions were beyond the pale. You made it necessary for Louisa and me to distance ourselves from you. We could not allow your antics to reflect poorly on us."

"All I did was warn Mr. Darcy of Lady Marjorie's treachery," said Caroline with a sniff.

"We both know that is not true, Caroline. You were plotting with her from the beginning. You were observed going to her house on more than one occasion."

"You were spying on me!" she cried outraged.

"None of that matters, now. I must deal with the current situation. How did you convince Aunt Honoria to allow you to travel here?" Caroline would not meet his eyes, and it appeared she did not intend to answer. "Tell me immediately!" Bingley barked.

"I forged a letter as if from you requesting that I visit."

"I am surprised Aunt Honoria believed you. It seems I shall have to inform her that I no longer wish to have any contact with you and advise her of your "talent" with handwriting."

Before anything else could be said, Mrs. Greenwood returned to the drawing room. "You wished to see me, Mr. Bingley."

"Yes, Mrs. Greenwood. What did this person say or do to make you agree to allow her entrance to my home?"

"She informed me she was your sister and showed me a letter inviting her to visit. I assumed you had forgotten to mention it to me. Is something wrong, sir?"

"Yes, I am afraid there is." The housekeeper's hands shook as she awaited her master's next words. "I have broken ties with Miss Bingley. She knew she was not welcome here, so forged that letter she presented to you. What room was she placed into upon her arrival?"

"I am sorry for my error, Mr. Bingley. I put her in the family wing, sir."

"Please escort her to another room—preferably something as far from the other guests as possible. The only comfort she will need is a fire, and I want a footman to stand guard at the door. Then send a maid to pack her belongings. She is not to leave her room. Also, would you send someone to Lambton to find out when the next coach leaves for York."

"Certainly, Mr. Bingley; right away, sir."

The housekeeper indicated that Miss Bingley should pass before her out of the room. When she did not rise to depart, Mrs. Greenwood stepped into the hall and spoke quietly to the butler. Soon the largest footman on staff appeared. He stepped up to Caroline and took hold of her elbow, pulling her gently to her feet. As he attempted to escort her from the room, she tried to shake loose and cried, "Unhand me!"

The footman looked to his master, whose head shook slightly. At the signal from his employer, he tightened his hold and propelled Caroline from the room. They followed the housekeeper up the stairs to Caroline's chamber. The footman gently pushed the woman into the room and closed the door, which was then locked by the housekeeper. She moved down the hall to the dressing room door. Entering she locked the door which connected with the bed chamber and then the hallway door, as well.

The housekeeper returned below stairs and issued orders to two of the maids to go pack Miss Bingley's belongings immediately. Pausing, Mrs.

392 of LINDA THOMPSON

Greenwood turned to the maid. "Pack all of Miss Bingley's belongings, except a nightgown and a traveling outfit. She will be departing on the next coach to York. Mr. Bingley wishes her confined to her room until her departure." The maid looked shocked at the housekeeper's words but hurried to do as requested.

Jane and Bingley knocked on the door to the sitting room attached to the Darcys' suite. Opening the door, Darcy put his finger to his lips as he beckoned for them to enter.

"Where is Lizzy?" asked Jane.

"I convinced her to rest. Where is Miss Bingley?"

"At present, she is locked in her bedchamber. She will remain there until being escorted to the coach that will take her back to York," answered Bingley.

"How did she get here?"

"She forged a letter to my aunt from me, inviting Caroline to visit. She used the same letter on the housekeeper to gain admission. I have since informed Mrs. Greenwood never to admit Caroline entry to the house in the future. I, also, sent someone to Lambton to find out when the next coach to York departs."

"I hope it is soon," was Darcy's emphatic reply.

"We will leave you to rest. Mrs. Greenwood said dinner would be at half-past six."

"We will see you at dinner," said Darcy as he held the door for them to exit.

"Until dinner."

Having finished dressing for dinner early, Bingley sat at the desk in his study, going over the correspondence that arrived during their absence. He looked up at a knock on the door. "Come."

The door opened and the butler entered. "Mr. Bingley, Joseph returned from Lambton. There is a coach departing at eight in the morning for York."

"Excellent. Please have the carriage ready by half-past six in the morning. I shall escort my sister to Lambton to purchase her ticket and one for Fletcher. Please ask him to be ready to accompany us. He will be joining my sister on the trip, then spend the night at my aunt's home in York before returning here."

"Everything shall be prepared as you have requested, sir."

A moment after the butler exited, he heard another knock. "Come."

Mrs. Greenwood entered the room. Looking somewhat nervous, the housekeeper said, "Sir, I am sorry to inform you that I have heard the sound of things breaking coming from Miss Bingley's suite."

"I should have expected it," said Bingley shaking his head. "Do not worry about it, Mrs. Greenwood. After her departure when you clean the chamber, notify me which pieces were destroyed, and I shall obtain replacements. I shall deduct the cost of the replacements from my sister's allowance. You need not worry about it any further."

"Yes, sir. Thank you, Mr. Bingley."

As the housekeeper departed, Bingley pulled out a sheet of paper and began a letter to his aunt.

The traveler's enjoyed a quiet meal before retiring for the evening. Before joining his wife, Bingley stopped at his sister's chamber. Mrs. Greenwood unlocked the door, and Bingley stepped inside. Giving Caroline an unrelenting look, he spoke. "We shall be departing here at half-past six in the morning. The carriage will take us to Lambton where I will buy you a ticket on the coach to York. The footman guarding your door will be traveling with you. He will ensure you arrive at Aunt Honoria's safely.

Please understand, Caroline, I do not wish to communicate with you or see you ever again." With that, Bingley turned and exited the room before Caroline could speak. Caroline stood staring after her brother. The treatment she had received since her arrival had increased her anger and desire for revenge. Despite being sent away so quickly, Caroline had learned something that might allow her to hurt the Darcys as deeply as she had been hurt. She vowed to cause them an unending pain that would cast a pall over the rest of their lives, perhaps even driving a permanent wedge between them.

Early the next morning the housekeeper and maid arrived to help Miss Bingley prepare for her departure. She gave them the silent treatment, which continued as she descended the stairs. Caroline refused to accept Charles' assistance into the carriage and rode the entire way to Lambton without speaking. If she had known her behavior was a relief to her brother, Caroline would have behaved in such a way as to cause him as much annoyance as possible.

His carriage pulled up in front of the entry to the Chestnut Tree in Lambton. Charles stepped down and offered his hand to Caroline. She again refused his assistance. Shaking his head, he turned and entered the inn; stepping up to the counter beside the door, he purchased a one-way ticket for Caroline and a round-trip ticket for the footman. He provided the tickets to Fletcher as well as bag of coins to cover incidentals during the trip, and his aunt's address. He also warned him to keep a close eye on Miss Bingley until she was safely delivered to his aunt's home.

Turning to Caroline, he said, "Good-bye sister. I hope you can find your own happiness."

When she did not acknowledge him, Bingley turned and exited the inn. He went directly to the express office and posted the letter he had written the day before. It should arrive in York before his sister. After completing his business, Bingley climbed into his carriage and returned home. He arrived just as the others were sitting down to breakfast. No one asked about his errand, but four exhalations of breath and equally relieved expressions greeted the small nod of his head.

The three days the Darcy's stayed at Ashford Hills passed pleasantly once their uninvited guest had departed. In the mornings, Bingley and Darcy attended to estate business, and Jane, Elizabeth, and Georgiana looked over the updates that had been made to the house, determining what rooms to focus on next, as well as looking at the samples and making the necessary selections.

At dinner on the last night the Darcys were in attendance, Jane and Bingley announced that they would be parents in early April. They joyfully celebrated the announcement with Jane and Elizabeth both expressing their pleasure that the children would grow up close in age and near to one another.

As the carriage reached the crest of the hill, the driver paused as usual. Darcy and Elizabeth stepped out of the carriage. The wind was bitterly cold, tossing about the capes on Darcy's greatcoat. Elizabeth clutched her bonnet to keep the wind from blowing it away. They moved to the edge of the ridge, Darcy standing behind Elizabeth and pulling her against his chest, his hands resting on her rounded stomach.

"I am so happy to be home," sighed Elizabeth.

Darcy gave her a gentle squeeze. "It thrills me to hear you call Pemberley home." She tilted her head, turning her face up to his. He leaned down and captured her lips in a gentle kiss, which he broke when he felt her shiver.

"Let us get you to the house, where I can warm you up properly." The look of passion in his eyes left no doubt in his wife's mind what method he would employ, so she gave him a provocative smile.

As the carriage pulled up before the door, it opened and several footmen rushed to assist them. The first one set the step and opened the carriage door. Darcy exited first, handing out Georgiana and then Elizabeth. Georgiana hurried into the house greeting Mrs. Reynolds with a hug, before mounting the stairs to her room.

As Darcy and Elizabeth entered the house, Mrs. Reynolds rushed forward. "Welcome home, Mr. and Mrs. Darcy. Oh, mistress, look at you," cried the housekeeper. Her hand stretched forward to touch Elizabeth's growing midsection, but recalling herself she pulled it back.

"It seems that I am growing at a rapid pace," said Elizabeth with a smile as her hand rubbed the small of her back.

"I have ordered you a bath, ma'am. It should be ready by the time you reach your room. I will send you some tea and biscuits to enjoy while you relax in the warm water. It will soothe the aches you are feeling," said the housekeeper in her motherly fashion.

Darcy looked on with a smile as he watched his housekeeper ensuring his wife's comfort. He offered Elizabeth his arm and escorted her to the door of her dressing room. "I believe we should dine in our rooms this evening. Could I tempt you to join me in our sitting room after your bath?"

"I can think of nothing I would like more, my love. We have not had time alone in several weeks. Though I loved spending time with our family and friends, I never wish to lose our private time. The time I spend alone with you is essential to my wellbeing."

"As it is to mine. You are the center of my world, and the time we spend together is the most precious thing in my life. So, will you care to join me?"

"I would like that very much. I will have Chalmers speak to Mrs. Reynolds to provide refreshments for two."

Honoria Bingley opened the express that had just arrived. She read her nephew's letter in growing horror and determined to keep the information in Charles' letters to herself going forward. The elderly Miss Bingley would also give Caroline a tongue-lashing upon her return home and restrict her activities and allowance even more than she had previously.

The day after the letter arrived, Caroline Bingley appeared on her aunt's doorstep. The anger and defiant attitude she displayed did nothing to improve her aunt's opinion of her niece.

Honoria called for her housekeeper before turning to the footman. "Thank you for ensuring my niece's safe return. If you will go with Mrs. Bland, she will provide you with a meal and a room for the evening."

"Thank you, ma'am."

Caroline walked towards the stairs as her aunt addressed the footman. "One moment, Caroline. I wish to speak with you."

"I am tired, Aunt. It will have to wait until the morning."

"I do not care if you are tired. You will come with me immediately." Honoria glared at Caroline until she grudgingly followed her.

"Sit down."

Caroline lowered herself into a chair, a mutinous expression on her face.

"Would you like to explain to me what you thought you were doing? Forging a letter from your brother, lying to me, going where you knew you were not welcome. Have you no pride, no self-respect? Caroline Bingley," her aunt said sharply, "you act as if you are better than everyone around you, but then you throw yourself at a man that does not want you—a man that is no longer available."

"He did want me before that chit came along. I know that he would have proposed to me had she not distracted him."

"Are you utterly lacking in sense? He has known you for years and has never shown any interest in you. Charles informs me he has repeatedly told you the man has no interest in you—that he never had any interest in you. Why is it you cannot accept that fact? Are you delusional? Do we need to have you committed?"

"How dare you speak to me that way?"

"It is evident someone needs to tell you the truth. You seem to be too blind to see it! You will not be leaving the house for at least a fortnight, and I shall withhold your allowance until I see considerable improvement in your behavior and attitude."

Caroline glared at her aunt but said nothing. "Go to your room!" said Honoria Bingley. "I cannot stand to look at your right now."

Caroline stormed from the room. When she reached her room, the sound of her door slamming reverberated thoughout the house, rattling the windows. Honoria merely shook her head in disgust.

Late that evening, Darcy and Elizabeth sat cuddled before the fire in their sitting room. Darcy's arm was around his wife's shoulder, absently stroking her arm. "We must take advantage of the time we have before our guests arrive for the holidays. I still cannot get enough of you, my love. I need your love, your touch, just as much as I need the air I breathe."

"I love you as well, my William. Then let us agree to dine together each day and to put aside our responsibilities by teatime, barring an emergency. From teatime on, we shall devote ourselves to each other."

"That is a promise I am happy to make you. He drew Elizabeth into his arms, kissing her with all the pent-up passion in him. Without breaking the kiss, Darcy gathered Elizabeth into his arms and carried her to their bed.

CHAPTER 25

THE MONTH OF November passed in a blur of activity. Darcy, as well as the entire staff of Pemberley, was constantly aware of Mrs. Darcy's activities and always at hand to offer assistance. They also ensured that she did not overdo and rested every afternoon. Frequently Darcy would search out his wife an hour or so before teatime and, taking her hand, escort her to their suite. Sometimes he would read to her until she fell asleep, other days, he would curl up on the bed with her, holding her in his arms until sleep overtook one or both of them. He also insisted they retire early so that she got as much rest as possible. Darcy knew it would be harder for her to get her rest when she was hosting so many guests.

One afternoon shortly after their return to Pemberley, Elizabeth lay wrapped in her husband's arms as she settled for the afternoon nap he required her to take. "William, did you see the way Caroline Bingley looked at me as she acknowledged my presence at Ashford Hills?"

"Yes, I did, and it seemed rather odd. It was not a glare as I would have expected, but a smirk."

"That is what I thought.

"What do you think caused such an unexpected look?"

"I have been wondering about that. The only thing I could determine was that she noticed the thickness of my figure, but that she did not attribute it to its proper cause."

"What do you mean?" asked Darcy in confusion.

"I believe she thought I had let myself go since capturing you." There was a definite grin on Elizabeth's face.

Darcy's look was incredulous. "Do you mean to tell me that Miss Bingley thought you were getting fat! Could the woman be any more insensible! Well, I can only say, thank heavens for her false assumption. I would not wish to see her reaction if she knew we were expecting a child."

"Do not even mention such a thing!" cried Elizabeth in horror.

A few evenings later, after they had retired for the night, another acquaintance was the topic of conversation.

"William, what would you think of inviting Michael Amesbury for the holidays? He is not close to his remaining family and will be alone for Christmas."

"How do you know he will be alone?"

"I do not know for sure; it just seems likely."

"Do you not think it would be presumptuous to include a new acquaintance at a family gathering?"

"But do you not think Kitty would enjoy his company?"

"Elizabeth Darcy, are you playing matchmaker?" She flushed slightly but made no answer. "Do you really wish Kitty to become attached to someone before she has an opportunity to experience a season? Do you not wish to have her meet many suitors so that she can truly know her mind before selecting her life's partner?"

"I do not think Kitty wishes for the drama and intrigue that often go with a season. It may at one time have seemed a romantic adventure, but I believe her thoughts on the matter have changed."

"What makes you say that?" asked William in surprise.

"It was something I heard her say the night we dined at the Clarendon with Mr. Amesbury." Elizabeth went on to tell her husband what she had overheard.

"I must say I am surprised."

"I was as well, but I am also very pleased with the maturity Kitty showed in understanding herself and the new society she was preparing to enter. It is such a change from the young woman she once was."

"If he is truly interested, he would be a good match for her, and he could easily care for her. I am not sure the size of his income, but I hear it is quite extensive. It may rival or even exceed my own." Elizabeth looked shocked at this statement.

"Well, then, what is your opinion? Should we invite him to spend Christmas with us, or at the very least invite him to the ball and to stay for the wedding?"

"Why not ask Aunt Gardiner. If Michael has continued to call upon Kitty in our absence, she would know how things have gone and what Kitty might feel about the situation."

"That is an excellent idea, my dear husband. I shall send off a letter first thing in the morning to solicit her opinion."

About a week later, she received her aunt's reply.

Dearest Lizzy,

I believe it would be appropriate to include Mr. Amesbury. He has called several times and on his last visit, he requested permission to court Kitty. Your uncle thought it best to deny the request due to Kitty's age and the fact she has not yet had a season, but he spoke with her first before making his decision. After listening to Kitty, he agreed to Mr. Amesbury's courting your sister, though he did inform the gentleman he would have to request anything more from your father. I do not believe it will be long before Mr. Amesbury joins the family.

I hope your return trip to Pemberley went well. We are looking forward to making a stop at Ashford Hills on our way north for the holidays. Mary and Kitty will be arriving at Pemberely on December fifth with your father.

We look forward to spending the holidays with you and plan to be there by December twentieth.

With love,

Madeline Gardiner

Elizabeth was delighted with her aunt's information. So she sat down to write out a formal invitation to Mr. Amesbury, inviting him to arrive at Pemberley on December twenty-first, to stay through twelfth night. In the note, Elizabeth included mention of the ball and the wedding, requesting his presence at both. She sent the letter express, and then sat down to write out the ball invitations with the help of Georgiana and Mrs. Annesley.

After completing the invitations, Elizabeth met with Mrs. Reynolds. First, they determined the rooms for all of the guests who would be staying at Pemberley throughout the holiday season. Then they went on to ensure that all of the guest rooms in the west wing would be cleaned and prepared to house any guests at the ball who would need to stay overnight. Lastly, they reviewed the menu for the ball, confirmed that the orchestra had been hired for the appropriate evening, and then went over the menu for the wedding breakfast.

When Elizabeth and Mrs. Reynolds met the following morning, they began to plan the meals for the time their family would be in residence. They also took an inventory of the items needed for outdoor winter activities and for games for the evenings after dinner. All in all, Elizabeth was very well pleased that all of the plans for the upcoming events were all in order.

One of the biggest joys for Elizabeth and William upon their return to Pemberley had been to check on the progress of the nursery. The painting had been done, the furniture refreshed, and the curtains and coverlet for the crib had been made. When Elizabeth opened the door for her first look at the room, she stopped a slight gasp escaping her lips. Darcy, at her shoulder, felt equally moved. The crib, dresser, changing table, rocking chair, and a pair of small tables had all been striped and refinished in a deep cherry color and gleamed in the sunlight streaming through the window.

Three of the walls had been painted a soft, sunny yellow. The third wall was a soft green. The curtains at the two windows and coverlet on the crib were adorable as well. The Pemberley seamstress had embroidered baby animals, teddy bears, blocks, dollies, tops, balls, and other children's toys in various colors on sturdy white cotton fabric. Mrs. Reynolds had even had the rocking chair cushions redone to match the other pieces.

Darcy wrapped his arms around his wife, pulling her back against his chest, as they stared at the room. "I can hardly wait to see our child resting in the crib. I can picture you sitting in the rocker, singing softly, the baby in your arms." Suddenly Darcy's face took on a stunned look. "What was that?" he asked in an awed voice.

Elizabeth turned her head and looked up at her husband's shocked face. "I believe that was your child agreeing to your statements."

"So this is what others have been able to feel for a few weeks now. Our daughter must have her mother's teasing nature making me wait so long to acquaint me with her presence."

"No matter boy or girl, I hope the baby will have my teasing nature as it is good for you to be teased regularly!"

Darcy leaned his head down and teased his wife's lips with a series of gentle kisses. He deepened the kiss for the briefest of moments before suddenly breaking it. He nearly laughed at the pout that appeared on his wife's face. "You are not the only one who can tease, my dear wife."

Darcy placed his hands on his wife's shoulders and turned her about to face him before backing her further into the nursery until she stood in the center of the room. He left her standing there as he turned and closed and locked the door. Darcy turned back to face a blushing Elizabeth, a roguish expression on his face. When he stopped, their bodies were touching, and she could feel his accelerated breathing gently stirring the curls that framed her face.

The eyes that gazed down at her were dark with passion as his arms came around her, pulling her as close to him as possible and lowering his head to drink deeply of her lips. By the time they both needed air, Elizabeth was surprised to find that her husband had somehow lowered them to the plush carpet covering the nursery floor.

Darcy held his weight on his arms as he lifted his head to gaze down into her eyes. "Thinking of you and our child fills me with a desire to love you here where the baby will live. I love you more than life, my dearest, loveliest Elizabeth." Darcy lowered his head and kissed her again, and that was the last that was heard from the couple for the remainder of the afternoon.

Word reached the house that a carriage had turned in at the gates. It was the day Mr. Bennet and his daughters were due to arrive. The weather was extremely frigid and the clouds had been threatening snow all day, but so far no precipitation had fallen. Darcy would not allow Elizabeth to greet their guests out in the cold, so she impatiently paced in the entrance hall for her family to arrive. Soon a flurry of servants appeared, letting Elizabeth know the carriage must be close. It was only a moment later that she could hear the crunch of wheels on gravel as the carriage came to a stop at the front steps.

Darcy sauntered in as Benton opened the door and several footmen exited to assist the guests. In a very short time, the efficient staff had the guests in out of the cold and were assisting them with their outerwear. Finally, Elizabeth was able to fly into her father's arms, hugging him tightly.

"Oh, Papa, I am so glad to see you. It has been too long."

Mr. Bennet hugged her briefly before taking her hands and stepping away from her. "Well, look at you, dear Lizzy," he said with a smile. "One would think you are about to make me a grandfather." Mr. Bennet chuckled at his tease.

Kitty and Mary stood waiting their turn to greet their sister. "Lizzy, you have changed a great deal since we saw you in London," remarked Mary.

"Indeed, you are so much bigger!"

Darcy, Elizabeth, and Mr. Bennet all laughed at Kitty's artless comment. "You are correct, Kitty," said Elizabeth ruefully. "I seem to be increasing almost daily. I cannot imagine how large I will be by the time the baby gets here!"

The group moved into the warm and welcoming drawing room as refreshments arrived. There were tea and hot chocolate as well as biscuits, fruit tarts, and small cakes.

"I am pleased that you arrived when you did, for I believe we will wake up to several inches of snow," remarked Darcy. "How were the roads you traversed?"

"They were a bit rutted but overall not too unpleasant. However the frigid temperatures were almost unbearable."

"Fortunately, you will be able to rest for several days before having to retrieve Lydia. The latest letter I received from her indicated that she was very excited to see the family again," Elizabeth told her father.

"I believe on the return from Winksley, we will go to Ashford Hills for a day or two. Her letter to me expressed a desire to visit Jane briefly before all of the family gathered," replied Mr. Bennet.

"That does not surprise me. Jane has indicated that Lydia has been very confused about mother's actions to those she professed were her favorites. It is no wonder that she wishes to speak to Jane as they were the two mother claimed as her favorites."

The conversation continued for quite some time. However, as Darcy had been unable to convince Elizabeth to rest before her family's arrival, he was determined to have her rest before dinner. "We are delighted you have safely arrived. However, you must excuse us now. Elizabeth needs to nap before dinner. Her excitement for your arrival disrupted her sleep last night, so she needs to rest now." He stood and rang for the housekeeper. When Mrs. Reynolds arrived, he asked her to show the guests to their rooms. Then Darcy offered his arm to his wife, who, with surprising submissiveness, took it and departed the room, calling over her shoulder that she would see them at dinner.

Mr. Bennet passed the next several days comfortably ensconced in Pemberley's famed library. Reviewing the wedding plans with Mary, Elizabeth delighted to learn her sister was well satisfied with all the arrangements made for her wedding day.

Elizabeth happily showed off the nursery to her sisters, who were delighted with everything they saw. They sat with Elizabeth in her private sitting room, sewing cloth dolls for the daughters of the tenants as well as working on blankets and clothes for the baby.

The day came for Mr. Bennet to leave to retrieve Lydia from school. Kitty had expressed a desire to go with her father, but Elizabeth and Mary had helped her to understand that Lydia needed time alone with both her father and with Jane before rejoining the rest of the family. Kitty was disappointed at the delay. She longed to see her sister and former best friend. However, Kitty was mature enough to understand Lydia's needed to talk to Jane and learn how best to deal with the hurt and disillusionment her mother inflicted upon her.

Mr. Bennet stopped the first night at the inn where the others had stayed after Mrs. Bennet's death. The next morning he arrived at Miss Bates' School for Girls to find Lydia ready and waiting for him. She greeted her father with a shy hug but was obviously pleased to see him. As they traveled from school back to the inn where they spend the night, Lydia regaled her father with the things she had been learning. Her bubbly personality was still present, but it was tempered by maturity and an understanding of the need for self-restraint. Lydia also spoke of the friends she made and her pleasure in the improved relationship she had with her sisters. She expressed excitement at being reunited with all of her sisters. They had a pleasant meal in their sitting room at the inn before retiring for the evening.

Mr. Bennet and Lydia broke their fast early the next morning and were soon on the road on the way to Ashford Hills. As the journey began, they spoke of inconsequential things, but the closer they came to the Bingleys' estate, the quieter Lydia became. Mr. Bennet allowed her to keep her thoughts to herself, but as he watched her anxiety grow, he felt he must speak.

"Lydia, my dear, I am not sure what thoughts are running through your mind, but there is no need to be anxious. I will not tell you how you should feel, but please believe me that any fault in what has occurred was your mother's, not yours."

Lydia's eyes welled with tears at her father's words. She tried to speak, but no words came out; eventually a whispered reply was heard. "Thank you, Papa."

Mr. Bennet leaned across the carriage and patted Lydia's hand. I am proud of the growth you have made in just the six short months you have been at school." Lydia's eyes again filled with tears that this time spilled over. Her heart swelled at her father's words, as she could never remember him complimenting her or being proud of her. Her shoulders straightened, and she smiled shyly at her father.

They completed their journey in silence, but Mr. Bennet was pleased to note that Lydia's anxiety seemed to have lessened. It was nearing six when the carriage turned into the drive leading to Ashford Hills. Unfortunately, it was too dark to gain much of an impression of their surroundings. That changed when the house came into view, as warm, welcoming light poured from several of the windows on the ground and first floor. As the carriage came to a stop, Greenwood, the Bingley's butler, opened the door, and Charles stepped out to greet his family.

"Mr. Bennet, Lydia, welcome to Ashford Hills. We are so pleased you came to see us. Please, do come in."

A footman held the door open as Mr. Bennet exited the carriage and handed Lydia down. He tucked her hand into the crook of his arm and guided her up the steps into the house. Once free of their outerwear, Bingley led them to the drawing room where Jane waited. Jane stood to greet her family, and Lydia ran into her sister's embrace.

"Oh, Jane, I am so happy to see you!"

"We are excited to see you as well. Other than William and Lizzy, you and Papa are our first guests. Would you like to rest before dinner or just refresh yourself before we dine?"

"I am starving," Lydia replied quickly.

"I am agreeable to dining immediately," replied Mr. Bennet with a chuckle.

Bingley pulled the bell cord, and Mrs. Greenwood appeared at the door to the drawing room. Could you please show our guests to their rooms and provide them with warm water to refresh themselves. We should be ready to dine in half an hour."

"Certainly, Mr. Bingley. If you would, please follow me." The housekeeper exited the room with Mr. Bennet and Lydia following. She led them to their rooms in the family wing, where warm water was already waiting for them. The family enjoyed a pleasant dinner and retired early as the travelers had had a long day.

The next morning after breaking their fast, Mr. Bennet rode out over the estate with his son. Bingley showed him the apple orchard and cider press. They saw the sheep grazing in several of the fields. While the gentlemen were gone, Lydia and Jane were in the morning room. Jane held a tiny gown in her hand and was embroidering a border of blocks around the bottom. Jane discreetly observed her youngest sister. She could see that Lydia wanted to speak to her, but could not quite figure out what she wished to say.

Finally, a hesitant voice said, "Jane, why did our mother not love us?"

"I think that she loved us in her own way, but, she could not put her fears for herself aside and put our needs ahead of her own."

"But how can a woman carry a child for so many months and not care for its well-being? Would she have loved us more if one of us had been a son?"

"Perhaps if she had not had to worry about her future, she might have been able to be more concerned for our happiness. However, that is merely speculation on my part. No one but Mama could truly answer that question, Lydia. The only thing we can do is to learn from her mistakes and strive to be better people ourselves."

"But, how do I deal with the feeling of betrayal?"

"We have each had to deal with Mama's betrayal as best we can, for she treated each of us so differently. Lizzy has always known she was not a favorite with Mama. Consequently, she decided that she would respect Mama for giving her life, but she refused to allow her to be a part of her life until Mama could treat her with courtesy and respect—even if Mama could never love her. Every person has a right to be treated with basic human kindness. I believe it was easy for Mary to come to the same decision as well. Except to criticize, Mama ignored Mary her entire life. Mary saw no need to recognize her either. As for Kitty, well, Mama did not see Kitty as her own person, but merely as your shadow. In fact, you treated Kitty very much the same way Mama did. As long as Kitty went along with what you wished, you were kind to her. However, if she showed any interests that you did not share, you belittled her. Do you remember how you behaved when she first expressed her interest in drawing?" Lydia flushed and looked at the floor, unwilling to meet her sister's eyes.

"Yes, but what about you? Mama always treated you well, she called you beautiful and said you would be the savior of our family."

"You are right. She did say all those things about me, but the first time I dared to openly disagree with her, she told me to shut up and called me ungrateful. She did not do me any favors by her words or her actions. She placed a huge burden on me. If Mr. Bingley had not come along and if we had not fallen in love, Mama would have pushed me at the first wealthy man who showed an interest in me. She would not have cared whether he were a decent man or a rake, so long as he could have provided a comfortable life for her and any unmarried daughters once Papa was gone. You know that she tried to force

Lizzy to marry Mr. Collins just so that she would not have to leave Longbourn."

"But should Lizzy not have sacrificed to protect our family?"

"No, that burden should have fallen to me as the eldest. However, Mama would not permit it. She wanted Lizzy to be unhappy and knew a marriage to Mr. Collins would accomplish that while providing for Mama's future comfort. Tell me, would you have willingly married him if Mama had selected you to do so?"

Lydia wore a look of horror on her face. "He was a disgusting, smelly man and lacked sense. I cannot imagine anyone wishing to marry him!"

"Your question seemed to indicate you felt Lizzy should have married him, but you just said you could not imagine anyone wishing to do so. Would you have wanted to see Lizzy forced into such a marriage? If Mama's desires prevailed, Mr. Collins would have had a say in your life, how much pin money you received, how you behaved, and what you could or could not do?"

"How could Lizzy's husband have had a say in such things?"

"If you resided in his home, you would have been under his guardianship. Mr. Collins could have punished you if he felt it was warranted."

"I would have run away if he mistreated me in such a way."

"If you had run away, he could have ensured that you could never come home. How would you have supported yourself, where would you have lived? It is important for you to understand, Lydia, that women have very few rights in this world. We are always subject to the demands of our fathers, husbands, brothers, uncles, or some other male guardian. Papa allowed Mama to have her way when he should not because he could not be bothered to check her and deal with her nerves and tantrums."

Lydia sat very still, looking out the window. Jane could almost see the thoughts churning around in her mind. "Lydia, I do not know if you can comprehend all that I have said. Nor, do I know how to help you understand your feelings. Perhaps, you should start by considering the things we talked about today; sleep on them. We can talk again tomorrow."

"I believe I will take a walk, if that is acceptable."

"Of course, you may, but please bundle up, for it is quite cold. Also, please do not go too far. According to our groundskeeper, the weather is threatening snow. I would not wish you to get caught out if the weather should turn."

Two days later, Jane and Lydia could again be found in the morning room. Jane had finished the gown she was embroidering and was today knitting a blanket. "Jane, I have been thinking about the things you said."

"And, have you come to any conclusions?" Jane waited patiently, covertly watching her youngest sister. "I realize that maintaining my anger and hurt at Mama is only hurting me. From our last encounter, I understand that Mama's love was conditional, and that was wrong. I have decided to adopt the philosophy of you and Lizzy. I will try to respect Mama's memory for giving my life and try to forget the selfish lessons she passed on to me. I will try to treat everyone with kindness as I have observed you doing all my life."

"I think you are making a wise decision, but you must be yourself. It is acceptable to follow my example, so long as the kindness you show is reflective of the person you are. We, sisters, are each very different in temperament. The way I treat others is based on my personality. Do you remember the affected way that Miss Bingley acted?" Lydia nodded. "Her insincere behavior was the reason she was unsuccessful in catching Mr. Darcy's attention as she desired. Be sure that you treat people honestly as well as kindly, otherwise it will not be believed."

"I will try to remember what you have said. Do you think my sisters, particularly Lizzy, will forgive me for my past behavior? I did do some awful things that allowed Mama to take her anger out on Lizzy before the wedding."

"I am proud of the way you have matured since you went to school, Lydia. I am sure they will also be proud of the changes you are making. They will see that you have grown up, and I am sure they will forgive any sincere apology you make. I believe this will be the best Christmas we have ever had. We will all be together, there will be no one causing unnecessary drama, and we will have the joy of seeing another sister married to a man she loves and who loves her in return."

"When I am struggling or confused, may I speak to you about it?"

"Of course, you may, Lydia. I am your eldest sister, and I love you. Give the others a chance. You will find that they want to be of assistance as well."

After three days at Ashford Hills, all the occupants departed for Pemberley. Bingley, Jane, and Lydia, were the first in a string of arrivals. The majority would not begin arriving until the next day.

While Darcy and Elizabeth were busy greeting Bingley and Jane, Kitty rushed to hug her younger sister.

"Oh, Lydia! I missed you so much!"

Before the sisters could exchange further words, Elizabeth turned to her youngest sister and extended a warm welcome to her, much to the girl's surprise. She was even more surprised by Darcy's pleasant greeting, even if he was somewhat more reserved.

Mr. Bennet quickly reclaimed his place in Pemberley's magnificent library. Darcy and Bingley headed for the billiard room, and Elizabeth led her sisters to her private sitting room. She called for refreshments and the sisters settled in for a good visit. Of course, Elizabeth and Jane first spoke about their mutual condition. They had just finished comparing notes when the refreshments arrived.

Turning to her youngest sister, Elizabeth said, "How did you enjoy your time at school, Lydia?"

"I did not enjoy it at first, but I did come to appreciate the opportunity." Lydia hesitated, "I owe all of you a very large apology. I treated all of you very poorly. Jane, Lizzy, when you tried to teach me to behave appropriately, I ignored you and accused you of not knowing how to have fun. Mary, I mocked you and your sermonizing, failing to understand that the words you chose were often the teachings of our Lord. I should have realized their importance and my need to adhere to the church's teachings. Kitty, I treated you the worst of all because my friendship was false. I wanted you to do what I said, and I failed to give any consideration to what you enjoyed doing. I am ashamed to say it, but I belittled your talent at sketching, because I was jealous of it."

All of her sisters opened their mouths to speak, but Lydia forestalled them. "I believe I have grown some since starting school, though I am sure I still have a great deal of growing to do. I have given a great deal of thought to what caused my behavior. I was immature, stubborn, and blinded by the words of our mother. I believed what she said of me and what she told me was acceptable. It was who I believed myself to be. However, I was not blind to the accomplishments each of you had that I did not. I knew that I could never be as kind and caring as Jane, or as smart and witty as Lizzy. I did not pay as much attention as I should to the tenants of our faith as Mary could and did. I made fun of Kitty's attempts at sketching, even knowing they were far better than anything I could ever do. Mother said I was pretty and lively and that I could have whatever I wanted, but that was not true. You all did not give me whatever I wanted. Papa did not give me whatever I wanted. And, sometimes getting what I wanted did not even make me happy. The most important thing I have learned is that I do not want to be like Mama, and I do not want to be the person she told me I was. I aspire to be more like all of you."

Lydia's sisters all looked at each other. Jane gave a small nod, and they all stood. Kitty pulled her younger sister to her feet, and Lydia was surrounded by her sisters in the warmest hug she had ever received. Soon all of them were in tears, and the tears eventually turned to laughter. Once all of them were seated, Lydia spoke again. "I do not deserve your forgiveness."

"Of course, you do. You have admitted to being wrong and apologized most sincerely. Besides, that is what sisters do—they love and support one another in one of the closest bonds there is. We have all come late to being as supportive of one another as we should. Jane and I were close, Kitty and Lydia were close, but we all ignored poor Mary. Perhaps it was our mother's influence that caused this, but whatever it was, it no longer matters. We are now the five

Bennet sisters, and we shall from this time forward support and love each other and do good wherever we can."

"Hear, hear!"

"Absolutely!"

"I second that!"

"I will do my very best at this always!"

The conversation in Elizabeth's sitting room continued all afternoon. As Darcy approached the sitting room door, he heard laughter ringing out. He knocked on the door, and when Elizabeth called out to enter, Darcy stuck his head around the door. "Pardon me for interrupting, ladies, but it is time for Elizabeth's nap." Elizabeth frowned at her husband, but her sisters just laughed and looked pleased.

"I am sure I can miss one nap without any ill effects, William. I am having a delightful time with my sisters."

"Your sisters will be here for more than a fortnight, my dear. You shall have plenty of time to visit. You do not have to cover everything on the first day of their visit."

"I believe that I shall join you, Lizzy. I am a bit tired, as well," said Jane.

"Yes, and I wish to spend some time with Mrs. Reynolds, if you do not mind, Lizzy," said Mary. "There is still much for me to learn. Then Georgiana wanted to practice some duets to perform for Christmas."

"Yes, Lizzy," added Kitty, "I want to spend some more time with Lydia. I will show her to the room you assigned her, and we will visit further."

"Are you all conspiring against me?" asked Elizabeth with a slight pout.

"No," said Jane, "four of the Bennet sisters are watching out for the fifth who will become a mother in just about six weeks." All of the sisters laughed. With a smile for her sister's Elizabeth rose and took her husband's offered arm. Then I shall see you all in time for tea."

The next morning, just before luncheon, the carriage arrived from Matlock. Traveling with the Earl and Countess were the Viscount and Lady Penelope, Lady Julia, Richard, and Anne de Bourgh. Excited greetings were exchanged all around before the visitors retired to their rooms to refresh themselves for luncheon.

The next group to arrive did so just before teatime. This time, there were, again, two carriages. The first carriage was a shiny new vehicle in the latest style and designed for comfort. It contained Mr. and Mrs. Gardiner and Michael Amesbury. In the second carriage rode the Gardiner children with their nurse and governess.

Into the front hall, the guests bustled with the children crying out to their favorite cousins. Again, happy greetings were exchanged. As the Gardiners and their children were bustled off to their rooms to change and refresh themselves, the Darcys had an opportunity to welcome Michael Amesbury.

"Welcome to Pemberley, Amesbury. We are very pleased you could join us for the Christmas season."

"Mr. and Mrs. Darcy, I am honored to have been invited to Pemberley. I thank you very much for including me in your family holiday."

"As you are courting my sister, Kitty, that makes you part of the family," said Elizabeth with a smile.

"It is a delight to be part of such a warm and loving family. It is a far cry from the one in which I was raised."

Elizabeth beckoned for Mrs. Reynolds to come forward. "Mrs. Reynolds, would you please show Mr. Amesbury to his room."

"Of course, Mrs. Darcy."

"Please join us for tea in the blue drawing room at three," said Elizabeth.

"I shall look forward to it."

When three o'clock rolled around, the blue drawing room was abuzz with conversation. All in residence at Pemberley gathered together, with the exception of the children, who had gone to greet the ponies. The staff provided tea and hot chocolate with an assortment of pastries, cakes, and biscuits, as well as dishes of strawberries, pineapple, and other fruits from the hot house. The conversation focused on the travels of the newcomers and the plans for the next several days.

"Is there anything I can help you with for the ball, Elizabeth?" asked Aunt Rebecca.

"Indeed, Elizabeth, you must allow us to assist you with anything that remains. I am sure that Darcy is keeping a close eye on you and not allowing you to over-exert yourself, but you must allow us to assist you now that we are here."

"Thanks to my superbly efficient staff, everything is well in hand. What I want most from this visit is to enjoy this time with my family. As we will not be in London for the season, it will be far too long before I can enjoy your company again."

The days leading up to the ball passed in a blur of busy activitiy.

CHAPTER 26

IN THE GREEN drawing room, the residents of Pemberley gathered awaiting the arrival of their hosts, as well as, and the guests who would attend Pemberley's first Christmas ball in more than 13 years. As the first carriage pulled up to the entrance to Pemberley, the guests moved to the ballroom, while Darcy and Elizabeth lined up to greet their guests. Almost all those invited had accepted the invitation to this momentous event. The couple took pride in welcoming their dear friends and many neighbors, including gentry from the surrounding counties.

At a slight break in the receiving line, Elizabeth looked up at William; she noted a frown on his face so she followed his gaze. Miss Parkington and her brother were approaching the head of the receiving line. She placed a gentle hand on her husband's arm and reminded him to smile. Miss Parkington stepped up to her host, her manner hesitant and her brother at her shoulder.

"Good evening, Mr. and Mrs. Darcy," said the young lady as she dipped a curtsey. I thank you for your invitation to this momentous event."

Darcy's reply was a crisp, "Good evening."

"We are very pleased you and your brother could attend, Miss Parkington. What a lovely gown you are wearing this evening."

The young lady replied politely, but she was staring at the magnificent creation her hostess wore. The crimson taffeta gown enhanced Elizabeth's complexion and the red undertones in her hair. On the skirt, snowflakes were stitched in silver thread. Sparkling crystals highlighted the snowflakes, making them shimmer in the light. The breathtaking Darcy rubies graced her neck. "I thank you for the compliment, Mrs. Darcy, but I believe your gown will outshine all others this evening. The color is lovely on you."

"How kind of you, Miss Parkington. I do hope you will enjoy your evening.

Elizabeth greeted Michael Parkington with her usual smile and received a look of grateful relief in return.

When, at long last, the reception line ended, Darcy offered his arm to his wife and escorted her into the ballroom. Tonight the deep green and gold of the ballroom was enhanced with red and silver. Garlands of pine and holly tied in red ribbon trimmed all the doors and windows. The non-mirrored sections of the walls held large wreaths made from laurel leaves and accented in ribbons of silver and gold. Bouquets of red roses from the hothouses stood about on various tables, adding their color and fragrance to the décor.

As they entered the ballroom, the first dance was announced, and Darcy and Elizabeth lined up with their guests. As the movements of the dance brought them together the first time, Darcy addressed his wife. "You were kind and gracious to Miss Parkington, my love. I found that difficult as she insulted my beloved wife when last they met."

"She is young and disappointed. She is also the sister of your dear friend, and she does not appear to think so highly of herself that she shall not overcome her disappointment. I shall always believe kindness the best weapon against such behavior. Had she proved to me like other *ladies* of our acquaintance, I should have addressed her differently."

The dance separated them, but when they drew close again, Darcy continued. "Miss Parkington did say something I must agree with."

"Oh," said his wife with a playfully arched brow.

"You do, indeed, outshine all others tonight. There are not enough words to describe your beauty. Not only is the gown quite spectacular, but you glow with love and joy. It is a tantalizing combination, and I shall have a hard time maintaining my composure in your presence when all I wish to do is sweep you up in my embrace."

"Though you cannot do so now, I hope the feeling shall last to the end of the evening." A look of passion filled her eyes and made his body begin to react in a most indecorous way.

"It shall certainly last!" was his roguish reply.

The ball progressed until the wee hours of the morning. The buffet was stupendous, the music entrancing, and the wine and champagne flowed freely. All in all, Pemberley's first ball in many years was a rousing success.

When the last of the guests departed and those staying had retired for the night, Darcy looked down into the bright eyes of his exhausted wife. Surprising her, he scooped her up into his arms and carried her to their suite. Darcy left her in Margot's tender care and went to change. Stepping into his bedchamber from the dressing room, he saw Elizabeth curled up in the middle of the big bed, sound asleep. He slid in behind her and wrapped his arms around her, pulling her to his chest. He kissed her temple and whispered, "Good night, my love."

Pemberley's tired, but ever efficient staff had a delectable breakfast laid out on the sideboard in the dining room for the guests to enjoy as they arrived. The young ladies, Kitty, Lydia, and Georgiana, who had remained at the ball until after the dinner break, were the first to arrive. They sat together at the table talking and laughing about all they had seen the night before. They remarked on the number of couple who made use of kissing boughs, the lovely gowns and jewels, and the number of handsome, eligible gentlemen, even though they had not spoken with them. Each of the girls had been permitted to dance with members of the house party, but no other gentlemen. Astonishing everyone, Mr. Bennet had danced once with each of his daughters.

In the master suite, the master and mistress of Pemberley were enjoying a postponed romantic encounter. Elizabeth's pregnancy had forced them to be creative in the ways they loved one another, but each liaison seemed more incredible than the previous one.

When Darcy and Elizabeth finally arrived in the dining room, most of the overnight guests were present. Many were finishing their meal as they planned to return to their homes as early as possible. The couple was afforded enough time to break their fast before they began saying farewell to the guests who only stayed the night of the ball.

After the final guests had departed, the residents of Pemberley dispersed to their various chosen pursuits and enjoyed a leisurely afternoon. As breakfast had been so late, there was no midday meal, so the group did not gather again until teatime.

Darcy and Elizabeth entered the conservatory, hoping to steal some additional time alone. They had taken no more than a few steps, when they heard the sound of laughter, followed by Richard's teasing voice.

"I do not know if I shall survive another six days until our wedding without your kisses, my dear Mary."

As his comment met with a shy giggle and then silence, Darcy and Elizabeth, smiled at each other and quickly exited the warmth of the conservatory. Eventually they ended up on the rug before the fire in Darcy's study, the door securely locked, where they were again able to enjoy the benefits of the deep and abiding love they shared.

As dinner was ending, Darcy stood to make an announcement. "We shall forego the separation of the sexes tonight for a special activity."

Murmurs ran around the table. It was Lydia who finally asked, "What are we to do?"

"Elizabeth and I wish it to be a surprise for a bit longer. However, we would ask that when everyone is through dining, they join us in the hallway outside the ballroom doors. Mr. and Mrs. Gardiner, please be sure that the children join us as well."

These comments only increased the murmuring and the confused looks. Darcy and Elizabeth smiled at each other at having such an unusual surprise for their family. The announcement seemed to curb any desire for additional food, and the company was scurrying away to prepare for whatever was to come.

Some ten minutes later, the entire house party was standing before the hosts in front of the closed ballroom doors. "As most of you know, my dear wife has a passion for reading. Well, during her reading in preparation for our first family holiday together, Elizabeth learned of a custom celebrated in Germany, and we decided to make it a part of our Christmas tradition beginning this year.

Darcy each took a door handle and turning them opened them wide. There is the center of the ballroom stood a fifteen-foot tall evergreen tree. There were several sofas and chairs positioned around the tree, and two tables piled high with boxes, spools of ribbon, and small candles. Two tall ladders sat nearby.

Exclamations broke out all around them as the family entered the room. Everyone broke into a chorus of "Oohs and aahs," followed by the children's voices raised in question.

"Why is there a tree inside?" asked Hugh.

"What are we going to do with a tree?" wondered Susan.

Elizabeth answered as she pulled out one of the books she had been reviewing that contained some pictures of Christmas trees in it to show the children. "We are going to decorate the tree and make it a part of our family holiday tradition," she explained.

The children were fascinated by the pictures and excited to begin.

"I saw a few of these during my grand tour," said Lord Matlock.

"I did as well," said the viscount. "They were all decorated in different ways and lovely to view."

The boxes were opened to reveal some glass ornaments imported from Germany, some gingerbread cookies made and decorated by Pemberley's kitchen staff, red and white flowers made of fabric, and some lace snowflakes.

There were also several pinecones the children had gathered from the estate grounds. With these, there were some glue and flakes of malachite, mica, and hematite with which to decorate the pine cones before hanging them on the tree. The company broke into small groups, working to add the different decorations to the trees. By ten in the evening, the decorating was completed. Everyone stood back to look at their handiwork. The tree was a beautiful sight, and everyone applauded. Little Rachel, who had been asleep on one of the sofas, stirred at the noise, but quickly settled again. The happy group departed for their bedchambers and a peaceful night's sleep. The children, and many of the adults, had sweet dreams of a happy Christmas day.

Darcy and Elizabeth woke early the next morning. "Happy Christmas, my dearest, loveliest Elizabeth. I am so delighted to be able to spend this Christmas with you. The separation last year was intolerable."

"Happy Christmas, my darling Will," said Elizabeth as she bestowed a gentle kiss upon her husband's lips. "Do we have the time to enjoy a Christmas cuddle this morning or must we rush to meet our family for breakfast?"

"There is always time for me to love you, and, if not, I shall make the time." Darcy kissed his wife softly at first, then deepened the kiss as the couple lost themselves to the passion they shared.

They arrived first in the dining room. Darcy had just placed Elizabeth's plate before her and was taking his seat when the other members of the family began to stream through the doors. Calls of "Happy Christmas" filled the air with each new arrival. Soon the entire family was seated at the table. The breakfast buffet included far more offerings than most mornings, including the cook's amazing cinnamon buns with almonds.

After breaking their fast, everyone returned briefly to their suites to get their outerwear and bundle up for the ride to church. Several inches of snow had fallen during the night, so when the family members stepped out of the house, there were four large, gleaming sleighs waiting to transport the group. Darcy, Elizabeth, Georgiana, Mary, and Richard stepped into the lead sleigh. The five remaining Fitzwilliams were in the second sleigh, followed by Mr. Bennet, Lydia, Kitty, Michael Amesbury, and Miss de Bourgh. The Gardiner family filled the final sleigh. The gentlemen all took up the reins and followed the Darcy sleigh as it headed for the Pemberley chapel. Mr. Millwood, the minister at Kympton, lead a special early Christmas service at the Pemberley chapel for the family, staff, and tenants before returning to his parish for the regular service.

Many of the flowers from the ball had been transferred to the chapel to decorate it for the Christmas service. The family party filled the first two rows on both sides of the isles and the tenants and servants who had been waiting filed in after the family.

The service included several hymns, allowing Darcy to enjoy his wife's lovely voice, and a reading of the Christmas story as found in the second chapter of the book of Luke. At the conclusion of the service, the Darcy party was the first to exit, but the master and mistress of Pemberley took the time to speak with many of those present, reminding the tenants of the gathering in the ballroom on Boxing Day.

When the party returned to the house, Darcy again asked them to join him and Elizabeth before the ballroom doors after refreshing themselves. When everyone appeared, they opened the doors to find the candles lit on the tree and a mountain of presents displayed on a piece of red and green plaid fabric surrounding the base of the tree. Elizabeth had arranged with Mrs. Reynolds to collect all the gifts and place them around the tree.

Everyone found a place to sit, and Edmund, Susan, and Richard were given the job of distributing the gifts. Little Rachel sat on a sofa between her parents with Hugh at their feet. Both were excited at the thought of all the presents. Darcy and Elizabeth were seated on a loveseat, as were the viscount and Lady Penelope. The unmarried young ladies were clustered together, with regular giggles coming from their direction. Mr. Bennet and Michael Amesbury were both seated slightly apart from the others, Mr. Bennet, so that he could take in the scene before him, and Michael, not wishing to intrude on such a special family celebration, though his eyes frequently rested on Katherine. His thoughts were on next Christmas, which he hoped would be their first together.

Once everyone received the gifts meant for them, the confusion began. Presents were opened and cries of "Thank you!" called out in a unceasing profusion of noise. Elizabeth had put together a selection of scents, lotions, and bath salts for all of the ladies in attendance, as well as some ribbons for her youngest sisters. Darcy had managed to obtain some excellent port for all of the gentlemen. William gifted his wife with a delicately-crafted jeweled brooch from which was suspended a small watch. A miniature portrait of her husband resided inside the watchcase. The note attached read:

To remind you to return to me quickly when you are exploring the beauties of our home.

Along with giving William a book he had been trying to purchase, Elizabeth had created and framed a sampler, which included some scriptures surrounded by flowers and vines, that read:

I found him whom my soul loveth. (2)
My beloved is mine, and I am his. (3)

Kitty and Lydia each received a new gown from their father (purchased with Lizzy's help, of course). There was music for Mary, Georgiana, Lady Julia, and Lady Penelope. Mr. Bennet received several books from Darcy and Elizabeth, a bottle of rare French Brandy from the Bingleys, and a picture from Kitty which Mary had framed. Lydia had embroidered some new handkerchiefs for her father. Knowing how much she had previously disliked the occupation, he was touched and impressed with her effort.

Kitty had embroidered some handkerchiefs for Mr. Amesbury, and in turn, he had given Katherine a book on the art of Michelangelo and da Vinci. Mary had purchased Richard a new crop and riding gloves, and he had presented her with a seal of her new initials surrounded by a ring of roses.

Along with the gifts from their parents, Elizabeth and Darcy presented Edmund with a chess set, Susan received a porcelain tea service, Hugh received a large set of colorful blocks, and a lovely cloth doll with two extra outfits was presented to little Rachel. There were many other gifts exchanged that morning, far too numerous to mention.

Late in the afternoon, the family enjoyed a sumptuous Christmas feast, following which most of the party felt that a nap was in order. Darcy and Elizabeth made their way to their bedchamber, where they curled up on the bed and spoke of their dreams for the future, before falling asleep in each other's arms.

The group came together again in the early evening. They passed the time by playing charades and snap-dragon before the ladies took turns entertaining them on the pianoforte and harp, often with Elizabeth's voice raised in song. Dessert was served before the music began, including a Christmas pudding and assorted other treats for the families' enjoyment.

The next day, Boxing Day, the majority of the servants were given a day of rest. Mrs. Mason, the Pemberley cook, had prepared several things in advance, so that the kitchen staff could enjoy time with their families on their day off. Mrs. Reynolds and Margot insisted on assisting Elizabeth as they did not wish her to over-exert herself at this time in her pregnancy. Elizabeth rose early and was seen descending the stairs to the kitchen, only to find the two ladies there ahead of her. Mrs. Mason had prepared everything to be served cold. There was an assortment of muffins and buns, and the kettle was on the stove, filled and ready to be heated for tea. Elizabeth added the butter and jams that were left ready to her tray and made her first trip to the dining room, arranging the items on the sideboard. Margot followed her, carrying a heavier tray.

Elizabeth arranged for the inn in Lambton to cater the mid-day meal. There were ham, roast beef, and goose with all of the trimmings. Platters of meats and bowls of all the sides appeared on the sideboard in the dining room for the family members, while the remainder was laid out in the ballroom for the tenant gathering.

Darcy and Elizabeth greeted the tenants as they arrived. Each of the families presented Elizabeth with a small gift, saying it was for the newest Darcy. Everyone was surprised to see the large decorated evergreen tree in the middle of the ballroom, and the children's excited comments filled the room. There was a table at one end of the room with gingerbread cookies, frosting, and other goodies. Kitty, Lydia, and Georgiana helped each child to decorate a cookie to take with them.

Once all the tenants had arrived, Darcy thanked them for their efforts and wished them blessings and good fortune in the coming year. Everyone enjoyed the bounteous meal and several toasts were offered to the Darcys. The table with the cookies rang with children's laughter. And as they departed, each family was given a basket of foodstuffs, some personal items for each family member chosen by Elizabeth, and a few coins.

Darcy and Elizabeth rejoined their guests in time for tea and enjoyed the time with their family. For the evening meal, a hearty stew appeared. Mrs. Reynolds heated it and transferred it to a large tureen before bringing it above stairs, along with some crusty bread for the family to enjoy. For the remainder of the evening, the family enjoyed cards, chess, billiards, reading and other activities.

CHAPTER 27

THE DAYS BETWEEN Christmas and the wedding of Mary Bennet and Richard Fitzwilliam passed pleasantly. More snow fell on Christmas night. The family members and guests were greeting by a sparkling white world that glistened in the morning sun. The children begged to be allowed to play in the snow and almost all those in attendance accompanied them. Lord and Lady Matlock, Mr. and Mrs. Gardiner, and Mr. Bennet preferred to enjoy the warmth of the manor house, instead.

After breaking their fast, the others retired to bundle themselves for the cold winter day before venturing out of doors. They divided into teams with each group building a snowman that would be judged by the adults later in the day. Mrs. Reynolds provided them with an assortment of hats, mufflers, carrots, buttons, and bits of coal to be used to create their snow friends. Of course, the snow play led naturally into a snowball fight, though Darcy forbade Elizabeth from participating. However, knowing she made a large, slow-moving target, she willingly stood to the side and cheered on the combatants. The group paused long enough to enjoy a warm luncheon before heading back out of doors. Darcy had the sleighs prepared and the sleds loaded on them before the group was taken for a short ride to the best sledding hill on the estate. Darcy even took Elizabeth and little Rachel down the hill on a sled himself. Kitty brought her sketchpad everywhere she went and did some sketches of the activities to help them all remember the joy of this holidays gathering. By the time the activities were over, the exhausted children almost had to be carried into the house.

Over the next days, there was more sledding, sleigh rides, and a picnic in the conservatory for the houseguests to enjoy. For Mr. Bennet, it was a particularly delightful time. He could not recall another occasion when all of his daughters had been so close or so happy in their togetherness. He realized what he had missed by not taking his home and his wife in hand much sooner. Recalling her behavior just before her death, he realized they may never have been able to achieve such closeness with Mrs. Bennet's presence. Longbourn would be a lonely place with all of his daughters gone. He would speak to Darcy. Perhaps he could find a governess for Lydia that would continue what she was learning at school, yet allow him to have her at home with him.

Finally, the morning of Mary's wedding arrived. There had been another light snowfall during the night. Darcy made sure the sleighs were polished brightly to carry all the guests to the chapel. A knock on the door to her room brought Mary awake. Surprisingly, the bride had slept well and was not experiencing any nerves. Though Mary still had moments of surprise that she had attracted the attention of such an intelligent, wonderful, kind man, she had no doubts that her life was meant to be joined with his.

At Mary's call to enter, Elizabeth swept into the room. "Good morning, Mary. How are you today?"

"Very well, Lizzy, and very excited."

"I have ordered a tray brought to your room and hope you do not mind my joining you as we prepare for the day."

"I should be delighted for the company," replied Mary with a serene smile more often seen on the face of her older sister.

They were interrupted by a knock at the door. Mary's new maid, Polly, who had accompanied her to Pemberley, entered with a breakfast tray with enough food for a small army.

"Lizzy, the two of us shall never be able to eat all of that!"

"I expect we shall have a visitor or two join us this morning."

She had barely finished speaking when another knock sounded. Polly opened it to see, Jane, Kitty, Lydia, Aunt Madeline, and Lady Rebecca all entering the room.

"We wanted to help you prepare," said Jane.

"I would like that," replied Mary. "This will be the last time we will all be together for some time."

Mary was quickly bathed and her hair washed by her maid before rejoining the ladies as they broke their fast while Mary's hair dried. The suite rang with laughter as they talked and remembered pleasant times from their past.

When her hair had dried, Polly seated Mary at the dressing table and began to style her hair. It was pulled softly back from her face with numerous ringlets streaming from the loose bun at the back of her head. Next, she was assisted into her gown, a soft, sage green that highlighted her eyes. A ring of small white flowers surrounded the curls piled atop her head. From beneath the curls, two layers of white

Brussels lace hung down the back to Mary's waist, the top layer was pulled forward to cover her head while in the church.

A knock at the door heralded Mr. Bennet's arrival. "Everyone is prepared to leave for the chapel. You ladies had best gather your wraps and go downstairs. I shall wait with Kitty and Mary."

Each of the ladies embraced Mary and wished her well before exiting the room. Polly moved to the foot of the bed and lifted a hunter green wool cape trimmed in marten. She placed it around Mary's shoulder and stepped in front of her to fasten it. Then Polly picked up a bouquet of cream roses and handed them to Mary. Kitty, who would stand up with Mary, wore a beautiful long-sleeved burgundy silk gown. Her bouquet contained the same cream roses mixed with burgundy ones. Mr. Bennet helped Kitty with a burgundy wool cape trimmed in beaver. Once the ladies were ready, they descended the stairs, where Mrs. Reynolds and Benton stood with two footmen, waiting to assist the group into the last sleigh.

In a matter of minutes, the sleigh arrived before the door of the chapel. Mr. Bennet stepped out and handed down Kitty, then Mary. The two footmen who had traveled with them on the sleigh opened the doors to the chapel. When the doors opened, the music, played by Georgiana, changed, and Kitty began to advance up the aisle. As she reached the halfway point, Mary and her father began the walk to where Richard and Darcy stood at the altar. The smile on Richard's face brought a rosy blush to his bride's. Her eyes shimmered with unshed tears, and a soft smile, one she only bestowed on Richard, lit her face.

They ceremony did not take long, and as Mr. Millwood pronounced them husband and wife, Richard picked Mary up and spinning her in a circle. When he placed her back on her feet, Richard leaned in and kissed her soundly. The blush on her face deepened, but her smile widened as she gazed at her adoring new husband.

The family and guests in attendance bundled back into the sleighs for the return trip to the house. Mrs. Reynolds and Benton greeted the couple, offering their best wishes to the newlyweds. Once freed of their outerwear, everyone proceeded to the dining room for the wedding breakfast. Mrs. Mason had prepared a feast, including ham, roasted beef, poached salmon, a delicate egg dish, savory muffins, and sweet rolls. She had, also, concocted a magnificent tiered cake made with cinnamon, nutmeg, and raisins.

Lord Matlock was the first to stand and offer a toast. "To Richard and Mary, may life bring you every happiness!" Mr. Bennet, the viscount, and Mr. Gardiner all offered toasts of their own.

Next Darcy stood. He reached for his wife's hand and gripped it tightly as he said, "Richard, Mary, I can think of nothing better to wish for you than that you know a stronger and more enduring love each day and that you will always be as happy as we are! To Mary and Richard!"

At the conclusion of the meal, the newlyweds boarded a sleigh that would take them to Pemberley's dower house where they would stay for a few days before returning to the house for Twelfth Night. The couple waved happily as the sleigh pulled away. They were not yet out of sight of the family when Richard gathered Mary to him and began kissing her. It was a kiss that did not end until the sleigh reached its destination.

It was New Year's Eve day, and Darcy was in his office going over the correspondence arriving since Christmas Eve. None of the pieces appeared to need urgent attention, so he set them aside and picked up the London paper included with the mail. Darcy glanced through the news and the accounts of the war before noticing an article on the death of a peer. Looking more closely at the article, he was shocked to see a familiar name. He pulled the bell pull for a servant. When Benton answered his summons, Darcy asked him to send Mr. Amesbury to him.

A short time later a knock was heard at the study door. "Come," Darcy called.

The door opened, and Michael stood on the threshold. "You wished to see me, Darcy?"

"I did, Amesbury. I am afraid I have some bad news for you."

Michael's brows puckered in confusion, as he said, "You have bad news for me? Is there something wrong with Miss Bennet?"

"No nothing like that. Please be seated." Darcy indicated the chairs before his desk. Once seated, he handed Michael the paper, indicating the article that caught his eye.

PEER KILLED IN DRUNKEN BRAWL

On Christmas Eve, Viscount Amesbury was observed drinking heavily and gambling in a gaming hall on the outskirts of London. He loudly accused one of his companions of cheating and a brawl ensued. It is unclear who delivered the punch that sent the viscount tumbling backward where he struck his head on the corner of the bar and slumped to the floor. By the time the brawl had been broken up, it was discovered that the viscount, who, it had been assumed had passed out, was, in fact, dead from the blow to his head.

Michael's face took on a stunned look, and he quickly turned to the gossip page. The death of a peer was sure to have raised gossip as well as the news article. Glancing down the column, he stopped when he saw what he was looking for and began to read again.

> *This columnist has learned that the recently married Viscount A died in a brawl at a disreputable gaming hall. Rumor has it the viscount has gambled away most of his fortune and was visiting this particular establishment to avoid those who knew of his financial state. Notice sent to his townhome uncovered that his new bride was not in residence. Apparently, all is not well with the newlyweds as they are not spending their first Christmas together. As you will recall, they decamped from London shortly after making a public spectacle at the theater. The viscountess has not been seen in London since that time. The reporter can only wonder whether it is the lady's spending habits that bankrupted first her father and now her husband. Though she may look lovely in widow's weeds, she will not find herself welcome to return to London.*

Michael sat back in his chair, looking stupefied. Darcy observed him for a few minutes before speaking. "It would appear you are now the Viscount Amesbury."

"It is certainly nothing I expected," the young man replied, still slightly dazed.

"Do you wish me to send servants to pack for you? I assume you will need to depart shortly."

"I would appreciate that Darcy. I, also, need to speak with Mr. Bennet and Kath – Miss Bennet, before I leave."

"Would you like me to have Mr. Bennet join you here? You may use my study for your conversation."

"That is very kind of you Darcy. I would appreciate your sending for him."

Darcy, again, pulled the bell cord, and Benton entered. "Is there something you need, Mr. Darcy?" the butler asked.

"Benton, would you please find Mr. Bennet and direct him to my study."

"Certainly, sir."

As they waited for Mr. Bennet's arrival, Darcy could not help asking, "What shall you do with Lady Marjorie?"

"I am not certain, but I believe I will find her a small cottage somewhere far from the estate and pension her off. She did not come to my brother with anything, so she has no dowry with which to support herself. I will not maintain her in the style to which she is accustomed, but I shall not leave her to starve either. If she is unwilling to accept my offer, I shall provide her with transportation to London where she can fend for herself," replied Michael with determination.

"I believe that to be a wise idea. As Miss Bennet's brother, I feel I must ask how you will handle things if she tries to use her wiles to manipulate you. I would not wish to see my sister hurt."

"That is why I wish to speak to Mr. Bennet –." He was unable to finish his thought as a knock came at the study door.

"Enter," called Darcy.

"You wished to see me, Darcy?"

"No, Bennet, it was Mr. Amesbury who wished to speak to you. I have offered him the use of my study for the discussion. Amesbury, I shall send the servants to pack for you."

Mr. Bennet directed a look of surprise at the young man, but before he could ask, Darcy closed the door behind himself. "You wished to speak with me, sir?"

"I did, Mr. Bennet. I had hoped to wait a few more days and speak to you before we all departed, but circumstances have arisen that require my immediate departure."

"I hope everything is well, sir."

"Unfortunately not. I have just learned from an article in the London newspaper that my brother died in an accident on Christmas Eve."

"I see. But why does that necessitate your needing to speak with me?"

"Mr. Bennet, I wished to ask your permission to propose to Miss Bennet. I realize that we will not be able to marry until the end of my mourning period. However, if we are engaged, Miss Bennet and I could correspond." Mr. Bennet looked thoughtfully but did not speak, so Michael continued. "I was not close to my brother, sir, so I will mourn for no longer than three months. Unfortunately, it was reported that he has bankrupted the estate, and I will have many things to deal with over the next three months, returning the house to a livable state and relocating my sister-in-law. I would wish to be able to marry at the conclusion of my mourning period, sir. I would marry her immediately, if you would allow it, but I do not wish to subject her to the intemperate behavior of my brother's widow."

"With all the expenses you have mentioned, will you be in a position, financially, that will allow you to take a wife so soon."

"I will, sir. With luck and hard work, I made a considerable amount of money during my time in India. I can easily settle fifty thousand pounds on Miss Bennet and have more than a sufficient balance to handle the other issues I mentioned."

Mr. Bennet's eyebrows rose significantly at the amount he mentioned settling on his second youngest daughter. Looking steadily at the young man, Mr. Bennet considered his words. "I will allow you to speak with Kitty. However, I would ask one thing of you. If she wishes for a longer engagement or more time to feel comfortable in your presence, you will grant it to her."

"Certainly, Mr. Bennet. Miss Bennet's wellbeing and happiness will always be my most important priority."

"I would recommend you go to the conservatory. I will send Kitty to you there."

Michael reached his hand out to the older gentleman and shook it heartily. "Thank you very much, Mr. Bennet. I promise she will always be loved and cared for."

"See that she is, young man, or you will have her brothers and sisters with whom to deal," said Mr. Bennet with a sardonic chuckle.

Michael was pacing before the wisteria covered bower in the conservatory as he waited for Kitty to arrive. He carefully considered what he would tell her as well as the manner of his proposal. Engrossed in his thoughts, he did not hear her quiet footfalls as she approached.

Kitty stopped when she saw him, and her features assumed a look of concern. By his attitude, it was easy to see that something was bothering him. After a few minutes in which he still did not look up at her, Kitty softly cleared her throat. "Ahem."

Michael turned. "Miss Bennet, thank you for joining me."

"It is always a pleasure to be in your company, Mr. Amesbury," said Kitty shyly.

"Will you please join me?" He beckoned to a cushioned seat within the arbor.

Kitty seated herself beside the gentleman and folded her hands in her lap.

"Was there something specific you wished to discuss?"

"Yes, there is." Michael slipped from the bench and kneeled before Kitty. "Katherine, you are gentle, loving, and kind, and I find myself bewitched by your presence. My love for you is boundless. Would you do me the very great honor of accepting my hand in marriage?"

Kitty's eyes brimmed with tears that spilled over onto her cheeks, as she took a deep breath to compose herself. "I would be honored to accept your proposal." Kitty softly added, "I love you too, Michael."

After placing warm kisses on the back of both of her hands, Michael rejoined Kitty on the bench. "Kitty, my dear, I must now speak to you about something much less pleasant."

"I could tell something was bothering you when I approached. What has happened to upset you so?"

"I have just learned that my brother died in a brawl."

"Oh, I am so sorry! Is there comfort I can provide you?"

"There is no need. You know from our encounter at the theater that we did not care for one another." Kitty gave a little shudder at the remembrance.

"I need to depart immediately. Apparently, my brother has bankrupted our family estate. I will need to see what can be done to rectify the situation. I will also have to uncover any outstanding debts he has and find out if there is a mortgage on the property."

"Where is your family home?" Kitty interrupted to ask him.

"It is in Northamptonshire, about equal distance from London to Derbyshire."

"I must also remove Lady Marjorie from the house and settle her somewhere else. I would marry you immediately and take you with me, but I do not wish to subject you to her poor behavior. Nor do I know if the house is in a livable condition."

"When shall I see you again," asked Kitty with tear-filled eyes.

"I am not certain. That is one of the reasons I begged your father for permission to ask you to marry me. Because we are an engaged couple, we will be able to correspond. While you are in London, you can look over paper hangings, fabrics, and furniture and plan how you would wish to redecorate the house."

"Tell me about the house."

"My family's manor house is on the small side, but there is an estate for sale next to it, that has a much larger house. If I were to purchase it, it would more than double our landholdings."

"Are the house and estate in good condition?"

"I am not certain as the previous owner also had financial difficulties. If I were to purchase the estate, we could choose to live in whichever house you preferred. I would even consider demolishing both houses, and we could build a brand new one, though we may wish to live in one of them temporarily."

Kitty looked at Michael uncertainly. Something was bothering her, but she could not quite determine what it was. "Who owed the other estate?"

"It belonged to the Earl of Dalbert."

"I see. So our choices are to live in your old home or the Dalbert house. Both are places Lady Marjorie has previously lived."

"Yes," said Michael hesitantly.

"Do you have pleasant memories of your family home?"

"Some. It was a comfortable place when my mother was alive. I am told I was much like her. My father, unfortunately, was a harsh man. He was diligent in directing his heir, but had no time for a lowly second son."

"I am sorry, Michael," Kitty said consolingly as she placed a gentle hand on his arm. "Tell me about the earl's home?

"It was a bit gothic for my taste. It is dark, with lots of small rooms and few windows. It even has a tower at one corner."

"It sounds as if you would not have any objection to the third option of building a place of our own?"

"None at all as your comfort and happiness are my primary concern. Would you feel it was too soon if we married in three months after my mourning period is over?"

"Not at all. I said I would marry you now and go with you, if you wished."

"I would like nothing better, but the business to which I must attend would separate us more than I would wish were I a new husband with a beautiful bride awaiting me at home."

"Then we shall marry in three months. Would you be opposed to marrying from Pemberley, if William and Lizzy would allow it? The baby is due in early February, and Elizabeth would most likely be unable to travel at that time."

"I would not mind in the least. Should we go and ask them?" Michael stood up and offered his hand to Kitty. As he drew her close, he said, "Before we go to join the others, may I kiss you?"

Kitty blushed profusely, but nodded her head in agreement. Michael leaned in very slowly until his lips met Kitty's. He broke the kiss quickly, but as her eyes remained closed he resumed the activity, increasing the pressure of his lips just slightly. As the kiss ended he drew her closer within the circle of his arms and rested his cheek on her hair.

"It is going to be a long three months." He felt the vibration of Kitty's soft laughter throughout his body, which only made him desire to kiss her again. Stepping away from her, he offered her his arm, and they went in search of the rest of the family.

The others were found relaxing in the blue drawing room. The smiles the new arrivals wore alerted the others they wished to share some news. Michael explained about the article and his brother's death. Kitty then told them of his proposal and their plans to marry in three month's time.

"William, Lizzy, we were wondering if you would allow us to marry from Pemberley since you shall not be able to travel by the beginning of April due to the new baby."

Darcy and Elizabeth looked at each other. He noted her slightly pleading look and nodded imperceptibly. Turning to the newly betrothed couple, Darcy said, "We would be delighted to host your wedding here at Pemberley. Did you have a date in mind?"

"We were hoping to marry on the third of April."

With that pronouncement, the congratulations rang out. Michael was unable to tarry long as he needed to depart for his family's estate. Kitty walked him out to his carriage, and with a kiss to her hand, he stepped in and was quickly on his way.

After Michael's departure, Mr. Bennet sought out Lydia. He found her sitting with Kitty in the conservatory. Kitty was smiling but teary, as Lydia reminded her that the three months until her wedding would pass quickly. I hope that I shall be able to miss a few days of school to attend the wedding."

"Yes, you must be here. I want you to stand up with me. We were the closest of sisters for many years, and I always dreamed of having you stand up with me."

"I am sorry for my actions. I never meant to drive you away. I am ashamed of the way I behaved, and you had every reason to separate yourself from me and my shameful behavior."

"I am just glad to have you back as my sweet baby sister."

Mr. Bennet, who had overheard this exchange, cleared his throat before advancing further into the room where the girls would see him.

"I did not intend to eavesdrop, but I must tell you that your words warmed my heart. I am sorry I did not act sooner to rectify the problems I had allowed to grow within our family. I am sorry for the time we all lost due to my lackadaisical attitude."

"Papa, you must remember what Lizzy always says," began Kitty. "Remember the past only as it gives you pleasure." The three of them spoke the words at the same time and could not help but laugh as they finished.

"Lydia, I was wondering if I might have a moment of your time?"

"Certainly, Papa."

Kitty stood, saying, "I shall go in search of Lizzy so that you two may talk."

Mr. Bennet moved to sit on the bench near his youngest daughter. "I wished to get your opinion about something before making a decision."

"You wish my opinion, Papa?" Lydia's voice spoke of her surprise.

Mr. Bennet shook his head ruefully. "I realized that I shall be returning to an empty estate. I wondered if you might prefer to have a governess and masters at home rather than return to school?"

Lydia was quiet for several minutes. It was obvious to her father that she was seriously considering his question. Eventually, Lydia answered. "As much as I would enjoy returning home, I believe it would be best for me to return to school, at least until the summer. I know I am making progress and that I have changed. However, I am not sure it is as deeply ingrained in me yet as it should be. Could we discuss this again when I return home for the summer?"

"Of course, we can, my dear. I am very proud of the thought you put into your answer. It is a sign of the growth you have made. However, I shall need you to write to me frequently. I am sure I shall be lonely rambling around Longbourn on my own."

"I promise to write you each week, Papa."

Mr. Bennet put his arm around Lydia's shoulder and pulled her closer to his side before placing a tender kiss on her forehead. "I love you, Lydia."

Her voice husky with emotion, Lydia replied, "I love you too, Papa."

The family enjoyed a festive dinner and a lively evening as they welcomed in the new year. The next day, Mr. Bennet and Lydia left to return Lydia to school. This time, Mr. Bennet permitted Kitty to join them. The sisters chatted happily throughout the trip. Mr. Bennet had to smile to himself as he observed them. There was a time he called them the silliest girls in the county, but what he now observed was two loving, intelligent young women reveling in each other's conversation and company.

The residents of Pemberley received an invitation to the Twelfth Night ball, the Marquess and Marchioness of Redvale were hosting that evening. However, only the seven Fitzwilliams and the Bingleys attended. Those who remained at Pemberley enjoyed an evening of quiet companionship.

The Gardiners would be departing in the morning, and they would take Kitty with them. Kitty was to order her trousseau and begin to look for items to decorate her new home. She had heard from Michael via express and would see him shortly. He requested the family stop in Northamptonshire, so that Kitty could view the two homes they discussed. If she did not like either of them, they would meet with an architect between meeting with his solicitors.

The Fitzwilliams, including Richard and Mary, would also be leaving. The Bingleys were anxious to return to their home as Charles needed to meet with his steward regarding the spring planting and the upcoming growing season. Mr. Bennet intended to return for Longbourn, as well, but Elizabeth convinced him to remain until the baby was born. He would travel to Ashford Hills with the Bingleys for a fortnight, then return to Pemberley.

And so it was that soon only the three Darcy's remained at Pemberley.

CHAPTER 28

AS THE SECOND week of January was drawing to a close, Derbyshire experienced one of the worst blizzards in its history. Throughout the storm, the wind howled, and the snowflakes swirled in little eddies. When the world was again quiet, more than three feet of snow had fallen, and the drifts were more than six feet deep. The manor house looked like a gray island in a white sea, a sea that went on as far as the eye could see. The bare trees stood like stark sentinels guarding the island's perimeter.

Ensconced before a roaring fire in the library, Elizabeth leaned against the arm of the sofa with her feet in Darcy's lap as his mellow baritone voice read to her from William Blake's, *Songs of Innocence and Experience*.

A gasp from his wife caused Darcy to pause, "Elizabeth, are you well?"

"I believe so. It was just a twinge in my abdomen." She rubbed her hand on her swollen stomach in small circles.

"I believe we should send for the midwife," was William's authoritative reply.

"William, I am not even sure what that was. The baby is not due for a few weeks yet."

"I am aware of that, my love, but it could take quite some time before anyone can reach us. I believe it would be wise if I were to send a sleigh to Lambton to retrieve Mrs. Bates and Dr. Elliott."

Feeling a sharp pain in her back, Elizabeth agreed with her husband's opinion. Darcy moved to the bell pull, and Benton was quick to answer.

"Benton, please send word to the stable to have a sleigh made ready. I would like three men to travel into Lambton to retrieve the doctor and midwife."

"Certainly, sir. Would you like me to send Mrs. Reynolds to you in the meantime?"

"I do not believe that will be necessary yet, but perhaps a rider should also be sent to Ashford Hills." The butler bowed and exited, his gait a bit quicker than his usual measured tread.

Darcy resumed his seat on the sofa and continued to read to Elizabeth. Three hours passed, and Mrs. Reynolds appeared in the library doorway carrying a tray. There were steaming mugs of soup, some fresh bread, cheese, and a pot of tea.

"Mrs. Darcy, how are you feeling," said the housekeeper in her motherly way.

"I am well, Mrs. Reynolds, though the pains that were mild and irregular at the beginning seem to be changing."

"That is to be expected if you are in labor. Are the pains more regular now?

"Yes, but they are not too painful."

"How often are the pains," asked Mrs. Reynolds.

"They are about every twenty minutes, but so far they are bearable."

"If they get closer together or if they become unbearable, you should notify me. You should also let me know if you feel any wetness. That is another sign that things are progressing. We will need to move you to your room and get you prepared to meet your little one. In the meantime, I shall prepare the birthing chamber."

As she attempted to move into a sitting position to enjoy the food that Mrs. Reynolds had brought, a stronger pain gripped Elizabeth, and she was forced to be still and gasped for breath.

Mrs. Reynolds stepped up beside her mistress and laid a comforting hand on her back, rubbing it gently. "That is not unusual, mistress, and a good sign. It means that the baby is closer to arriving." Elizabeth just nodded, but she could not deny that she was a little fearful.

After the housekeeper left the library, Elizabeth sat up next to her husband. Leaning into his shoulder, she whispered, "William, though I am anxious to hold our child in my arms, I am also somewhat frightened. I know it is not what is considered appropriate, but would you stay with me throughout my labors?"

"I do not care what society considers appropriate. Since meeting, we have faced our challenges together; this experience will be no different. There is nowhere else I would rather be, and, in any case, I would have asked you to let me remain." Darcy placed his arm around his wife's shoulders and pulled her gently to him. He placed a gentle kiss on her temple as he whispered, "We can do anything together, my love; remember that."

"Do you think the midwife will arrive in time?"

"I sent for them early to ensure that they would, but if they do not, Mrs. Reynolds and two of the maids have assisted with deliveries in the past. You will not be alone in this."

"I do hope Jane will arrive in time. I am sure I will need her calming influence." Elizabeth attempted a laugh, but another pain gripped her."

Elizabeth was only able to manage a few sips of her soup and a cup of tea. When they finished eating, Elizabeth requested they take a walk through the gallery. Arm-in-arm with her husband, they moved from the sitting room. Elizabeth looked at each ancestor and asked Darcy to tell her something about them. They stopped before the oldest picture in the gallery. Elizabeth concentrated on the portrait as she listened to Darcy's soothing voice.

"Alexander Philip D'Arcy, a younger son, came to England with William the Conqueror. He received the lands that made up Pemberley from William I. The King had wished to bestow a title as well, but D'Arcy had declined. Family legend said that Alexander told William he had not supported the king's cause for such an honor. 'I do not desire to raise myself above my brother in France. I wish only for the chance to build a home and raise a family of which I can be proud. I wish to love and work my lands and to watch them grow. I wish to raise righteous, God-fearing sons, who will strive to do their best for King and country.'" Darcy paused as Elizabeth experienced another pain. "What the king did not know," continued Darcy with a chuckle, "is that Alexander did not wish to be forced to bow to the inconsistencies of a king as he would be as one of his nobles. Alexander hoped that with the seat of government so far from the lands that eventually came to be called Pemberley, he would not be subjected too often to the whims of the monarch."

Elizabeth gave a cry and dropped to her knees. Darcy noted the darkening color of her skirt and the puddle that appeared on the floor around her. Calling out to the footman stationed at the gallery's entrance, he cried, "Have Mrs. Reynolds meet me in the mistress' chambers." Turning to his wife he spoke softly, "I believe our child is becoming more anxious to make his appearance. I am certain he wishes to behold his beautiful Mama." As he spoke, Darcy knelt beside his beloved wife and gently lifted her into his arms. Standing, he strode off down the hall towards Elizabeth's bedchamber.

Darcy deposited Elizabeth on the bed in her bedchamber, stepping away to allow Mrs. Reynolds and Margot to assist her into a dry nightdress. When the ladies had completed their task, he sat on the edge of the bed and held Elizabeth's hand tightly. Margot built up the fire in the room before disappearing into Elizabeth dressing room. Darcy could hear her moving about, but he could not observe what she was doing. He could hear the sound of doors opening and closing nearby and the sounds of feet moving about, but everything was out of the range of his vision. Darcy could only wonder about the preparations taking place.

The firm grip of his hand distracted him as he realized Elizabeth was suffering from another pain. Darcy cast a worried look at Mrs. Reynolds. The midwife and doctor had not arrived, and it appeared that Elizabeth's pains were growing stronger and getting closer together.

"Mr. Darcy, do you have your watch with you?" Mrs. Reynolds inquired. Darcy nodded. "Would you please watch it and tell me the time between the pains." Again, Darcy nodded. Mrs. Reynolds knew that having something to focus on would help to keep the master calm. She knew he would not leave his beloved wife, yet seeing her in such pain would distress him, so she needed to keep him from becoming a distraction or difficulty. Darcy removed his watch and began to closely watch his lovely wife. When the next pain began, he noted the time.

As the pain concluded, Mrs. Reynolds addressed Elizabeth. "Mrs. Darcy, how are you fairing?"

"The pains are increasing in intensity, but it is still manageable."

"Please, ma'am, do not feel you must be silent through the pains. Yell if you must," the housekeeper encouraged her.

Elizabeth's pains continued for another two hours before she found she could no longer maintain her composure. She cried out as the pains increased and squeezed Darcy's hand with increasing pressure. Throughout the pain, Darcy whispered words of love and encouragement to her. "You are so brave, my dear Lizzy. I love you so much. Just think, all of this work will soon allow you to hold our child in your arms. I am so proud of you, my love." Occasionally, her husband found it necessary to briefly let go of her hand so that he could flex his fingers and attempt to restore the circulation to them.

After a particularly intense pain, a knock was heard at the door. Mrs. Reynolds moved to open it and was as relieved as her master to see the midwife and doctor in the opening.

Doctor Elliott moved to stand behind Darcy as the midwife immediately moved to check her patient. "How are you feeling, Mrs. Darcy? I am pleased to be here on such a momentous day. The next generation of Darcys joins the world today."

"Considering the weather, we are grateful to have you here with us." Elizabeth managed to utter her rather breathy response between pains. "I am well, but I do hope it will be soon."

After washing up, the midwife, Mrs. Bates, was able to complete her examination during the doctor's interchange with Mrs. Darcy. It was clear the baby would very shortly make his appearance in the world.

"I believe we should move Mrs. Darcy to the birthing chair. Mr. Darcy, please carry your wife to the chair and then leave us," Mrs. Bates directed.

A new pain struck Elizabeth just as Darcy prepared to lift her. Looking at Mrs. Bates, Darcy spoke firmly. "I will happily carry her, but I will not be leaving her. She asked me to remain with her throughout the birth, and that is where I will be."

The midwife opened her mouth to argue with him but quieted as Dr. Elliott placed a hand on her arm and shook his head. Mrs. Bates gave a little sniff, as Mrs. Reynolds led her to the birthing chair. She was busy laying out the equipment she would need as Darcy sat Elizabeth down in the chair.

Darcy could now see that Margot had been busy preparing for the baby's birth. The fire in the bathing chamber burned brightly, and the heat filled the small room. The birthing chair sat in the middle of the tiled floor. He saw a footstool on the hearth upon which sat several towels. A small table was, also, placed before the fire. Upon it lay a blanket Darcy had observed Elizabeth making. Upon the blanket rested a nappy and gown for the baby. Darcy further noted a small basin containing warm water and a soft rag; on the hearth close to the fire sat several buckets of hot water.

Darcy took up a position on the right side of Elizabeth's chair, and Mrs. Reynolds moved to the left side. As the next pain occurred, Mrs. Bates instructed Elizabeth to bear down with all her strength. Elizabeth groaned loudly as she did as the midwife had asked. Darcy continued his stream of loving, encouraging words, unsure as to whether Elizabeth could hear him or not. With one final push, the baby arrived in the midwife's hands, and a lusty cry pierced the air. It is a boy!" cried Mrs. Bates.

Margot stood next to the midwife with one of the warmed towels and took the baby from her. Moving closer to the fire, Elizabeth's maid began to clean the baby, giving him his first bath. Darcy was stroking the hair from Elizabeth's forehead as they both watched their new son.

A cry of pain from Elizabeth startled everyone. As Mrs. Bates attempted to determine what had caused Elizabeth's cry, Jane Bennet's voice was heard from the mistress' chambers. Hearing her sister cry out, Jane followed the sound to the dressing chamber. Jane entered the room just as Mrs. Bates announced there was a second baby. Jane quickly moved to take Mrs. Reynolds place at her sister's side, adding her words of love and encouragement to her sister. Mrs. Reynolds rushed to the nursery to find an additional gown, blanket, and nappy. As Dr. Elliott was now examining the cleaned and diapered baby, she handed the items to Margot, who held them close to the fire, hoping to warm them quickly.

With another cry from Elizabeth and Mrs. Bates order to bear down, Mrs. Reynolds grabbed another of the warmed towels and moved to stand beside the midwife, preparing to receive the next baby. This time, it was Mrs. Reynolds who announced the birth of the child. "The young master has a sister!"

As Margot was now dressing the heir to Pemberley, Dr. Elliott, dumped the used water from the basin and filled it with clean water for Mrs. Reynolds to wash the little miss. Mrs. Bates was delivering the afterbirth and Darcy and Jane were both still speaking with Elizabeth. At the midwife's direction, Darcy placed Elizabeth in the bathing tub, which had been filled with the buckets of warm water. At a word from Mrs. Reynolds, Margot directed the master into the mistress' bedchamber and placed his son into his arms. Darcy sat down on the side of the bed and stared at his first born as silent tears ran down his face.

It did not take long before an exhausted Elizabeth was cleaned, dressed, and returned to her bed. She was sitting up against the headboard upon a mound of pillows. Darcy placed their son in Elizabeth's arms as he received his daughter to hold. Darcy moved to sit on the bed beside his wife. "Our family has doubled in size today. You gave me not one child but two—a most beloved son and daughter. I love you more than words can say, my dearest, loveliest Elizabeth. You and our children are my world, and I am the richest and most blessed of men. How can I ever thank you, Elizabeth, for the amazing gift you gave me this day."

"Thanks are not necessary, my darling husband. Having you and our children is more than thanks enough."

The couple was interrupted by a knock at the bedchamber door. Margot moved to open it, revealing the proud grandpapa and doting aunts and uncle. Georgiana rushed towards the bed and sat on Elizabeth's other side as she gazed at her nephew and niece, exclaiming over how small they were. Jane and Bingley moved to stand near Darcy's side of the bed with Mr. Bennet opposite them.

Elizabeth held the baby out to her father saying, "Would you care to meet your grandson?"

Mr. Bennet accepted the small bundle and gazed upon the small face of his first grandchild. "I cannot see his eyes, but he appears to bear a strong resemblance to his father, right down to the dimples in his cheeks. Does this handsome young man have a name?"

Elizabeth looked at her husband, who nodded. Turning back to her father she said, his name is Andrew Thomas William Darcy." Upon hearing the name, Mr. Bennet looked up from his grandson to his dearest daughter, tears glistening in his eyes."

Darcy had handed his daughter over to Jane. She moved to stand next to her father so that he could see his granddaughter. "Lizzy, she is the spitting image of you as a baby. What will you call this beauty?"

This time, Darcy answered. "Her name is Elizabeth Anne Darcy, but we plan to call her Beth."

With a chuckle, he added, "She looks like you, Lizzy, and will bear your name. I wonder if she will give her father as much trouble as you gave me?"

The soft laughter of those in the room seemed to wake Master Andrew, who gave a lusty cry. Handing the baby back to his mother, the visitors left the room so that Elizabeth could feed her son.

As she settled the child at her breast, Darcy remained beside her, holding their daughter and observing his son nursing. The picture it created filled the master of Pemberley with an overwhelming feeling of love and gratitude, and he offered up a silent prayer of gratitude to God for preserving his beloved wife and blessing him so abundantly. As the dinner hour approached, Mrs. Reynolds knocked softly on the door of the mistress' chambers. Hearing no reply, she quietly opened the door to see the master and mistress asleep on the bed, their children nestled between them, sleeping soundly. The peaceful scene brought tears to the housekeeper's eyes as she observed the love between the new family and knew that love would fill the halls and lives of those who resided with the walls of Pemberley.

The day after the births, Darcy began writing letters to their extended family, telling them about the arrival of the twins. In each home where a letter arrived, rejoicing occurred. The news even reached the gossips of London, who of course reported the information in the papers.

The Bingleys stayed for a week after the birth, but Mr. Bennet decided to remain until Kitty's wedding. He frequently corresponded with his steward to ensure that all was well at Longbourn, but he could not deprive himself of the joy he received from watching his grandchildren grow and thrive.

It seemed as if the twins changed almost daily, but they were, indeed, the spitting images of their parents. Andrew had Darcy's dark wavy hair, dark eyes, and dimples. He even seemed to have Darcy's serious nature. He was a quiet baby who seemed to take in everything around him. On the other hand, Beth had her mother's riotous curls and chocolate brown eyes, which seemed to sparkle with mischief from the moment of her birth. She was a bright, happy baby. They both brought tremendous joy to the lives of all those who lived at Pemberley.

Pemberley seemed filled with new life and joy. It was not just the addition of the Darcy twins, but the love and joy that filled the lives of all those who resided within its walls. Elizabeth recovered quickly and refused to remain in bed for the six weeks expected of her. After two weeks, she insisted she be allowed to move about between their suite and the nursery. A week later she was demanding access to the library and music room as well. Though Darcy worried for her health, Elizabeth seemed to glow with vitality. Soon she had returned to her daily meeting with the housekeeper in her study and was busily answering correspondence from those who had sent letters of congratulations after learning of the birth of the twins. Most of the letters arrived with gifts for the newest members of the Darcy family. The arriving gifts overflowed the table in the family drawing room on which they sat. As the weather was extremely cold, it was decided the christening would be held just before the wedding of Michael and Kitty when all the family would again gather at Pemberley. Elizabeth was amazed to note that small gifts seemed to appear almost daily and could only assume they were from the staff. As soon as Darcy and Dr. Elliott allowed her to move freely about the house, Elizabeth set aside time each day to open a few gifts and write a note of thanks.

The whole of the estate and the communities as far as Lambton and Kympton were pleased to know the Darcy family would continue in the parts for another generation.

CHAPTER 29

CAROLINE'S LIFE SINCE returning to York had been more tedious than ever before. He aunt was furious with Caroline for her deception, and she was no longer privy to the news and letters that came from her brother. Cut off from society as she was, she had begun reading the London newspaper even more assiduously than before. It was the middle of February when she saw a small notice announcing the arrival of the Darcy twins. Furious that Elizabeth had been blessed with not only an heir for Darcy but a daughter as well, Caroline seethed. Somehow she must find a way to ruin the Darcys. She no longer held any desire for Darcy. Her only desire was to revenge herself on both of them.

She brooded for days and finally a plan came to her. She nearly cackled with glee at the idea that had occurred to her. If successful, her actions would devastate the Darcys and likely drive them apart as well. Her first step was to be on her best behavior. She needed Aunt Honoria to be less suspicious and watchful if she was to be successful. As a result, she wrote letters of apology to her brother, sister, and the Darcys. She presented them to her aunt and requested that she mail them. Aunt Horatia accepted the letters but did not commit to sending them. For the next several days Caroline was polite and helpful whenever in her aunt's presence. However, as everyone slept, she set about obtaining the items she would need to complete her plan. Caroline discovered where her aunt kept her household monies and knew what day of the week that Aunt Horatia replenished them. She also found an old bottle of laudanum and secreted it away in her room.

Finally, the day came when Caroline set her plan in motion. As she brought the tea tray from the kitchen that evening, she managed to put an extra large dose of laudanum into the servants' teapot. Then as she prepared a cup of tea for her aunt, she slipped a large dose of the medication into the cup.

As her aunt became sleepy from drinking the drugged tea, Caroline solicitously helped her to her room. She managed to get the sleeping lady onto her bed, where she lightly bound her hands and feet, before placing a gag in her mouth. Caroline exited the room, locking the door behind her and taking the key. Next, she went into her aunt's study and took the funds she kept there. Hurrying to her room, Caroline changed into some clothes she had managed to remove from the laundry. She had acquired a rough, work shirt and wool pants. To these Caroline added her sturdiest pair of boots, and her warmest cloak and sat down to wait. When there were no further sounds in the household, she slipped down the servants' stairs and arrived in the kitchen to see the staff asleep, their heads down on the table. Caroline locked all the doors connecting the kitchen to other rooms before letting herself out the kitchen door taking all the keys and the housekeeper's ring with her. She quietly entered the stables and hid all the keys among the straw on the floor. She knew no one would be about as the stable hands had been in the kitchen with the other servants, fast asleep. Caroline struggled briefly but managed to saddle one of the carriage horses. With money tucked safely into her boots, Caroline mounted the horse and slowly made her way from her aunt's neighborhood. Once away from the more populated section of town, she whipped the horse into a gallop, heading south towards Pemberley. Riding through the night, she stopped at an inn, partook of a meal, and secured a room to rest for a while. After two days of traveling, Caroline reached the area surrounding Pemberley.

Caroline visited Darcy's estate often enough in the early years of their acquaintance to be familiar with the routine of Darcy's staff. Often on those visits, she would claim the need to rest. While other thought Caroline asleep in her suite, she would sneak through the house, learning its layout and the location of the hidden servants' passages. On one particular visit, she managed to make an imprint of the kitchen door key and have a copy made for herself. This key would allow her to successfully carryout her plan.

She remained hidden in the woods of Pemberley throughout the afternoon and evening, though she was forced to suffer a drenching from a rain shower. Finally, the hour was advanced enough that she would be able to enter the house. Entering though the kitchen door, Caroline slipped into the servants' passages. Attempting to compromise Mr. Darcy on one of her earlier visits, she knew Mr. Darcy now stationed a footman in the hallway near his bedchamber. Caroline exited the servants' passage into a bedroom a few doors down from where the footman stood duty. Knocking over a chair in the room she occupied, Caroline was able to draw the servant to investigate. He opened the door, and by the light of his candle, could see the overturned chair.

As the footman moved further into the room to investigate, Caroline brought a small marble statuette down on the back of the footman's head. He slumped to the floor at her feet, and Caroline quickly ripped strips from the bed sheets and used them to bind the man's hands, feet, and mouth. Taking up the footman's candle, she stepped into the hall, closing the door behind her, and moved stealthily to the door she knew led to the nursery. Opening the door as quietly as she could, Caroline looked into the room. She saw the two cribs and moved towards them. She hoped she would be able to determine the daughter from the son as, to her, all babies looked alike when they were this young. One of the cribs was empty, causing Caroline to fear discovery. Ignoring her plan to suffocate the girl child, she grabbed the baby from the other crib and moved towards the stairs to make her escape from the house.

Elizabeth was unsure what had caused her to awaken, but she felt a strong need to see her dear children. Slipping quietly from Darcy's bed and embrace, she passed through their sitting room and into her bedchamber. Moving in the direction of the nursery, she opened the door into the room as the door to the hall closed behind Caroline. Surprised to find a candle burning, Elizabeth moved quickly to the cribs. Discovering them both empty, she threw open the door to the room the wet nurse used. Seeing only Beth and the wet nurse, she cried anxiously, "Wake Mr. Darcy! Someone has taken Andrew! Then lock yourself in this room and keep Beth safe."

Elizabeth turned on her heal and head towards the door to the hallway, grabbing the candle as she passed. The nurse jumped up and rushed to the master's chambers, yelling Mrs. Darcy's message from the doorway before rushing to lock herself and Beth safely in her room.

Darcy woke at the wet nurse's words, but it took him a moment for the words to register. Grabbing his dressing gown he rushed into the hallway looking for the footman. Not seeing anyone, Darcy quickly moved off down the hall for the stairs leading to the lower level. Not knowing who was in the house or if they were armed, he moved as quickly and quietly as possible. By the light of the candle Elizabeth had placed on a nearby table, he could see Elizabeth struggling with an assailant at the top of the staircase one floor down. As he rushed to his wife's aid, he saw her pull Andrew from the intruder's arms. Elizabeth attempted to turn and run, but the intruder managed to grasp her shoulder, halting her progress. The interloper turned Elizabeth around to face him. A hat pulled low over the eyes of the housebreaker prevented Elizabeth from getting a good look at the person. She kept a tight hold on the baby, preventing the assailant from regaining possession of her beloved son, but hampering her ability to protect them both. Consequently, the intruder got a firm grip on Elizabeth's upper arms, in spite of her attempts to twist free. Elizabeth was forced to release one arm from around her son to try to break the stranger's hold on her. Caroline managed to finally get a good grip and was leaning into Elizabeth menacingly, intent on throwing her and the child down the stairs. Darcy reached them just in time. With a cry of "Elizabeth," he managed to pull his wife to safety. Off balance, the intruder went head first down the stairs. The body came to rest on the marble tile of the hall floor, the head tilted at an unusual angle. Darcy stood clutching Elizabeth and Andrew to his chest as he stared at the body below them.

The noise of Darcy's cry and the body tumbling down the stairs managed to rouse other members of the household. Georgiana and Mr. Bennet appeared on the upper landing, and Benton and Mrs. Reynolds followed closely by Gregson and two other large footmen came up from below stairs. It was Gregson that moved to examine the body. Not finding a pulse, he turned the body over. The hat fell back from the face, and those gathered round the body gasped in shock. Benton looked up to his master and mistress and said, "It is Miss Bingley." Disbelief was evident in his voice.

Pandemonium broke. Darcy barked out orders for his staff to remove the body and send immediately for the Bingleys. He called for Gregson to attend him, then escorted Elizabeth and Andrew back to the nursery. Darcy directed Gregson to find the footman who should have been in attendance outside their rooms. Knocking on the door, Darcy called for the wet nurse, Mrs. Hansen, to open the door. He ushered Elizabeth, who still held tightly to Andrew, Georgiana, and Mr. Bennet inside, instructing Mr. Bennet to lock all entrances to the nursery and to keep watch over the ladies. He was not to let anyone enter until Darcy returned.

Elizabeth collapsed into the rocking chair in the nursery, Andrew in her arms, and began to sob. She had fought like a tigress to protect her son, but now that the immediate danger had passed, she was overcome with the realization of what could have been lost that night. Georgiana rushed to comfort her sister, and as her tears subsided, Mrs. Hansen put Beth into her mother's arms, as well. Elizabeth held a babe in each arm as she rocked and sang softly to them.

After more than an hour, Darcy returned. "A comprehensive search of the house revealed no other intruders. Dr. Elliott should arrive shortly. He will check you and Andrew thoroughly, then see to Chaney, who was on duty in the hall this evening. It appears

Miss Bingley lured him into one of the other bedchambers and bashed him in the back of the head before tying him up. I have also sent for the Bingleys."

"Poor Charles. He will be devastated by his sister's latest behavior. I hope it will not upset Jane too much in her delicate condition," worried Elizabeth.

Darcy suggested Georgiana, Mr. Bennet, and Mrs. Hansen retire and try to get some additional rest. The ladies complied, but Mr. Bennet decided to dress and wait for his eldest daughter and her husband to arrive. He wished to be of comfort to them, if he could. Darcy and Elizabeth, each carrying one of the twins, took them into their bedchamber and rested together on the bed as they awaited the doctor's arrival. Elizabeth and the children had all managed to doze off, wrapped securely in the arms of their husband, father, and protector.

When a knock came at the doorway, Darcy softly called for the visitor to enter. Mrs. Reynolds opened the door, admitting Dr. Elliott. She followed closely, closing the door quietly. Darcy explained that someone had attempted to kidnap his heir and that Elizabeth had tangled with the interloper. The doctor leaned over the bed, carefully examining the sleeping Andrew.

"As he is not crying and appears to have no signs of bumps or bruising, I feel safe saying he is perfectly fine and will have no memory of this difficult night."

Elizabeth had roused at the soft voices and was heard to whisper, "Thank the Lord for such a blessing."

"I must agree with you, Mrs. Darcy. Now your anxious husband wishes for me to examine you." Knowing Darcy would not find any peace until the doctor pronounced her well, Elizabeth submitted to the examination. Dr. Elliott's only findings were signs of bruising on Elizabeth's upper arms, where Miss Bingley fingers dug into her flesh.

Once relieved of his worst worries, Darcy resettled Elizabeth and the twins in his bed before asking Dr. Elliott to accompany him to his study. Once in the privacy of Darcy's sanctuary, he explained more fully about who the intruder had been. "This news will be devastating to the Bingleys. I was hoping you would help in a slight deception to save their reputation."

"What is it you wish me to say, Mr. Darcy?"

"I merely wish it to be known that the visting Miss Bingley, for some unknown reason, was moving through the house in the dark and must have stumbled and fallen down the stairs, resulting in her death. I do not wish it to be know that she attempted to kidnap my children as the Bingleys would be ostracized." As an afterthought, Darcy added, "I hope that she did not harm her aunt or the woman's staff in her escape from York. That might be too much of a burden for Bingley to bear."

"I can agree with your request. Perhaps we should call the constable so that he too may learn about Miss Bingley's unfortunate accident."

"Perhaps you are right. I shall send a groom to Lambton for Mr. Oliver."

The sun was just rising as the Bingleys and the Hursts, who had arrived a few days earlier for a visit at Ashford Hills, arrived at Pemberley. Darcy indicated there were rooms prepared and suggested that Jane and Louisa might like to rest.

"William," said a concerned Jane, "you did not send for us in the wee hours of the night so that we could rest at Pemberley. What has happened? Are Elizabeth and the children well?"

"Something unusual did occur, Jane. Mrs. Reynolds, please take the ladies to the master sitting room and alert Mrs. Darcy of their presence. As the ladies followed Mrs. Reynolds, Darcy led the gentlemen into his study. He poured three glasses of brandy and handed one to each gentleman before seating himself behind his desk with one for himself.

"I am afraid there is no easy way to tell you what has happened here tonight."

"Are Elizabeth and the twins well, Darcy?" Charles' voice carried a note of anxiety.

"Fortunately, they are unharmed save for some bruising to Elizabeth's arms."

"For heaven's sake, what happened?" cried Bingley.

"I sorry to say, Miss Bingley broke into my home and attempted to kidnap Andrew. Fortunately, some instinct woke Elizabeth, and the loss was discovered quickly. She asked the wet nurse to wake me and gave chase to the unknown intruder. I reached them just as Miss Bingley attempted to push Elizabeth, who now had Andrew back in her arms, down the stairs. I grasped for Elizabeth and was fortunate enough to save her from falling. However, Miss Bingley was off balance and fell down the main staircase. Her neck was broken, and we only discovered it was she when we turned the body over after determining that there was no heartbeat."

Bingley's face drained of color, and his hand began to tremble. Hurst was not much more composed, but he managed to remove Bingley's glass from his hand and set it on the desk before it slipped from Bingley's nerveless fingers.

"Oh, Caroline. What drove you to such madness?" cried an anguished Bingley as he dropped his head into his hands.

"Perhaps that was it, Bingley. Perhaps Caroline had lost her grip on reality? You know she refused to listen to anything anyone said to her. She believed only that which she wished to believe, no matter what one said to her."

"But how shall we survive the shame of this incident. Jane and I shall have to leave Derbyshire when it becomes known that my sister attempted to kidnap the heir of Pemberley."

"Charles, there is no need to worry. I have spoken to Dr. Elliott, and we developed a reasonable explanation." Darcy told Charles the agreed upon story. There will be no mention of the kidnapping attempt."

"I thank you for that Darcy, but how can you wish to be in my presence after what my sister tried to do?"

"Bingley, I have always tolerated your sister's behavior for your sake. Why would that change now? If you had known her plans or been here at the time, you would have done everything you could to prevent her from causing any harm. I know that. I know you are a dear and trusted friend, now, also, my brother. Nothing will change that."

Bingley could only stare at his friend in surprise. However, Hurst added, "For Louisa's sake, Darcy, let me express my thanks for your consideration of our families."

"You are my friends, and I trust I would receive the same assistance for the two of you. I do have one concern, Bingley, and that is for your aunt. I am sure she would have notified you of Caroline's departure had she been able to do so. Perhaps you and Hurst should accompany the body to York for burial and be sure that you aunt is well."

"I pray she has not done anything that will again put our family on the brink of disgrace."

The gentlemen had just departed the study to seek out their wives, and Darcy asked for Benton, Mrs. Reynolds, and Gregson to attend him. Upon their arrival, Darcy told him the agreed upon story and asked that they repeat it to the constable upon his arrival. Darcy had barely finished speaking when a knock was heard at the front door. Benton left to answer it and returned to announce the magistrate, Mr. Oliver.

After everything had been explained, the magistrate departed satisfied that the death had been nothing more than an accident.

The next day, Bingley and Hurst saw Caroline's body loaded onto a wagon that would follow them to York. They rode ahead as quickly as they could, stopping only to change horses. They arrived in the mid-afternoon on the second day. Upon arriving at his aunt's home, no one answered his knock, and Bingley's fears began to mount. There would be no hiding a large number of deaths, if Caroline injured them during her escape. Bingley silently cursed his sister.

The men made their way to the mews behind the house, tethering their horses in the stables. Bingley led the way to the kitchen door. It, too, was locked, but the men could hear voices inside. Knowing where his aunt hid a key to the kitchen door, Bingley quickly retrieved it and let himself into the kitchen. All of the staff appeared to be well but confused. The last they could remember was drinking tea on Wednesday evening, then waking up locked in the kitchen with all of the keys missing. Several of the men put their shoulders to the door separating below stairs from above stairs but could not break through the heavy door. One of the grooms rushed to the stables and retrieved an ax, which made short work of the door. Bingley rushed above stairs calling his aunt's name, but heard no reply. Mounting the stairs two at a time he reached the first floor and went directly to Aunt Honoria's room. He again required assistance to break the door in, and found his aunt lying upon her bed bound and gagged. A note was dispatched requesting the doctors attend them. He pronounced her weak but healthy, and assured the gentlemen she would return to her former state of health in but a few days. The doctor was curious about what had put his patient in such a state, but no one was willing to enlighten him.

After broth, bread and tea had been brought to his aunt, Bingley explained what had occurred while she was tied up. Aunt Honoria was extremely grateful that none of her staff had been hurt and that Caroline's plans had been thwarted without causing injury to anyone but herself.

Bingley and Hurst stayed with Aunt Honoria and made plans for Caroline to be laid to rest immediately after the arrival of the cart carrying her coffin-encased body. Once the plans were completed the two men ate a quick meal before retiring to rest their exhausted bodies.

The funeral was held the afternoon of the following day, with only Bingley and Hurst in attendance. Before departing, Bingley arranged for several thousand pounds of his sister's dowry to be sent to his aunt to compensate her for all of the trouble, and to ensure her servants did not speak of what had happened. The two gentlemen returned to Pemberley as quickly as they departed, both needing the comfort that only their wives could provide.

CHAPTER 30

EVERYONE IN THE family knew of the attempted kidnapping, so immediately upon arriving at Pemberley, the first thing they wished to do was see the twins for themselves. Once assured of their wellbeing, the incident was never discussed out of respect for the Bingleys and the Hursts.

The house was bustling with people. The preparations for Andrew's and Beth's christenings and Kitty and Michael's wedding were completed, and the family greatly anticipated the two events.

The Bingleys and Tim Whitman, Darcy's neighbor since childhood, had been selected to be Andrew's godparents and Richard and Mary Fitzwilliam along with Georgiana were to be Beth's godparents. After a search of the attics, Mrs. Reynolds had produced the christening gown made for the Darcy heir by Lady Anne Darcy. Both Darcy and Elizabeth were emotional at the thought their son would wear the same gown Darcy had worn for his christening. Lady Anne's delicate stitching had held up well over the years. The heavy white satin of the gown and lace trimming had been well preserved. Lady Matlock had purchased a beautiful lace gown for

Beth in London and presented it to Elizabeth for the baby to wear at her baptism.

The churching service for Elizabeth occurred several weeks earlier, so she sat in the Darcy pew with her husband, holding her daughter in his arms. Mr. Bennet and Georgiana shared the pew with her and Darcy. As the rector called for Andrew to be presented, Elizabeth handed Beth to her grandpapa. Then she and William stepped forward to present their son. The Bingleys and Mr. Whitman joined them around the font.

Mr. Millwood asked the godparents a series of questions wherein they promised to ensure the child is raised in the teachings of the church. After they made their promises, Mr. Millwood took the baby in his arms and asked the godparents to name him. "Andrew Thomas William Darcy," they replied. Then dipping his hand into the water of the baptismal font, Mr. Millwood said, *"Andrew Thomas William Darcy, I baptize thee in the Name of the Father, and of the Son, and of the Holy Ghost. Amen."* (1) Several prayers were offered on behalf of the child and then everyone returned to their seats.

Mr. Millwood then called for Beth. Elizabeth took Beth from her grandpapa, and Darcy handed him Andrew. This time they presented their daughter to Mr. Millwood. Mary and Richard Fitzwilliam and Georgiana moved to stand beside them at the font. The service was repeated for the Darcy's daughter, again ending with Mr. Millwood saying, *"Elizabeth Anne Darcy, I baptize thee in the Name of the Father, and of the Son, and of the Holy Ghost. Amen."* (1)

At the conclusion of the church service, the Darcys, along with the family and invited friends, returned to Pemberley for a luncheon. The twins calmly received a great deal of attention before sleep overtook them. The gifts had already been opened because of the need to delay the baptism. Elizabeth decided to display the many gifts the children had received. Central to the display was a pair of pictures, one of Andrew and one of Beth. They had been drawn by their Aunt Georgiana and colored by their Aunt Kitty. Elizabeth was delighted with them, and she and Darcy teasingly argued over whose office they would grace.

The day after the christening, Michael and the gentlemen of the family met in Darcy's study to learn more about the conditions Michael had found upon arriving at his family estate in January. "The house was nearly crumbling from neglect, and only the butler and housekeeper remained. They both inherited their position from their parents, who served my father and grandfather. Mrs. Moore, the housekeeper, was in quite a state. It seems that Ralph and Marjorie argued fiercely before he left for London. Apparently, he pushed her, and she struck her head. It knocked her unconscious, and though she lived for four days, she succumbed to her injury. I had her buried at her father's estate that borders my family home. I went from there directly to London to meet with the solicitors. I arranged to purchase the earl's estate and was able to visit the home with Kitty. We had original discussed knocking down both houses and building something new, but when Kitty saw Dalbert Manor, her artistic eye saw some potential in it. Instead of knocking it down, we are having some remodeling done. We are going to open up some of the smaller rooms, removed some of the dark wood, and add some windows. As a surprise to Kitty, I am having the uppermost room in the turret turned into an art studio, adding windows all around.

I hope it will be a place Kitty can sketch and paint to her heart's content. Kitty has also picked out new paper hangings, paints, and fabrics, and some of the more ostentatious features are being removed. Perhaps we can host the family next Christmas." Michael said hopefully.

"I am sure we would all enjoy that," replied Darcy.

"Indeed, it will make a much easier trip from Rosings," added Richard.

"I am having my old family home torn down and a tenant house built on it. I will turn the lands that belong to the original Amesbury Hall into an additional tenant farm."

"That sounds like a wise idea," Darcy remarked.

As the gentlemen discussed the more pertinent aspects of the matter, Kitty enjoyed telling her sisters and aunts about her new home and the changes she was having made to it. She, too, mentioned hosting the families for Christmas.

Two days later, Pemberley hosted the wedding of Kitty Bennet and Michael Amesbury. Kitty wore a gown of palest aqua. Silver stitching decorated the neckline, sleeves, hem, and train. She wore a white bonnet trimmed white flowers and ribbons to match her dress. As a finishing touch, Kitty wore a dazzling set of diamonds made from the stone Michael find in the mine in India. Lydia, who stood up with her sister, was in a gown of Prussian blue and wore a wreath of matching blue and white flowers in her hair with ribbons streaming down her back.

The groom wore black with an embroidered silver waistcoat and white cravat. Standing with Michael was a friend from his childhood. Michael's face glowed with happiness as he watched Kitty coming towards him on her father's arm. The ceremony was exactly like that of the three sisters who had gone before her. Each of her married sisters had their fingers entwined with those of their husbands and tears in the eyes. Lydia's eyes held tears as well, as she hoped to be loved one day as dearly as her sisters all were.

The wedding breakfast was another monument to the talent of the cook and staff of Pemberley. The decorations were beautiful, the food delicious, and happiness and joy pervaded the atmosphere. About one o'clock in the afternoon, the bride and groom departed for their new home. They would spend their first night there before traveling on to Brighton for a fortnight. The family and guests all waved from the steps of Pemberley until the carriage was out of sight.

EPILOGUE

IT WAS THE twenty-fifth wedding anniversary of Fitzwilliam and Elizabeth Darcy, as well as of Jane and Charles Bingley. Settled around the dining table in the formal dining room at Darcy House, Darcy could not help but smile at the faces before him. The heir to Pemberley, Andrew, was to be wed at the end of the month. His twin sister, Beth, had been married for three years and had twin sons of her own. He and Elizabeth had four more children, Bennet Nicholas, age three and twenty; Joshua Charles, age one and twenty, Eleanor Jane, age eight and ten; and Jenny Diana age five and ten. Bennet had excelled at school and would be taking over one of the smaller estates Darcy owned. Joshua had two more years of school and was preparing for a career in the church.

Georgiana had made her debut the year following the twins' birth. Her beauty and fortune attracted a considerable attention, but Georgiana did not find anyone that touched her heart. It was not until her third season that she met Christopher Burton-Smythe, the eldest son of the Duke of Ashburton, whose estate was in Warwickshire. They married after a six-month courtship and engagement and were now the proud parents of three sons and two daughters.

The Bingleys remained at Ashford Hills. Jane's first child had been a son, Charles William, Charlie to the family, who was now helping to manage the family estate. Following Charles was Madeline, Lydia, and Margaret. The youngest Bingley was another boy, named Stephen. Eleanor Darcy and Lydia Bingley would be making their London debuts together this season.

Richard and Mary Fitzwilliam had shared their home with Anne de Bourgh for seven years until her death. She had enjoyed the freedom from her mother's demands and spent as much time with her extended family as possible. She found great joy in the love of her constantly growing family. Anne had been conservative in her spending, though she did spoil the children at Rosings, and left a large fortune to be shared evenly between all of her cousins' children. Richard and Mary had three daughters and after a long break between pregnancies, finally gave birth to a boy, Richard Henry. Jonathan Fitzwilliam was now the Earl of Matlock as his father had died of heart trouble two years earlier. The Dowager Countess of Matlock divided her time between Matlock and Rosings, enjoying as much time with her grandchildren as possible. She still traveled to all of the family gatherings and was able to play grandmother to her many nieces and nephews by marriage, as well.

The Viscount and Viscountess Amesbury were one of the richest couples in the country. They preferred the quiet of their country home and only traveled to London when necessary. When there, they attended only events given by their family and closest friends and were renowned for the charitable works.

Lydia, did, indeed, leave school after she completed her first year. She kept house for her father and had a governess to further her education and instruct her on how to conduct herself in society. It was initially uncomfortable for her to mix with her old neighbors in Hertfordshire. Lydia worked very hard to change the opinion they had of her from her youngest years. She did not find herself comfortable in the more sophisticated society her sisters' enjoyed, though she loved spending time with her sisters and their families. When Lydia was twenty years of age, the Beaumont family purchased Netherfield Park. The second son, Laurence, was quite taken with the daughter of his nearest neighbor. He and Lydia often met at card parties, assemblies, and dinners held in the neighborhood. After six months he asked her for a courtship, to which she agreed. Three month's later, he asked Mr. Bennet for Lydia's hand in marriage. Mr. Bennet was pleased with the pleasant, intelligent young man. During Mr. Beaumont's discussion with Mr. Bennet, he asked the young man how he would feel about changing his name to Bennet and becoming his heir. Thomas Bennet invited them to live with him after the marriage and learn more about running the estate. When he was comfortable with the management, Mr. Bennet would turn the estate over to him and Lydia. They currently had four young children, and Mr. Bennet delighted in his freedom to divide his time traveling about England visiting his daughters and grandchildren. This happy circumstance was made possible when, three years after Mr. Collins traveled to Australia, they received word of his death. As his heir, Elizabeth deeded Longbourn back to her father, at Mr. Bennet's suggestion, for Lydia and her husband.

The only couple at the table that was not actually family were Lord and Lady Wescott. It was

Lord Wescott's honorable actions that protected Elizabeth and allowed them to marry. As a consequence, the couples had become close over the year. Wescott had turned around his family fortunes, and he and Evelyn were the proud parents of one boy and two girls. Lord Wescott worked closely with his son, instilling in the young man the pride in his family name and home, as well as the importance of integrity. He did not wish his son to grow up to be the man he was before, but to be an upstanding, honorable gentleman.

Darcy looked again over the table and could not help but smile at the joy that filled the room. The joy that filled his life and brought all of these people together began with Elizabeth's unforgettable laugh.

FOOT NOTES

(1)   1662 Book of Common Prayer, as printed by John Baskerville between 1760 and 1762.

(2)   The LDS version of the KJV Bible, © Copyright 1979 by Corporation of the President of The Church of Jesus Christ of Latter-day Saints, Salt Lake City, Utah, U.S.A., Old Testament, *Song of Solomon 3:4*

(3)   The LDS version of the KJV Bible, © Copyright 1979 by Corporation of the President of The Church of Jesus Christ of Latter-day Saints, Salt Lake City, Utah, U.S.A., Old Testament, *Song of Solomon 2:16*

AUTHOR'S NOTES

The games mentioned in the Pemberley picnic scene are actual games of the times. Below is a brief description of what the games entail.

- Battledore and Shuttlecock is similar to modern badminton

- Graces was played mostly by young ladies, who each held two sticks and tried to catch a small hoop that was tossed between them.

- Bilbocatch is similar to the ball on a string that you catch in a cup to which the string is attached.

Part of the character, Michael Amesbury's fortune came from a diamond mind in India.

In reality, there were two major diamond mines in India.

- The first one the Kollur produced at least ten notable diamonds, including The Hope Diamond, which resides in the Smithsonian in Washington, D. C. This mine stopped producing in the mid-1800's.

- The other mine, near Panna, India, has not produced any really large diamonds. Diamonds from this mine come in four colors: Clear/Brillant, a faint orange tint, a greenish tint, and sepia colored. Diamonds from this mine are collected by the district magistrate and auction yearly during the month of January. This mine is still producing.

OTHER TITLES FROM THIS AUTHOR

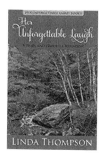

Dark curls and an unforgettably sweet laugh were all he knew of his sister's rescuer. Later, a second glimpse showed her to be lovely, and he heard her melodious laugh again. Darcy wondered what it would be like to meet this remarkable, and remarkably lovely, young woman. Would the spirit that caused her to go to the aid of a stranger be able to bring some joy to his lonely life? Would they ever meet, or would he always be left wondering?

Little did Fitzwilliam Darcy know that his trip to Hertfordshire to help his friend would bring him face to face with the lovely young woman whose unforgettable laugh had haunted his dreams for the last several years. Would she be anything like the woman he had built up in his dreams? Would he be able to avoid Miss Bingley long enough to discover more about this mysterious young woman?

Dark curls and an unforgettably sweet laugh . . .

In Book I of the series, Her Unforgettable Laugh, a trip to Hertfordshire brought Fitzwilliam Darcy face-to-face with the woman who had haunted his dreams for five years. Their chance meeting led to a courtship, in spite of those who wished to separate them. Now Elizabeth Bennet is traveling to London where she will be introduced to Darcy's family and the ton. How will Elizabeth be received? Will their love flourish and grow or will new trials overwhelm them?

"You must marry her," the stern voice said. "I need to gain control of her inheritance before she reaches her next birthday. It need not be a long marriage, but marry her you must."

Alone in the world, Elizabeth Bennet had to rely upon herself. She knew escape was the only way to

ensure her safety. With the help of Longbourn's faithful servants, Elizabeth disappeared from her home and the odious heir. She was determined to find a way to support herself and remain hidden until after her birthday.

Fortune smiled on Elizabeth when a series of events offered her the position of companion to Georgiana Darcy. In spite of her position, Elizabeth found herself attracted to her new employer. Could he ever see her as more than his sister's companion? Sometimes Elizabeth thought Mr. Darcy might care for her, too, but would his attraction—if that is what is was—survive when he learned the truth about her?

Hidden away at Pemberley, would Elizabeth be able to remain safely concealed until coming of age? What surprises did the future hold for her?

22140428R00298

Printed in Great Britain
by Amazon